Requiem
for
Richard Cory

Lawrence Fischman

Gram's Group, Ltd.
Dallas, Texas

Requiem for Richard Cory

Gram's Group, Ltd. books may be ordered through booksellers or by contacting:

Gram's Group, Ltd.
18 Royal Way
Dallas, Texas 75229
972/419-8318 or on Facebook®

ISBN: 978-0-9857232-0-0 (sc)
ISBN: 978-0-9857232-1-7 (dj)

Printed in the United States of America

Other books by Lawrence Fischman –

The French Artillery Officer
The Skeleton in the Closet (anticipated publication date – Aug. 2012)

Prologue

Richard Cory

Whenever Richard Cory went downtown,
We people on the pavement looked at him:
He was a gentleman from sole to crown,
Clean favored, and imperially slim.

And he was always quietly arrayed,
And he was always human when he talked;
But still he fluttered pulses when he said,
"Good morning, and he glittered when he walked.

And he was rich-yes, richer than a king
And admirably schooled in every grace:
In fine, we thought that he was everything
To make us wish that we were in his place.

So on we worked, and waited for the light,
And went without the meat, and cursed the bread;
And Richard Cory, one calm summer night,
Went home and put a bullet through his head.

Edwin Arlington Robinson,
American (1869-1935)

i

REQUIEM FOR RICHARD CORY

Chapter One

Somewhere between routine and ritual, that is Tilbury Town. But that's the way most townspeople like it. Although the Great War is taking place across the ocean in France they eagerly follow its progress, cheering on Blackjack Pershing and their Doughboys. France is a place everyone had heard of and could find easily enough on the big globe in the main reading room of the public library at the south end of Water Street. Although too much complaining would have been unpatriotic, Tilbury Towners did grumble from time to time about shortages of flour, of cloth, of shotgun shells and deer rifle ammunition. Shoes too were in short supply, even with a shoe factory right there in town. The only time, though, when they felt keenly the effects of the war was when the *Kennebec Journal* published its periodic list of Maine boys who'd made the ultimate sacrifice for their Country or had been blinded or maimed in the ultimate absurdity that was trench warfare. From Augusta down-river to Bath, from Camden all the way down to Kennebunk, everyone had a relative or knew someone who'd lost a son, a brother, or a cousin, or had received news that a local boy had been gassed or had lost a leg to a machine gun.

But that first Sunday morning in August the war was just something the grown-ups tucked away in the backs of their minds in favor of enjoying a lazy summer Sunday. The kids, with the impending start of the school year in the backs of their minds, were busy squeezing as much out of every minute of summer as they could. That morning they either played at soldiering or played nurses and front-line ambulance drivers. By eight o'clock most everyone was up enjoying the cool morning in anticipation of the heat of the day that would come later. The devout were making ready to leave for one of the town's several churches. Those choosing to express their piety in other ways on that particular Sunday were sitting down to a leisurely breakfast or the women of the household were busy preparing picnic baskets for an outing downstream along the grassy banks of the river.

Among the latter, Gladys Brimmer was peeling already-cooked red potatoes for potato salad. Believing it her patriotic duty, she was using mayonnaise and French's mustard, hard-boiled eggs and scallions rather than the German-style salad for which she was justly renown at the pot-luck suppers put on by the ladies of the Congregational Church. Her husband of nearly twenty years, Amos Brimmer, came in the front door and headed back to the kitchen. Most every Sunday morning, weather notwithstanding, Amos walked the three blocks to the newsstand in the Palace Hotel (formerly the "Rhinelander Hotel") on Water Street to purchase a Sunday *Boston Globe* or a *Maine Sunday Telegram*. Whichever it happened to be, he and Gladys would spend the better part of the day reading and dreaming their day-dreams. As was his habit, Amos had the paper folded, crumpled Gladys would say, under the stump that was the remainder of his left arm after the mill accident some years back. As was also his habit when the kids weren't around, he kissed the back of Gladys's neck and rubbed her bottom with his remaining hand. Indeed, when Gladys would complain that he crumpled the paper by folding it under his stump, he'd reply that the only reason he did it was so he'd have his hand free to do what he was at that moment doing a bit too vigorously to suit Gladys's mood.

Gladys turned around and gave Amos a maybe-later kiss on the cheek, "What was all the commotion? I heard the sirens all the way back here in the kitchen. Is there a fire?"

"Not that I could see," Amos replied, a note of resignation in his voice. "It was Sheriff Dowdy with a car-load of deputies, and another car-load behind them. Came tearing down Main Street headin' south like a German submarine had surfaced in the river or something."

At that moment Clarence the Brimmers' twelve-year old came in the back door to get a drink of water. He and the other boys on the street had been fighting the battles of Belleau Wood and Chateau Thierry against the forces of the gang from two streets over. They'd been at it a while and had decided to take a break. His eyes got wide as he processed the last part what he'd just heard his father say. After a quick gulp of water drunk from his cupped hands placed under the kitchen tap which Gladys had obligingly turned on for him, he headed back out to spread the alarm.

A few minutes later an armistice had been quickly negotiated with the other gang and everyone ran home to get their bicycles—those who had them—or to beg incredulous parents to get in their automobiles—those who had them—or to otherwise get down to the river as soon as possible. By the time the news made its way around the immediate neighborhood and spilled over into the adjacent streets, the report had gained enough credibility that a good number of Tilbury Townsmen had armed themselves—those who had ammunition took their guns—the others axes, pitchforks and buck knives and headed toward the center of town. There they milled around for a while as though waiting for orders. Finally someone suggested that they head for the ice plant and make their stand there. Cyrus Barker, a Spanish-American War veteran, added that there were hay bales to use as barricades. Someone else suggested that they slide the remaining inventory of large blocks of ice into the river thinking that maybe the sub would strike one and go down like the *Titanic*.

To the great relief of the ice plant manager, the notion that a block of ice, even one weighing 300 pounds, could sink a submarine is put to rest by a few of the men who worked at the Bath Iron Works, the huge shipyard downriver at Bath. After nearly an hour of tense waiting, word finally came that it wasn't the Germans at all; evidently something had happened down at Oakdale Hall and that's where the sheriff was heading when he'd so disturbed the tranquility of the morning.

By the time the make-shift brigade disbanded the as yet unknown emergency at Oakdale Hall was the source of no little concern and a great deal of speculation. Oakdale Hall is the great manor house standing on the crest of a small hill just south of town. The lord of the manor is Richard Cory. Richard Cory is a bachelor, a circumstance that flutters the hearts of every nubile female, miss or missus, who resides in Tilbury Town. The only other inhabitants of Oakdale Hall are Esther Dubrowski the head housekeeper and Deaf Silas the stone-deaf stable hand whose surname is known to no one, perhaps not even recalled by Deaf Silas himself. Over the years there had been maids, a cook and kitchen helpers, gardeners and field hands but they all lived either in town or on neighboring farms. Indeed, until the war, Richard Cory had been one of the leading employers in the area, right there alongside the shoe factory, lumber mill and ice plant (in each of which, it was rumored, Richard Cory owns a substantial interest.)

First the German submarine scare, then the unusual event—whatever it was—at Oakdale Hall, left the routine of a fair-weather August Sunday in tatters. Somehow, word had gotten to the pews and was being whispered behind open prayer books up and down the aisles. Even before the sermons and closing hymns had ended men, women and children, in all a good part of the population of Tilbury Town, were promenading up and down Water Street pausing to greet one another and to share their relief or disappointment. (They were about equally divided between those who were glad that the war had not been brought to their doorstep, and those whose blood had been set to boiling by the thought of having an opportunity to settle the score for the *Lusitania*.)

Around ten o'clock, with the sun already warming the streets, some enterprising high-schoolers set up a lemonade stand under the awning shading the front windows of Stein's Furniture Store. They were making good money at a nickel-a-glass to be put toward the senior class trip down to Boston at the end of the up-coming school year. The speculation reached an almost unbearable level as Molly Brimmer was deftly combining threats and promises to persuade her little brother Clarence to run home to see if there were any more lemons. Just then one of the sheriff's vehicles — the Ford, not the Buick (Only the sheriff drives the Buick.) — came 'round the corner from Brunswick Avenue in a four-wheel power drift and roared away south on Water Street with Doc Goodson bouncing around in the rear seat clinging to his medical bag with one hand and trying to hold on to his straw panama hat with the other.

By two o'clock when the deputy returned Doc Goodson to his home and office on Brunswick Avenue the gravity-like pull of routine and the seasonable heat of the day had pretty much cleared Water Street as Tilbury Towners went about their Sunday plans trusting that in good time they'd be made privy to whatever had taken place at Oakdale Hall. Several of those who were unable to contain their curiosity tried calling Doc Goodson, but after telling the first several callers that Sheriff Dowdy had enjoined him to say nothing and that he was inclined to do as he was told, Doc Goodson stopped answering his telephone. Fortunately, there were no medical emergencies that night which might have had a bad outcome owing to Doc Goodson's self-imposed unavailability.

But then, around eight o'clock that evening Tilbury Town's modern communication systems were taxed beyond their limits when Reverend Sloane's wife Vashti reports seeing the Black Mariah from Davis & Son's Funeral Home lumbering south toward Oakdale Hall, Ulysses Davis himself at the reins. Davis & Son Funeral Home was something of a source of civic pride in that the Davises were the only black family in Tilbury Town. Ulysses's father Jefferson Davis had walked all the way to Maine from Virginia, his deed of manumission secured in an oil-skin pouch sewed into the lining of his coat. He'd found work assisting the town mortician, mainly digging graves and building plain pine coffins for those who couldn't afford more luxurious accommodations for their eternal rest. Eventually he'd learned enough about the business of death to get a license from the state and had taken over the mortuary after providing a most tasteful and well-attended funeral for the late proprietor and buying out the deceased's heirs (none of whom wanted the business) at an inflated price which Jefferson Davis paid punctually and in full over several years.

At birth Jefferson had been given only the name "Jefferson" and upon being granted his freedom near the end of the Civil War he like others of his background had out of expediency and perhaps in a spirit of magnanimity simply adopted the surname of his former owner which happened to be "Davis" although no relation to the President of the late Confederate States of America. No one had bothered to explain the irony of his name, so Jefferson Davis never gave it a thought. After settling in Tilbury Town, in time he'd traveled down to Boston and brought back a wife Beulah herself the daughter of freed-slaves. Beulah soon produced a son and at her insistence they named him Ulysses Grant Davis. Jefferson, a widower now for a decade, mostly left the running of the business to his son whose duty that Sunday night was to remove the remains of the deceased from Oakdale Hall to the Davis & Son embalming room but do nothing to the corpse except to keep it in an ice packed container until further notice.

When Davis returned to his premises around ten o'clock a good size crowd had gathered in his viewing parlor and had spilled out on to the sidewalk and lawn, where some heedless ones were standing in the flower beds on either side of the main entrance. Davis and his assistant turned the team around and backed the hearse, its curtains securely drawn closed, into the attached barn. They locked the barn doors and in the dark moved the body into the basement workroom. Completing Sheriff Dowdy's instructions they removed the clothing and placed the body in the large zinc-lined box packed with ice and kept for the purpose of temporary storage of the deceased until suitable funeral arrangements can be made. Davis went upstairs into the living quarters and returned with a shotgun which he placed in the sweaty hands of his young apprentice enjoining him to brandish it if necessary, but not to fire it except in the most dire of circumstances. As an added precaution he broke open the breech and removed the two number seven bird-shot rounds from the side-by-side barrels. He left the shells with the young man with instructions that he is to fire in the air but only if his own life is unmistakably in danger.

Davis then went upstairs to the main level and into the parlor. As soon as he appeared the crowd grew silent and readily acceded to his request that everyone repair to the lawn where he would say all that he could. This proves to be little more than what Doc Goodson had been authorized to say. He did, however, confirm that he'd removed one deceased person's body from the Oakdale Hall premises. He was not at liberty to say the name of the person or whether the deceased was male or female, young or old, inhabitant of the premises, visitor or intruder. Nor was he permitted to state his opinion as to the apparent cause of death, whether by natural causes or by violent means. The last thing he said as he bid everyone good night is that he was expected to be at the county courthouse at ten o'clock in the morning to give evidence before a coroner's jury at a formal inquest.

Chapter Two

By nine o'clock Monday morning, nearly every adult in Tilbury Town whose presence was not absolutely required at the mill, the bank, the shoe factory, post or telegraph offices or other place of employment had made the short trip up to Augusta, the seat of Kennebec County as well as the state capital. Completed in 1830 of unpolished gray granite quarried just down the road in Hallowell, the Kennebec County Courthouse stands on State Street at Court Street just north of the Statehouse grounds. Befitting the importance of the proceedings within, the ground-floor entrance façade has three rectangular granite columns, a metaphor for the four-square treatment of those who pass between them. These columns are surmounted by three more granite columns fronting the building's second floor. These are in the Doric style reflective of the plain, forthright manner in which proceedings are conducted in the Supreme Judicial Court located within on the second floor. Mounted on the building's pitched roof is a square bell tower whose roof is supported by eight much smaller columns, these in the ornate Ionic style calculated to symbolize some as yet unexplained civic virtue, or perhaps merely reflecting nothing more than the architect's whimsy.

There being no business before his court that day, Judge Cranston E. Gribble, judge of the Supreme Judicial Court, had consented to the use of his courtroom to accommodate the large crowd, thereby more than trebling the space available for spectators over that provided by the smallish first-floor room usually employed for this type of proceeding. Not long after ten o'clock, the bailiff, also on loan from Judge Gribble, bade those assembled to rise and the coroner took his unaccustomed place on the judge's bench.

The coroner, Ebeneezer Blaine Ingersoll, in his youth had stood barely five feet three inches tall. Now into his seventh decade, he barely makes it to five feet and that only in his high-button shoes. Judge Gribble, on the other hand, is a rather gangly six-footer. In extending the hospitality of his courtroom, his honor had neglected to instruct his staff to adjust the seat height of his high-back swivel chair. As is the case with court staff everywhere, taking the initiative in any matter was neither a job requirement nor a job virtue. Thus the chair remained configured for Judge Gribble's elongated frame. As a result, when seated, Coroner Ingersoll's feet dangled several inches above the floor making it difficult for him to control either the pitch or the yaw of the formidable chair. His first attempt to lean back resulted in the chair tipping over backwards coming to rest at a 45-degree angle against the claret-colored heavy velvet drape covering the doorway leading to the judge's chambers. Once the chair had been righted and Coroner Ingersoll had regained his balance, if not his dignity, as the bailiff stood by, his lips pursed with indecision, Weldon Bailey, a mechanic at the shoe factory, came forward from the audience and adjusted the chair elevation screw so that Coroner Ingersoll's feet could now touch the floor, if just barely. This solution, as might be expected, created another equally vexing problem: Owing to the lowered seat, Coroner Ingersoll could not see over the bench to the first of the two rows of counsel tables inside the bar, and the occupants of the seats could not see him. After a few minutes of mooting about various suggestions, a solution to the dilemma was finally arrived at. It consisted of again raising the level of the seat and situating several volumes of the *Maine Reports,* purloined from the County law Library, at the coroner's feet so now he could see and be seen without further risking of life, limb or dignity.

In keeping with the solemnity of the proceedings, other than a few muffled snickers which were met with disapproving glares and finger-to-lips admonitions, the crowd had maintained a respectful silence. Coroner Ingersoll bade everyone be seated so that the proceedings could begin. This being a non-adversarial hearing, the only persons at the first row of counsel tables to the Coroner's right were Sheriff Dowdy and the District Attorney for Kennebec County, Bascom Pommus, III.

Coroner Ingersoll was not a judge, or even a lawyer. Nor did he have any medical training other than as a sixteen year-old enlistee in the Union Army in which he served as an orderly in a field hospital for a few months prior to Appomattox and a few more months thereafter until his mustering out. Although he'd never seen much less performed an autopsy, he was as expert at necropsy as any veterinarian. Many years before he'd been appointed county coroner, building on his army experience, he'd learned the art of taxidermy and it was this trade that had provided his livelihood. Because his compensation as coroner was not fixed by state law, but was set by the county fiscal body, even with his veteran's pension it was not a living wage. It was his skill at taxidermy, an always-in-demand trade, coupled with his army pension that had moved the county commissioners to appoint him. Given that his services as coroner were called upon only infrequently, and that the cause of death was more or less self-evident in those deaths that fell within his purview, it was all in all a mutually satisfactory arrangement.

Adjudging that all was in readiness, Coroner Ingersoll settled his wire-rim glasses on the bridge of his nose and requested that the clerk call the case. A coroner's inquest is not a record proceeding; there is no court reporter to record and transcribe what transpires during the course of the hearing. The clerk is therefore charged with the duty of not only calling the case, but also recording the names of the jurors and witnesses as well as the jury's verdict when it is received. But since she was not trained in recording testimony, her functions were limited to noting appearances and the identification and admission of exhibits. Rising from her desk in front of the bench, the clerk, Martha Parsons, herself the widow of a Civil War veteran, cleared her throat and called out in a strong voice, "Case number 18-CI-03; *In the Matter of the Death of Richard Cory.*"

What had theretofore been the consensus of speculation was now a reality; it was indeed Richard Cory who'd died sometime yesterday or the previous Saturday night. Recognizing the inevitability of the outburst of conversation that ensued in the spectator benches, Coroner Ingersoll let it continue for about a minute. Then, not having one of his own to wield, he took the liberty of borrowing Judge Gribble's gavel which he proceeded to pound vigorously on its round pallet until the bailiff, not wishing to account to Judge Gribble for a broken gavel, reached up and stayed the coroner's hand. It took a stern look over his shoulder by the sheriff to finally silence the agitated crowd.

With decorum restored, the coroner asked the district attorney if he was ready to proceed, and receiving an affirmative answer went on to the next order of business: Selection of a coroner's jury. This body, six in number, after hearing such evidence as the district attorney is pleased to present, would return a verdict as to the cause of death and if the death were not of natural causes, whether the death appeared to be accidental or the product of a willful act. Finally, if the death was found to be not of natural causes and thus either accidental or willful, the jury would determine whether the deceased died at his own deliberate hand or as a result of his own misadventure or some other person was responsible.

District Attorney Pommus rose from his seat at the counsel table. With a bow toward the bench and a "May it please the Court" befitting a trial in the Supreme Judicial Court, he turned toward the audience crowding into the spectator gallery and lining the walls at the rear and sides of the courtroom. Foolscap pad and pen in hand, he began his *voir dire* examination by addressing the audience as though all, ladies (who of course were ineligible to serve) as well as gentlemen, were potential jurors. His first question to the venire was, "Were any of you personally acquainted with the deceased Richard Cory during his lifetime? Please raise your hand." Everyone responded by raising his or her hand. Of course everyone in Tilbury Town knew Richard Cory and virtually everyone had the warmest of feelings toward him. Indeed whenever he appeared on the streets of the Tilbury Town, impeccably attired, slim and erect in bearing, always with a smile and a tip of his hat to the ladies, nearly everyone who passed him felt their day brighten for having been in his imperial presence, no matter how briefly. However, inasmuch as *voir dire* is taken to mean, in forensic English, "to speak the truth," in that spirit it must also be noted that at least a few of the men of Tilbury Town covertly begrudged Richard Cory his esteemed status. Be that as it may, whether by design or inadvertence, District Attorney Pommus asked no one to state whether their feelings toward the deceased were favorable or otherwise, or would in any way affect their ability to sit as a "fair and impartial juror."

For his next question, District Attorney Pommus asked, "Do any of you claim to have personal knowledge regarding the manner in which the deceased Richard Cory met his death?" Whether the district attorney had hoped to dramatically end the proceeding before lunch-time by having the guilty party — assuming that there in fact was one — rise and confess all, or had some other purpose in asking such a fatuous question, was the subject of much table talk over the noon recess. In any event, when no one raised a hand in response, the prosecutor asked his search-your-heart question that he used in every case: "Does anyone know of any reason why you could not render a true and impartial verdict based upon the evidence presented in court and according to the instructions given you by the judge, er, that is, the coroner?" Again, no hands went up, the only manual activity being attributable to a few of the ladies who were using their hand-fans to counter the heat generated by the warm sun and crowded courtroom.

Having exhausted his repertoire of *voir dire* questions, District Attorney Pommus had a sudden and relatively rare inspiration: "Very well, ladies and gentlemen, is there anyone present who does *not* wish to serve on this jury? Please raise your hand." At this, even the fans stopped moving lest the motion be mistaken for something else. This was a wholly foreign experience for District Attorney Pommus. In the usual trial, his *voir dire* examination followed by that of defense counsel produced an abundance of reasons why this potential juror or that one could not serve on a given case. Here he'd not been able to ask the court, sorry, the coroner, to excuse anyone.

Ever the wily courtroom veteran, District Attorney Pommus, after a brief *sotto voce* conference at the counsel table with Sheriff Dowdy, turned to the bench and announced, "If your honor (this time he did not pause to correct himself) pleases, we will accept the six gentlemen seated in the first row to my left." And so it was that Weldon Bailey and five other men seated in the front row, left side, were seated in the front row of the jury box as the coroner's jury in the inquest over the body of one Richard Cory, late of Tilbury Town, Maine. The clerk, at Coroner Ingersoll's direction, then had the six rise and swore them to a true verdict render according to the evidence and instructions given them.

These steps having been accomplished, the clerk, again at Coroner Ingersoll's behest, summoned forward all those present who intended to give testimony in the proceeding. These were Sheriff George Dowdy, Dr. Philip Goodson, Mr. Ulysses Grant Davis, Esther Dubrowski and "Deaf Silas" (last name unknown). These individuals were sworn *en masse* to tell the truth, the whole truth and nothing but the truth in the matter now pending before the court (it would have detracted from the solemnity of the oath to correct this inconsequential misstatement) and in which they'd been summoned to give testimony. As Coroner Ingersoll was about to invite District Attorney Pommus to call his first witness, the district attorney rose from his place at the counsel table and addressed the coroner, "If you please, Mr. Coroner, the State invokes the Rule."

Coroner Ingersoll looked down at the district attorney clearly having no idea what   Pommus meant. "The 'Rule?' What rule is that, Sir?"

"Invoking 'The Rule' means that I'm asking that you sequester the witnesses and instruct them not to discuss their testimony with one another or with anyone else."

"Can I do that? You've never asked that before. What's the purpose? They all know what they saw yesterday."

"It's done in every Supreme Judicial Court trial, Your Hon…Mr. Coroner. Keeps the witnesses from letting what other witnesses may have seen influence their own testimony."

"Very well," he paused as the bailiff whispered that there were rooms used for that purpose located just outside the main doors to the courtroom, "the bailiff here will show you where to wait. You folks just go with him."

District Attorney Pommus rose to interject, "You need to tell them not to discuss their testimony with anyone, Mr. Coroner. Oh, and if you don't mind, Sheriff Dowdy'll be the State's representative as well as my first witness, so he can stay."

"Yes, yes. You folks please do what Mr. Pommus here just said. Now go along with the bailiff so we can get this case started." Coroner Ingersoll took off his eye-glasses and made a show of cleaning them with a pocket handkerchief which he then proceeded to use to mop his perspiring forehead.

In a minute or two, the bailiff returned from his mission and Coroner Ingersoll again with only the slightest shading of exasperation in his voice asked, "Are we now ready to proceed, Mr. Pommus, or do you have anything else that we need to take up first? I expect that the folks in the jury box and in the audience are as curious as I am to find out what happened down there yesterday. Maybe we can even finish up by lunch-time. I'm sure they'd like that as well."

"Just what I was hoping myself," came the reply. "With that in mind, I now call Sheriff Dowdy to the stand."

Sheriff Dowdy quickly left his seat at the counsel table and took the seat on the witness stand situated between the judge's bench and the jury box. As if addressing a stranger for the first time, District Attorney Pommus began as he always did, "Please state your name for the record, Sir."

The sheriff rolled his eyes, "George Anderson Dowdy."

"And you are the duly elected and serving sheriff of Kennebec County, Maine"

"Yes, Sir, I am. Have been since January, 1901," a response that elicited a snicker or two from the spectators' gallery.

"Indeed, Sheriff Dowdy. And may we assume that you were serving in that capacity yesterday between 7:00 a.m. and 10:00 p.m. Eastern Daylight-Saving Time?"

"Yes, you may, Sir."

"Did your office receive a call to come to Oakdale Hall around seven-thirty yesterday morning?"

"Yes, Sir. The Sunday desk sergeant had just come on duty, relieving the night man. He took the call," he glanced at his notebook, "from a Miss or Missus Dubrowski. She said come quickly, Mr. Cory's been shot. Well, as you might expect, the sergeant got pretty excited and called me right away. I told him to not say what this was about to anyone—I wanted to keep things under control; that's part of my job, keeping things under control—just call in all the men who were not assigned to duty that day and have them report to the jail as soon as possible. I told him I'd be in my office in fifteen minutes and to have everyone except those on jail guard-duty to assemble in my office.

"Well he carried out my instruction right enough and by the time I got to the jail at five minutes before eight we had a pretty good turn-out. Not knowing what might be waiting for us at Oakdale Hall, I took three men in the car with me and had five more follow in another car. We took out south through Tilbury Town to Oakdale Hall and got there right at eight forty-nine. Pretty good response time, I'd say." Sheriff Dowdy beamed at the spectators.

"Did your desk sergeant say whether Miss…or Missus (Pommus couldn't help rubbing that one in)…Dubrowski had said anything else, for example, that Mr. Cory was alive or dead?"

"No, now that you mention it, I don't recall that he did. Guess I'll have to ask him, or you will."

"Maybe I will," Pommus shot back. Despite this being a non-adversarial proceeding and despite the sheriff being a so-called "friendly" witness, the district attorney, evidently enjoying himself, pressed on. "Didn't say whether the housekeeper said whether it was Mr. Cory'd shot himself, or it was someone else?"

Sheriff Dowdy, apparently not expecting to be cross-examined by his own side shifted his ample rear end around in the witness chair and gave Pommus a shut-up glare.

District Attorney Pommus and Sheriff Dowdy are both elected officials. They belong to different political parties, not an infrequent circumstance in Maine. Moreover, in addition to their political rivalry, they have to compete for their respective departments' shares of the county budget every year, a contest that would have caused friction even between the most congenial of political bed-fellows. So although the next election year was not until 1920, it never hurt to embarrass the other party's elected officials when the opportunity presented itself as it just had. And as a bonus, doing so would provide additional leverage in the annual grovel before the county commissioners at budget time.

Without the constraints that might have been imposed by a judge or opposing counsel, Pommus pressed on. "Tell us, Sheriff Dowdy," Pommus cleared his throat, "what was the scene when you arrived at Oakdale Hall yesterday morning at approximately eight-forty in the morning?"

"It was '*exactly* eight forty-*nine*,' I said. We drove up the driveway and parked in front of the house. The housekeeper (Sheriff Dowdy was apparently being careful not stick his chin out on the miss-or-missus knowledge gap again) met us at the front door which she opened as we were first coming up the steps. She led us into a front hallway and from there into a large parlor to the right of the hallway. I believe she called it a 'music room.' Well, whatever it is, we went through a double doorway, the lintel is curved and comes to a point in the middle..."

"Yes, yes, go on," Coroner Ingersoll interrupted.

Sheriff Dowdy looked up at the bench and gave a slight shrug. "Yes, Sir, your honor...I mean Mr. Coroner. Not knowing what to expect, I had my hand on my side-arm as did the rest of my men on their own weapons. Well, of course, that wasn't necessary as there was no one in the room beside us, the housekeeper and Mr. Cory, and anybody could see that he was not a threat to anyone.

"Well I approached Mr. Cory..."

"You mean the *late* Mr. Cory, don't you, Sheriff Dowdy?" District Attorney Pommus asked mildly.

Another sharp glance from the sheriff was met with the faintest of smirks by Pommus. "Well, until I got close enough to see him, I couldn't truthfully say that, could I, Mr. District Attorney?"

"A fine distinction, Sheriff Dowdy. Thank you for making it for us." At this, the District attorney's half-formed smirk quickly receded. "At what point did you determine that Mr. Cory was in fact the *late* Mr. Cory?"

"Well," Sheriff Dowdy smiling slightly at having evened the score with Pommus continued, "he was seated in an upholstered armchair near the fireplace. There's the chair and a low coffee table. There's a settee on the opposite side of the coffee table. The chair and the settee face each other just in front of the fireplace. He looked like he was asleep. His head was down with his chin almost touching his chest. When I got up in front of him I could see a bullet-hole in his right temple and there was a revolver, a .22-caliber Smith & Wesson six-shot single-action, Model 17 in his right hand which was dangling over the arm of the chair.

"I removed the revolver from his hand; his finger was inside the trigger guard and it was pretty stiff—*rigor mortis* I'd say—making it hard to pry the weapon out of his hand. As soon as I did that, I instructed one of my men to go with the housekeeper, Dubrowski, and use the house telephone to call Doc Goodson and to take the Ford and go fetch him. I then felt for a carotid pulse, something I've learned to do," he again shot a self-satisfied look at the spectators, "and found that there was not one."

"Are you sure *rigor mortis* had set in? Isn't that something we'd best leave for Doc Goodson to tell us? You'd not be wanting to steal the march on him, would you, Sheriff Dowdy?"

"I've been in this job a good many years, Mr. Pommus. I think I can recognize *rigor mortis* when I see it."

"Perhaps, Sheriff Dowdy, perhaps you can." Pommus evidently was willing to call that one a draw. "But why don't you just tell us what you did next."

"Well, two things: First, I had several of my men search the premises just in case it was an intruder shot the deceased and might still be lurking about. Second, I had a couple more deputies look around, see if they could maybe find a suicide note. While they were doin' that, I opened the breech of the revolver and checked the cylinder."

"What, if anything, did you find?" Pommus asked.

"The cylinder holds six rounds. I found five live rounds, .22-longs they were, and the sixth chamber, the one in front of the firing pin and lined up with the barrel, contained a spent round, also a .22-long. I unloaded the weapon, and then held it up to my nose so I could smell the barrel in order to determine whether the weapon had been fired recently."

"And…," Coroner Ingersoll started to ask.

"You can't always be absolutely sure that way, because it's always possible that the revolver's owner didn't take proper care of it such as cleaning it after every use. But I'd say, based on my experience, that the weapon had been fired recently."

Pommus shot his cuffs and fingered the lapels of jacket. Turning to the jury, he asked, "And would you also say Sheriff Dowdy that the recent firing resulted in the bullet wound you observed in the deceased's right temple?"

"Well," Sheriff Dowdy also turned toward the jury, "that would certainly be the most likely conclusion to be drawn from the evidence."

Pommus paused and tugged at his chin. "Indeed, Sheriff Dowdy. And may the jury understand that you, based on your years of experience in law enforcement, drew that conclusion?"

"I suppose he could have died of a heart attack or something and then someone came along and shot him to be sure he was dead," Sheriff Dowdy paused to chuckle at his own witticism. But seeing that no one else shared his sense of humor, he quickly put on his most officious face. "Yes, Mr. District Attorney, that'd be my conclusion. Mr.

Cory died of a wound caused by a single round fired from a .22-caliber weapon, the very one I found in his hand when I saw him as I described earlier in my testimony."

"Is it your further opinion that the gunshot wound that caused the death of Richard Cory was inflicted by Mr. Cory himself?"

"Considering that the weapon was still in his hand, there was no evidence of a struggle, no evidence of an intruder, and the housekeeper did not report that she'd heard any arguing or ruckus of any sort, even though my men did not find a suicide note, I do believe that Mr. Cory took his own life. I should add, Mr. Pommus, that there was a decanter of brandy and an empty glass—I believe it's called a 'snifter,' you know, one of those glasses that's fat around the bottom and narrow at the top—on the table just in front of Richard Cory's body. I'd say that he took a pretty good snort to sort of work up his courage to shoot himself."

"Thank you for that added bit of information about the brandy decanter, Mr. Dowdy. If I understand you rightly, it's your view that Mr. Cory drank the brandy to steady his nerves before he shot himself."

"That's correct, Mr. Pommus."

There are two vitally important rules of examining a witness, especially a hostile one: Never ask a question to which you do not already know the answer, and quit while you're ahead. By reason of painful experience, District Attorney Pommus was well aware of these rules. Never-the-less, he couldn't help violating both. "Did I understand you to say you found no suicide letter?"

"No, Mr. Pommus, you must have misunderstood. I said *my men*, in searching the obvious and accessible places where one who intended to take his own life and wished to declare that intention to those who might come across his earthly remains in the event he successfully carried out that intention, found no such writing in any form." Sheriff Dowdy leaned forward both hands gripping the railing that forms the front of the witness box. "While I have every confidence that *my men* went about their assigned task with their usual diligence, and that they did, in the performance of that task, do a thorough job, the possibility remains that there may exist such a memorandum of Mr. Cory's intent in some concealed place, such as a wall safe. So in the interest of stating the truth as my witness oath binds me to do, I wish to make it clear that I personally made no such search and no such document came to my notice during my time at Oakdale Hall. And, in the interest of telling the *whole* truth, as I am likewise bound to do, my men found no such document, leastwise that they brought to my attention."

By now District Attorney Pommus's animus toward his political rival had rendered him oblivious to the coroner, the coroner's jury, the spectators' gallery, and indeed to anything except his antagonist seated in the witness box in front of him. "Very well, Mr. Sheriff, do I understand then that thus far no suicide letter or equivalent document has thus far been found?"

"That is a correct statement, Mr. District Attorney."

"Well, then, let me ask you this: In the 'diligent' — I believe that's the word you used — search conducted by your men, did they come across any letter or other document that would shed any light on why Mr. Cory would wish to end his life by means of a bullet through his head last Saturday night or in the early hours of Sunday morning last? Or did they perhaps come across anything that would indicate that someone else desired him dead and acted upon that desire?

Coroner Ingersoll had taken about all of District Attorney Pommus that any man ought to be subjected to, especially on an empty stomach. "That's *two* questions, Mr. Pommus. And when the sheriff answers those, that'll be the last questions you'll ask him. You said when we started that you expected to be through by lunchtime, so whether you're done with whatever it is you're trying to do, or not, we're going to lunch and when we reconvene, you can put on Dr. Goodson and your other witnesses, although I can't for the life of me see why you need to. Sheriff Dowdy, now you go ahead and answer Mr. Pommus's questions, if you remember 'em and if you know the answers. And if you do, please make your answers short."

Sheriff Dowdy looked up at the coroner, "Yes Sir, I will." Turning back toward the jury, he continued. "We found some documents; I suppose you'd call them. There was some sort of account ledger, and there was one letter. Both items were removed into the custody of my office. Whether any of them has anything to do with Mr. Cory's death remains to be seen."

"What kind of…"

"That's all, Mr. District Attorney. This inquest is in recess until 2:00 o'clock. Jurors, you're excused until then. I'm also supposed to tell you not to discuss the case, but I expect you won't listen to me. Hardly anyone does." Coroner Ingersoll carefully rose gingerly stepping down off the *Maine Reports*, and made his way off the bench.

Chapter Three

By 2:15 the principals, the coroner, the jury, the district attorney and Sheriff Dowdy, along with enough of the morning session's spectators to fill the gallery, if not the standing room, had taken their places. The clerk had again called the case, and District Attorney Pommus had indicated his readiness to proceed. "The State calls Dr. Philip Goodson," he intoned. Doctor Goodson was already in the courtroom seated in one of the spare chairs situated inside the bar behind the State's counsel table. He took his place in the witness box and the district attorney, after briefly consulting his time-piece, began. "You understand Doctor Goodson that you're still under oath from this morning?"

"Yes, Sir, I do."

"Then please state your name for the record."

"Philip Goodson; no middle name."

"You are a physician, are you not?"

"Yes, Sir."

"Please give us a brief summary of your professional background."

"Baccalaureate degree in science from Union College, Schenectady, New York; medical degree, Harvard College Medical School, Boston Massachusetts; internship and residency, Massachusetts General Hospital, Boston, Massachusetts; military service, Walter Reed General Hospital, Washington, D.C. Went in a captain, came out a major. Been in private practice in Tilbury Town ever since."

"Quite an impressive resume, Dr. Goodson."

"Thank you, Mr. District Attorney."

Coroner Ingersoll leaned forward. "I'm well aware of Doc Goodson's qualifications, Mr. Pommus. And I'm quite willing, as are we all, to accept his medical opinion in regard to the death of Mr. Cory, just as we defer to his judgment in regard to the health of the living. Now could we please get to the part about Mr. Cory?"

"Absolutely, Mr. Coroner," Pommus gave a slight submissive bow as he'd learned to do on the not-infrequent occasions when he'd been admonished by the judge. "Very well. Dr. Goodson, did you have occasion to go to Oakdale Hall, the home of the deceased, Richard Cory, yesterday morning?"

"Indeed I did, Sir. It was a few minutes after ten o'clock that I arrived there."

"And how did you happen to go there?"

"Please Mr. Pommus," the coroner injected. "We've already heard how Sheriff Dowdy had one of his men go to fetch Dr. Goodson. Please get to what you've put him on the stand for."

This time, not even a hint of a submissive bow. "What did you see when you arrived?"

"I was brought immediately to the music room by the sheriff's deputy. When I entered the room, I saw Sheriff Dowdy and several of his men standing around an armchair in front of the fireplace. At that time I did not see Mr. Cory, nor did I see anyone in obvious need of medical attention or who was beyond the need for medical attention."

"You mean…"

"Yes, Sir. The deputy that called told me only that I was urgently needed at Oakdale Hall and that a car would be at my home to bring me there in a few minutes. The deputy that came to fetch me said he was ordered not to say anything about why I'd been summoned; only that it was urgent. Once we got started in that direction, he was too busy driving and I was too busy trying not to get thrown out of the vehicle going around corners to have any more conversation.

"I approached Sheriff Dowdy and we shook hands. As we did, I saw Mr. Cory for the first time. As I stood next to Sheriff Dowdy, I couldn't see any gross trauma. His head was down with his chin resting on his chest. His left hand was in his lap, and his right arm was extended down outside the arm of the chair. From his facial pallor and the absence of any movement of his diaphragm, he did not appear to be breathing. I immediately went to him to check for a carotid pulse. It was then that I saw what appeared to me to be a gunshot wound to the right temporal region of his skull. Although it appeared to be unnecessary, I went ahead and checked for a carotid pulse and did not detect one. To be absolutely certain, I also took a small mirror from my medical bag and held it close to his nose and mouth. I also opened the front of his shirt and applied my stethoscope to see if there perhaps was a heartbeat, however faint."

"I take it there was none?"

"That is correct."

"How was Mr. Cory attired?"

"He was wearing a smoking jacket. I believe the fabric is called "brocade." It was gold in color with black velvet lapels. The jacket was open at the waist. Underneath, he wore a white dress shirt. All the studs were fastened except for the collar which was loose. His bow-tie was undone and hanging open around his neck. He was wearing black formal trousers, the buttons of which were undone."

This last bit of information produced gasps and blushes from a number of the ladies still in attendance. This provoked several sharp raps of Judge Gribble's gavel until decorum was restored. "Order! Order!" Coroner Ingersoll sputtered as the bailiff, who was having his customary afternoon nap in his chair next to the jury box, came to his feet.

"Will there be any more such testimony, Mr. Pommus? Shall I have the bailiff clear the spectator gallery?"

"I, I don't know, Your…Mr. Coroner. I had no idea that Dr. Goodson was going to say what he said." Pommus glared at Sheriff Dowdy. "The sheriff neglected to mention that fact to me in his report."

"Dr. Goodson?"

"I don't know, Eb…I mean Mr. Coroner. I'm just telling what I saw; answering the questions Mr. Pommus puts to me."

"Well, in the interest of the whole truth being told, I suppose you must. But if you've got any more details of that nature, before you give them please let me know so that I can invite the ladies to excuse themselves first."

"Yes, of course. I'll try to do that."

"Did you notice anything else that was of significance to you in regard to his appearance?"

Determined to maintain his professional detachment, Dr. Goodson ignored the urge to respond "Other than the bullet wound in his head and the fact that he was dead?" Instead, he continued, "He was still wearing patent leather dress shoes, but that would not be remarkable considering that he was still wearing formal evening attire as I said. As far as the body itself, other than the apparent gunshot wound to his right temple, and its after-effects, there was nothing remarkable about his appearance."

"Thank you, Doctor. I'll come back to the after-effects in a minute. First let me ask you this: You say the wound was to his right temple, is that correct?"

Dr. Goodson nodded.

"Please say yes or no, Dr. Goodson. Wouldn't want any of the jurors to mistake a nod for a shake."

"Sorry, gentlemen. Yes, the wound was to the right temple."

"Do you know whether Richard Cory was right or left-handed?"

"Well, I'd have to say that he was right-handed, but it's possible that he was ambidextrous; that is, he could use both hands. I remember seeing him once or twice at the golf club, although we never played together. I do recall that one time he was in a foursome in front of me. It seems to me that he swung his driver right-handed. I also received a Christmas card from him every year and the handwriting, if I recall rightly, is that of a right-handed person. Of course he could have had a secretary or someone else address the card and inscribe a greeting, but the handwriting, as I think about it, was always the same, a man's handwriting, not a woman's. In fact, the "e" at the end of the word 'Avenue' and at the end of the word 'Maine' were both what's called a "Greek *E*" instead of a cursive 'e'. I always thought that an unusual affectation. Anyhow, that makes me pretty sure that the handwriting was the same every year. And I don't recall that Mr. Cory had a male secretary, certainly not one who'd been with him eight or nine years running. So my best guess is that Richard Cory is…was right-handed."

"Very good. Thank you, Dr. Goodson. Now have you ever attended an apparent suicide by gunshot before?"

"I saw a number of them at Mass General and also at Walter Reed, at least thirty or more. Since I've been in practice in Tilbury Town, I've seen a few gunshot deaths that might have been suicides but weren't."

"Isn't it usually the case that a right-handed person will shoot himself in the right temple as opposed to trying to shoot himself in the left?"

"In the great majority of cases, that's true. However, I've seen and read about cases where the deceased — it's almost always a man — has shot himself and tried to make it look like someone else fired the shot. Usually they do that where there's life insurance involved and the beneficiary can't collect if the death's a suicide. Or maybe there's a double-indemnity provision in the case of accidental death, so they try to make it look like an accident."

"Yes, of course. But let's move on to the case at hand." District Attorney Pommus looked up hoping to receive some sign of approbation from Coroner Ingersoll. Disappointed, he continued. "So if I understand your testimony, you've seen more than thirty gunshot wound deaths in your professional career?"

"More than a hundred all told."

"Do you know whether Richard Cory as of yesterday suffered from any condition, say a weak heart, or a bad liver or some such?"

"Well, he didn't come to me on a regular basis. It's therefore possible that he may have been attended by another physician for such a condition. I did see him back in the spring; I treated him for a separated shoulder. Said he'd fallen from his horse. Didn't look like that kind of injury to me, but it was obvious that he'd suffered a mild separation. Anyway, I reintegrated the joint—it was his left—and that was that. Since he said he'd fallen off a horse, I insisted on examining him to see if there were any other injuries, like a concussion or ruptured spleen, or perhaps a broken rib that might perforate a lung or even his heart. He said okay, so I gave him a pretty thorough going over. I didn't notice any abnormal heart or lung sounds. His blood pressure was well within the normal range; his eyes, ears, nose and mouth showed no evidence of disease. His pupils reacted normally and equally to light and a sensory neurological examination was also equal and normal. I couldn't accurately test his grip, because I didn't want to aggravate his injured shoulder. So based on that examination, and based on the fact that he'd never consulted me about any serious symptom before, I'd say that until late Saturday night, Richard Cory enjoyed robust good health. Even his teeth were perfect; nary a filling that I could see."

"You said 'until late Saturday night?'"

"Yes, Sir. When I did my superficial examination to see if he was possibly still alive, I determined that *rigor mortis* was pretty well set in. That must have been right around half past ten. *Rigor mortis* usually starts about three hours after death occurs and reaches its maximum at about twelve hours. He was getting pretty stiff by the time I got to him, so I'd say he'd been dead about eight to ten hours. I wanted to get a rectal body temperature—that would have helped with the time—but Sheriff Dowdy said we'd best not."

"So again, if I understand what you're telling the coroner and this jury, Richard Cory died of a self-inflicted gunshot wound between midnight and two o'clock in the early Sunday morning hours?"

"No, Sir, I said nothing about self-inflicted."

Before Coroner Ingersoll could break Judge Gribble's gavel, the bailiff and Sheriff Dowdy were both on their feet calling for quiet in the spectator benches. The jurors, at least half of whom had all but dozed off, heedless of Coroner Ingersoll's admonition not to discuss the case until all the evidence was in, began an animated conversation punctuated by numerous "It can't be's" and "I told you so's," so that it took a full ten minutes for a semblance of decorum to be restored.

During that interval, District Attorney Pommus and Sheriff Dowdy engaged in an intense half-whispered, many-gestured conversation, the gist of which was Dowdy to Pommus: "You damned fool; why'd you have to ask *him* that. You had *my* testimony!" Pommus to Dowdy: "Don't you call me a 'damned fool'. You're the one sent for him to inspect the body and assured me that a small-town doctor like Goodson would see that Cory'd shot himself. Now we've got to hear the rest of what the good doctor has to say."

The *tête-à-tête* was cut short by Coroner Ingersoll. "Well, well, gentlemen. Now we do have an interestin' situation here. Sheriff Dowdy's of the opinion that Richard Cory did away with himself. On the other hand, we've got Doc Goodson here who's seen over a hundred gunshot deaths, sayin' that it weren't Richard Cory pulled the trigger at all. And with Sheriff Dowdy's assurance that there weren't a suicide note, I'd say the jury needs to hear why Doc Goodson's of a mind to call it a homicide and not a suicide."

"If I may say something, Mr. Coroner," Dr. Goodson rose in the witness box and turned toward the judge's bench. "The absence of an apparent suicide letter…or 'note' if you prefer…did not influence my thinking. Some doctors in academic medicine have done studies and found that a letter or note is left in less than twenty-five percent of confirmed suicide cases. And that includes gunshot suicides and suicides by hanging, poison and jumping off bridges or tall buildings."

"Thank you for pointing that out, Dr. Goodson. Gentlemen of the jury, you'll want to take that into account in your deliberations.

"Mr. Pommus, are you ready to continue asking your questions? It's getting a bit late in the day. Since we were unable to finish before lunch as you indicated you intended, I'm sure I don't want to keep the jury past their dinner. County commissioners'll have a fit if they have to pay for the jury's dinner."

District Attorney Pommus brushed aside Sheriff Dowdy's restraining hand on his elbow. "Yes, Mr. Coroner. As you remarked earlier, Sir, we all respect Dr. Goodson's expert opinions, both in every-day health matters as well as forensic medicine."

Sheriff Dowdy, so that the spectators could not see his red face and bulging eyes, sat facing the witness box his elbows planted on the counsel table and his face resting in his hands.

Turning to the witness, District Attorney Pommus began, "Sheriff Dowdy testified this morning…"

"Wait just a minute, Mr. Pommus. You had me 'invoke the Rule' or whatever you called it just this morning. I was given to understand that the whole idea was to keep one witness from hearing what another was saying. And now you're about to tell Doc Goodson what Sheriff

Dowdy testified to this morning. Why…"

"No, no, Mr. Coroner. It's okay if I do it. The rule doesn't bind the lawyers in the case, just the…"

"Now if that ain't the silliest damn thing…Oh! Sorry, ladies. Please pardon my coarse language." Several fans in the spectator benches were pressed to lips to stanch the titters that would have otherwise emanated.

"You lawyers. If you're trying to pull a fast one here, Mr. Pommus, it'll go hard…"

District Attorney Pommus gripped his lapels and turned his profile to the spectator benches. "I assure you, Mr. Coroner, as the duly elected and serving district…" an audible "not for long" came from one of the back rows…"attorney, it would be beneath the dignity of my office to misstate the law, even in this," he paused, "*quasi*-judicial proceeding. Now may I continue?

"Very, well, Mr. Pommus, but consider yourself warned. If you've stepped over the line, by whatever powers that are vested in me…"

"Thank you, Mr. Coroner. Now, Dr. Goodson, as I was about to say: Sheriff Dowdy testified this morning that when he first approached Mr. Cory he was seated in the chair just as you described; his chin was resting on his chest, his left hand was in his lap and his right hand draped over the right arm of the chair. When he went to check for a carotid pulse—just as you did—just like you, he noticed the gunshot wound in Mr. Cory's right temple. The only difference between what he saw and what you saw is that Mr. Cory had a .22-caliber," Pommus paused to consult his notes, "Smith & Wesson revolver in his right hand." Turning to Sheriff Dowdy, he said, "You said this morning that his finger was inside the trigger guard. Was it his index or trigger finger?"

"Trigger finger, or index finger. Yes, I'm sure of that."

Coroner Ingersoll scratched his chin for a moment. "Mr. Pommus, under your 'Rule' is Sheriff Dowdy still under oath?"

"Yes, Sir, he is."

"Gentlemen of the jury, then you may consider in your deliberations, if we ever get to that point, what Sheriff Dowdy just said…about it being Mr. Cory's trigger or index finger that was inside the trigger guard of the revolver…just as though Sheriff Dowdy'd said it from the witness stand."

"Yes, thank you Mr. Coroner." District Attorney Pommus

instinctively gave his slight bow toward the bench.

"Now if Sheriff Dowdy's telling the truth…"

Sheriff Dowdy was out of his chair grabbing District Attorney Pommus by the shoulder, "Why you no-account buffoon, I'm gonna…" At that Sheriff Dowdy drew back his fist and threw a round-house right that managed to clip the end of District Attorney Pommus's nose resulting in a gout of blood that splattered the district attorney's foolscap pad as well as the front of the sheriff's dress uniform. In attempting to get free of the sheriff's grip, the district attorney tore the jacket of his best courtroom suit. When he finally did get loose he ran around the front of the counsel table. As he and the sheriff were playing "pop goes the weasel" around the table, Coroner Ingersoll, standing on the stack of law books, was banging Judge Gribble's gavel to no apparent effect, until it finally cracked at the neck with the head landing in the second row of the jury box, just missing the head of juror number three.

The bailiff, a superannuated deputy but still on the sheriff's departmental payroll, weighing his duty of loyalty to his employer and his clear duty as the person in charge of courtroom security and decorum, managed to get in front of the district attorney so as to place himself in between the sheriff and the district attorney.

As the co-equal guardians of the public peace and safety in Kennebec County were trying to catch their breath, Coroner Ingersoll managed to croak, "This matter will be in recess for fifteen minutes. This may be only a *quasi*-judicial proceeding, but you Mr. District Attorney, and you Mr. Sheriff can take your political differences and deal with them somewhere else. *Not* in this courtroom!"

Chapter Four

While Dr. Goodson tended to District Attorney Pommus's nose in the men's lavatory, the sheriff had used the phone in the clerk's office to call his own office and then returned to the courtroom, this time seating himself at the vacant defense table. So when Coroner Ingersoll, using the head of Judge Gribble's gavel, rapped for order twenty minutes later, a uniformed sheriff's deputy tapped District Attorney Pommus on the shoulder and handed him several pages headed "Incident Report Form" along with a small cardboard box about the size of a shoe box, a ledger-type book, a manila folder and an envelope marked "taken from Oakdale Hall, the date and the initials G.A.D". The district attorney glanced at the form and rippled through the manila folder contents, looked briefly in the box and then placed them all on the counsel table next to his foolscap pad.

"Before we begin, Mr. Coroner, I wish to say that I did not intend to impugn the sheriff's veracity. I meant only that we should take Sheriff Dowdy's word that there was a gun in Mr. Cory's right hand when the sheriff first examined him. I'm sorry that anyone took offense at my choice of words. Surely Sheriff Dowdy would not fabricate something of that importance, especially since a number of his deputies were present and would no doubt come forward to contradict him, should his testimony be in error."

"Why you…" Sheriff Dowdy was on his feet again and took a step toward the district attorney. He stopped, either because he saw the bailiff placing his hand on his side-arm or because his political survival instinct took hold. Instead he turned to face the spectator benches, "Folks, I've been your sheriff for nearly eighteen years. During that time not once has anyone even thought to question my truthfulness or integrity — until now. And I hope you'll excuse my strong reaction. But I'd say that any one of you would have acted the same way if you'd been called a liar by some self-serving politician passing himself off as a representative of the people. Then he steps up and tries to tell you he didn't say what you all heard him say barely twenty minutes ago. And then he suggests to you that the only reason I'd be telling the truth is that there were others present who would come forward to call me a liar. I just had my office turn over our file together with the evidence collected at the scene to the district attorney. From now on he can handle it any way he chooses. My belief is Mr. Cory took his own life and that's that.

Mr. Pommus here is just stringin' this out for whatever political gain he can get out of it. I, for one, will have no more of it." His piece said, the sheriff returned to his seat.

"That's enough from the both of you. Any more carrying on and I'll recess this inquiry and ask the attorney general's office to send somebody over who'll do a proper job and leave politics out of it. I want to hear what Doc Goodson has to say, and I expect the jury and the other folks do as well. Mr. Pommus are you ready to proceed, or do I call a recess?"

"Oh no, Mr. Coroner. Since Sheriff Dowdy's turned the matter over to my office, there'll be no need for further delay. Dr. Goodson, would you please re-take the witness stand?"

After Dr. Goodson had resumed his seat in the witness box and Coroner Ingersoll had reminded him that he was still under oath, District Attorney Pommus continued, "Before the recess, Dr. Goodson, you expressed your disagreement with the sheriff's opinion that Mr. Cory'd taken his own life. Are we to understand that you're of the opinion he did not do so?"

"That's correct, Mr. District Attorney."

"Well, Sir, tell us what led you to form that opinion."

"Several things." Dr. Goodson looked up at the coroner, "Is it okay if I just tell what makes me think Mr. Cory's death was not a suicide?"

"Indeed, and if Mr. Pommus or I have any questions, we'll hold 'em 'till you're done. Please go ahead."

"Thank you, Eb." Turning to the jury box, he continued, "The first thing I noticed that's inconsistent with suicide..." He paused and looked up at Coroner Ingersoll. "Eb, I'm going to have to mention again about his..."

"You mean his trousers being..."

"Yes, what I said this morning."

"Go ahead, Phil. I think by now with what all's gone on already, everybody's pretty much past being shocked, so say what you need to say, and I'll apologize to the ladies present for you."

"Okay. Ladies, please excuse my having to describe such an embarrassing matter. When I was still in medical school and later during my internship and residency, in order to make some money to supplement my scholarship and later my intern's and resident's salary, I worked as often as I could for the Suffolk County — that's Boston — medical examiner's office. Most of the time my work was washing the bodies when they brought them in for autopsy, cleaning the autopsy table and mopping the blood and body wastes from the floor. Sometimes I'd help with the autopsy; the medical examiner'd let me make the Y incision in the deceased's chest and abdomen. Sometimes I'd weigh the organs when he removed them."

At that, there was a small commotion in the back of the courtroom. "Pardon me for interrupting you." Coroner Ingersoll was standing on his law-book perch. "Looks like one of the ladies in the back has fainted. Would you mind taking a look to be sure she's alright? Mr. Bailiff, will you help Doc Goodson out? Maybe carry her out to the benches in the hall; get her a glass of water. Does anyone else feel faint? Mr. Pommus, you're looking a little green. Do you need to step out?

"No thank you, Mr. Coroner," District Attorney Pommus replied without much conviction. "Perhaps I'll join the bailiff in assisting the unfortunate lady and maybe have a drink of water myself. My throat's a little dry as it sometimes gets when I'm speaking as much as I have today."

"Fine; you do that. Take your time. I think we can manage 'till you get back."

District Attorney Pommus rose in his seat and started to reply, but instead put his hand over his mouth and dashed from the courtroom.

Following the recess during which the "unfortunate lady" had been restored to sentience by a whiff of smelling salts from Doc Goodson's medical bag everyone had resumed their places, including the lady and District Attorney Pommus. Dr. Goodson resumed his seat and his testimony. "Well, later on, during my residency and when I was at Walter Reed, I would often go with the deputy medical examiners to the scene where the body was discovered. So I also saw a number of male gunshot suicides *in situ*...that is, I mean, where they occurred. Sorry for the Latin; I'll leave that to the lawyers from now on."

"Thank you, Phil. I'm sure everyone appreciates that."

"The point is that in all the male gunshot suicides I've seen, I've never seen one where the deceased unbuttoned his trousers first. In fact, I don't expect that any man who was going to do away with himself would want to be found with his trousers unbuttoned or in any state of disarray. He may unbutton his collar, just as I found Mr. Cory. But a man would never unbutton his trousers or leave them unbuttoned.

"It's much like what happens in female suicides, which are usually by an overdose of a sleeping potion or by poison. Almost invariably, a woman of even modest means will put on a favorite dress, fix her hair and apply make-up so as to be found looking her best. Even in the case of gunshot suicides, a woman will be more likely to shoot herself in the chest — aiming for her heart — than to risk spoiling her appearance by a gunshot wound to the head.

The district attorney rose in his place at the counsel table in an effort to make himself relevant. "Thank you, I'm sure, for that information, Dr. Goodson. But are we to understand that because he was discovered with his trousers unbuttoned you believe Richard Cory was murdered?" Pommus smirked at the jury and resumed his seat.

Doctor Goodson shook his head in disgust. "It is possible that Mr. Cory's trousers being unbuttoned had something to do with his murder — indeed that's quite likely — but that's not the sole reason for my conclusion that the gunshot wound to Mr. Cory's temple was not self-inflicted. May I continue, Mr. Pommus?"

"It's not up to me, Dr. Goodson," Pommus sat down dejectedly.

"Well it *is* up to me." The coroner leaned forward in his chair. "Go ahead, Phil. And as for you, Mr. Pommus, I said we'd hold any questions until Phil...Dr. Goodson...is through. If you interrupt again, I'll have the bailiff handcuff you to that chair and stick a gag in your mouth. Do I make myself clear?"

Pommus started to rise and give one of his obsequious bows, but decided to remain in his seat. "Yes, Mr...."

Coroner Ingersoll raised from his chair, balancing precariously on the stack of law books, "Whoa, Mr. Pommus. I said not another word. Phil...Dr. Goodson...you were saying..."

"I was saying that there are other strong indications that Richard Cory did not pull the trigger. Most important of all, the gun was not held pressed to the flesh of Mr. Cory's temple. It had to have been fired from a distance, albeit a short one. Say two to four inches. And..."

"You know that because...Sorry Phil, that kinda just slipped out. Since Mr. Pommus has shut up, I'd best do the same. Please go ahead."

"I know that because of the size of the powder stippling around the wound. A gunshot suicide will always press the barrel against his head, or chest, wherever he plans to shoot himself. He doesn't want to take the chance of missing, you know, having the bullet carom off his skull instead of penetrating. Also, it serves to steady the weapon.

"When a revolver is fired, not all of the propellant...the gunpowder... burns. The unburned powder and the ash or residue that's left from the powder that did ignite is pushed out the barrel along with the bullet. When the barrel is pressed up against the skin, as in the case of a suicide, the stippling is very small making a very compact, uniform ring, maybe a quarter to nearly half an inch in width around the entrance wound, depending on the bore of the weapon. Most of the unspent powder and powder ash goes into the wound and not around it.

"On the other hand, when the shot comes from close range, the unspent powder and powder residue make a much larger pattern around the entrance wound and very little goes into the wound itself. Depending on the caliber and type of weapon and the distance, a close-range shot can leave a pattern—often star-shaped when a revolver is used—as much as a couple of inches from one point of the 'star' to the opposite one.

"Now I looked closely at Mr. Cory's entrance wound. There was a star-shaped pattern of black material, undoubtedly gunshot residue, around the entrance wound. This can only mean that the barrel of the revolver was held a few inches from Mr. Cory's temple and that the barrel was not pressed against the skin. In my experience, as I testified earlier, that strongly—I'd say virtually conclusively—indicates that Mr. Cory was shot by someone else.

"There are two other factors that strongly suggest that Richard Cory did not fire the weapon that put the hole in his head. First, a revolver is a reliable but messy weapon. By that I mean in addition to all the stuff that comes out the barrel along with the bullet, there's also a residue of spent and unspent powder that comes out of the space between the firing chamber and the barrel. In a well-made revolver—such as a Smith & Wesson—the gap is only a millimeter or so. But it's enough that some of the residue will be expelled from the side of the revolver and end up on the hand of the person who fired it. I found no such traces on Mr. Cory's right hand.

"Second, a .22-caliber long rifle bullet typically contains forty grains of lead. The muzzle velocity of this type of revolver with a six-inch barrel..." Goodson paused..."it is a six-inch barrel isn't it Mr. Pommus?" Pommus reached into the box and held the weapon up. "Yup, that's a six-inch barrel. So the muzzle velocity is something like one thousand, eighty feet per second. Now there is a formula for calculating this that's pretty exact, but for our purposes I think probably everyone on the jury's fired a handgun or rifle, or a shotgun at sometime in his life. So I assume that they're all familiar with the recoil or kick when such a weapon is fired. In any case, even with a bullet as small as a .22-caliber long-rifle, there's going to be some kick. Also, to a lesser extent there's going to be some movement of the target away from the gun muzzle as the target absorbs the energy of the bullet."

All the jurors along with the spectators nodded in agreement as the district attorney and sheriff studied their respective fingernails.

"Because of the recoil, or kick if you prefer, it's pretty unusual in my experience for a suicide to still be holding the gun. When someone's shot in the brain, as the bullet pierces the skull, its energy creates a cavitation-like effect. I mean the energy of the bullet creates a larger path through the tissue than the diameter of the bullet. In the case of a .22 long-rifle with a muzzle velocity of at least one thousand, eighty feet per second, fired at close range, as the bullet travels through the brain matter it creates a path that is at least twice the diameter of the bullet. Now this cavity goes back to the diameter of the bullet just as quickly as the bullet passes through the tissue, but before it does it interrupts the function of the brain much more than just the damage created by the path of the bullet. So the brain, in effect, shuts down and as a result peripheral motor nerve responses shut down immediately. This means, in plain English, that the brain is no longer sending signals to the hand, thus the hand cannot continue to function. In other words, as soon as the bullet entered Mr. Cory's brain, his hand no longer had the ability to hold the revolver. In my opinion, if Richard Cory'd fired the shot, the revolver would have fallen from his hand either next to the sofa, or as much as a foot away.

"Also, it's likely that the impact of the bullet would have forced his head in the opposite direction, that is, to his left. While the impact from a .22 long-rifle wouldn't have necessarily toppled him over, I would expect at least some turning of his head to his left. And as I noted, his chin was down toward the mid-line of his chest, not pushed to one side.

"So taking all that into account, it's my professional opinion that the gunshot wound that caused the death of Richard Cory was not self-inflicted."

When Dr. Goodson had completed his testimony, juror number one, Weldon Bailey, stood up. "Your honor, I mean Eb, no... I mean Mr. Coroner, we'd all like to inspect the body of Mr. Cory...I mean the deceased. We think we got what Doc Goodson was sayin', but then with Sheriff Dowdy being of a different mind, it'd sure help us to make up ours. Can we do that?"

Well, I...Mr. Pommus, any objection? Mr. Dowdy, you have any problem with that?"

Pommus, totally out of his depth, managed a "No, Mr. Coroner,

I don't suppose there's any rule that prohibits it. And if it'll help the jury, then we have no objection."

"It's up to you," Sheriff Dowdy allowed. "My office has washed its hands of the whole thing. I don't care how many degrees Doc Goodson has or how many suicides he's seen. I know what I saw and in my opinion Richard Cory killed himself. If you and the jury want to believe all that stuff about 'muzzle velocity' and 'cavitation' or whatever he called it, well that's your right. But I say Richard Cory died of a self-inflicted gunshot wound and you can look at his corpse until the flesh rots away, and I still won't change my mind."

"Bailiff, please ask Mr. Davis to step in here a minute, would you?"

Ulysses Davis, escorted by the bailiff stood in front of the bench, clearly uncomfortable in the unfamiliar and rather intimidating surroundings. Rotating his derby hat nervously in his hands he managed a "Yes, Sir. How can I help? All I did is pick up the remains as Sheriff Dowdy tol' me to do and bring him to my place just like he said. Did I do something wrong?"

"Oh no, Mr. Davis, you did exactly right. I just want to ask if Mr. Cory's remains are in the same condition as when you removed them from Oakdale Hall last night."

"Yes, Sir, Mr. Ingersoll. Only difference is that Sheriff Dowdy tol' me to remove the deceased's clothing and pack the body in ice until further instructions. That's just what we — my apprentice and me — done. Except we had a devil of a time gettin' him — Mr. Cory that is — into the ice box on account of the *rigor mortis*. So he is almost exactly like he was when we took him from Oakdale Hall."

"Will he remain that way overnight so that the jury might have a look at him in the morning?"

"Yes, Sir. I do believe he will. 'Course his skin gonna be pretty wrinkled from being packed in ice, and I expect he'll need a shave by then…"

"You mean his beard will continue to grow even though he's dead?"

"Yes, Sir. That's why we always give a man a shave before the funeral if there's gonna be an open casket."

"Well, other than wrinkled skin and possibly needing a shave, has there been any change in the body? Was his head packed in ice as well?"

"No, Sir, we couldn't get his head into the ice on account of the *rigor mortis*. We'd of had to break his pelvis and knees to do that, and I didn't want to do nothing like that without Sheriff Dowdy telling me it was okay."

"Very well, then, I'm going to adjourn this inquiry until tomorrow morning at nine o'clock when we will reconvene at Mr. Davis's funeral parlor. Gentlemen of the jury, you are to be there at nine o'clock sharp. Mr. Pommus, if you think you're up to it, you can come as well. Sheriff Dowdy, since you've recused yourself from the case, you don't have to be there, but you can or you can send a deputy if you'd rather. Dr. Goodson, you need to be there. Ladies and gentlemen in the spectator benches, I doubt that Mr. Davis's embalming room will accommodate very many of you, so I'm going to say that no spectators will be allowed. We'll reconvene here tomorrow at eleven o'clock and I promise to give those of you who choose to come back a full report on what took place in your absence.

"Mr. Bailiff, please tell the housekeeper, Miss or Mrs. Dubrowski, whichever it is, and 'Deaf Silas' that they're excused and to be back here at eleven o'clock tomorrow morning. Also remind 'em not to discuss the case with anyone. Oh! And gentlemen of the jury, that goes for you as well. You're not to discuss the case with anyone until all the evidence is in and I've told you that you may begin your deliberations.

Chapter Five

Promptly at nine o'clock the inquest reconvened in the Davis & Son visitation parlor. Rather than going straight to the embalming room, the group, which now included a deputy from Sheriff Dowdy's office, allowed themselves to be diverted by the aroma of fresh-baked doughnuts and coffee—something of a luxury with the current war-time rationing—graciously laid out for them by Daisy Davis, wife of Ulysses. Some minutes later, Mr. Davis led them down the rear staircase to the basement embalming room and the by now pretty-well macerated corpse of Richard Cory.

Davis's assistant, Adolphus Presley, had been standing watch, or sitting watch as it were, next to the zinc-lined box that looked like an oversize coffin, Davis's shotgun across his knees and the two bird-shot rounds in the pocket of his shirt. Having been awakened by the cadre of men coming down the stairs he came to a semblance of attention, awaiting further instructions from Mr. Davis, his "boss" or "tutor." He wasn't sure which, so he always just referred to him as "Mr. Davis." Even though Presley was in effect, if not in law, an apprentice, surely referring to Ulysses Davis as "master" would have been viewed by all— Mr. Davis especially—as most inappropriate. In any case, torn between, on the one hand, the smell of fresh doughnuts and the sight of powdered sugar on the mustaches and beards of a couple of the jurors, and on the other hand the opportunity to participate in a real coroner's inquest, if only to assist Mr. Davis in handling the corpse, he stood hesitating until Mr. Davis asked, "Adolphus, you tell Coroner Ingersoll and these other gentlemen, you been here with the body ever since Sunday night?"

"Yes, Sir.'Cept when I needed to…you know…"

"Well other than that, you were here the whole time? Anybody else come in here while you were here, or when you came back from…?"

"Yes…I mean, no, Sir. Nobody here but me. You come down a couple of times to check everythin's alright. Miss Daisy, she come too a couple of times bring me something to eat and drink. And late yesterday morning Mr. Jefferson, he come down, ask me what all's goin' on. Well I tol' him about Mr. Cory being shot and all. That wasn't wrong, was it?"

Receiving no reply, Adolphus continued, "He say he want to see the body, so I raise the lid on the box an' he look in for a minute or two, shake his head 'an gone back upstairs."

"Then no one, yourself, Mr. Jefferson Davis, Mr. Ulysses Davis,

Mrs. Davis, nobody's touched the body since you and Mr. Davis put him in the ice chest Sunday night?"

"Yes, Sir Mr. Ingersoll. That's 'xactly right. Ain't been nobody touched him at all."

Dr. Goodson asked, "Would it be possible to remove him from the box? I think it'd be easier for everyone to see what I'm talking about if he were laid out on the table there."

"Course, Dr. Goodson. Adolphus and I can do that. Adolphus, you help me take the lid off the box and let's lay him out like we were going to embalm him." Davis and his assistant, one at each end, lifted the lid off the box and stood it against a wall. Three of the jurors standing closest to the box couldn't resist getting an early glimpse of the body and were rewarded with much more than they bargained for. Because most of the ice had melted, the corpse was now floating in a bath of very cold water. When Richard Cory had been shot apparently he was sitting down just as Sheriff Dowdy'd found him. Owing to the last vestiges of *rigor mortis,* which can last more than thirty-six hours after onset, the body was still somewhat bent forward at the waist. Also, *livor mortis,* the pooling of the blood in the lowest portions of the body after the heart stops pumping, resulted in the blood pooling in the tissues of the buttocks and the lower extremities. This pooling of the blood naturally made the lower portion of the body heavier than the upper half. The end result was that when the box lid was removed, the upper half of Richard Cory's corpse popped up to a semi-sitting position, water dripping from his upper torso as though he'd just emerged from a bath.

This unexpected life-like appearance of Richard Cory caused District Attorney Pommus to faint which resulted in his striking his nose on the edge of the embalming table. It also resulted in Norman Beasley, one of the jurors and a deeply religious man, to flee the premises by the nearest stairway, that being to the rear entrance, shouting over his shoulder that Lucifer himself must be in possession of poor Mr. Cory and he'd have no more of this blasphemy.

Being without a gavel, Coroner Ingersoll found a wooden crate to stand on and began shouting "Order! Order!" while clapping his hands as loudly as he could. The remaining jurors had moved to the other side of the room, as far from the animated corpse as possible. In a few minutes the blabbering had subsided and Dr. Goodson had once again ministered to District Attorney Pommus's nose after first administering a dose of ammonium carbonate, which, given the delicate state of the district attorney's nose, must not have been the most pleasant of ways in which to be awakened from a swoon. Dr. Goodson found a bottle of medicinal brandy in his bag and started to offer it 'round. Coroner Ingersoll, at first dubious about the propriety, relented and took the first draught, then passing the bottle to the remaining jurors who gratefully followed his example. District Attorney Pommus, seated on a closed coffin his head between his knees as Dr. Goodson had instructed, declined.

As Mr. Davis and his assistant started to remove the corpse from the box, Coroner Ingersoll held up his hand. "Best wait a bit, Mr. Davis.

"Mr. Pommus? Mr. District Attorney? Can you hear me?"

District Attorney Pommus raised his head and rested it in his hands, his elbows on his knees. "Yes, Mr. Coroner, what is it now?"

"Appears as though Norm Beasley's not interested in earning his fifty-cents in juror's pay for today's service. Should I send the deputy here to bring him back, or can we continue with just the five that's left?"

"I'm sorry; I just don't know the answer to that. Never had it come up before."

"Well, it's come up now for sure, 'less you want the deputy to bring Norman Beasley back here. I expect he'll have to put him in handcuffs and leg shackles to do it."

District Attorney Pommus took hold of the embalming table to pull himself to his feet. He then realized what he was holding on to and released his grip which caused him to fall back to his seat on the coffin. That particular coffin was one of Davis & Son's least expensive models. The reinforced bottom could bear three hundred pounds or more, not that there were many three-hundred pounders in Tilbury Town and its environs, but better safe than sorry. However the top was flat rather than concave and thus not designed to bear a sudden concentrated weight heavier than perhaps a modest floral tribute to the deceased within. As a result, the sudden pressure of the district attorney's two hundred or so pounds cracked the top along its long axis so that District Attorney Pommus ended up wedged in the coffin at its shoulder point gasping for breath and in a good deal of pain. The deputy sheriff and the wide-eyed Adolphus Presley managed to extricate him. A cursory examination by Dr. Goodson detected no injuries that would likely require hospitalization, so they seated him in Presley's chair next to the telephone alcove which Mr. Davis has recently installed to accommodate a second instrument so that he could take calls while working without having to go upstairs and risk fouling Mrs. Davis's kitchen with the smell of formaldehyde.

Pommus managed to give the operator the number for his office and in a few moments had one of his two assistants on the line. He repeated the coroner's question to the assistant who likewise did not know the answer off the top of his head. Anxious to please his boss and to recover from not knowing the answer, the young man offered to look up the answer in the law library and call back in a few minutes.

Although the last approximately twenty-four hours had been among the worst in District Attorney Pommus's life, even through the pain and horror, his political survival instincts, just like the sheriff's yesterday, took over. He was not about to render an opinion on so arcane a question as whether a verdict by less than a six-person coroner's jury would be valid. This he quickly justified in his own mind by the fact that his assistant, although a recent graduate of the Yale College of Law, was too inexperienced to be relied upon in a matter of such importance. On the other hand, his mind racing through the permutations, if I get an opinion from an authoritative source other than my office, if the opinion's in error, someone else will have to bear the brunt of the County Commissioners' wrath over the scandalous waste of taxpayers' money and I'll not have to explain to the voters why I didn't know the correct answer to such a simple question. So with only a moment's hesitation the district attorney suggested that the young assistant instead place a 'phone call the attorney general's office and report their opinion on the issue as soon as possible.

Around ten-thirty, the assistant district attorney called back to report that he'd been unable to contact anyone in the attorney general's office willing to express an opinion for the record, but he'd researched the subject and was able to report that inasmuch as a coroner's inquest is not a criminal prosecution or other adversary proceeding, the constitutional right to a jury trial was not implicated so that the matter at hand could proceed with only five jurors. Resigned to his fate, District Attorney Pommus then terminated the call and informed Coroner Ingersoll that he could, were he disposed to do so, continue with the inquest.

Granted their leave by Coroner Ingersoll, Mr. Davis and his assistant pried Richard Cory's remains from the box and lay him on the embalming table, a cloth draped across his private parts for the sake of modesty. Coroner Ingersoll and the remaining jurors crowded around the head. Dr. Goodson put his thumb to the right side of the corpse's nose and pressed down as much as he could so that the right side of the head was turned right-to-left making the entry wound more easily visible.

"See here, gentlemen. Just as I said yesterday there's gunshot residue in a crude star-shaped pattern. It's large enough so that one point of the star runs into the hairline back toward his ear and there's another that runs up from the wound nearly to the hairline of his forehead." As the jurors were each in turn confirming at close range what they'd seen from a foot or two away and that Dr. Goodson had just pointed out to them, Dr. Goodson produced a swab from his medical bag. Reaching across the table he inserted the swab into the wound to a depth of about an inch. "Now look at this. I testified yesterday that there would be little or no residue inside a non-contact wound." He extracted the swab and held it so all could see that there was almost none of the gray-black powder residue, only some dark reddish-brown fragments of what was certainly dried blood.

Coroner Ingersoll stepped back. "Well, gentlemen have you seen enough. It's gettin' along toward eleven o'clock. I promised we'd start up again at the courthouse at eleven and it looks like we're going to be a mite late as it is."

Percy Bodfish, juror number five, formerly number six, raised his hand tentatively. "No disrespect to either Doc Goodson or yourself, Eb, but is there some way that we can see what the wound would look like if the gun was held up again' th' skin. I don't want to desecrate the body, but is there some other way?"

"I don't..." Coroner Ingersoll started to reply.

"How about this, Eb?" Dr. Goodson turned to Mr. Davis. "Do you think Mrs. Davis could spare an empty flour sack? Now we'd have to put a hole or two in it, so I don't suppose it'll be much good for holding flour afterward. 'Course we'd also need the gun and some bullets. Mr. Pommus, could you call your office and have it sent over?"

"Would that be legal, Mr. Pommus?" Coroner Ingersoll's demeanor betrayed no hint of how he wanted his question answered.

District Attorney Pommus sat for half a minute or more his hands clasped in his lap and his eyes tightly closed. Finally he shrugged his shoulders and addressing no one in particular, "Well, as the saying goes, 'in for a penny...'" Turning to Adolphus Presley, he said, "Young man would you get me the telephone again, please."

Shortly before noon Enoch Matthews, the young assistant district attorney who'd so capably answered the question regarding the propriety of continuing with only five jurors, was escorted down to the embalming room clutching the cardboard box that had been turned over to his boss yesterday afternoon. In the meantime, Adolphus Presley had been delegated the task of filling the five-pound flour sack with dirt and mulch from the Davis' front flower beds. The sheriff's deputy, being the most experienced with handguns, volunteered to fire the weapon as Dr. Goodson instructed. A make-shift firing range was assembled out of the empty wooden crate and the shattered coffin lid so that the flour sack was resting on the crate and the two halves of the coffin lid were braced behind to absorb the bullets as they passed through the sack.

When all was in readiness with everyone except the deputy standing on the far side of the room the deputy aimed the revolver and fired two rounds into the sack, the first with the muzzle presses tightly against the white fabric and the other holding the muzzle approximately three to four inches away. As might be expected in a room with a tile floor and tile wainscoting to near shoulder height, the noise from the shots left everyone momentarily deaf. When the participants' ears stopped ringing, everyone eagerly crowded around the flour sack. Just as Dr. Goodson had predicted, the first round left a neat ring of residue around the hole where the first bullet penetrated the cloth. The residue from the second round was more widely diffused in the same star-shaped pattern as the wound to Richard Cory's head.

As the deputy sheriff returned the revolver to Enoch Matthews, Dr. Goodson seized the deputy's right wrist. "See here, gentlemen, there's also a fine spray of residue on the back of the deputy's hand between his forefinger and thumb." The deputy held up his hand so the jurors could see. Coroner Ingersoll asked, "Does that happen whenever you fire a revolver?"

"Why yes Sir. I suppose it does. Lessen' of course you wear a glove."

District Attorney Pommus now possessed of a clear-eyed view as to where this inquest was heading, jumped on the band-wagon lest he be left behind along with Sheriff Dowdy. "Adolphus, would you please empty out the flour sack? Take care not to smudge the bullet holes; I think we'd best hang onto it as evidence. Matthews, you go with him and take custody of the sack. You be careful as well. Fold it and put it in the box with the revolver. Oh yes; one other thing: Adolphus, you'd best give Mr. Matthews here Mr. Cory's clothes. Since Doc Goodson thinks the trousers being unbuttoned may have something to do with his death, best take the clothes along too.

"Mr. Coroner, I think we've done all we can do here. Perhaps we'd all like a short break for lunch, then if you're of a mind, we can resume at say two o'clock. Would that be suitable? As you requested when I called my office, I also instructed my secretary to inform the bailiff that we'd be a while so that the folks who came back at eleven for today's proceedings would know not to wait around. I assume that most of them went to lunch…"

"And others likely gave up and went home," Coroner Ingersoll added. Turning to the jurors, the coroner continued, "Gentlemen, I know this is mighty inconvenient for everyone. You've got jobs or businesses to get back to as do we all. In fact, Phil, you haven't seen a patient now for the better part of two days; at this point there's nothing more you can do for Mr. Cory. I'm sure that there'll be folks among the living needin' to see you. So unless any of you jurors have any more questions for Dr. Goodson, I'm going to excuse him now and let him get back to his practice. And I don't suppose we'll be needing anything further from Mr. Davis either. I assume you have no objection to Dr. Goodson and Mr. Davis being excused, do you Mr. Pommus?"

"Oh no, Mr. Coroner, Dr. Goodson's free to go with the thanks of my office and the good citizens of Kennebec County. The same for Mr. Davis. And my thanks to his assistant and especially Mrs. Davis for her gracious hospitality. I expect you'll be handling the funeral and interment, Mr. Davis?"

"Don't know, Mr. Pommus. That'd be up to the next of kin. Hadn't been anyone contact us just yet."

"Well gentleman, then it's settled. We'll reconvene in the courtroom at two o'clock. I'll give you my instructions then and you can start your deliberations. I should think that those won't take very long with what all we've heard yesterday and seen for ourselves today."

"One thing, Mr. Coroner. Since the verdict's likely to be homicide, I'd like to put the housekeeper and the stable hand on the stand to see if they know anything that would further aid our inquiry."

"Now hold on, Mr. Pommus. I'm as interested as you in finding out who *may* have murdered Mr. Cory, but that's not the job of this inquest, at least as I understand it."

"Yes, Mr. Coroner, perhaps that's true. But since Sheriff Dowdy's renounced any interest in pursuing the investigation—that is, in the event the jury returns a verdict of homicide—I think we ought to develop as much evidence as we can as soon as we can, lest the culprit destroy other evidence or make good his escape altogether. You have my word as your district attorney, Mr. Coroner and gentlemen of the jury.

Two more witnesses and we'll be done."

"Seems the district attorney has a point, Mr. Ingersoll." Seth Horner, juror number two, spoke up

Coroner Ingersoll caught himself before he could blurt out, "It's about time." Instead he asked, "Do you gentlemen mind putting your affairs on hold for the rest of the day? If you're agreeable, I'll give Mr. Pommus one hour. After that, you can begin your deliberations and we can bring an end to this proceeding."

Chapter Six

Somehow word of the extraordinary happenings at Davis & Son had spread so that by two o'clock the spectator benches were once again full with half a dozen late-comers forced to stand. At five after, Coroner Ingersoll had taken the bench and the sheriff's deputy, Walter Isaacson, who'd been so helpful that morning, was seated at the State's counsel table nearest the jury box. The jurors were all seated; the only absence was District Attorney Pommus.

In order to temporize and to keep his word given yesterday, Coroner Ingersoll began to provide the spectators with a recapitulation of what had transpired at Davis & Son that morning. He gave a thorough and lucid account, omitting only the extraordinary manner of Richard Cory's emergence from his temporary resting place and the effect it had on District Attorney Pommus and on Norman Beasley whose absence was explained as the result of a sudden illness. These omissions caused a few sly grins among the jurors who were delighted that Coroner Ingersoll decided to skip over those features of the morning's proceeding leaving to the jurors the pleasure of reporting later in fuller detail.

Having completed his report, Coroner Ingersoll was in the process of sending Deputy Isaacson to bring the district attorney to the courtroom *instanter*, placing him under arrest if necessary. As though on cue, the district attorney came bustling in to the courtroom looking like he'd just won reelection by a lop-sided margin. "My apologies, Your...Mr. Coroner, gentlemen of the jury. But while you were at your lunch, your district attorney," Pommus paused to tug at the lapels of his jacket, "and his staff—you met Mr. Matthews this morning—were hard at work putting together the evidence I'll be presenting to you."

"No more evidence, Mr. Pommus. You save that for the grand jury if you ever find somebody to charge with the crime, assuming there was one. You said you wanted to hear from the housekeeper and the stable hand, and I going to hold you to that."

"Yes, Mr. Coroner, and I mean to keep my word. Mr. Bailiff, will you please bring in Silas."

"Deaf Silas" appeared to be about the same age as Coroner Ingersoll, perhaps a few years older. Like the coroner his height had diminished with age so that he stood stooped-shouldered at less than five and one-half feet tall. He had an unkempt gray-white beard and his hair hung down to his shoulders. His tanned face was wrinkled with age and life's disappointments. His clear blue eyes peered out from behind wire-rimmed spectacles. He wore faded denim overalls over a plaid shirt and scuffed gum boots that he'd bought by mail-order from a maker in nearby Freeport. In one hand he held a beat-up fedora and in the other an antique wood and brass ear-trumpet.

Once "Deaf Silas" had taken his seat in the witness box District Attorney Pommus began with his usual "Please state your full name, Silas."

"What's that? This ear trumpet ain't much good, Mister. If you'll move closer and talk slow, I'm okay at lip readin' so that'd probably be best if you mean to ask me questions."

"Very well, Silas. Mr. Coroner, may I approach the witness?"

"Why are you askin' me? He said come closer, didn't he?"

"Well, Sir, that's the way we do it in the Supreme Judicial Court. You always have to ask the judge's permission before you can approach the witness."

"As you wish, Mr. Pommus. I suppose that's just bein' polite. Yes, go ahead. You may approach the witness."

"Thank you, Mr. Coroner." District Attorney Pommus walked around to the front of the counsel table and stood in front and just to the side of the witness box so that the jurors could see the witness. "Now, Silas, is this better?"

"Yup."

"Please state your full name for the jury."

"For the who?"

"For the jury, those five men sitting there," Pommus gestured with a sweep of his arm.

"Oh, I got you. My name is Ellsworth Henry Silas."

"You mean…your last name is Silas? I thought that was your first name. Everybody does…did."

"Nope. It's my last name."

"Well, then I suppose we need to call you *Mister* Silas from now on."

"Don't much matter; Silas'll do.

"I'll stick with Mister Silas, if it's all the same to you. It's more respectful."

"You're askin' th' questions. If you want to call me 'Mr. Silas,' and it'll make you feel better, it's okay with me."

"Good. I'm glad we got that settled," Coroner Ingersoll interjected. "Now would you mind askin' him if he knows anything about what happened down at Oakdale Hall Saturday night, early Sunday morning.?"

"Yes, Mr. Coroner." Pommus gave his obsequious bow. "Just a couple more preliminary questions." Turning back to the witness, Pommus asked, "May I ask how you came to lose your hearing, Mr. Silas?"

"Yup."

Pommus looked blank for a moment. "Okay, how'd you lose your hearing, Mr. Silas?"

"Artilleryman. Civil War. First Maine Heavy Artillery Company I, Seventeenth Maine Infantry. I was a loader. Stuffed our ears with cotton, we did. Even stuck our fingers in our ears. But it done no good. Time I was forty, my hearing was all but gone. So I got pretty good at readin' lips. Men with big mustaches give me trouble, but otherwise I get by okay."

"We all thank you for your gallant military service, Mr. Silas. But let me move on. How long have you worked at Oakdale Hall, Sir."

"How long?"

"Yes, Sir; how long?

"Reckon a bit more'n two years. Came some years after the housekeeper lady, Mrs. 'Browsky' or something like that. Never could get that straight."

"Then Mrs. Dubrowski's married?"

"Can't say. Never seen no man with her. Maybe she's not. I just called her 'missus' and she never seemed to mind."

"Thank you, Mr. Silas. Now tell us your duties at Oakdale Hall."

"Stable hand. I take care of the horses. I also keep his motorcar shined and ready. It's a good thing he has the motorcar. Wouldn't be much else for me to do. We got only two ridin' horses left and just two old draft horses for the hay wagon. Used to have a whole stable full but Mr. Cory give most of 'em to the Army. Guess he figured they needed horses more'n we did. I keep the stable clean. Saddle a horse for Mr. Cory. Sometimes he'd have some guests. So I'd saddle them up too. Didn't have many lately, I guess that's why Mr. Cory sold off all but two of the ridin' horses. He was right fond of them horses, but he didn't do much riding lately."

"Not since he fell and separated his shoulder?"

"Since what? I don't think I heard you right. Say again."

"Mr. Cory fell off his horse back in the spring and suffered a separated shoulder. He was treated by Dr. Goodson for his injury."

"First I heard of it, Mr....what's your name? You never did say's I recall."

"Pommus, Bascom Pommus, Third. I'm the district attorney of Kennebec County."

"Okay, Mister Third..."

"No, no. My last name's Pommus. The 'third' means my father and grandfather were also named Bascom Pommus."

"Well Mr. Pompus, far's I know, Mr. Cory's never fallen off his horse. Some folks used to come ridin' out at Oakdale, now that's different. 'Specially when they'd get all liquored up. There's times a horse'd come back to the stable without a rider. All wild-eyed and half scared to death. Then I'd have to hitch up the wagon and go out to find whoever'd fallen off. Bring 'em back in and help 'em into the house. Then Missus Browsky she'd take over from there. Don't remember we ever had to call a doctor or anything. Most of 'em, they'd just sleep it off and be fit to go next day.

"But Mr. Cory? He rode like one of those Johnny Reb cavalry officers. An' I sure seen my share of those. So I'd be hard pressed to believe Mr. Cory fell off a horse, 'less I seen it with my own eyes."

"Any other duties?"

"That's about it. Sometimes Mr. Cory'd have me fill the hay wagon with hay. He'd have a bunch of folks come up to the house in the evening and about sundown they'd all pile into the wagon and go for what they'd call a 'hay ride.' Always took a big wicker hamper with 'em. Full of food and whisky I guess. Took at least two of 'em to carry it. Anyway, they'd usually be gone couple hours or more. Most times I'd be gone to sleep. And with my hearin' bad as it is I'd never hear 'em come back. But when I woke up in the morning, the horses'd been unhitched and put in their stalls and all I had to do was take the hay out of the wagon and put it back in the rick. Reckon Mr. Cory'd taken care of the horses himself. Asked him about it one time; he said not to worry about it."

"Did Mr. Cory pay you a salary?"

"Yup."

"Mind telling us how much?"

"Yup."

"Well...I...Mr. Coroner, would you please instruct Mr. Silas that he must answer my questions?"

"I might if I knew why you're askin' him how much he earns. What's that got to do with Richard Cory's death? You reckon maybe Mr.

Silas there killed Mr. Cory over money?"

"Well, stranger things…Never mind. I withdraw the question.

"Let me ask you this, Mr. Silas: Do you know whether Mr. Cory had any visitors late last Saturday night or in the early Sunday morning hours?"

"Nope."

"Does that mean that Mr. Cory had no visitors, or you just don't know?"

"Don't know."

"Now I'm confused, Mr. Silas. Does 'Don't know' mean that you have no knowledge as to whether Mr. Cory had any visitors during that period?"

"Means I don't know if he had any folks come to see him, or not. Why don't you ask Missus Browsky? She'd likely know."

"Thank you Mr. Silas. I'll try to remember to do that. One last question: did Richard Cory own a .22-caliber Smith & Wesson revolver?"

"Yup."

"How do you know that?"

"Kept it in a chest in the stable. Used to take it with him sometimes when he'd go ridin' alone. Said it was for snakes. He was terrible afraid of snakes."

"But there are no poisonous snakes in Maine, Mr. Silas. You're sure that's what he said?

"Yep, that's what he said. I kinda' wondered about it myself. I did see what I think was a timber rattler a few years back, but that's the only one I've ever seen. But that's what he said and there weren't no point arguing about it; I just worked there. If he'd wanted to keep an elephant gun 'cause he was afraid of elephants, well, that'd be his business far as I was concerned."

"Thank you again, Mr. Silas. Mr. Coroner, may this witness be excused?"

"Yes, Mr. Silas, you're excused."

"What's that he said?"

"He said you're excused, Mr. Silas. You're free to go. Wait, Sir. I need to ask you one more question."

"I thought you were through with Mr. Silas, Mr. Pommus. How many more 'one last questions' you gonna have?

"This is it, Mr. Coroner: Mr. Silas, what are you and Mrs. Dubrowski going to do now that Mr. Cory's gone?"

"Don' rightly know th' answer to that one, Mr. Pompus.

Somebody's got to take care of the horses. Motorcar won't need much lookin' after. I don't think anybody'd be drivin' it. Reckon I'll just stay around doin' what I been doin' until someone tells me to stop. Don' know about Missus Browsky. She 'n' I didn't talk much with my hearin' bein' so bad and she sort of keeping to herself. We'd eat meals together sometimes, but neither of us'd say much. Reckon that's another question you'll have to ask her."

Chapter Seven

"As its final witness, the State calls Esther Dubrowski."

Esther Dubrowski, summoned by the bailiff, made her way through the swinging doors dividing the low railing that separates the counsel tables, witness and jury boxes and judge's bench from the spectator benches. She is a tall woman, at least five feet, eight inches, big-boned but not heavy. Dressed in a simple ankle-length gray cotton dress, she wears her henna and gray hair in a bun tied at the nape of her neck. Her face, unadorned by make-up, is a strong one: Firm, prominent chin, high cheek-bones, and narrow gray-green eyes beneath thin brows. She looks around the room in quick, darting glances taking in everything as though committing each face and each feature of the courtroom to memory. After acknowledging Coroner Ingersoll's reminder that she's still under oath, she takes her seat in the witness box her hands folded in her lap.

"Please state your name."

"Esther Dubrowski."

"Is it miss or missus Dubrowski?"

"Missus, I suppose. I am a widow."

"What was your late husband's name?"

"Tadeusz Dubrowski."

"Where were you born, Mrs. Dubrowski?"

"Oestrelenka, Prussia. It is small town that is in the part of Poland occupied by Prussia. But I do not call myself a German. I am a Pole. I hate the Germans."

"When did you come to America?"

"1892."

"Why did you come?"

"I am young girl; fifteen, maybe sixteen years. My parents send me to marry my husband. He was from Oestrelenka also.

"My parents very poor; father was a...how do you say?"

"How do you say what, Mrs. Dubrowski?'

"Rag picker, junk man. He has push cart; can not afford to own horse. Problem is, in Oestrelenka everyone is poor. So don't have much to give or even sell to junk man. Dubrowski is a widower, first wife died. Don't know from what. He knows my family. Says needs new wife; doesn't need dowry. My father thinks one less mouth to feed says I must go to America; be new wife of Tadeusz Dubrowski. Dubrowski, he pays for passage. So that's why I come here."

"Does 'here' mean to Maine?"

"No, I go Chicago; that's where lives Tadeusz Dubrowski. He is a *schneider*."

"A what?" asked Coroner Ingersoll.

"A *schneider*. He makes women's coats."

"Oh, you mean a tailor," District Attorney Pommus volunteers.

"*Tak*. I mean 'yes.' A tailor."

"Thank you, Mrs. Dubrowski. Do you have any children by your marriage to Mr. Dubrowski.?"

"A daughter. She is now grown."

"You say she's an adult?"

"Yes."

"Where is she?"

"This I do not know. We lose contact. I not hear from her in many years. Lives Colorado, Texas, maybe. Someplace...I don't know. Why do you ask about my daughter?"

"Just trying to get a little background, Mrs. Dubrowski. I'm sorry if that makes you uncomfortable. I'll change the subject.

"Let's talk about your late husband. Or does that make you uncomfortable as well?"

"What is to talk about? He is dead."

"Did you love your husband?"

"What I 'love?' I was his wife. I try to be a good wife. I give him a child, my...our daughter."

"When did Mr. Dubrowski pass away?"

"Sometime in nineteen hundred. I don't remember the exact date."

"How old was your daughter then?"

"Maybe seven years-old. She is born 1893."

"So that'd make her about twenty-five years old today?"

Esther Dubrowski paused and dabbed her eyes with a handkerchief she'd taken from her small reticule handbag. "I'm sorry. Excuse me. Thinking about my daughter makes me very sad."

"Yes, Mrs. Dubrowski; I understand."

"You do, Mr. Pommus? Well I don't quite understand why you're askin' this woman all these questions that don't seem to me have a bless'd thing to do with Richard Cory's death. Now you either move along to something that does, or I'm going to cut you off right now."

"May I approach this witness, Mr. Coroner?"

"Mrs. Dubrowski, you mind if Mr. Pommus sidles up there next to you?"

"No, is okay, Your Honesty."

"Your what, Ma'am?"

"I think you mean 'Your Honor', Mrs. Dubrowski," District Attorney Pommus suggested.

"Please pardon me, Sir. Sometimes I not get right these English words."

"Quite alright, Mrs. Dubrowski. But in any case I'm not a 'Your Honor.' 'Mr. Coroner' will do just as well. Now Mr. Pommus, is there some reason you need to be standin' there in the lady's face?"

"Just to show her this, Your…I mean…Mr. Coroner." Pommus took a small velvet box from the side pocket of his suit and handed it to Esther Dubrowski. "Go ahead, Mrs. Dubrowski, open it up."

"Just a minute there, Mr. Pommus. What's in that box, and where'd you get it? Here, hand that to me before you go askin' questions about it."

"Yes, Mr. Coroner." Pommus took the box back from Mrs. Dubrowski and handed it to the bailiff who handed it to Coroner Ingersoll.

"Well, Mr. Pommus?" Coroner Ingersoll opened the box, adjusted his glasses and peered inside.

"That box and its contents were taken from the right-hand pocket of Richard Cory's smoking jacket—the one Dr. Goodson described yesterday—by Mr. Matthews of my office. It was recovered when Mr. Matthews and my secretary were going through Mr. Cory's effects removed from Davis & Son's premises this morning. They were doing so at my direction in order to make an inventory in case an accounting is needed later in some other proceeding.

"When the box was discovered in my office, I telephoned Mr. Davis to ask if he knew anything about it. He told me that Adolphus, his assistant Adolphus Presley, had discovered it when they were moving Richard Cory's body. Seems it was wedged half-way down between the seat cushion and the arm of the chair so no one had seen it before they moved the body. Young Presley, so he told Mr. Davis and Mr. Davis told me, assumed that it'd fallen from Mr. Cory's pocket at some point so he put it back there and had forgotten to mention it to anyone."

"Then why are you bringing it up now? Do you think it has some connection to Richard Cory's death?"

"That, Mr. Coroner, remains to be seen. I was hoping that Mrs.

Dubrowski could shed some light on how and why Mr. Cory came to possess it. May I proceed?"

Coroner Ingersoll handed the box to the bailiff who returned it to Mr. Pommus. "Go ahead, Mr. Pommus, but do keep it brief. Either Mrs. Dubrowski knows something about it or she doesn't. And there's no point in takin' the rest of the day to find out."

"Well, Mrs. Dubrowski, Coroner Ingersoll's given his permission. You may open the box."

Taking the box from District Attorney Pommus's hand, she held it open for a few moments and then shut it with a loud snap. "No, I do not know what is this." She held the box out expecting the district attorney to take it back.

"Are you sure, Mrs. Dubrowski? Maybe you should look again." Pommus took the box from her hand opened it and removed the contents holding the object up for the jury and the spectators to see. "It's a brooch, isn't it Mrs. Dubrowski?"

"*Tak*…yes; it is a…how you call it? A brooch."

Still holding it up, Pommus continued, "It's made of black onyx, would you agree?" Not waiting for a reply, he continued his description, "The onyx stone's in the shape of a rectangle, about an inch and a half long, half an inch, maybe three quarters, tall. Correct?" Again not waiting: "There's a large diamond — at least it appears to be a diamond — in the center. I believe it's called a 'marquis-cut'?"

"This I do not know, this 'marquis-cut'. I never have any jewelry."

"Well, that's okay, Mrs. Dubrowski. None of the rest of us have had anything like this either. But it also has two rows of smaller stones…I presume they're also diamonds…all around the onyx. Am I describing it accurately?"

"Yes, yes; I believe so." She again dabbed her eyes with her handkerchief. "But why you keep asking me these questions? I already tell you I never saw this…this brooch before. You say Mr. Cory has in pocket or on chair where he sits. Maybe so, but I know nothing about it. Certainly he didn't buy it for me."

Snickers and murmurs in the spectator benches. Coroner Ingersoll raps the head of the gavel for order.

"Well, I think we can take your word for that." Pommus favored the spectator benches and jury box with his most self-satisfied smirk. "But do you know for whom Mr. Cory did purchase the brooch."

"No, no. I tell you I know nothing of this."

"Very well then, Mrs. Dubrowski, let us change the subject." Pommus picked up a document from his place at the counsel table. "May I again approach the witness, Mr. Coroner?"

"You can, but let me remind you that you're also approaching the end of your allotted time."

"Thank you for reminding me, Mr. Coroner, I'll be as brief as I can."

"No, Mr. Pommus, you'll make it brief, period."

After his rote obsequious bow, Pommus handed Mrs. Dubrowski the paper he'd taken from the counsel table. "Tell me, Mrs. Dubrowski, do you recognize this?"

Esther Dubrowski took the paper from the district attorney and after a perfunctory glance handed it back. "No, I not seen this paper before."

"Mr. Coroner, may I publish the document to the jury?"

"Publish?"

"Read it to the jury, Sir."

"I don't know about that, Mr. Pommus; lady said she'd never seen it before."

"Well, perhaps if I read it aloud that'll refresh her recollection."

"Let me read it first; then you can read it to the jury if I say so."

"May I approach the bench, Mr. Coroner?"

"How else you gonna hand it to me, Mr. Pommus?"

District Attorney Pommus handed the document to the coroner who pushed his eyeglasses up on his forehead, read for a few moments and then handed it back to the district attorney. "I don't see what an eight-year old letter addressed to "To Whom It May Concern" has got to do with Richard Cory's death, Mr. Pommus. Can you explain that?"

"Yes, Mr. Coroner, if you'll allow me to read it to the jury and then ask Mrs. Dubrowski a few questions about it, I think it'll be clear to everyone in this room that it has very much to do with Richard Cory's death."

"Well, I will allow it, but if you can't tie it to Richard Cory's death pretty quick, then I'm going to excuse Mrs. Dubrowski and close the evidence. Do you understand me Mr. Pommus?"

"As you wish, Mr. Coroner. May I continue?" Not waiting for an answer, District Attorney Pommus turned until he was partially facing the jury box and partially the spectator gallery. "This letter, so I am informed by Sheriff Dowdy's men, was found in a file cabinet in the library of Oakdale Hall during the search made by the sheriff's men for a suicide note. It was in a file marked 'veterinary bills.' Obviously, as you'll learn in a moment, gentlemen of the jury, it was incorrectly filed.

"I will now read it to you in its entirety. The letterhead reads 'G. Miller, P.O. Box 44, Joliet, Illinois.' The letter is dated August 18, 1910. As you heard, it is addressed not to a specific person, but '*To Whom It May Concern.*' I will now read you the text: '*This letter will introduce the bearer, Esther Dubrowski. Mrs. Dubrowski was with us from August 1, 1900 until the present date. During her tenure with us, she always performed her assigned duties in an exemplary manner. She is very refined in her personal habits. She got along well with others. Based on our time together, I am pleased to recommend Esther Dubrowski for any private household or commercial establishment executive house-keeping position. Very truly yours,* and it is signed '*G. Miller.*' Pommus handed the letter to Weldon Bailey so that he could read it and then pass it along to the other jurors. After each juror had an opportunity to inspect the letter, Pommus took it back and turned back to the witness box.

"Tell me, Mrs. Dubrowski, do you recognize *this* document?"

Esther Dubrowski sat stone-faced. Finally she answered in a barely audible voice, "Yes, Sir. It is reference letter for when I go to work by Mr. Cory."

"Who is G. Miller, Mrs. Dubrowski?"

"He was secretary to manager where I work before I come here."

"Why'd you leave your position? It seems to me that you were well-liked and did an outstanding job, Mrs. Dubrowski. Why leave a good position to move to Tilbury Town — which we'll all agree isn't exactly Chicago or Poland — was something wrong, or did you just want to make a change?"

"I want to make change."

"Come now, Mrs. Dubrowski. How'd you hear about Oakdale Hall?

"I read in newspaper advertisement."

"What newspaper, Mrs. Dubrowski?"

"Long time ago; I not remember now."

"Then tell us what kind of establishment was it where you worked for ten years in Joliet, Illinois."

Esther Dubrowski sat for a full minute as if trying to compose herself. Finally, with a shrug of her shoulders, she responded, "Why you ask me, Mister? You know answer already. Go ahead and tell the people."

"I'm not a witness, Mrs. Dubrowski. They have to hear from you."

She held her head up and again dabbed at her eyes. "Okay, Mister. It is Illinois State Penitentiary for Women."

"And were you employed there as a matron or in some other position?"

"Must I say, Your…Mister Coroner?"

"Yes, I think you must, Mrs. Dubrowski."

"No, I am inmate."

"You…you were a prisoner?" Pommus turned to the spectator gallery and gave them a look of mock surprise. "What was your crime? Must have been pretty serious for you to have served ten years."

"I was convicted of murder, but I…."

Coroner Ingersoll let the murmuring go on for a minute or so and then rapped the gavel head for order.

Pommus continued, "No 'buts,' Mrs. Dubrowski. Either you were convicted of murder, or you were not. Whom did you murder, Mrs. Dubrowski?

"I kill Tadeusz Dubrowski, my husband. He is…was…terrible man…a *shiker*…a drunk He beats me when he is drunk on slivovitz which was nearly every night."

"Is that why you killed him, because he beat you?"

"Yes, no. I kill him because he start behaving toward our daughter the way no man should behave with a seven year-old child…especially one that is his own daughter." As the murmuring began again, Esther Dubrowski stopped dabbing her eyes and sat up straight in her chair, relieved that she no longer had to carry her burden in secret.

"How did you kill your husband, Mrs. Dubrowski?

"I shoot with gun."

"Whose gun, Mrs. Dubrowski?"

"His. He keep in house. I am afraid he gets drunk and shoots someone so I hide gun where he can't find. Then one night he very drunk is touching my daughter. I tell him he must stop. He pushes child to floor; starts beating me with brass candlestick. I get gun and shoot him."

"How many times did you shoot your husband, Mrs. Dubrowski?

"I…I don't know this. I shoot one time, he keep coming at me so I shoot again and again until gun not shoot more."

Mr. Miller says that according to the Chicago Police Investigation Report, you shot your husband, Mrs. Dubrowski, a total of six times. Is that right?"

"I don't know. After I shoot, I take child and run to neighbor apartment. They call police. I not see him again after that."

"Okay, Mr. Pommus. We now know that eighteen or nineteen years ago, Mrs. Dubrowski killed her husband. Sounds to me, and likely most of the folks here, that he needed killin'."

"Perhaps so, Mr. Coroner, but perhaps not everyone wants to have a convicted murderess living in his home. During the recess yesterday, I contacted the Joliet, Illinois police department by long-distance telephone to see if they had any information on 'G. Miller.' They're the ones who told me that Gallus, 'G-a-l-l-u-s,' Miller is the secretary of the Illinois Department of Correction. And they kindly gave me his phone number at the prison. I then called Mr. Miller and asked him what he knew about Mrs. Dubrowski. He said he thought the name was familiar, but would pull the file to be sure and I should call him back in half an hour's time. I did so and he gave me the information that Mrs. Dubrowski has just confirmed. He told me that he frequently writes such letters for deserving parolees. For obvious reasons, he does not use letterhead that would immediately identify the person as an ex-convict. He told me that Mrs. Dubrowski had been sentenced to twenty years, but had been a model prisoner and was accordingly paroled after serving about half her sentence.

"But what else he told me is also most interesting. It seems that the Esther Dubrowski file was already in his office. He told me that he'd received an inquiry about Esther Dubrowski from someone in Maine just a few weeks ago. It was a letter, post-marked Augusta, Maine, from someone named 'Major F. Sharp' return address General Delivery, Augusta, Maine. He said he'd not gotten around to responding to it because he had been on vacation from which he'd returned to his duties just Monday of last week.

"And there's more, Mr. Coroner, gentlemen of the jury. Mr. Miller was most interested to learn that Mrs. Dubrowski is now living in our community. It appears that by leaving Illinois, Mrs. Dubrowski violated the terms of her parole, that and by failing to report to the authorities every two weeks as she was also required to do. Accordingly, when Mr. Miller asked if I knew her whereabouts, he was greatly relieved to learn that I was going to have a few words with her as soon as he and I finished our conversation. He said a fugitive warrant would be prepared immediately and forwarded to us by Western Union so that she could be returned to her 'former place of employment' to complete her obligation to the People of the State of Illinois."

"Then you'll want Sheriff Dowdy to take custody of Mrs. Dubrowski as soon as she's done here so that she can be sent back to Illinois?"

"That is correct in part, Mr. Coroner. I'll be asking Deputy Isaacson to take Mrs. Dubrowski into custody, but I don't think it'll be to await her return to Illinois."

"Then you think she may have had something to do with Richard Cory's death?"

"Let me ask a few more questions, then perhaps we'll know for sure.

"Mrs. Dubrowski, it was your employer Richard Cory who was making the inquiry about you past, was it not?"

"No!"

" He was concerned that you might find out he was inquiring, so he used a false name and gave 'General Delivery,' Augusta, as his return address."

"No, you do not know this!."

"You discovered what he was doing. Perhaps he left Mr. Miller's letter out on his desk inadvertently, or perhaps he made a carbon copy of 'Major F. Sharp's' letter and left that letter out where you came across it. Or perhaps you made a habit of rifling through Richard Cory's correspondence and private papers as a precaution against just such an eventuality as…"

"I tell you, I know nothing of…"

"You found the letter and knew at once your days at Oakdale Hall and of freedom were about to come to an end."

"This is not so, you make this…"

"It is not me who is fabricating a lie, Mrs. Dubrowski. It is you who are fabricating, you who have been living a lie for the last eight years."

"I tell truth, I make oath."

"So you now want to add perjury to you list of crimes, Mrs. Dubrowski?

"Mr. Cory showed you the brooch Saturday night. You had already made up your mind to kill Richard Cory, didn't you? You decided to do it that night and steal the brooch so you could sell it for enough to live on until you could escape back to Europe when the war ends, or perhaps escape to South America…"

No, I didn't…"

"No more lies, Mrs. Dubrowski. You served Richard Cory the brandy that was found on the coffee table in front of the chair where Mr. Cory was sitting. You knew that he'd been out to dinner and likely had a cocktail or two before dinner and perhaps wine with dinner, maybe even an after-dinner drink as an aid to digestion. So when he returned home, he was perhaps a bit tipsy already. He then showed you the brooch and in doing so sealed his fate. You brought him more cognac which he drank. You also brought him his smoking jacket."

"Am I correct so far, Mrs. Dubrowski?"

"No. you are wrong. I am upstairs in my quarters. I do not hear him come home. I am listening to phonograph. Paderewski is playing Chopin etudes. I have all Paderewski's recordings."

"Perhaps you were for a while. Being experienced with men who've had too much to drink, you knew that Richard Cory would likely fall asleep in his chair. You waited until you were sure he was asleep, and then you got his gun.

"Where'd you get the revolver, Mrs. Dubrowski?"

"From desk in library where he keeps…"

"Yes, Mrs. Dubrowski, go on. What did you do with the gun? Isn't it a fact that you then went into the music room and shot the sleeping Richard Cory to death?"

"No, I…"

"Come now, Mrs. Dubrowski, you admit you got the gun with which Richard Cory was murdered. Are you going to tell us that you took him the gun so he could shoot himself?"

"I…I, stop it please! No more of your questions. Yes, I took gun from desk and I shoot Richard Cory in his sleep!"

"And you put the gun in his hand so everyone would think he'd put a bullet through his own head."

"Please, I said what you wanted to hear. Isn't that enough?"

"Not quite, Mrs. Dubrowski. You searched him to find the brooch, didn't you? You couldn't find it in his smoking jacket, so you tried to search the pockets of his trousers. But in order to do that, you had to unbutton…"

"Yes, yes!

"Then you went back to your quarters. Did you get a good night's sleep, Mrs. Dubrowski, or did you stay awake all night trying to figure out what to do?

"I…"

"Doesn't matter, Mrs. Dubrowski. Whichever it was, you waited until morning to call the sheriff's office and made up your mind to try and brazen it through. If it hadn't been for Doc Goodson, you just might have gotten away with it.

"You couldn't destroy the letter. You needed it as a reference in case someone started asking questions. You thought that before anyone could check, you'd be long gone from Tilbury Town. So instead of burning it, you deliberately 'misfiled' it with the veterinary bills. Do you deny it, Mrs. Dubrowski?

"I will not answer any more questions. You can do with me what you will."

As District Attorney Pommus turned to the spectator benches and gave them his stern champion-of-justice look, Coroner Ingersoll gestured to Deputy Isaacson. "Reckon you'd best take her into custody, Deputy Isaacson. And see that no harm comes to her while she's in the custody of Sheriff Dowdy. I will hold you personally responsible for her safety. That understood?"

"Yes, Sir." Deputy Isaacson produced a pair of handcuffs and approached the stoic Esther Dubrowski. "Please stand up, ma'am. You need to stand up and turn around so I can handcuff you. I'll have to keep you in handcuffs until we get over to the women's lock-up where a matron can search you for weapons."

After Esther Dubrowski had been handcuffed and led from the courtroom by Deputy Isaacson, Coroner Ingersoll turned to the jury. "Well, gentlemen, it's been a long an' interestin' day. I believe we're now ready for me to give you your instructions and for you to render your verdict. I don't reckon that'll be too difficult.

"If you agree with Sheriff Dowdy's opinion, and believe that Doc Goodson's talkin' through his hat, then you need to find that Richard Cory died of a self-inflicted gunshot wound. I didn't hear any evidence that'd make me think it was accidental. So if you think like Sheriff Dowdy that Richard Cory's the one put a bullet in his own head, then your verdict must be one of suicide.

"On the other hand, if you believe Doc Goodson, then your verdict must be one of homicide. In that regard, you can also consider Mrs. Dubrowski's testimony, particularly the part where she admitted being the one shot Richard Cory. But it's not your job to determine Mrs. Dubrowski's guilt or innocence. That'll be for a grand jury, and then if they indict her, it'll be up to a jury in Judge Gribble's court. All you need to do, if you think that someone other than Richard Cory put that bullet in his head, is to render a verdict of homicide.

"The bailiff will now show you to the jury room where you can do your deliberatin'. When you're done, just knock on the door and he'll bring you back in. Now if any of you need to take a personal convenience break, this is the time to do it. Just don't discuss the case until all of you are present in the jury room and the bailiff's closed the door."

"Excuse me, Mr. Coroner," Weldon Bailey held up his hand. "Do we need to go through all that? Can't we just confer here and announce our verdict?"

"Well, if that's the way all of you want to do it, I suppose it's okay. Mr. Pommus, any objection?"

"No, Mr. Coroner, that's acceptable to me."

The jury leaned toward one another for a few moments. Then Weldon Bailey addressed the coroner. "We're unanimous, Mr. Coroner, we find that Richard Cory's death was a homicide."

"Gentlemen, thank you for your service. Mrs. Parsons will record your verdict. If you will each give her your addresses, she'll see that the county pays you for your two days of service. This proceeding is adjourned."

Flammonde
(Abridged)

The man Flammonde, from God knows where,
With firm address and foreign air,
With news of nations in his talk
And something royal in his walk,
With glint of iron in his eyes,
But never doubt, nor yet surprise,
Appeared, and stayed, and held his head
As one by kings accredited.

He never told us what he was,
Or what mischance, or other cause,
Had banished him from better days
To play the Prince of Castaways.
Meanwhile he played surpassingly well
A part, for most, unplayable;
In fine, one pauses, half afraid
To say for certain that he played.

What was he, when we came to sift
His meaning, and to note the drift
Of incommunicable ways
To make us ponder while we praise?
Why was it that his charm revealed
Somehow the surface of a shield?
What was it that we never caught?
What was he, and what was he not?

We cannot know how much we learn
From those who never will return,
Until a flash of unforeseen
Remembrance falls on what has been.
We've each a darkening hill to climb;
And this is why, from time to time
In Tilbury Town, we look beyond
Horizons for the man Flammonde.

Edwin Arlington Robinson
American (1869-1935)

Chapter Eight

That Friday, while District Attorney Pommus was eloquently summing up the State's case against Esther Dubrowski in front of the July Term of the Grand Jury in and for Kennebec County—a process that was taking far longer than it should have given that the woman'd confessed to the crime—her lawyer, although he did not know at that moment he was her lawyer, was lamenting to himself—there being no one else in the office to whom he could lament—the meager state of his finances. Thomas ("Just call me Tom") Hardwicke, the manager of the Farmers & Merchants Bank of Tilbury Town, had called yesterday afternoon to politely but firmly inform him that the bank would not honor any more overdrafts drawn on his account and to inquire when they might expect a deposit to cover the current debit balance. As he'd done for the past two weeks, Quincy Adams, the soon-to-be lawyer for Esther Dubrowski, replied with an earnest but purposefully vague promise to address the problem as soon as possible. The call ended with the banker again politely but firmly suggesting that Quincy (they were after all on a first-name basis) make a more diligent effort to collect the receivables due from his clients, and Quincy again pressing Thomas to send more paying clients his way.

Like Dr. Goodson, Quincy Adams (third cousin, several times removed from his namesake John Quincy Adams) possessed abundant qualifications for his occupation, that being a small-town lawyer: Baccalaureate degree in classics from Brown University; Harvard Law where he was articles editor of the *Harvard Law Review* and *cum laud* graduate; summer clerk and then upon graduation associate lawyer at Trout & Dickson, Attorneys and Counselors, principal office in Boston. Trout & Dickson's principal expertise and field of law upon which its formidable reputation is built is patent, trademark and copyright law. After three plus years of helping draft patent applications and once in a while helping prepare for a patent infringement trial in federal court, Quincy Adams took his leave of Trout & Dickson to set up his own office in Tilbury Town, drawn by its small-town atmosphere yet proximity to Augusta and but a day's train ride to Boston on the Maine Central connecting in Portland to the Boston & Maine.

Adams's office is a two-room suite on the second floor of a building on Water Street situated a few doors down from the F&M Bank. The first floor is occupied by the Red Rooster Café, an establishment owned and operated by Dorothy Allagash a lady who has seen many summers and who proudly maintains her native heritage by wearing her gray hair parted down the middle and plaited into two braids that hang down over her clavicles. "Aunt Dorothy" as everyone calls her is also Adams's landlady and his part-time employer who can always be counted on to put aside an extra daily special in exchange for Adams's after-hours scullery service.

The shingle, for indeed it is literally a shingle, identifying the Law Office of Quincy Adams hangs over a doorway next to the entrance to the Red Rooster. The office is reached by a narrow stairway leading to a hallway that runs from the head of the stairs to a door at the rear of the building used as an emergency exit in the event of fire or the unexpected appearance of persistent law book salesmen sent by the publisher to collect Adams's delinquent account. The floor covering on the second floor is worn and mostly discolored brown linoleum. The walls are smoke stained beige over warped wainscoting. Electrification was accomplished around the turn of the century. Illumination is provided by bare light bulbs hanging precariously from the ceiling. At the head of the stairs on the right side of the hallway there is a frosted glass door marked "Law Office" opening to Adams's reception room. The lettering on the reception room door is left-over from the previous occupant who had given up on the practice of law in Tilbury Town and gone to work as a Casco Bay lobsterman out of Portland.

Adams's private office is accessed through a second frosted glass door between the reception room and his office. There is another solid door leading from Adams's private office to the hallway. Its obvious purpose is to allow a client to leave without having to go back through the reception room and a possibly awkward encounter with another client. In addition to its ostensible purpose, it also provides a convenient way for Adams to reach the rear door undetected when stealth is called for. Adams's private office has one window looking out over the alley that runs along the back of the buildings fronting on Water Street. The wall between his office and the hallway is adorned with his licenses and diplomas. The opposite wall is lined with plain, one-by six pine bookshelves holding the volumes comprising the United States Code (a parting gift from Trout & Dickson), the Maine Statutes-at-Large (not yet fully paid for) and a few treatises such as *Pomeroy on Equity* (small balance still owing) and the *Maine Reports,* the official reports of cases decided by Maine's highest court (which he would continue to receive as long as he could pay for each volume as it is published).

As it is for all but three afternoons per week, that particular

Friday the reception room is empty of both clients and a receptionist to receive them. Tuesday, Wednesday and Thursday afternoons are when Camille Winters, Aunt Dorothy's seven a.m.-to-noon waitress and Adams's part-time secretary, file-clerk, bookkeeper and receptionist, continues to loyally report for duty despite not having been paid by Adams since the first of July.

At the end of June, Adams had drafted a somewhat complicated timber lease for which he'd been paid with a good check from the satisfied client. As a result, he'd been able to pay Aunt Dorothy some of the back rent due her, pay Camille Winters and go over to Stein's where he splurged on a General Electric table-model electric fan which was now situated atop a file cabinet and doing its best to blow the warm air around the office and out the open back window. Because of the noise made by the fan motor, Adams did not hear the outer office door open and thus was startled by the sound of metal tapping on the glass of the door to his office. The metal proved to be, as soon as Adams was able to croak, "Come in," a signet ring worn on the fourth finger of the right hand of a man (obviously a gentleman) attired in a blue seer-sucker suit over black-and-white wing-tip shoes, a white shirt, yellow bow-tie and straw boater. He was clean-shaven, and if one had to guess, in his late thirties.

"You are Quincy Adams, attorney-at-law?"

"Yes, I am. How may I be of service?"

"I would like to discuss engaging your professional services." He handed Adams a plain business card, just a name, no address or phone number. "As you can see from my card, my name is Emil Flammonde. I have only recently come to Tilbury Town. I am residing for the time being at Mrs. Norman's boarding house. I believe you reside there as well, although I don't recall having seen you at dinner."

"Nor do I recall having met you, Mr...Mr. Flammonde. Did I pronounce that correctly?"

"Yes, you did."

"Please have a seat." Adams gestured to one of the two client chairs at the front of his desk. "What brought you to Tilbury Town, and more particularly what brings you to my office?"

Flammonde took out his pocket handkerchief and wiped the thin layer of dust from one of the chairs and sat down. "As to the first, I am investigating business opportunities in the area, and as to the second, I wish to retain your services."

"I should be delighted to represent you, Mr. Flammonde. Is it a merger or an acquisition that you have in mind?"

"At the moment neither, Mr. Adams. I wish to engage you to represent someone else."

Adams did his best not to look disappointed as in his mind's eye he saw a four-figure check grow wings and fly out his rear window. "Who would that be, Mr. Flammonde?"

"Esther Dubrowski. I'm sure you're aware of the dire circumstances in which she finds herself at the moment."

"Only what I've read in the newspaper and what little gossip I've heard in the café downstairs. But from what little I know, she's in need of someone with a great deal of experience in criminal law. And frankly, with her having confessed while under oath at the coroner's inquest, I doubt that Clarence Darrow himself could get her anything less than a life sentence, much less acquitted. I myself have no criminal trial experience; I've handled a few misdemeanors which were resolved by plea agreements, and that's all. In fact, I've had little trial experience of any kind outside the field of patent law."

"I am well informed as to your credentials, Mr. Adams; yet I came here in the belief that you will accomplish more than the modest goal of saving her from a life sentence, you will, in the end, bring about her complete acquittal."

"At risk of appearing frivolous in regard to such a grave matter, Mr. Flammonde, the sign on my door says 'Law Office', not 'miracle worker'."

"Then you wish to decline the engagement?"

"No, I would welcome an engagement of such notoriety, especially if it were a remunerative one. However, I fear the defense of Mrs. Dubrowski is far beyond the scope of my training and experience. Thus I'm concerned that I might not be capable of providing adequate representation."

"Have you seen District Attorney Pommus try a case, Mr. Adams?"

"Point well taken, Mr. Flammonde. But he does have, in addition to a sworn confession, at least one very able young associate, not to mention all the resources of the State of Maine at his disposal.

"Your point is well taken also, Mr. Adams. Yet, having sat through the entirety of the coroner's inquest, I am convinced that her cause is not necessarily lost and wants only someone with skill and determination to be the lady's champion."

"Her 'cause?' Then you believe that she's innocent? What about the confession?"

"Yes, I do believe she is, if not wholly innocent—and by that I refer to her short-changing the People of the State of Illinois of their full measure of justice—at least innocent of the charges laid against her in connection with the death of Richard Cory. As to the former, I suspect that if she'd had competent representation in the matter of the death of her late unlamented husband, she'd not be in the precarious situation in which she now finds herself. And as for the death of Richard Cory, I'm convinced beyond any doubt that her confession is false and she is completely innocent."

"Have you spoken with Mrs. Dubrowski? Why do you believe her confession to be a false one?"

Flammonde reached into the inner pocket of his jacket and took out a small leather cigar case. "Do you mind if I smoke, Mr. Adams?"

"Oh, no, please feel free. There's an ash tray in the corner next to the file cabinet." Adams started to get up to bring it to his visitor.

"Please don't trouble yourself; I can get it." Flammonde rose and located the ashtray and moved it so that it stood on its weighted base and slender neck next to his chair. After extracting a cheroot from his case and lighting it, he continued, "The answer to your first question is 'no.' I've not spoken with the lady; she knows nothing of my interest. And a condition of your engagement, should you see fit to accept it, is that my role must not be divulged, even to her. As to your second question, her 'confession' is at variance with the facts in at least one material respect."

"That is…?"

"She didn't know where Cory kept the revolver. As you may have read, District Attorney Pommus invoked the Rule—I'm sure you're familiar with the term—so Mrs. Dubrowski was not in the courtroom when 'Deaf Silas' testified. Because he had so little information to offer in his preceding testimony, and because Pommus asked the question about the location of the revolver almost as an afterthought, the newspaper reporter didn't mention in his article that Mr. Silas testified quite differently regarding where the revolver was kept…"

"What'd Mr. Silas say about where…?"

"He said Richard Cory kept it in a chest in the stable. He'd carry it with him when he rode horseback. Something about his being afraid of snakes. On the other hand, Esther Dubrowski testified, as I'm sure you read in the newspaper, that she'd gotten the revolver from Richard Cory's desk in the library."

"Couldn't it be that Mr. Silas is the one who's fabricating or at least mistaken?"

"That is possible, of course, but I think not. Why does the judge in every trial instruct the jury that they are the sole judges of the credibility of the witnesses and the weight to be given their testimony? Jurors seem to develop an intuitive ability to decide whose testimony to believe when there's a conflict. From your limited trial experience I'm sure you have developed that same sense of when a witness is telling the truth and when he — or she — is either mistaken or lying. To me, Silas's testimony had the ring of truth about it. On the other hand, I believe that Mrs. Dubrowski's so-called 'confession' was made up on the spur of the moment. She most likely had no idea where Mr. Cory kept the revolver; she may not have even known that he owned one."

"You are certainly entitled to your opinion, Mr. Flammonde, but the five men on the jury evidently saw it otherwise."

"Not so, Mr. Adams. Not that juries always follow the judge's instructions. But in this instance, Coroner Ingersoll greatly to his credit carefully charged them that it was not their duty to determine Esther Dubrowski's guilt or innocence; they were only to consider her testimony, along with that of Dr. Goodson and even that of Sheriff Dowdy in deciding whether Richard Cory took his own life or was the victim of a homicide.

"They very well could have discarded the opinion of Sheriff Dowdy, supported as it was by his *ipse dixit* alone. Likewise, they may have given little or no weight to the outburst of a brow-beaten, hysterical woman and relied solely on the testimony of Dr. Goodson. Again, owing to the lateness in the day and the sensational testimony that preceded the coroner's instructions, I believe the newspaper reporter was most derelict in his duty to report every important aspect of the proceeding."

"What you say, Sir, sounds reasonable enough, but it is at best a conundrum which cloaks an even deeper mystery. I will grant from what you say and from what I've read and heard elsewhere, that Mrs. Dubrowski may have been hysterical at the time, or at least worn down by Pommus's badgering, but that doesn't mean that she was wholly bereft of her ability to act in a rational manner when it concerned her own self-interest. Thus I must ask the inevitable question: Why would a sane person confess to the premeditated murder of such a well-known and highly-esteemed person as Richard Cory?

"Even making allowances for gaps in the press coverage, and from my very limited exposure to criminal law, without the confession,

Pommus made at best a flimsy circumstantial evidence case based upon possible but by no means certain opportunity, and a motive that is no more than speculation. I mean, who knows whether Mrs. Dubrowski feared that she'd be sent back to Illinois? Perhaps the original reference letter was in fact misfiled. Who will come forward to identify Richard Cory as...what was his name?"

"'Major F. Sharp.'" Flammonde stubbed out his Cheroot sat back in his seat and smiled. "You see, counselor, you're not such a naïf in the world of criminal jurisprudence after all."

"That's generous of you, Mr. Flammonde, but my analysis only serves to underscore the importance of my question: With the evidence against her so weak — something that she may well have known, given her prior experience in a similar circumstance — why would she confess? Why not, as Pommus is quoted as saying, 'brazen it out?'

"Are you thinking that she might enter a plea of insanity? From what little I remember from my criminal jurisprudence course, the *M'Naughten* Rule requires that the accused by reason of some mental disease or defect be unable to distinguish right from wrong, or being able to distinguish, lacks the ability to conform his conduct to the social norm. And again relying on my soupcon of knowledge, I don't think there's sufficient evidence to even warrant submission of the defense to a jury. Perhaps if she were to be seen by an alienist and if she were being defended by someone with experience in presenting the insanity defense..."

"On the contrary, Counselor. It is my belief that Mrs. Dubrowski is as possessed of her wits as any person whom you might encounter on the streets of Tilbury Town. And I assure you that I do not mean to disparage our good neighbors, Sunday morning's submarine scare notwithstanding. It is my considered opinion that Mrs. Dubrowski's confession is a desperate attempt on her part to protect someone else, a someone about whom she cares a great deal and a someone whom she fears may be implicated, if not the actual person who placed the revolver next to Richard Cory's right temple and pulled the trigger.

"When she first began her testimony, she was calm and answered Pommus's questions in a direct and forth-right manner, making some allowance for her English language short-comings. It was only when Pommus approached her that her demeanor changed. I too do not mean to be facetious, but I doubt it was Pommus's cologne that so disconcerted her. As soon as she opened the jewelry box, all of the starch went out of her. I do believe that she'd have confessed to being the

Kaiser's mistress if Pommus had asked her to."

"From our conversation thus far, Mr. Flammonde, I've developed a considerable respect for your knowledge of the law and of trial practice, as well as your ability to read people. May I assume that you are a lawyer as well as a businessman?"

"An accurate deduction on your part, Mr. Adams. I am indeed trained in the law although my career in academe is not nearly as distinguished as your own. Moreover, it's been many years since I've accepted a brief. Now with that admission, do my conjectures carry sufficient weight to pique your interest in the plight of Esther Dubrowski?"

"Why not undertake the representation yourself?"

"Because of my unshakeable faith in you and because it best suits me to remain in the penumbra. Besides, I am not admitted to practice in Maine, and have no desire or need to become so. "

"As you wish, Mr. Flammonde, but I'd like to return to the question of Mrs. Dubrowski's motive to confess. For whom could she be covering? Her husband's dead; indeed were he alive, it's unlikely that she'd cross the street except to spit in his eye, much less risk incarceration for life to avoid his being placed in the same peril. And, if I recall her testimony as it was reported, she's been alienated from her daughter since she was first imprisoned. She said she doesn't even know where the young woman is. Of course she may have some other relative in this country, but that seems far-fetched."

"As to the husband, of course you're right. And possibly as to the daughter as well. I think the key is to find out the story of the brooch. When she opened the box on the witness stand, it was as though Pommus had handed her a venomous snake; she couldn't wait to close the lid and get it out of her hands."

"Uncovering the story behind the brooch may prove to be rather a difficult challenge. If Mrs. Dubrowski's covering up for someone, it would defeat her purpose to admit that fact and it's even less likely that she'll name that someone."

"Well, Mr. Adams, do you think you can find out her secret?"

"I would like to defer responding to that question until you answer one more of mine."

"About your fee?"

"No. Before we discuss that subject, if indeed we reach that point, I'd like to know what motivates your evidently keen interest in the fate of Mrs. Dubrowski. Is it you she's covering for?"

"Dear me, no. Your cynicism is at a level far beyond your years at the bar. No, I knew Richard Cory by name and reputation only. And if it were me who is the beneficiary of Mrs. Dubrowski's willingness to sacrifice her life, why would I be here asking you to represent her? Out of a sense of remorse? Why not just let Judge Gribble appoint some jackleg to sleep walk through the trial letting Pommus put on his dog-and-pony show. That way, without breaking a sweat, her lawyer can collect his paltry few dollars at the end of the day as he wishes her God's mercy and a pleasant remainder of her life?

"Indeed, were I sitting on your side of the desk, I'd have asked the same question. Therefore I take no offense..."

"Nor was my question intended to give offense, Mr. Flammonde. It's just that in my experience, limited though it may be, no one offers to pay what will certainly be a substantial sum of money to fund a lawsuit out of the goodness of his heart and not in the expectation of some more tangible return on the investment."

"Well, in answer to your question, I will tell you this and only this: I am interested in finding out who did in fact murder Richard Cory and why. My reasons for wanting to discover this information need not concern you. I do, however, guarantee that the people for whom I work are honorable, and when your engagement is concluded, you will not have the slightest reason on our account to be embarrassed for having undertaken it."

"How do you know that Mrs. Dubrowski will have me as her lawyer?"

"That, Mr. Adams, will be the first of many challenges you will have to overcome. But, as I said earlier, I wouldn't be here if I didn't think you were the man for the job. Now, do you wish to discuss your retainer and fee?"

"Despite my present fiscal circumstances, of which I'm sure you're aware, I would not accept this case—assuming Mrs. Dubrowski will have me—without such assurance on your part as you've just given. Although we've just met, you strike me as a man of your word. So I'm willing to risk that which is most valuable to me: My good name. And I assure you that whatever we may agree upon as my fee, it is not enough for me to compromise my name. That said, I must tell you that this defense will be costly. I will need to spend more time than you might think necessary delving into the substantive and procedural laws of Maine applicable in criminal prosecutions. While Pommus probably hasn't opened a law book in the last decade, his associate Enoch

Matthews can be counted on to be prepared on the law.

"Unless Matthews goads him into doing so, I do not expect that Pommus will be willing to spend much of his budget on further investigation of the facts, especially since this fiscal year ends August thirty-first, and the commissioners have not yet approved the county budget for next year. Nor, after his confrontation with Sheriff Dowdy, do I expect he'll ask for any help from that quarter."

"Nor would I expect he'd get any if he asked," Flammonde grinned as he replayed the scene in his mind.

"We, on the other hand, will need one or more competent investigators nearly full-time. And from experience, I can tell you the good ones aren't cheap. You get what you're willing to pay for."

"That will not present a problem. If you accept that I possess the necessary skills and have associates who are my equal and more, you will have all the investigative resources you need."

"Again, I take you at your word. But what about your business interests?"

"I will continue as I have been. If I do not, my usefulness will be compromised. I assure you that Mrs. Dubrowski will be my first priority." Flammonde reached in the pocket of his suit and removed an envelope which he handed to Adams. "Will two thousand, five hundred suffice as a retainer? Since it's in cash, I'll need a receipt."

Chapter Nine

When Adams arrived at the Kennebec County jail, it was nearly time for the prisoners' evening meal which is comprised of an under-size lobster and a baked potato, these being the cheapest foods available. Furthermore, since he was not on the list of persons authorized to see her, the jailer on duty at the public entrance said that he would have to ask the watch commander's permission. Finally, Adams was informed, Mrs. Dubrowski presently had a visitor who would be leaving as soon as the prisoner-trustees began their rounds with the food carts.

Having brought nothing with him other than a business card and a foolscap pad, Adams resigned himself to reading the wanted posters and court docket sheets posted on a cork board on the wall opposite the barred window to the turn-key's enclosure to pass the time until it was his turn to meet with his prospective client. Only a few minutes had gone by when he heard the steel door leading to the cells open. He saw a bearded man in a somber black suit and wide-brimmed black hat emerge and start toward the exit. The turn-key motioned Adams to come to his window. "That's the fellow was her visitor. Give me your card, counselor, and I'll go ask the watch commander about letting you in soon's they're through eatin'."

Handing over his card, Adams thanked the deputy and started after the man who'd just left. He caught up with him just as he'd gotten outside heading in the direction of the railroad station. Adams touched the man on the shoulder, "Excuse me, Sir, the deputy said you'd been to see Esther Dubrowski. Could I have a few words with you?

The man turned around, clearly annoyed, "I'm sorry, Sir, I do not have time. I must catch the train back to Portland. In any case, I cannot speak to the press about Mrs. Dubrowski. Now, if you'll excuse me..."

"But I'm not a reporter, Sir, I'm a lawyer."

"Do you have a business card?"

Adams reached into his pocket. Realizing that the jailer had taken his only card, Adams shrugged, "No...I mean...yes, but I gave it to the deputy."

"A lawyer? What kind of lawyer are you? You have only one business card..."

"I assure you, Sir, I have a good supply in my office. However, I came to see Mrs. Dubrowski, and not for the purpose of soliciting business from any and all who might be in need of a lawyer."

"Well, why Mrs. Dubrowski? From what I know of the law, she's certainly in need of a lawyer. Indeed that's why I myself went to visit her. That and to check on her well-being. I am Rabbi Gerson Klein, of Portland. What is your name, young man?

"Quincy Adams, Sir. You are Mrs. Dubrowski's pastor...er...spiritual adviser?

"My, such a distinguished name, 'Quincy Adams,' for such a young lawyer."

"You, Rabbi Klein, are not the first to make that observation. But you've not answered my question as to your relationship to Mrs. Dubrowski."

"Mrs. Dubrowski comes to our services fairly often and has been generous within her means in supporting our congregation. I read of her arrest in the Portland newspaper yesterday, and came here as soon as I could. But what brings you to Mrs. Dubrowski's defense, Mr. Quincy Adams? You must be aware that her financial resources are quite limited."

"I've been engaged to represent Mrs. Dubrowski."

"And she knows this?"

"Er, no, not yet. Indeed one of the most difficult aspects of this engagement will be to persuade Mrs. Dubrowski to trust me and allow me to defend her."

"So if she did not engage you, and I know this to be a fact because as I left her I promised to see what I could do to raise funds from among my congregation members for her defense, who did?"

"I'm sorry, Rabbi, a condition of my engagement is that I not disclose by whom I am retained. I can only tell you that this person is firmly convinced that she is innocent, and wants to see justice done. Moreover, he has convinced me that she is innocent as well."

"This is most unusual, Mr. Quincy Adams. A lawyer suddenly appears like a *golem* and says he's come to defend this unfortunate woman. And he won't say who is paying him to do so.

"How am I to know that you are who you say you are and that you are what you purport to be? Although I am not a lawyer, I make note of the fact that you use the word 'innocent'and not the term 'not guilty.' If you have chosen your words carefully as a good lawyer must do, then I gather you are telling me that you, and the party who engaged you, believe that Esther...Mrs. Dubrowski did not in fact kill Richard Cory. Am I correct?"

"Your parsing of words, Rabbi Klein, is most perceptive and entirely correct. I...we...believe without reservation that Mrs. Dubrowski had no hand whatever in the death of Richard Cory, her purported confession notwithstanding. Come back to the jail and see Mrs. Dubrowski with me, Rabbi. If I do not convince you of my *bona fides*, then tell Mrs. Dubrowski to send me packing."

"Alas, Mr. Quincy Adams, this I cannot do, at least not at the present moment. I must catch the next train back to Portland which leaves in little more than twenty minutes. As you may know, our Sabbath begins at sundown, so I must be back to attend to my rabbinic duties before then.

"I propose this instead: I will give you a note to take with you to give to Mrs. Dubrowski, assuming that the jailers will allow you to see her. You must promise me that you will do no more than introduce yourself, tell her that you believe she is innocent...you see, I too choose to use your word...and that you and I will come back to meet with her on Sunday. Make it after you attend your own worship service, if you are so inclined, because I'll not be able to meet you until at least the noon hour assuming that the Central Maine's on time."

The rabbi grasped Adams's hand as though to shake it. Instead, taking Adam's elbow with his left hand, he drew him close reading his face for even the smallest sign of artifice. Finding none, Rabbi Klein removed a small notebook and pen from his pocket, wrote a brief note and handed it to Adams. "I wish you *ein gutten shabbas*, Mr. Quincy Adams. Until Sunday..." Rabbi Klein released Adams's hand turned and resumed his walk to the train station.

When Adams returned to the jail, the turn-key told him that the watch commander wished to see him. The jailer unlocked the steel door between his kiosk and the hallway leading to the cells. He then opened the steel door leading to the lobby and stood aside as Adams entered. "Regulations, Mr. Adams, I need to search you for weapons and contraband. Would you please step over this way?" He motioned to a small alcove. "No briefcase, Sir? I don't recall a lawyer coming here didn't have a briefcase."

"No, I don't have anything much to put in one at the moment."

The jailer patted the pockets of Adams's suit. "Not carrying a weapon or drugs, are you?"

"No, Sheriff, I only plan to visit Mrs. Dubrowski, not make myself a long-term guest."

"Thank you for your cooperation, Sir. You'd be surprised what some folks try to sneak in here. Now, if you'll follow me, I'll take you to my watch commander."

The watch commander's office is a windowless room hardly larger that the turn-key's kiosk. In addition to a small desk and the low-back swivel chair occupied by the watch commander there is an armless wooden chair in front of the desk. The deputy sheriff motioned for Adams to be seated. The deputy finished reading and initialing a few papers and then laid them in a wire mesh out-basket. He picked up Adams's by now somewhat frayed card and turned it over a couple of times in his hand as though looking for something he'd missed in his first reading. "I'm told you want to see Mrs. Dubrowski, Counselor; is that true?"

"Yes, it is."

"Are you her lawyer?"

"I have been engaged to consult with her, but no, she hasn't yet agreed to employ me."

"Well that's a most unusual situation." The deputy looked again at Adams's business card. "We get lots of lawyers comin' around tryin' to drum up business, but I don't recall seein' you before."

"I'm sure you do have a good deal of that type of traffic, Deputy…"

"Isaacson, Walter Isaacson."

"Yes, Deputy Isaacson, thank you. It's true; this is my first visit to your…facility.
I do not maintain an active criminal law practice…"

"Pretty tough case to be gettin' your feet wet with, isn't it Counselor?"

"That may be true, Mr. Isaacson, but isn't that a decision best left to Mrs. Dubrowski and myself?"

"I don't mean to stick my nose into other people's business, Counselor; it's just that Coroner Ingersoll had me pledge to see that no harm comes to her while in our…'facility'…as you call it. And I'm sure you'll be pleased to know that when I give my word, I take it seriously."

"I am indeed, not only for Mrs. Dubrowski's sake, but for my own peace of mind as a citizen and taxpayer in Kennebec County. But tell me, Deputy Isaacson, since you may be the only public official who at the moment has Mrs. Dubrowski's welfare in mind, what do you think of her?"

"Nice lady, I mean if you can set aside her habit of shooting to death the men she lives with. No trouble, doesn't talk much. Doesn't say anything but 'good morning' or 'good afternoon' to the matron on duty. Doesn't talk to any of the other prisoners, except for two juveniles that are awaiting their date with Judge Gribble who'll send 'em off to the girls' reformatory and the tender care of Miss Boyles and Dr. Smedley.

"Esther, Mrs. Dubrowski, so the matrons tell me; spends all of her time with those two girls, and not much else. Actually, she's been a big help keeping those two hell-cats in line. I can tell you they'll miss her once Reba Boyles and that Dr. Smedley — they're the ones run the reformatory — get their hands on 'em."

"Perhaps it's maternal instinct. Maybe she sees them as proxies for her own estranged daughter. But tell me frankly, Deputy Isaacson, you were in court last Tuesday, do you think Mrs. Dubrowski's guilty?"

"Not for me to say, Counselor. I just lock 'em up and keep 'em that way 'till they bond out, serve their time, get shipped off to prison or even once in a while get tried and acquitted. Guilt or innocence, that's up to Judge Gribble and the jury. But I did hear her confess to it on the witness stand. In fact, so I'm told, she's intendin' to plead guilty at her arraignment Monday afternoon. Also hear Judge Gribble's going to appoint J. Patrick McGarrity to represent her."

"I don't think I know J. Patrick McGarrity, Deputy Isaacson."

"Don't expect a fellow like you'd have run across him that is unless you're in the habit of falling off bar stools and sleeping it off in our drunk tank."

"That doesn't sound good at all, Deputy Isaacson."

"Couldn't agree with you more, Mr. Adams. And that's why I'm going to bend a few rules and let you see Mrs. Dubrowski. Just continue down the hall to the elevator. Guard that runs it, he'll take you up and when you get there he'll call the matron on duty to let you in."

As Adams rode up in the tiny hydraulic elevator the jail-house aroma, a mixture of sweat, cigarette smoke, disinfectant, human waste, hopelessness and fear that is the unmistakable trade-mark of every jail and penitentiary, became so pervasive that Adams found himself trying not to breathe. Feigning a sneezing attack, he used his pocket handkerchief to cover his nose until he could become acclimated to the stench. Noticing Adams's effort, the guard offered, "Smell's kinda bad, Counselor, 'specially this time of year. But you eventually get used to it so it don't bother you so much. Anyways, it ain't quite as bad on the women's floor.

"Here we are and you can see yourself what I mean. Just a second; I need to call the matron to let you in." The guard picked up a telephone ear-piece and turned the crank on the old-fashioned wall phone. "Maude, that lawyer-fella's here. Chief Isaacson says let him in." He replaced the receiver, took out a ring of keys and opened a steel door opposite the elevator door. "Just step in there, Mister. Soon's you do I'll lock the door from this side, 'n' then Maude...Maude Woods...she's the matron on duty, can open the door on the other side so's you can go on in. When you're done, Maude'll let you out her door. Then you just ring that electric call button there on the wall 'n' I'll come up and get you."

"Thank you, Deputy. I don't expect to be very long."

When the deputy had closed the door and turned the lock, Adams turned around to see a forehead above large close-set eyes that were looking at him through the small, chicken-wire reinforced glass window in the door on the opposite side of the one-person vestibule in which he was now locked. The forehead and eyes disappeared and a moment later he heard the key turn in the second door. Once it was opened he saw that the forehead and eyes belonged to an elderly woman with the beginnings of a dowager's hump in her upper spine and legs as bowed as any cowboy in any photograph he'd ever seen.

Evidently she'd been standing on a small stool kept near the door for just that purpose. She quickly toed out the stool of the way so that it came to rest next to a wooden rocking chair. In addition to her singular frame, her thinning, frizzled gray-over-black hair was cut short, almost mannishly short, and stood on end as though she'd received an electrical shock. Her wrinkled face and hands showed an abundance of bluish veins and reddish capillaries.

She wore a shapeless tan-colored garment, the same hue as the male deputies' uniforms. On her right sleeve there was a sewn-on patch that read "Kennebec County Jail Matron." She wore a heavy brown belt at her waist. Appended to the belt on one side was a ring of keys, in the back a set of handcuffs and on the other hip a regulation billy-club.

"Please walk in front of me. I'll tell you when to stop. Walk only on the outside of that green line running down the corridor. You don't, then one of 'em's liable to grab you by the ankle and you'll end up with a mighty sore leg when I have to use my club to knock their hands away. 'Happens lots of times. Them, they don't mind gettin' their knuckles bruised, but you lawyers don't seem to like gettin' rapped on the ankle-bone at all.

"That's far enough; next cell's the one." Adams stood next to the outer wall as Matron Woods unhooked her billy-club and used it to rap on the bars. "Esther, that lawyer-fella's here.

"Now you, Mr. Lawyer, you need to stand back against the outer wall. You can sit on the floor if you want, but keep your back against the wall and keep your knees up. She's got a couple 'o wild ones in there with her. They get hold o' you, and you'll wish to the devil you'd listened to what I'm tellin' you. I'll be settin' back at the front, just keepin' an eye on things."

"You mean there's not a private room…or cell…for lawyers to meet with their clients?"

"Nope, this is it. If it don't suit you, I'll just let you back out and you can go complain to Sheriff Dowdy, or even the county commissioners, all the good it'll do you. You don't need to worry about me overhearin' what you say. For one thing, I'm too far away 'less you start shoutin' at one another. And for another thing, it ain't none of my business. Now are you gonna talk to Mrs. Esther here, or do you want to go back down? Up to you."

"Thank you, Matron. I'm sure that there's nothing you can do about it at the moment. Perhaps the bar association can petition the county commissioners, and maybe in the next budget they'll find a way to provide a consultation room."

"Well at least you're right about the first part; ain't nothin' I can do to fix it. Just let me know when yer done."

Adams peered into the dark cell and saw Esther Dubrowski standing against the back wall. "Mrs. Dubrowski? My name is Quincy…"

"Yes, Mr. Lawyer; I know your name from the card the deputy show me earlier. Is 'Adams,' like the President." She took a tentative couple of steps closer to the front of the cell.

"Yes, ma'am, like the President. Actually two Presidents, father and son. Distant relations. However, I'm only a small town lawyer."

"Why you want see me, Mr. Adams, lawyer of small town?"

"I want to defend you against the charges that are brought against you in connection with the death of your late employer Richard Cory."

"Why do I need lawyer? I had lawyer last time; he does nothing and I'm sentenced to twenty years. You think you can do better than twenty years? Besides Deputy…Mr. Isaacson…tell me judge will give me lawyer, no cost. Do you know I have no money to pay you? Why you work for no money? You do not look like rich man to me; too thin. Can't you even afford food?"

"I've brought you a note from Rabbi Klein." Adams began

reaching in his pocket to hand her the note.

"No, wait!" She whispered. "Must not let matron see you give me anything; is against rules. I get caught, I'm sent to solitary confinement. This I cannot allow. You read to me instead."

Adams extracted the note from his pocket and opened it. After a moment he looked up. "I'm sorry, Mrs. Dubrowski, I can't read it. It's in some kind of German dialect. I can read Greek and Latin, but not German."

"Is Yiddish."

"Wait, I can make out some of this. I see my name, 'Adams *ist ein mensch*.' Then it…"

"He says you're an upright…an honorable man. A high compliment from *Rebbe* Klein. How do you know the *Rebbe*?"

"I met him only a short while ago. He was leaving just as I was coming to see you. I could not get in to see you during mealtime, so I was waiting when he came out. The turn-key told me that the rabbi had been visiting you. So I approached him outside and we talked for a few minutes. At the end of our conversation…he had to leave to catch the train back to Portland…he gave me this note and said something about *ein gutten*…"

"*Shabbas;* he was wishing you a pleasant Sabbath. What else did he say?"

"He had me promise to just introduce myself and to tell you that I believe you're innocent. If you agree, he and I will come back to see you on Sunday, just after noon, depending on whether the train from Portland is on time."

"But I don't want a trial; I want to plead guilty. And the court will give me a lawyer, even though I don't need or want one. What difference does it make to me whether I spend the rest of my life in prison in Maine or in Illinois? If I go back to Illinois, I'll have to serve the rest of my sentence and more for violating my parole. I have no family either here or there. I am at peace with the fact that I'll never again see the outside world…never again listen to Paderewski play Chopin…never again see my daughter, hold my grandchild…" These words were forced out between sobs that brought Matron Woods out of her rocking chair and down the hallway.

"Everything all right? I think maybe it's time for you to go, Lawyer Adams. Don't want to get her upset 'cause it gets the others all riled up. They'll be mewlin' and cryin' all night."

"Is all right, Matron. See, I not cry any more. Mr. Adams, you tell

Rabbi Klein that for his sake, I'll see you both Sunday afternoon. But I'm making no promises other than I will be right here."

Chapter Ten

"So she agreed to let you represent her?" Flammonde had hardly settled in his chair and taken out a cheroot.

Adams leaned forward his forearms resting on his desk. "Well, yes and no."

"Meaning?

"She said that I could be her lawyer on three conditions: One, that she will do nothing to aid in her defense; two, I must also represent the two young women...girls actually...that share her cell; and three, that I'm not to request bail for her unless her cell-mates are released from custody as well."

"Now ain't that interestin' Counselor. She say why?"

"Says that they're good girls. Haven't committed any crime; they're just runaways. Ran away from home. According to Mrs. Dubrowski, the girls' father died...tuberculosis they said...mother re-married. Then the mother died; cancer got her. New husband must have been like Mrs. Dubrowski's husband. Girls...they're twins by the way...names are Colleen and Bridget O'Brien...said the step-father and step-uncle started molesting them a year ago...mother not yet a week in her grave at the time."

"Easy to see why she's taken them under her wing. But what are you going to do about condition number one?"

"You mean what are *we* going to do, don't you Mr. Flammonde? Don't forget that you're the one who got me into this."

"Me and my twenty-five hundred dollars." Flammonde flicked the ash off his cigar.

"Well that plus the fact that you promised me all the investigative help I need."

"Easy, Counselor. I haven't forgotten my promise. But let's not bicker about how we got here. The question of the moment is: where do we go from here?"

"That's easy; I'm going to the arraignment at two o'clock at which time I will enter my appearance as Mrs. Dubrowski's lawyer and she'll enter a plea of 'not guilty.' At least I got her to agree to that."

"Do you think that Rabbi Klein will be of any help?"

"Well, Mrs. Dubrowski trusts him. Wait a minute...how'd you know I met Rabbi Klein?"

"An acquaintance of mine told me that the rabbi went with you to see your client yesterday afternoon."

"An acquaintance?"

"Just someone I know in Augusta."

"Just someone you know in Augusta that likes to hang around the county jail keeping tabs on who comes and goes? Look, if we're going to be working on this together, you need to be completely candid with me."

"Okay, Counselor. He's someone who's helping me in my investigation of local business opportunities and who's agreed to help in this matter as well. That's all you need to know just now. Remember, you've agreed to trust me and you'll have to continue to do so even if it's sometimes not exactly to your liking. Don't worry, I'm not reading your mail or rifling through your client files, few though they may be."

"I suppose I must, but you're not making it any easier. I've got a client who won't tell me anything I can use to defend her. And I've got a colleague who won't tell me much that's of use either. I feel like an actor in a stage play; everyone else knows the plot and I don't even know my lines. How am I going to defend this woman with nothing more than a belief in her innocence?"

"If you don't object, I have a couple of ideas."

"You mean more lines for me to learn?"

"If you insist on putting it that way, Counselor. Do you want to hear them, or not? Time grows short, and you'll have to put one to use, assuming you wish to do so, at the arraignment."

"And that idea is…

"Move that Judge Gribble recuse himself."

"On what grounds? Apart from the fact that he probably won't recuse himself and that my moving for his recusal will not endear him to our…no, my…client, I've got to practice in his court for the foreseeable future. Even so, I'd run the risk of his permanent enmity if I thought that it might help Mrs. Dubrowski. But I just don't see him recusing himself."

"How about the fact that he gave the eulogy at Richard Cory's funeral?"

"You went to the funeral? Or did you hear it from another acquaintance?"

"Heard it myself, in person."

"Anybody else at the funeral, I mean other than the entire population of Tilbury Town?"

"You got that part right. In fact, I was a bit surprised that you weren't there. Davis & Son put on a spectacular show."

"I was up here reading up on criminal law and procedure. You mean it was open casket?"

"It started out that way, but the crowd was so big they had to move it from the funeral home to the cemetery. Never seen so many flowers. There were even home-made bouquets. Whether that's 'cause some folks couldn't afford to send flowers from a florist or because the florists had run out is hard to say."

"Why didn't they move it to his church?"

"Seems which church was *his* church was a matter of some rather heated debate among Tilbury Town's men of the cloth. Evidently Richard Cory gave generously to all the churches, but none is able to claim him as a member. Indeed, so I hear, none of the clergy-men could claim to have ever seen Cory at one of their services. Anyway, in order to avoid a rather unseemly fight, it was agreed that an ecumenical service would be conducted at the cemetery with each clergy-member participating. If ever a fellow got a more spirited send-off than Richard Cory, it must have involved angels coming down from on high to lift the departed straight to St. Peter's gate."

"Anyone else of interest there?"

"If you mean of interest to the matter at hand, I really can't say."

"'Can't' or won't?"

"Just not sure. Out of that bunch of people, it's more likely than not that whoever did in Richard Cory was there at the funeral, unless of course she was unable to attend, her being locked up tight in Sheriff Dowdy's jail. But nobody I'd put my money on just yet."

"What's your other idea?"

"Find out who benefits from Cory's death."

"That should be easy enough, assuming that he made a will. Someone's bound to be showing up pretty soon to file it for probate."

"I've thought of that and I've made a small financial arrangement with a deputy clerk in the probate court to let me know soon's that happens.

"Mr. Flammonde, You promised me that I'd not be embarrassed by representing Mrs. Dubrowski. I hardly think that bribing court clerks is in accord with your pledge."

"As you wish, Counselor. No more bribing government employees, at least without your say-so."

"But hold on a minute." Adams stood up and walked to the window smoothing his hair off his forehead. "Why would Esther Dubrowski want to plead guilty, or at least not put up a defense? If she's the beneficiary of the will, and she murdered Cory she couldn't inherit under the will as a matter of law. So if she's not the beneficiary under the will, do you think she would plead guilty so that someone else—the murderer—could inherit under the will?"

"A mighty good question, Mr. Adams. The only problem is where she said she got the revolver. If she really did do it, why make up the story about where she got the gun? Do you reckon she's calculating enough to have assumed that whomever she got for a lawyer would figure out that her confession was a lie because of the gun?"

"Seems far too risky to me. You say you've never met the lady, so she can't have expected you to appear *deus ex machina* with an envelope full of cash and ..." Adams walked around his desk and stood over Flammonde who was still seated and in the process of reaching for another cheroot. "I do recall rightly that you said you'd never met Esther Dubrowski?"

"Yes and…"

"And you've never had any contact with her, direct or indirect, whatsoever?"

"Yes, Counselor, that's correct. No contact, direct or indirect, whatsoever."

"But you knew who she was, her position in Richard Cory's household?"

"True. As I told you I'm here investigating business opportunities. Richard Cory is…was…said by all to be a man with many business interests. However, I could find out nothing about him through public records or queries to state agencies despite having made certain financial arrangements not unlike the one with the probate clerk, the one of which you so rightly disapprove. Evidently he does not bank in Tilbury Town, Augusta, Portland or any place else in Maine. In short, Richard Cory was like a man from Mars somehow come to earth and one day just appeared as the squire of Oakdale Hall and Tilbury Town.

"As I make it my business to find out everything I can about a man in whom we are interested, I naturally made inquiry into his household arrangements. That's how Mrs. Dubrowski came to my attention. In time, I would have approached her, either with financial incentives or in some other way, but as you know events overtook my plans."

Adams took his suit jacket off the coat rack near the door. "I need to be starting for Augusta. Are you coming to the arraignment?"

"I see no reason to do so, and I'd just as soon not call unwelcome attention to myself, an outsider so to speak, by appearing to take an undue interest in the fate of Mrs. Dubrowski. Incidentally, what do you plan to do about her second and third conditions?"

"I'll speak with Enoch Matthews after the arraignment and find out what I can about the girls. I'll have to enter an appearance as their attorney over in the clerk's office first, but that shouldn't take long. As for the third, bail, I doubt that it will be much of an issue. There's no chance that Judge Gribble's going to set bail on a murder charge for a defendant with Mrs. Dubrowski's baggage. What are you going to be doing?"

"I'm going to see what I can find out about the brooch. As I said last Friday, I believe it's got something to do with Esther Dubrowski's willingness to spend the rest of her life in prison. I think I'd like to find out what."

Chapter Eleven

When Adams arrived in the courtroom Esther Dubrowski was seated in the jury box along with several other women and the two girls, Bridget and Colleen O'Brien. They were all attired in the drab gray dresses with the words "Kennebec County Prisoner" stenciled on the back. The garments must have been made by convict labor at the state prison for women. They were, Adams mused, like hand-me-downs passed on from one generation of prisoners to the next. The next-generation prisoners seated in the courtroom that afternoon were all manacled and their feet in shackles. There was a long chain looped between each prisoner's legs so that none of them could even attempt to hobble away on her own. This chain was fastened to a steel u-bolt set in the floor at one corner of the jury box. This arrangement allowed each prisoner to stand when addressing the court, but otherwise she is unable to move in any direction. As a further precaution, the "jail-chain" as it was referred to is presided over by Matron Maude Woods.

District Attorney Pommus was seated at the front counsel table. To his right was Assistant District Attorney Matthews, case files in a stack in front of him. A third man, whom Adams did not recognize, was seated at the rear counsel table reading a document and making notes on a pad. Adams went around the front of the counsel table and stood in front of Pommus who was sitting with his hands folded in front of him apparently lost in thought. "Excuse me, Mr. District Attorney, my name's Quincy Adams. I'll be representing Mrs. Dubrowski." Adams held out his hand which Pommus gripped tepidly and let go.

"Quincy, how are you?"

"Good, Enoch. How about you?"

The man seated at the other table stood and Adams had a twinge of nausea in his gut. The man was average height and build. His face was badly scarred from measles, chicken-pox or perhaps childhood acne. He had a black patch over one eye, and there was a puffy scar running from above the covered eye socket down his cheek to his chin. In contrast to his disfigured face he wore an expensive-looking black linen suit and a clerical collar above a black clergyman's vest. He walked to where Adams was standing. "Mr. Adams, my name is Horatio Christmas. I'm the deputy attorney general in charge of criminal prosecutions." He held out his hand which Adams took and held for a moment, the chill of it running up Adams's arm. "I look forward to working with you in the *State versus Dubrowski* matter."

"Working with me, Reverend...er... Mister Christmas?"

"Yes, indeed, Mr. Adams. District Attorney Pommus has requested that the attorney general's office take the lead in the prosecution. By the way, you can call me either 'Reverend Christmas' or 'Mister Christmas' whichever you prefer. Indeed when we meet informally, please feel free to call me 'Horatio' and I shall call you 'Quincy.' I'm sure we shall get along just fine."

"All rise," the bailiff parted the heavy drapes covering the door leading from the courtroom to the judge's chambers. The prisoners rose as one with much clanking of their shackles and chains. "The Supreme Judicial Court of Maine in and for Kennebec County is now in session, the Honorable Cranston Gribble presiding." Judge Gribble took his seat and glanced at the stack of folders which Martha Parsons handed up to him from her desk at the front of the bench.

Judge Gribble looked over at the jury box and down at the counsel tables. "Be seated, gentlemen. Bailiff, the defendants may be seated as well. The clerk will call the first case."

It took the better part of two hours for Judge Gribble to work his way through the docket until only Esther Dubrowski and the O'Brien twins remained. None of the other defendants had attorneys, and prior to the hearing each had professed a desire to plead guilty. These plea cases were all handled by Enoch Matthews who Adams thought looked increasingly uncomfortable in his role as lead worker on this assembly line of justice. A couple of the defendants tried to offer at least mitigating circumstances, if not legally-cognizable defenses. But Judge Gribble was having none of it. In each case the clerk would swear in the defendant and then Judge Gribble would go through the guilty plea ritual: "Are you pleading guilty because you are guilty?"

The defendant eyes tearing up and looking steadily at the floor responded in a barely audible voice, "Yes."

"Yes what?"

"Yes, Your Honor, Sir."

"And for no other reason?"

"Yes, Your Honor."

"And the district attorney's made no promise of leniency from the court or offered any other inducement to you to plead guilty?"

"Yes...I mean...no, Your Honor."

"You understand you have a right to a trial either before the court or before a jury?"

"Yes, Your Honor."

"And you voluntarily want to give up that right?"

"Yes, Your Honor."

"Very well, I accept your plea of guilty and based thereon find you guilty of…" He would then flip through the file until he came to the indictment and read the offense to which the defendant had just pleaded guilty and of which he'd just found her guilty…"theft, assault (or whatever happened to be the charge).

"Sentencing will be three weeks from today. Until then, the defendant…" he would look at the file again for the defendant's name…"(Defendant's name)" is remanded to the custody of the Sheriff of Kennebec County, Maine. Next case."

Martha Parsons read out: "Number 18-07-4-J; *State versus Bridget O'Brien*; Number 18-07-5-J; *State versus Colleen O'Brien*."

"Mr. Bailiff, bring these defendants forward."

It took a few minutes for Matron Woods to unlock the chain that bound the defendants and for the girls, still handcuffed and shackled, to stand before the bench, the bailiff standing just behind them. While this was being done, Judge Gribble was thumbing through the files. When he was through, he looked down and remarked, "I see that the two of you are back again. This time charged with attempted escape. Which of you is Colleen and which is Bridget?"

"I'm Colleen," the girl on the judge's left answered, her eyes down-cast as she'd seen the other defendants do.

"And you'd be Bridget?" Judge Gribble looked to his right.

"Yes, Sir. She's my sister Bridget."

"I asked her, young lady. You are to speak only when spoken to. "Are you Bridget O'Brien?"

"She doesn't speak, Your Honor. She stopped talking right after our ma passed. I talk for both of us. I guess that's maybe because I'm the oldest."

"I thought you were twins."

"We are, Your Honor; I'm ten minutes older."

"Well how do you and she communicate with one another?"

"I don't know, we just do. We always seem to know what the other's thinking."

"You say she stopped speaking when your mother died?"

"Just after, Sir."

"Do you know why she stopped?"

"No, Sir; she just did."

"Well if you and she always know what the other's thinking how come you don't know why she stopped speaking?"

"I'm sorry, Your…Your Honor, I just don't."

"Can she nod her head?"

"Yes, Sir, but she won't."

"Are you telling this court that she's willing to let you speak for her?"

"Yes, Sir…Your Honor. May I ask something?"

"No you may not…"

"But it's…Bridget needs to go to the toilet really bad, Your Honor. Please…"

"Very well. Matron Woods, you better take 'em before there's an accident in my courtroom. The bailiff'll watch the rest 'till you get back. Court will be in recess for ten minutes."

"All rise," the bailiff intoned as he took Maude Woods's seat at the end of the jury box.

Adams, who'd been seated at the defense counsel table walked over to the prosecution table. "Uh…Reverend Christmas, do you suppose we might have a word in private before Judge Gribble comes back. It's about the Dubrowski case."

"In private, Mr. Adams? Shouldn't the public's business be conducted in public? And what about your client, does she waive her right to be present? And what of District Attorney Pommus? It would look most unseemly if we left him out. He is still attorney of record for the State."

"I don't have a problem with Mr. Pommus being present, nor Mr. Matthews either. But let me confer with my client for a moment and I'll see if she'll consent to waive her right to be present. After getting the bailiff's permission to have a whispered conversation with Mrs. Dubrowski, Adams returned to the counsel tables. "Yes, my client waives her right to be present."

"Will she make that waiver on the record when her case is called?"

"Yes, I'm sure she will. Would you mind if we adjourned to one of the witness rooms?"

"No, that would be fine. Mr. Pommus, is that acceptable to you?" Pommus nodded and started to rise from his chair along with Enoch Matthews. Reverend Christmas put a restraining hand on Matthews's shoulder. "Perhaps you'd best wait here, Enoch. Come fetch us when Judge Gribble's back on the bench. I'd ask the bailiff, but he would appear to have a full plate keeping an eye on the jail chain until the matron returns."

The witness room is a windowless square with two armless wooden chairs against each wall except the wall with the door. The only other furniture is a couple of metal floor-standing ash trays that were overflowing with cigarette and cigar butts. Scattered on four of the six chairs were sections of last week's *Kennebec Journal*, a frayed copy of a Sears mail-order catalog and a couple of falling apart, months-old copies of the *Saturday Evening Post*. District Attorney Pommus, in an effort to be relevant, picked up the reading material and laid it on one of the chairs. When the three men were seated, one on each wall, Adams started to speak first. "Gentlemen, I appreciate your meeting with me like this. I…"

Pommus butted in, "If you're going to ask for a plea agreement…I assure you this will be a very short meeting. The people of Tilbury Town and all of Kennebec County wouldn't…"

"Hold on a moment, Bascom, let's hear what Quincy has on his mind. There will be time enough to answer him after we've listened to him."

"You mean you'd consider a reduced sentence? There's not a chance in Hades that I'll…"

"Bascom, will you let Quincy have the floor for a minute?" Christmas held a hand, palm outward, in the direction of Pommus as a shut-up gesture. "Go ahead Quincy."

"Thank you, Reverend…"

"We're in private, so please call me Horatio. Will you do that, Quincy?"

"I'm happy to Rev…er… Horatio." In fact, a guilty plea is about the farthest thing from what I want to discuss as anything could be. But in case Judge Gribble comes back sooner than expected, let me tell you that I do intend to enter a plea of 'not guilty.'

"You mean 'not guilty by reason of insanity' do you not? I'm sure you're aware there is a difference, Quincy."

"Yes, Horatio, I did take criminal law in law school. In fact the professor was rather obsessed with the insanity defense; he spent fully half the class time having us students discuss the flaws in the *M'Naughten* Rule. Then the final examination covered everything about criminal law except the *M'Naughten* Rule.

"Actually I'd like to get you to agree to a change of venue, say to Cumberland County, Portland."

"You must be joking. The crime occurred in Kennebec County,

and that's where she's going to be tried."

"Now hold on Bascom; let's hear Quincy's reasons for changing venue. Quincy?"

"Thank you Horatio. In truth, the thought came to me just before the recess. My original intention was, and if necessary will still be, to move for Judge Gribble to recuse himself."

"Because?"

"Because of the appearance of impropriety. I don't know if you're aware, but Judge Gribble gave the eulogy at Richard Cory's funeral."

"Bascom, you were there; did his honor come to bury Richard Cory, or to praise him?"

"Well, it was pretty clear that Judge Gribble was deeply moved. I was standing close by with the rest of the dignitaries, the mayor, and so on, and I'd have to say I maybe saw a tear or two in the judge's eyes. But that could be just for appearances sake. I'm sure Judge Gribble'd be completely fair…"

"Perhaps so, Bascom, but Quincy does have a point. It's for the sake of appearances, to borrow his thought that Quincy says that Judge Gribble ought not to try the case. In the public's eyes, the appearance of justice and due process are just as important as the attainment of justice. But Quincy, you said you were prepared to move for recusal, not that you were necessarily going to. You mentioned a change of venue."

Despite Reverend Christmas's fearsome appearance and august title, Adams was beginning to feel that possibly the reverend actually believed that the prosecutor's first duty is to seek justice and not merely rack up convictions. Silently he thanked District Attorney Pommus for inviting the attorney general's office to take the lead in prosecuting Esther Dubrowski. Whether it was Pommus's initiative or the decision was thrust upon him by others, in either event it gave Adams the first glimmer of hope. "My thought is that a change of venue would be more palatable to Judge Gribble, instead of a recusal motion. Again, it's for appearances sake."

"On what grounds?" Christmas leaned forward, evidently keenly interested.

"Four that have occurred to me so far. One, we're certain to get a fair number of Tilbury Town residents on the jury panel. They all knew Richard Cory and from what I know of my own experience they held him in high esteem. Also, look how many turned out for the funeral and sent flowers whether they could afford them or not. They're all going to want someone to be punished for taking his life, although they're unlikely to say so. That means I'll have to use all my peremptory challenges just keeping the deceased's friends and neighbors off the jury.

"Second, the State's only witness to the *corpus delicti* of the offense—that Richard Cory's death was a homicide—is Dr. Goodson, a popular, highly respected physician who is probably the family doctor for most of the *venire*. No matter how effectively I cross-examine him, and frankly, I'm not sure how I'd do that, is any juror not going to accept his word?

"That leads me to the third reason: Sheriff Dowdy. He believes that Richard Cory's death was a suicide. His testimony's enough for me to argue reasonable doubt. But even those people who were not at the inquest have heard about his altercation with District Attorney Pommus. In light of that, what juror is going to believe him?

"Lastly, who in Kennebec County hasn't heard that Esther Dubrowski confessed to shooting Richard Cory and that she's been convicted of murder in Illinois? Even if I don't put her on the stand, the jury's bound to know that she's a 'murderess.'"

"Perhaps so, Mr. Adams, but they're going to hear her confession anyway."

"Maybe so, Mr. Pommus, or maybe not."

"You make a very difficult case to answer in regard to change of venue. I take it you also have a strategy for keeping the confession out."

"Truthfully, Horatio, at the moment I don't. I'm kind of taking things one step at a time."

Enoch Matthews knocked on the door once and stuck his head into the room. "Judge's back on the bench and feeling lonesome. He sent me to fetch you three, and sent Mrs. Parsons to see what's keeping the O'Brien sisters and Matron Woods. They're not back either."

"Thank you, Enoch. Mr. Pommus, Mr. Adams and I will be there in a moment." Turning to Adams, he held out his hand. "Quincy, you've just got your client a change of venue assuming, that is, that Judge Gribble goes along. But there's an old saying: 'be careful what you ask for, you may get it.' Some of those judges down in Portland make Judge Gribble look like Old Saint Nick. Remind me and I'll get you a list of the better restaurants in Portland. I hope you're fond of lobster. Now let's go either make Judge Gribble happy or grumpier than he already is."

The lawyers returned to their places at the bar. Judge Gribble rearranged the remaining files in front of him and began looking around the courtroom like he'd misplaced his gavel.

"Reverend Christmas, I'm sorry to keep you so long. Had I known you were appearing for the State, I'd have had my clerk move your case to the head of the list when she made up the docket."

"Thank you, Your Honor, but we've put our time to good use. I've had the opportunity to meet Mr. Adams and…"

"Who's Mr. Adams?"

"I am, Your Honor, Quincy Adams. I'm representing Esther Dubrowski."

"You are? I don't recall appointing you. I appointed J. Patrick McGarrity. In fact, where is McGarrity?"

"I don't know, Your Honor. I have been retained to represent Mrs. Dubrowski and…"

"Retained by whom, Counselor?"

As Adams was trying to think of a polite way to tell Judge Gribble that whoever was paying his fee was none of the Court's business a female scream echoed down the deserted hallway outside the courtroom. "Bailiff…no…you, Matthews, go out in the hall and see what the devil's going on."

Matthews made his way out of the courtroom to the sound of yet another scream. In a minute or so he came back. "Your honor, it seems that the O'Brien twins have escaped. It was Mrs. Parsons who screamed. She may need medical attention because she's hysterical. I went into the women's room and found Matron Woods handcuffed to one of the toilet stalls with a wad of toilet paper stuffed in her mouth to keep her from raising the alarm. The O'Brien sisters were nowhere to be seen. If the bailiff will give me his handcuff keys I can go let Matron Woods loose and she can tell what happened."

"Bailiff, you do that. And you keep a sharp eye on the rest of them. I'm going to call Sheriff Dowdy. This is unprecedented; prisoners escaping custody while in my courtroom. There will be a full accounting when this is done. Court's in recess."

In a few minutes the second floor of the courthouse was an ant farm of activity. Sheriff Dowdy had issued orders to search the courthouse from basement to cupola. An ambulance had been called for Mrs. Parsons whose hysteria had not abated in the intervening time. Now Sheriff Dowdy and Matron Woods stood in front of the bench awaiting the inevitable remarks from Judge Gribble who first had one other item of business to handle. "Mr. Adams, I'm postponing your client's arraignment until two o'clock tomorrow afternoon.

"Sheriff Dowdy, I want you to have two of your men escort the prisoners back to the jail. I don't want any of them to get ideas about escaping by hearing how those two hellions did it. Do you think you can manage that without losing any more of them?"

Sheriff Dowdy quickly drafted two of his men who happened at that moment to be in the courtroom searching under the spectator benches. As the prisoners were being led out through a rear door of the courtroom to a holding cell in the back hallway, Adams looked at his client and for the first time since he'd met her saw a trace of a smile on her face.

Chapter Twelve

On the day following the arraignment, Adams and Flammonde were seated in Adams's office sipping ice tea poured from a pitcher brought up from the Red Rooster by Camille Winters. Miss Winters was busy in the outer office dealing with telephone calls from Tilbury Townspeople expressing their displeasure at Adams having undertaken the defense of Esther Dubrowski. Adams's taking on the case had been reported in the morning's *Daily Kennebec Journal* as a side-bar to the lead story reporting the O'Brien twins daring escape from custody. The reporter had been in the courtroom throughout the previous afternoon, intending to write his story about the Dubrowski arraignment. His patience had been more than rewarded.

Flammonde had read the story, but Adams had not. "It must have been quite a sight, Counselor, Sheriff Dowdy and Matron Woods standing there in front of the judge like a couple of defendants about to be sentenced to twenty years. The Richard Cory Case has not been one of Sheriff Dowdy's finest moments in law enforcement."

"Yes, and Matron Woods has probably had better days on the job as well. As she told it to Judge Gribble, she made Bridget leave the stall door open while using the toilet so Matron Woods could keep an eye on her. Matron Woods had to take off one of the handcuffs in order that Bridget could...you know...and soon as Bridget finished, Colleen came up behind Matron Woods and put her hands over the matron's head and started choking the matron with the handcuff chain. When Colleen made her move Bridget got up, grabbed a handful of toilet tissue and stuffed it into Woods's mouth so she couldn't call for help. Not that she'd have been able to with Colleen choking her nearly to death.

"Then Bridget grabbed the handcuff keys and took off her other handcuff. They used Bridget's handcuffs to chain Woods to the lintel over the toilet stall door. Her arms were stretched over her head so she couldn't remove the toilet paper from her mouth. Her toes were barely touching the floor. Then they undid Colleen's handcuffs, got rid of their leg shackles and headed for parts unknown."

"How'd they get away without anyone seeing them? They were dressed in prisoner uniforms weren't they?"

"That's right, and Sheriff Dowdy's only explanation was that the courthouse was pretty empty at that time of day. Seems all the county offices closed at four o'clock. The commissioners did that—cut back the employees' hours—as way to cut their pay.

"Anyway, after Judge Gribble spouted a while longer he got the sheriff to promise that from now on the prisoners on jail chains would be allowed to use the toilets in the jail before coming into his courtroom. So I suppose some good may come of it. But I fear the price the O'Brien girls will have to pay for that good deed will be a steep one."

"I wonder how they've managed so far not to get caught. Seems like a couple of girls running around downtown Augusta with "Kennebec County Prisoner" in bold letters on their backs would grab someone's attention. Do you think they had an accomplice?"

"Two young girls, not from around here. Their only friend herself a prisoner. I doubt it, Counselor. My acquaintance in Augusta did tell me before I came up to your office that the Augusta police took a report from a citizen that someone had stolen two dresses off a back yard clothes line early this morning. Could be a coincidence, but…"

"Well, I wish them good luck. Mrs. Dubrowski seems more concerned about them getting sent to the girls' reformatory than she is about her own fate. From my conversation with the deputy sheriff…Walter Isaacson…I got the impression that the two that run the reformatory are not who you'd want taking care of your own children. But in any event, until Sheriff Dowdy catches up with them, I suppose I'm down to just one client."

"And what about that client? How'd the arraignment go? You haven't said whether Judge Gribble recused himself."

"The arraignment was…an arraignment. Mrs. Dubrowski acknowledged that she is in fact Esther Dubrowski, the defendant charged in the indictment. She said she understood the charge against her. I waived reading of the indictment and entered a plea of 'not guilty.' I must admit, however, that I didn't follow the script when it came time for the recusal motion. Instead of moving for recusal, I moved for a change of venue. The State concurred, and Judge Gribble didn't have much choice but to grant it."

"Well done, Counselor." Flammonde raised his empty glass in a mock toast and took out a cheroot. "I'm amazed that Pommus went along."

"He didn't have much choice either. That man Horatio Christmas, head of the attorney general's criminal division, he's the one made the decision."

Flammonde stopped lighting his cigar and discarded the match in the ash tray. "Horatio Christmas? My word, Counselor, you do know how to pick your opponents."

"I'm sorry, but I don't recall having been consulted in the matter."

"Nor do I believe that District Attorney Pommus was consulted any more than you were. Do you know who Horatio Christmas is?"

"He said he's head of the attorney general's criminal division."

"And that's true. But do you know why he became a lawyer and how he got to be the State's chief prosecutor?"

"No, but I expect I'm about to find out." Adams stood up and poured himself another glass of tea, taking the little bit of ice that remained in the pitcher.

"As you've gathered," Flammonde paused to light his cheroot, "Reverend Christmas is indeed an ordained minister of the Gospel. Not a very pleasant fellow to look at, even before he lost his eye."

"How'd that happen?"

"Patience, Mr. Adams, I'm coming to that. The Reverend Christmas had a pulpit, in Augusta, long before you settled in Tilbury Town. And a grand pulpit it was. Pews packed every Sunday, not just Palm Sunday and Easter. Collection plate full to overflowing every week. Indeed, Reverend Christmas was doing quite well doing God's work.

"Although he's far from a handsome man...the ravages of childhood chicken-pox, I believe...he does...or at least did...have a certain charm. But his strength was as a preacher of the Gospel. He could preach hell-fire and brimstone in one breath and the healing, forgiving hand of God in the next. So compelling were his weekly sermons that women were known to swoon and sinners come forward to confess their sins and beg for salvation in front of the congregation."

"So why'd he get out of the salvation business?"

"He hasn't. He's just changed how he goes about it. Do you think Miss Winters would object to getting us another pitcher of tea?"

"Probably not. I'm sure she'd welcome a break from dealing with the telephone. In fact, as an inducement, I'll ask her to join us, if you don't mind."

"That seems a fair trade, Counselor. By all means, make the offer."

Miss Winters was indeed glad for the respite from repeating the same "every person is innocent until proven guilty, even Esther Dubrowski, and everyone accused of a serious crime, even Esther Dubrowski, is entitled to a lawyer." A few callers would attempt to argue one or both points, and others would simply agree and ring off with "well any lawyer who'd represent that harridan is not going to get any of *my* business." Miss Winters had procured another pitcher of ice tea, and as a lagniappe, a plate of fresh cookies. After a frosty greeting to Emil Flammonde, she took the second client chair and Flammonde resumed his biography of Horatio Christmas.

"Like some Biblical parable...the Book of Job comes to mind...The Lord put Reverend Christmas's faith to a est. One night when the Reverend was out performing some pastoral duty or another, a burglar broke into the Reverend's home and began terrorizing Christmas's wife. If I recall correctly, the intruder ravaged the poor woman and stabbed her numerous times with a buck knife. The Reverend returned home just as the fiend was leaving and grappled with the man. As his Parthian shot, the intruder slashed Reverend Christmas down his face from forehead to chin, costing Reverend Christmas his left eye, not to mention that dreadful scar that remains even today.

"So he turned to the law?" Miss Winters asked.

"Not right away. For several months the police and the sheriff continued to question, often without the highest punctilio of regard for the civil rights of the gentleman being questioned, every burglar, petty thief and vagrant that came to their notice. Of course none would own up to the crime, and many had iron-clad alibis: They were incarcerated at the time of the crime. Eventually, one man was taken into custody and was charged with the murder of Reverend Christmas's wife, Eve. The charge was based on his possession of a cameo locket that Reverend Christmas identified as having been given by him to his wife Eve on her birthday, a few months prior to the murder.

"The grand jury returned a true bill of indictment charging the man...I wish I could remember the name...with burglary as well as murder. Somehow, through a foul-up in the clerk's office, the district attorney's office or both, the defendant was allowed to plead guilty to burglary, for which he received a five-year sentence. Since he had pleaded guilty to one count of the indictment, jeopardy attached and they could not then try him for murder because of double jeopardy."

"Was the judge Judge Gribble and the district attorney Pommus?"

"I believe Pommus was an assistant at the time and possibly was the one who handled the guilty plea. And yes, Judge Gribble was the judge who flipped through the file in his typical perfunctory manner and allowed the defendant to plead guilty to the lesser charge."

"I can imagine the public outcry," Adams paused in the midst of chewing a cookie.

"Actually, there wasn't one. The bureaucracy closed ranks and managed to stifle any press coverage. Reverend Christmas, perhaps sensing the futility of doing so, declined to make the miscarriage of justice public. Instead, he chose another means of seeking justice for his murdered wife."

"He went to law school and became a prosecutor?"

"Indeed, Miss Winters. He closed his church and sold the building. He finished the required law school course work in less than half the required time, was admitted to the bar and went to work in the attorney general's criminal division."

"I assume that since he heads that division, he's good at what he does," Adams offered."

"That would be a given, Mr. Adams. I am made to understand that he's not lost a murder case, and he's tried more than his share."

"I can see him as being very effective in front of a jury, but how is he on the law?"

"Don't think that because he is single-minded in his zeal to prosecute murderers that he's a slouch when it comes to knowing what's in the law books. Do you have *Wigmore on Evidence?*"

"No, I wish I did. It'll probably be my next acquisition for my library, as soon as I pay for the materials I have. Why do you ask?"

"When Professor Wigmore has a question on the law of evidence I'm told he asks Reverend Christmas. That said, I'm also told that he's equally expert in criminal procedure as well as the substantive law of crimes in Maine.

"I suppose he has no warm feelings for either Judge Gribble or District Attorney Pommus and that's why he agreed to the change of venue."

"I can't help thinking you're right, at least in part, Counselor. However, there's another aspect to chief prosecutor Christmas and that's his abhorrence of having any of his convictions overturned on appeal."

"So that's why he agreed to the change of venue? Dare I assume that he won't try to railroad Esther Dubrowski into a life sentence?"

"That would be a fair assumption, Counselor. She will get a very fair trial, much fairer than at the hands of Judge Gribble and District Attorney Pommus. But while you and I may believe Esther Dubrowski is innocent, you'll have quite a job convincing a jury of that. And don't forget, in closing arguments, Christmas gets the last word."

"May I ask a question?"

"Of course, Miss Winters." Flammonde took a long drink of his ice tea.

"What happened to the man who pleaded guilty to burglary?"

"Well, most all of that story's no more than speculation, and it's unlikely the truth will ever be known. But it seems that Reverend Christmas started a prison ministry just a month or so after the guilty plea. He'd go to the prison to preach on Sundays, and often went several times during the week all in the interest of saving the souls that wanted salvation. He'd counsel with prisoners in small groups, and sometimes one-on-one. Somehow, the man who'd murdered the Reverend's wife became one of the one-on-one prisoners with whom the reverend would counsel. Then after maybe half a dozen visits from the reverend, the murderer hung himself in his cell. It was just after that that Reverend Christmas closed down his prison ministry and went off to law school."

"And what of your efforts to trace the brooch?"

"Not nearly so successful as your efforts in court, Counselor. But why don't I take you two to dinner? It's been a long, if productive, day. Miss Winters?"

Camille looked at her boss not knowing how to respond. Reading assent in his expression, she said, "Well, if we make it the Red Rooster. I really must be home early as I have to be at work by six-thirty in the morning."

"Excellent. Then it's a date. Come Miss Winters, we'll leave Adams to lock up." Flammonde stood and offered his arm to a flustered Camille. "I'll tell you both of my misadventures in searching for the brooch, and I do have one other bit of interesting news."

"Which is?"

"Sorry, Counselor, it'll have to wait until we've ordered."

It took Adams only a minute or two to turn off the fan and lights gather the pitcher and the empty cookie tray and lock the office. When he got downstairs and into the cafe, Flammonde was just finishing holding Camille's chair for her and gently arranging it at the table all under the suspicious eyes of Dorothy Allagash and the wide-eyed amazement of the evening waitress. Adams introduced Flammonde to Aunt Dorothy as a new client for whom he is handling several business matters. He had to interrupt their work in order to attend the Dubrowski arraignment, and as a result they were working late and decided to break for the evening meal.

Aunt Dorothy, while rattling off the evening's bill of fare, continued to eye Flammonde with suspicion as though assessing his ability to pay for three dinners. Orders were quickly placed, pot roast for Adams and Flammonde and baked cod for Camille Winters.

When Aunt Dorothy left to place the orders and to supervise their preparation, Flammonde delivered on his promise. "First the positive news; notice I didn't say 'good news.' The will was filed for probate this morning by the named executor: Chivas McDade Smedley."

"Why he's the director of the girls' reformatory. You know, the one Deputy Isaacson is none too fond of."

"One and the same, Counselor. I was able to get a brief look at the dispositive provisions before the will was sealed pending the hearing on admitting it to probate. It appears that Richard Cory, in a final act of benevolence, left virtually his entire estate, Oakdale Hall included, to a trust for the benefit of wayward girls. Dr. Smedley is the co-trustee along with Reba Boyles, the executive assistant administratrix and second in command under Dr. Smedley. The co-trustees have unfettered discretion in how the corpus of the trust shall be managed and its income and capital gains either expended or added to corpus."

"You said 'virtually all his estate,' Mr. Flammonde. Were their other legatees?"

"Yes, Miss Winters. But why don't you two start calling me Emil, at least when we're together like this or in the office?"

"But I've never called Mr. Adams anything but 'Mr. Adams.' Is that proper?"

"Oh, I think we can make an exception with Mr. Flammonde…I mean Emil. He's right, you know; we're going to be working together a good bit, so I'd say some level of informality is warranted."

"Good, I'm happy that's settled." Flammonde lifted his ice tea glass, "Camille, Quincy, I think we're going to make a grand team." After they'd clinked glasses toasting their new relationship, their food arrived and they busied themselves with Aunt Dorothy's finest cuisine.

After a few minutes, Emil lay down his knife and fork. "To answer your question about the other legatees, Camille, if I read the will correctly—the clerk was anxious that I get through and clear out—Cory left one thousand dollars to each full-time employee working at Oakdale Hall at the time of his death. So I suppose that Mrs. Dubrowski and Mr. Silas will each get one thousand dollars, unless of course Dr. Smedley decides to withhold Mrs. Dubrowski's legacy pending the outcome of her trial. Then, even if she's acquitted, I expect he'll refuse to pay in the hope that she'll sue so that he can attempt to prove her guilt to a jury applying the lesser preponderance-of-evidence standard of proof required in civil cases."

"Do you really think, Emil, that Dr. Smedley is that much of a pinch-penny?"

"I really know little about Dr. Smedley's spending habits, Quincy. But I expect that he will claim that it is his fiduciary duty, as executor and trustee, to see that not one penny goes to Richard Cory's murderer."

"Well, if nothing else, it does rule out inheritance as a motive for Esther Dubrowski to have murdered Richard Cory or for her to be covering for someone else who stood to benefit substantially for Richard Cory's death."

"I agree, Quincy. Unless she's a murderess-for-hire, I think we can rule out Mrs. Dubrowski's having murdered Richard Cory in order to benefit a trust, even if it is for the benefit of wayward girls."

"I'm interested in hearing about the brooch, Mr. Flammonde…excuse me…Emil. But I really need to be getting home."

"Five minutes, Camille. I promise. I checked only one store today, Nicholson & Ryan on Water Street in Augusta. They disclaimed any knowledge of the piece, and I think the manager was being truthful. Of course I had only a sketch that I'd made from memory, and I saw it for less than a minute from rather far away. In truth, I based the sketch largely on the description recited by Pommus during his questioning of Mrs. Dubrowski. So if his description is wrong, so's my sketch.

"Perhaps the store manager didn't want his firm associated with such a notorious piece? After all, Nicholson & Ryan is the oldest, largest and most prestigious jewelry emporium in Augusta. "

"You could well be right, Camille, but a wise person once said 'the only thing worse than bad publicity is no publicity.' If you doubt that, just wait and see what the Dubrowski case does for Quincy's practice. Soon enough he'll be needing you and one or two more secretaries on a full-time basis. But be that as it may, I'm going to Portland tomorrow, maybe I'll have better luck there."

Flammonde looked at his watch. "I see my allotted five minutes is up. Let me pay the bill and then, since it's dark out, Quincy and I will see you home and then it's off to Mrs. Norman's for the both of us."

Chapter Thirteen

Flammonde cracked open a claw and extracted a piece of meat which he dipped partially into the small dish of drawn butter. "How'd your meeting go with the judge? What's his name?"

"Beauchamp; Judge Franklin Beauchamp. It's spelled 'B-e-a-u-c-h-a-m-p' but he pronounces it 'Beechum'. Couldn't wait to correct me on that, so I guess I sort of started out on the wrong foot. Would have been nice of the clerk, or Christmas for that matter, to give me a hint in advance."

"I'd wager that Christmas knew what was coming and enjoyed watching you step on your tongue."

"The judge didn't seem too put out about it. Said I'd probably get it right next time." Adams took another paper napkin from the dispenser and wiped the combination of brine and butter off his fingers. Good lobster, but for a dollar-fifty? They'll be charging that much a pound before too long."

"Well, it's the war Counselor; drives up the price of everything. Labor's in short supply. Even a deck hand on a fishin' boat can make eight, ten dollars a day these days. And wait until the war's over. Before the country can get back to peace-time production of goods and services you'll see the price of just about everything—from baby diapers to coffins, and all in between—going higher than anyone'd think possible. But other than mispronouncing his name, how'd you and the judge get along?"

"Okay, I guess. But he and Christmas seemed awfully thick. And if that's not enough to make me nervous, the judge set the trial date for the third Monday in September. That doesn't give us a lot of time. I started to ask for more, and then Christmas put in his two-cents worth reminding me—and the judge—that a defendant's entitled to a speedy public trial under both the U.S. and Maine Constitutions, and he put the emphasis on the word 'speedy' in saying it. I left there with the feeling that Judge Beauchamp and Deputy Attorney General Christmas may have had a word or two about the case before His Honor called us back in chambers."

"Well, Counselor, except for maybe York County, you've about run out of places in Maine to try your lawsuit. Are you going to try a recusal motion? Judge's liable to take more offense at that than your mispronouncing his name."

"I don't know, Emil, I thought about it. But Christmas'll get up on the stand and say that he and the judge didn't discuss the case at all; they were discussing some bench-bar get together or something like that. Even worse, he'll testify that I threatened a recusal motion on Judge Gribble, and that I'm just using this as a tactic to delay for the sake of delay. You know the old defense lawyer's maxim: 'They can't convict your client until they try him.' The judge'll deny the motion and I'll have gained nothing."

"Is that old maxim something you learned in law school?" Flammonde signaled the waitress for coffee and took out one of his cheroots. "Anything else happen?"

"Judge wants any pre-trial motions — with briefs — and our witness lists in ten days."

"Do you have any motions in mind?"

"Maybe one: A motion *in limine* to keep Christmas from bringing up Dubrowski's Illinois conviction in the event she takes the stand."

"Counselor, are you really thinking about putting Dubrowski — Esther Dubrowski — your client — on the stand? That criminal law professor of yours needs to have his tenure reexamined. All she'll do is confess…"

"And that's exactly what I'm counting on."

"You want to put your client on the stand to confess that she committed the crime with which she stands charged? Dear me, how law school's changed since I sat for the bar examination."

"That's my only hope; that she'll get on the stand and say the same thing she said at the inquest. I may have to ask Judge Beauchamp to let me treat her as a hostile witness. Then I can cross-examine her and expose the inconsistency between her confession and the facts. That together with Sheriff Dowdy's testimony ought to be enough to create reasonable doubt."

"The only reasonable doubt it'll create is regarding your competence to defend a murder case. But okay, suppose for argument's sake you do try to pull this off. How are you going to keep out the prior conviction if Christmas offers it for impeachment?"

"I've got two thoughts: One, it's too remote in time. It is, after all, almost twenty years old. I haven't researched *Wigmore* yet, but I'm hoping he takes my side."

"Well you can be certain that Christmas won't and I'd venture to say neither will Judge Beauchamp. What's your second basis?"

"That one's an even further stretch. I'm thinking about arguing that the Illinois conviction's void because she didn't have competent counsel. In other words a constitutional argument based on the Sixth and Fourteenth Amendments."

"Interestin' idea, Quincy. But I see two problems with it. First, aren't you collaterally attacking a judgment of a sister state? How can one court refuse to respect a final judgment of another court, particularly when it's, as you've admitted, almost twenty years old? Aren't you going to run into a finality-of-judgment, public policy argument? And what about the full faith and credit clause of the Constitution? You can't ignore that.

"But even if you get past those hurdles, how are you going to prove that the defendant was denied counsel? She said she had a lawyer. You're going to have to show that her lawyer was incompetent. How are you going to show that the outcome of the Illinois case would have been any different if Clarence Darrow had been defending her? To get anywhere with that you're going to have to put her on the stand. What if the if judge doesn't believe her? To do a proper job, you're going to have to re-try the Chicago case in the context of a pre-trial motion.

"I don't see the judge allowing that, and even if he did, I don't think he'd keep the conviction out. Nor do I see any appellate court overturning him. However, I've got another thought you might consider."

"And that is…"

"A motion *in limine* to keep out the confession so that you don't have to put her on the stand, and the jury doesn't get to hear that she's been convicted of murder once before."

"I told Pommus and Christmas that I was going to do just that. They asked me how, but I just played coy. Do I dare assume you've thought of some way for me to keep it out?"

"Actually, no. But anyone who can come up with the change-of-venue motion, and almost convince me that you could keep out the prior conviction, is bound to come up with something. Now, Counselor, I must bid you good day. I'm off to try another jewelry merchant or two here in Portland."

Having more than two hours before the afternoon train back to Tilbury Town, Adams decided to attempt to pry some more information out of Rabbi Klein. He found the synagogue in Newbury Street and was greeted by a janitor who also acted as a sort of door-keeper. The door-keeper was wary of a *goy* calling on the rabbi in the middle of the afternoon without an appointment. But when Adams identified himself as Esther Dubrowski's lawyer, the man could not do enough to make Adams feel comfortable in the unfamiliar house of worship. In a short while the man led Adams to Rabbi Klein's study, a substantial room shrouded in dark velvet curtains with heavy German-style furniture and oriental carpets. With book-filled shelves all around, the room identified itself as a place devoted to the pursuit of learning.

After rising to come around the front of his desk to shake Adams's hand, the rabbi guided Adams to a seating area and bade him to be seated on an overstuffed sofa upholstered in a dark velvet fabric. The rabbi sat in a matching chair placed at a right angle to the sofa. "Please forgive me for meeting you in my shirtsleeves, but this heat is hard on an old man such as me. Would you care for some iced lemonade, Mr. Adams?"

"Yes, thank you, Rabbi Klein that would be most welcome."

Rabbi Klein rose and returned to his desk where he pressed an electric buzzer which was answered in a minute or two by a tiny, elderly woman. "Mr. Adams, this is Mrs. Nachamovich, my assistant. Except for my rabbinical duties, it is she who keeps the *shul* operating as efficiently as it does.

"Jenny, this gentleman is Esther Dubrowski's lawyer, Quincy Adams by name."

Adams rose and waited, as a gentleman should do, for Jenny Nachamovich to offer her hand, or not, as she pleased. When the hand was not proffered, Adams contented himself with a "Pleased to meet you, Mrs. Nachamovich."

"And I you, Lawyer Adams. The *rebbe* says you are a man of great learning in the law and that you will do your best to see that Mrs. Dubrowski receives justice. I wish you *nachas* – good fortune – in this undertaking. *Rebbe* would you and Mr. Adams like some fresh lemonade with ice? I was just making a pitcher to bring in to you when you pressed the buzzer."

"Yes, indeed, Jenny. Thank you."

When Jenny Nachamovich left and Adams resumed his seat, Rabbi Klein asked, "So, Mr. Adams, what brings you to Sharrey Tphiloh all the way from Tilbury Town on such a hot day?"

"I had a court appearance this morning in connection with the case. I take it you're aware that venue for the trial has been transferred from Augusta to Portland?"

"Yes, this I knew from the newspaper, the *Portland Press Herald*. This is a good development, is it not?"

"That, I'm afraid, remains to be seen. But I certainly think so. I'm the one who asked for the change. However, the prosecutor, Horatio Christmas, when he agreed not to oppose the change of venue, did remind me of the adage 'be careful what you ask for, you may get it.' And I don't know whether he said that in jest or as a serious warning.

"I gave several good reasons for wanting the change, any one of which would have been enough to sway an impartial judge. After watching Judge Gribble handle his guilty-plea docket for two hours, I did not like what I saw. But even before that I was concerned about the judge's ability to be fair, considering that it was he who delivered the eulogy at Richard Cory's funeral.

"All things considered, I think I made the right decision. No matter which judge in Portland got the case, it had to be an improvement over Judge Gribble. I was hoping that District Attorney Pommus would stay on the case, but apparently the attorney general's office, Reverend Christmas, had already shoved Pommus aside."

As soon as Mrs. Nachamovich set the lemonade tray on the coffee table and left, Rabbi Klein asked, "What of this Reverend Christmas? Isn't prosecuting criminals a rather unusual occupation for a supposed man of God?"

Adams took a welcome sip of the lemonade and touched the cold glass to his forehead. "Apparently he conceives this as his ministry, his means of doing God's will."

"And he knows God's will how?"

"Apparently God speaks to him." Adams related Christmas's background as Flammonde had told it to him.

"It is a *shande* – a shame – what happened to Reverend Christmas. But I don't see that as justification for appointing one's self as God's earthly instrument for the punishment of sinners. This I think God does for Himself. But enough of the Reverend Christmas, what happens next?"

Adams told Rabbi Klein the details of the conference with Judge Beauchamp. "After I had lunch at a lobster pound on the wharf, since I have some time before my train back to Tilbury Town, I thought I'd take a chance that you'd be in and would be able to spare me a little of your time."

"This, for Mrs. Dubrowski's sake, I am happy to do. How can I be of help?"

"Would you mind answering a few questions?"

"Such as?"

"How long have you known Mrs. Dubrowski?"

Rabbi Klein pulled at his chin a moment. "Let me think. I am here since nineteen oh four. She was not here when I arrived, so it must have been later. Yes, she came in I think nineteen ten. Is that right?"

"I think so. She testified at the coroner's inquest that she'd been with the Richard Cory household about eight years."

"So maybe I met her not long after she arrived."

"When you first met her, was she already employed by Richard Cory?"

"I don't recall; why do you ask this?"

"I suppose, Rabbi Klein, to be honest with you, because I want to know, and don't know how to ask is: Did you know of her background? Her life in Illinois? Her conviction and parole?"

Rabbi Klein took a sip of his lemonade. "See, that wasn't so hard, Quincy Adams. No, Esther told me she came from Poland and had been living in America since she was in her teenage years. She never mentioned her past life, but I knew...I could sense...that her life was not without *tsuris*."

"I'm sorry, Rabbi, without what?"

"Oh, that's right; I forgot. Esther told me that you are literate in Greek and Latin, but not Yiddish. '*Tsuris*'; it means troubles, sorrow."

"I'll try to add to my Yiddish vocabulary. From my client I now know '*mensch*,' from Mrs. Nachamovich, *nachas* and from you I've just learned '*shande*' and '*tsuris*'.

"Who knows, Quincy Adams, perhaps you'll be the first in your distinguished family to become a *bar mitzvah*."

"A *bar*..."

"Never mind, Mr. Adams, that will take too long to explain, and you've got a train to catch. What else can I tell you about your client? Here, take some more lemonade."

"Did she ever talk about her work, about Richard Cory?"

"Only that she was the head of the domestic staff. I didn't get the sense that she either enjoyed her work or was dissatisfied. It was a job. It provided for a decent way of life that evidently suited her."

"Did she ever discuss Richard Cory?"

"No, I don't recall that she did. You need to understand, Mr. Adams, unlike our Catholic brethren, we don't have a penitent-priest confession ritual. We seek absolution collectively through our prayers on *Yom Kippur*, which comes but once a year. So unless a congregant comes to me for help in coping with some crisis or difficulty in his or her life, I don't have much opportunity to get involved in the private lives of the congregation. I try to help but only when I'm asked.

"Of course I know more about the lives of some members — those with whom I have almost daily contact — such as the lay officers and the board of directors. And in dealing with them, I must constantly remind myself that they are volunteering their time and are generous with their checkbooks, so I make allowances.

"I also learn things from the gossip that gets passed around at secular functions, the lay Sisterhood, for example. And I always meet with the bereaved family when there's a death so that I can personalize the funeral service. It doesn't matter what a *mamser* he was in life, I can usually find something good to say. There, Mr. Adams, you've got yet another Yiddish word: '*mamser.*'

"Meaning?"

"Meaning a 'bastard.' It's used just as in English: To describe a bad person."

"A very useful word, Rabbi Klein. But I must go soon and I know that my coming here without an appointment must be diverting you from what you need to be doing. So I have only two more questions: One, did Mrs. Dubrowski have any friends among the congregation; and two, did she ever speak with you about her daughter?"

"No, I did not know she had a daughter until I read the account of the inquest in the Augusta newspaper, the *Kennebec Journal.* As to friends in the congregation, again I can be of no help. She did not belong to the Sisterhood, of this I am sure. She only comes to services, maybe once, sometimes twice a month and on the High Holy days, *Rosh Hashanah,* the New Year according to the Hebrew calendar, and *Yom Kippur*, the Day of Atonement.

"As you may know, in our branch of the Jewish Faith, Orthodox, men and women do not sit together in our sanctuary. You may be familiar with the Society of Friends, the Quakers. They also sit separately, although for a much different reason. In the case of we Jews, the reason…and this may be only apocryphal, not in the literal sense, but meaning 'of obscure origin'…is that the early priests and later rabbinate feared that the ladies would provide too great a distraction from the men's prayers. So we relegate the fair sex to balconies and loges, while the men remain front and center. I personally find the custom of dubious efficacy and unquestionably demeaning to both men and women. Be that as it may, in our *shul* the men sit downstairs and the women upstairs. My eyesight isn't what it once was so I don't see who is with whom in the balcony as well as I did in years past. However, I do recall that Esther would usually sit with the same woman; I don't know who she is. All I recall about her is that she is younger than Esther. I recall this because it seems to me that they didn't sit next to the other women, but always a little apart from the others. I'm sorry I cannot be of more help to you. I will ask Mrs. Nachamovich, and perhaps the president of the Sisterhood, and if I learn anything, I will let you know at once.

"And now, before you leave, I must ask you two questions, Mr. Adams: Do you still believe that Mrs. Dubrowski is innocent—there, I've used that word again—and is she going to allow you to properly defend her?"

"As to the first question, yes, Rabbi Klein, I still believe that she's innocent. As to the second question, I think it is in Mrs. Dubrowski's best interest that I not press her because to do so may only strengthen her resolve to accept an unjust fate."

Chapter Fourteen

Flammonde shed his jacket and hung it on the coat rack next to Adams's. "Where have you been?"

"At the county law library reading about confessions."

"Ah, yes. The law library: Last refuge of the desperate lawyer. Did you learn anything?"

Adams held up a foolscap pad and rippled through several pages of notes. "Your telephone message said you had news on the subject of the brooch."

"Don't be peevish, Counselor. I like law libraries, and I respect the people who use them. It's just that I've been gnawing on the confession problem and vice versa and I can't seem to find any basis upon which to keep the blasted thing out. The only solution, it seems to me, is you've got to all but produce the murderer in open court; either that or you're going to have to convince Esther Dubrowski to repudiate the confession. Any luck on that front?"

"I take it you know that I saw her today. Your busy-body friend, I assume? And no, she still refuses to give me anything with which to mount a defense. I all but accused her of covering up for the killer, and she terminated the interview. She got up went to her bunk, lay down and turned her face to the wall. If we, and a jury, are going to ever know the truth, it'll not be from the lips of our client."

"We may be a half-step in the direction of knowing the truth. May I ask Camille to join us? We may need her help in taking the next half-step."

"As you may have noticed when you came in, the 'phone's stopped ringing every two minutes and she's actually doing some productive work. I'm pleased to admit your prognostication was correct; the Dubrowski case has started to bring in a bit of business. I've gotten two new matters, a will and a divorce. Both clients are women. They each said they thought they could place their trust me since Esther Dubrowski trusts me. I wonder what they'd think if I told them the truth. But yes, ask her to join us if you think she can help. It seems that your charming manner has made quite an impression on Miss Winters."

Camille allowed Flammonde to hold her chair for her, flattered by the gentlemanly gesture which was a welcome contrast to the attention she frequently received from some male customers of the Red Rooster. Flammonde started to take out a cheroot. "Do you mind,

Camille, if I smoke one of these?"

"No, I'm used to it. My father and my two brothers who are still at home are pipe and cigarette smokers. But I'm anxious to hear your news. When you telephoned, you said that you have news of the brooch. Have you found the woman for whom it was intended?"

"Not yet, Camille. That's why I asked for you to join us. I did learn the identity of the jeweler who made the piece. Do you know Cross Jewelers in Congress Street in Portland?"

"Well, I suppose. It depends on what you mean by 'know.' I've been by the store several times and looked in the window. But as far as buying anything there, there's no way I could afford it, and so far, no gentleman of my acquaintance has offered to take me there on a shopping spree."

"Is that who made the brooch?"

"I have it on reliable authority, Quincy. Yes, the workrooms at Cross created the bauble in question."

"They told you? Did they also tell you the name of their customer?"

"Neither; they were identified to me by a competitor. I was on my way to Cross when I passed a small jewelry store also in Congress Street, M. Hirschorn & Son. More or less on a whim, I stopped in and asked for 'M. Hirschorn.' The clerk went to the rear of the store and in a moment another man came out and asked if he could be of assistance. I asked him if he was 'M. Hirschorn.' He said no. Although his name is Martin Hirschorn, his late father, Mordecai Hirschorn was the 'M' of M. Hirschorn & Son. I told him that I'd seen a piece of jewelry, a brooch that I admired very much, and was thinking of purchasing one similar to it for my fiancé.

"He asked me to describe it, so I showed him the sketch that I'd made. As soon as I did, he told me that if it was made anywhere in Maine, it would have been by Cross. He added that his wholesale diamond merchant had offered him the center stone, marquis-cut, about two and three-quarters to three carats, as a loose unmounted stone. Hirschorn was not interested in buying the stone, even though it was well-priced, because he couldn't see any immediate need for a stone that size. He told the wholesale merchant that when the war was over, then maybe he'd be in the market for a stone of that size and quality."

"Quality?"

"Yes, it seems that diamonds are priced not only by size, but also cut, color and the absence of flaws. Mr. Hirschorn told me that if it's the same stone, he would have graded it very high for color. He added that the stone has no flaws visible to the unaided eye and that the marquis cut is expensive because much of the stone is lost in the cutting."

"So on the strength of that you concluded that Cross made and sold the brooch. But you still don't know the buyer?"

"Patience, Counselor. I'm coming to the most interesting part. It seems that I'm not the first person to inquire of Martin Hirschorn regarding the brooch. To his recollection a woman, a young woman, came to him in late July and asked him to look at the brooch and…"

"She actually had it with her?"

"Yes she did, Camille. She wanted to know whether it was valuable. Mr. Hirschorn surmises that a suitor had given it to her and she was trying to determine whether the jewels were genuine. He told her that the stones were in fact the real McCoy and he placed the retail value at ten thousand dollars, at the very least. When he said that, instead of a huge smile, or perhaps tears of joy, the young lady grew very pale and began breathing in shallow, rapid manner so he had a clerk bring her a chair and a glass of water. She recovered in a few minutes, thanked him and left.

"Mr. Hirschorn remarked to me that he's been in the jewelry business all his life and he's never seen a woman react with such antipathy upon being told that she was the recipient of such a unique and valuable piece of jewelry."

"How'd he know that she was the intended recipient of the gift? Perhaps her husband bought it for a mistress and she found out?"

"A cynical but never-the-less valid question, Quincy. But Mr. Hirschorn discounts that as a likely circumstance because the young woman was not wearing a wedding band or even an engagement ring."

"I still wouldn't rule it out. But in any case, we don't know whether Richard Cory was the purchaser from Cross. Nor do we know the identity of the woman or whether the brooch, the woman or both are involved in Cory's death."

"Hear me out before you dismiss my endeavors as unproductive."

"Sorry, Emil. It's just the case. It's gnawing at me as much as you. We just can't seem to find the right tool whether it's the law, the facts or something else to break this thing open."

"Maybe things aren't as glum as you think. I asked Mr. Hirschorn to describe the young woman. He was dubious at first, but I persuaded him that I wanted to be sure that she was not one of my fiancé's close friends. It would never do to have them both show up at the same ball or restaurant wearing nearly identical pieces of jewelry. That, I said in my most earnest manner, would be even worse than having them both appear at the same occasion in the same gown.

"With this assurance that my motive for inquiring was entirely benign, he described her as being fairly tall, at least five, six with dark, copper-colored red hair and dark brown eyes. He added...how shall I say it with a lady present...ah, yes, that she is pleasantly proportioned from stem to stern."

Disregarding Camille's sharp look, Flammonde continued. "He placed her age as in her twenties. She was not wearing gloves. That's why he was able to notice that she was not wearing a wedding band. He added that she was not wearing any other jewelry. Nor did she wear much, if any, make-up. He described her as being dressed fashionably and noted that her garment was well cared-for except that her cuffs were shiny and beginning to fray just the tiniest bit.

"From that he gathered that she was not a lady of leisure, but almost certainly worked to earn her living. Because his business demands such sensibilities on his part, I would venture that Mr. Hirschorn has a good eye for ladies' fashions and appearance so we may take his description and conclusion as being accurate."

Camille brushed a stray wisp of hair back over her ear. "What you say is true, Emil, but where does that leave us? That description would more or less fit perhaps a hundred women in Portland. And if his guess as to her age is off by a few years, perhaps hundreds more."

"Then too," Adams added, "she might not be from Portland. With what little time we have left, we can't stroll about the streets of Portland giving the eye to every likely-looking woman whom we encounter. And if we did, we'd probably be arrested as a couple of mashers within the first hour."

"I think we may entrust the task to Camille."

"You want *her*..."

"You want *me*..."

"Wait, wait," Flammonde held up his hands palms out, "not both of you at once. I believe that we'll be able to narrow our search considerably. As it was late in the day, I waited, window shopping up and down Congress Street, until closing time. I approached the clerk who'd greeted me when I first came in the store. I offered to buy him a beer or two, it being such a hot afternoon and all. Seeing that Mr. Hirschorn and I had gotten along amiably, he was willing to accept my offer of hospitality.

"Once we'd downed a pint of summer ale and ordered a second, I told him the same tale that I'd spun for his employer. I told him that I needed to be absolutely sure that the young lady and my fiancé did not travel in the same social circles because of the potentially disastrous consequences that would ensue. I literally begged him for the sake of my future happiness and that of my fiancé, to tell me if he knew anything more about the young lady who had visited his employer's store.

"I rightly surmised that M. Hirschorn was unlikely to have more than one salesman other than himself, what with the man-power shortage brought on by the war. I was correct; indeed it was my drinking companion who'd brought our mystery woman the chair and glass of water. He confirmed Martin Hirschorn's description and added one invaluable detail: He'd seen the lady in question at the synagogue on several occasions. In fact he'd asked his aunt and cousin if they knew her, hoping that would lead to an introduction. The aunt and cousin recalled having seen her, but for all their interest in finding a suitable match for their unmarried male relative, they were unable to help."

"So it's your intention to post a colleague or two to lurk outside the synagogue to see if she shows up and if so follow her home?"

"I'm ashamed to admit, Quincy, that the very same thought crossed my mind. However, I discarded it as impractical and too risky. I cannot imagine that my 'lurkers' as you so aptly describe them would go unnoticed. Two strange men, or even one, hanging about the synagogue before and after worship services would justifiably raise quite a few hackles and would likely lead to an unproductive confrontation at the very least.

"Well, Emil, how do I fit in?"

"You, my dear colleague, will be our lurker. Only you'll not be hiding behind a tree or lamp post, you'll be inside the house of worship."

"Except for the Steins…the furniture store down the street…and I know them only to say 'hello'…I don't think I even know anyone who's Jewish. I wouldn't have the faintest idea how to behave."

"Don't worry, Camille. By sundown on Friday you'll be a veritable Queen Esther." Flammonde reached over and patted her forearm.

"Quincy, it's Wednesday. We have only tomorrow and part of Friday to prepare Camille for her incursion. Do you think you can spare her tomorrow if I pay her wages? Camille, what about Aunt Dorothy?

Do you think she will be too inconvenienced if you take a day off?"

"Aunt Dorothy won't be a problem," Quincy offered. "I can help out in the kitchen in the morning and during the lunch-time rush. That'll leave Aunt Dorothy free to work the front."

"There. Then it's settled. Camille, I've bought you a few things that will help alter your appearance." Flammonde reached down beside his chair and picked up a battered briefcase. "First, a wig." Flammonde reached into the briefcase and removed a brown woman's wig. "I borrowed...or I should say 'rented'...it from the property room custodian in the Bowdoin College Drama Department. I need to return it on Saturday."

"Another one of your trivial cash incentives?"

"You could say that, Quincy, if you insist on examining the transaction that closely.

"However the next item is an outright purchase. This morning I returned to M. Hirschorn and Son and called upon my erstwhile drinking companion of last evening. I told him that it was not unlikely that my fiancé and the woman he described would know one another since they attended the same place of worship even though my fiancé does not live in Portland. He congratulated me and assisted me in picking out this piece."

Flammonde removed a velvet box from the briefcase and handed it to Camille. "Go ahead, open it. There's nothing inside that's liable to bite you."

Camille cautiously opened the box and extracted a gold chain which supported a lavaliere of gold set with small diamonds. "What is it?" She held the chain up to her throat so that the pendant lay on the ruffles of her white blouse just above her breasts.

"It's the Hebrew word '*chai*'. It means 'life.'"

"Is it some sort of amulet, to ward off evil?"

"No, Quincy. Your education in the classics too much affects your thinking. An amulet suggests some sort of pagan belief, something that the Hebrews abandoned over five thousand years ago. Actually it is a simply an expression of that which Jews value so highly."

"Meaning that they value life, Emil?"

"Just so, Camille."

"Isn't it a rather expensive trinket for what we all hope will be but one evening's wearing?"

"It's yours to keep, Camille. Consider it a bonus for extraordinary service. I shall so report it to my employer."

"Emil, you seem to know quite a lot about the symbol and the Jewish reverence for life. So let me ask you this: Esther Dubrowski is Jewish. Why is she so determined to throw away her life?"

"That's an easy question, Quincy. She doesn't think she's throwing it away. By protecting whomever it is that she's protecting, she undoubtedly feels that she's getting full value for her sacrifice. The hard question is who is that person? And through Camille's efforts, perhaps we'll find that out. Camille, are you game?"

"I don't know, Emil. In the first place, I've never done anything sneaky in my life, unless you count occasionally pilfering one of my brothers' cigarettes. But more than anything, I don't think I can accept a gift of a piece of expensive jewelry, which this obviously is." Camille held the piece by the chain, admiring it.

"I understand your concern, Camille, but it's not a gift. At least it's not a gift in the sense that the brooch was undoubtedly intended. I can't very well return it; that would be unfair to Mr. Hirschorn and his employee who sold it in good faith. Indeed Mr. Hirschorn might not take it back, or if he did, it would be only for store credit in which case I'd have to buy you something else which would be equally expensive and equally unacceptable to you. Moreover, if I try to take it back he may begin to doubt my story and bring unwanted attention to my activities. And that I assure you would incur far greater consternation back at the home office than the size of the line item on my expense report."

"So you really give me no choice, do you?" Camille's eyes began to well up as she reached in her handbag for a handkerchief.

"Now just a minute, Emil…Mr. Flammonde. I let you seduce me with a four-figure retainer. Against my better judgment, I've not pressed you to identify your employer or to disclose your true motive for wanting to find out who murdered Richard Cory. I've swallowed hard, but swallowed none-the-less, your underhanded ways of obtaining information as well as your keeping tabs on my comings and goings. But at this I draw the line. Will you stick at nothing to gain your ends, whatever they may be?

"I'm sorry, Mr. Flammonde, I cannot allow Miss Winters to participate in this masquerade against her will. It's, it's…"

"Quincy, wait. It's my decision, not yours. I think that Mr. Flammonde is right about the jewelry. Since Richard Cory had it in his possession when he was murdered, he is more likely than not the original purchaser from Cross. As you may now realize, if you didn't know it before, not every woman is willing to barter her…her…virtue for a trinket, no matter how expensive. The woman for whom he bought it apparently rejected it because she was suspicious of Cory's motives in giving her such an expensive gift. That's why it was in his possession when he was fatally shot. If he did not commit suicide, and we all agree he did not, then someone murdered him.

"It could be that his possessing the brooch when he was shot is only a coincidence. On the other hand, perhaps the woman who spurned his gift had another suitor. And suppose that suitor found out that Richard Cory'd been trying to poach his girl. He is consumed with jealousy and hatred. However, this suitor lacked the nerve of Harry Thaw, so instead of shooting his rival in a public place before a hundred witnesses, he follows Cory home and confronts him. They argue and…no, they wouldn't have argued."

"You're right, Camille, they wouldn't have argued. If they'd argued, then Cory would have been shot in the chest or between his eyes." In spite of his anger at Flammonde, Adams couldn't help but get caught up in Camille's hypothesis.

"What's more likely," Flammonde took up the thought, "is that the assailant followed Cory to Oakdale Hall and found him passed out on the sofa. The murder was a so-called 'crime of opportunity'. Instead of confronting Cory, he decided to do away with him."

"That means," Adams now finished Flammonde's thought, "that he must have been to Oakdale Hall before in order to know where Cory kept his revolver and known that he could get to it without fear of waking Mr. Silas."

Camille fastened the gold chain around her neck. "This means that if we're to find the murderer of Richard Cory, we must find the woman who would drive a man to such desperate measures."

"And once we find her, maybe we'll be able to figure out for whom Esther Dubrowski is covering. And that will certainly explain the why."

"You're right of course, Quincy. And if you can come up with a better plan than mine, taking into account the small amount of time remaining to us, I'd be more than happy to adopt it as I'm sure Camille would be as well."

"Emil, Camille has a point. My objection to your plan is not entirely that Camille'd be in any sort of physical danger attending the religious services. I expect she'd be perfectly safe inside the synagogue. The worst that can happen if she's exposed is they'll ask her to leave. My concerns are: First, that Camille will be engaging in a subterfuge which is wholly against her nature, even though it's in furtherance of a worthwhile cause.

"Second, although there's no risk to her safety in the synagogue, what about when she leaves? If against all odds the woman actually appears at the prayer service and Camille recognize her, what happens next? Confront her? Follow her home? If you post one or two of your operatives where Camille can give them some sort of signal, then we're back to my initial thought which you so tactfully derided a few minutes ago."

"Counselor, your skill at dialectics leaves me in awe. But lest we debate our scheme…"

"You mean *your* scheme, don't you?"

"Of course. *My* scheme, if you prefer. In either case, I have one more item in my bag of tricks." Flammonde reached again into his briefcase and extracted a leather box which he handed to Camille. "Go ahead, Camille, this gift is one that you can return when it's no longer needed. Only take care when you have it on your person."

"A pistol." Adams leaned over so he could see the contents of the box as Camille opened it.

"Actually, Quincy, it's a derringer. Forty-one caliber, two-barrel single-action Remington."

"That it is, Camille. You certainly know your firearms."

"Having grown up in a household with a father and four brothers who hunt every week-end during the season and talk about hunting and little else during the off-season, yes Emil, you could say I know a little about guns. In fact my father has a small collection which includes a Philadelphia Deringer; you know, like the one used to assassinate President Lincoln.

"Although I come from a gun-toting family, I'm no Annie Oakley. I dislike guns intensely. I know how to handle one but avoid doing so as much as possible." Camille removed the weapon from the box grasping the grip between her thumb and forefinger. "Is it loaded?"

"No, I checked it when I put it in the box."

Camille examined the chambers to confirm what Flammonde had said. "Do you really think this necessary?"

"Again, Quincy's thoughts are my own. You're certainly in no danger inside the synagogue, but what about on the street? If you succeed in identifying this woman, you can't just follow her home. What if she's in an automobile or carriage? What if she's in the company of someone, say Richard Cory's rival? What if she decides to have a late supper or merely detoured for an ice cream cone?"

"I've been thinking about that since you first brought up my role in this business. Obviously, if by some lucky chance she is there and I identify her, somehow I've got to meet her and at least learn her name. And if I'm going to make her acquaintance, why do I need this?" Camille closed the box and handed it back to Emil.

"Camille, I really wish you'd take it. If I were going to do what you're going to do, I would want some protection against the dangers you've just postulated. We don't know who killed Richard Cory or why. Until we know who this woman is and how she fits in, if the derringer adds even the thinnest layer of protection, I want you to have it with you. I could not live with myself if anything were to happen to you. By bringing you into this, even though it was Emil's suggestion, I feel that I'm the one putting you in harm's way. "

"Quincy Adams, that's the nicest thing you've ever said to me, and I think you mean it. But it's my decision, and I intend to see this through. Emil, give me back the damn gun. I assume you intend to provide me with at least a couple of bullets?"

Chapter Fifteen

Adams's Model T clattered up Winthrop Hill on the northwest side of Hallowell. His business card had at least persuaded the gate-guard to telephone someone in the administration office who in turn had authorized the guard stationed in a kiosk at the entrance to the grounds just at the crest of the hill to allow Adams into the grounds. Following the guard's instructions Adams drove past the temporary wooden picket fence that surrounded the construction site of the prosaically-named "Central Building," noting that someone must have taken the turn too fast and ran off the gravel track knocking down a number of the pickets. Just past the construction site he came to the building identified as the Administration Building for the Industrial School for Wayward Girls, Maine's reformatory for female juvenile delinquents. As he parked his vehicle he saw several inmates picking berries off the cultivated blueberry bushes that seemed to be the principal landscaping of the facility.

Once inside the building he saw several more girls on their hands and knees scrubbing the worn wooden floor of the reception area. The youngest of these appeared to be no more than eight or nine years old. Adams approached the counter which divided the reception area from a clerical area and the corridor leading to what Adams presumed were the offices of the officials who ran the place and in the world of adult penology would be called "wardens." A plump girl with a heart-breaking case of facial acne, one of two inmates seated at typewriter-desks behind the counter, finally noticed Adams after he'd cleared his throat a second time. "Yup?" she said indifferently.

"I'm Quincy Adams; I'm here to see Dr. Smedley."

"You the lawyer the guard called about from the outside gate?"

"Yes, I am." Adams held out his business card which the girl took by the edges as though holding a day-old mackerel.

"Sit over there." She pointed to an armless wooden chair situated under a large wall-mounted wood-frame Regulator clock.

Adams did as instructed. The floor-scrubbing detail had finished their task and moved on to the corridor and offices beyond. The absence of the swishing brushes left the only sounds in the room the staccato tap-tap coming from the machine of the two-finger typist remaining behind the counter, and the metronomic ticking of the Regulator clock. Holding his briefcase in his lap, Adams embraced the sound of the clock and in a minute or two had drifted off to sleep. In his dream he was again the rebellious ten-year-old sent to the principal's office where he sat awaiting whatever grim punishment was to be meted out to him for yet another infraction of the rules of classroom decorum.

"Mister, Mister Adams, Mister…"

Adams shook himself awake to the sound of his name being repeated by the clerk-inmate who'd taken his business card. "Yes, yes I'm Quincy Adams," he responded having not quite come fully out of his dream. Glancing at his watch he noted that he'd been waiting over thirty minutes.

"Come with me and I'll take you back to Miss Boyles's office."

Adams went through the swinging half-door in the counter and followed the girl down the hall. They stopped in front of a door marked "Miss Boyles." She knocked lightly and stood back. After a couple of minutes her knock was answered with an "Enter."

Adams did as bidden. The office was a large one, at least half again the size of his own. The large woman behind the institutional-looking oak desk was smoking a cigar whose aroma—or perhaps 'stench' would be a better word—pervaded the air despite the open window and the lazily-turning ceiling fan. "Sit," The woman nodded toward a chair the twin of the one Adams had just vacated. As Adams seated himself in front of the desk the woman put her cigar in an ashtray. "I'm Reba Boyles, executive assistant to Dr. Smedley. What do you want here?"

"Actually, I came hoping to have a few minutes of Dr. Smedley's time to ask him a few questions."

"What about?"

"Richard Cory, Ma'am. I understand Dr. Smedley filed Mr. Cory's will for probate…"

"What concern is that of yours, Mr. Adams?"

"I intend no disrespect to you, but I really prefer to take up my business directly with Dr. Smedley, Miss Boyles."

Reba Boyles leaned forward, her enormous breasts piling up on the top of her desk. She gave Adams the glare that must have frightened the starch out of hundreds if not thousands of girls over the years no matter how hardened they were by the system. She almost succeeded with Adams. "Well you are impertinent, Mr. Adams, most impertinent. Dr. Smedley is an extremely busy man and doesn't have time to waste with the likes of…of…lawyers." She folded her ham-like arms across her chest as though daring Adams to contradict her.

"Then he'll probably thank you for allowing me to speak with him here instead of his having to waste perhaps hours if not days of his time waiting to testify in response to a subpoena that I'll serve on him if necessary."

"Don't you come in here threatening me or Dr. Smedley, young man. We run a state agency here. The attorney general will defend Dr. Smedley against having to appear in court in response to a subpoena. Don't you think others have tried that tactic and failed?"

Adams played his last card: "I'll tell you what Miss Boyles," Adams reached into his briefcase and took out one of the few things in it. He handed Boyles Horatio Christmas's card. "Call Horatio Christmas, he's the head of the attorney general's criminal justice division, and ask him whether Dr. Smedley ought to spare some time out of his busy schedule to speak with me. If he says 'no' then I'll be on my way. If he says 'yes' then you need to go find Dr. Smedley and tell him Quincy Adams is here to speak with him."

Boyles left the card on her desk where Adams had put it. As Adams sat with his fingers crossed below her line of sight hoping that she wouldn't call his bluff, Boyles ran her large mannish hands through the sparse hair atop her head. Finally she pressed a buzzer and in a few moments there was a knock at the door. "Enter," she barked.

Acne-girl took a couple of tentative steps into the office. "Edna, you stay here and keep an eye on Lawyer Adams until I get back. Don't talk to him, just keep an eye on him; see that he doesn't touch anything or go snooping around on the top of my desk. He does anything like that, you press the security buzzer and someone'll be here in a minute to take care of Mr. Adams. You understand me, girl?"

"Yes, Miss Boyles, I understand real good."

"There's one thing you can tell him, girl, and that's if you press that security alarm and I get here before security does, he'll wish that security had gotten here first."

"There's no need, Miss Boyles. Your warning, although wholly gratuitous, is adequate. I take you at your word. I promise not to move a muscle until I'm given leave." This last undertaking was given as Adams stared straight out the window so that Miss Boyles would not see the grin on his face.

After maybe twenty more minutes, a tiny girl with stick-like arms and legs appeared in the open doorway. When Adams turned around to look at her she smiled at him and lisped through her missing two front teeth, "Edna, Miss Boyles said to bring the gen…gentleman to

Dr. Smedley's office and be quick about it. And she said be sure to close her office door behind you." Her commission having been completed the girl ran off giggling down the hall.

Dr. Smedley's office was but two doors further down the hallway. Again Edna knocked and awaited permission to enter. When permission finally came, Edna carefully opened the door and stood aside for Adams to enter, and when he did she closed the door just as cautiously and trundled off back to her regular duties.

Chivas McDade Smedley might have been Reba Boyles's sibling. They were the same height and were about equally bald, the only difference being that Smedley's thin hair was streaked with silver whereas Reba Boyles's was colored with what might have been lamp-black and Smedley had huge bushy eyebrows, whereas Boyles had only dark pencil lines. Adams judged their weight to be about the same, each enough for two normal-size persons. They each wore black, Boyles wool crepe, and Smedley worsted wool over a wing-collar shirt, black tie and white waistcoat. Smedley wore pearl-gray spats over his shoes and Boyles wore heavy black shoes that would have looked stylish on a tackle for the Harvard varsity eleven.

Smedley came forward his right hand extended. "Mr. Adams. So pleased to make your acquaintance. Obviously you've already met Miss Boyles," He nodded in her direction while she glowered at Adams. "Please have a seat," he gestured toward a large arm chair at the front of his desk which Adams surmised normally held Reba Boyles's bulk when she and Smedley had their meetings.

"I'd rather take this other chair, if you don't mind, Dr. Smedley. I've a bit of a back problem which seems to be aggravated by overly-comfortable chairs." As he said this Adams took a straight-back wooden chair such as he'd been seated in twice before from the side of Smedley's desk and moved it around to the front. Adams decided that for the time being he would refrain from rubbing Miss Boyles's nose in her being overruled by her boss.

"Miss Boyles says that you wish to question me about Richard Cory."

"Question you seems rather adversarial and formal, Dr. Smedley. I usually save that for the courtroom. All I want to do is ask you a few questions."

"Then by all means let's have it your way. I assume that since this is informal you have no objection to Miss Boyles remaining?"

"No, certainly not. Miss Boyles is most welcome to stay. I know you're both very busy, so I'll be as brief as I can."

"Thank you, Mister Adams. I assure you we appreciate that. Now, what do you want to know?"

"First, about your relationship with Richard Cory. Since you filed the will for probate, I make the assumption that you are named as executor, or perhaps the two of you are executor and executrix. If my assumption is correct, then you and Mr. Cory must have been very close, or at least he placed a great deal of trust in you to name you as his surrogate. If Oakdale Hall is any indication, Mr. Cory must have left a sizable estate the administration of which would be a daunting responsibility for anyone, especially someone such as yourselves who are so consumed with your responsibilities here.

"I'm not here to pry into the Richard Cory estate's business. I mention these assumptions only as background to ask you how you came to know Mr. Cory and what is…was…the nature of your relationship?

"Reba…Miss Boyles and I came to Winthrop Hill in nineteen oh eight, just a few years after these facilities were completed. As you saw when you arrived, we're in the process of completing a new facility which unfortunately is badly needed as we've very much outgrown our present ones."

"And you met Richard Cory then? How did you meet?"

"It wasn't immediately, was it Reba?"

"No, it was several months later. It was about the time Mr. Cory purchased Oakdale Hall and took up residence there. He'd been living abroad, as I recall."

"Yes, Reba is correct. I recall that our first meeting was when the legislature was in session. I was testifying before a criminal justice subcommittee trying to get our appropriation for the ensuing fiscal year increased. I don't recall what business brought Mr. Cory to the statehouse that day, but in any event after I was excused by the committee, he approached me and introduced himself. He said he was impressed by my testimony and wondered what he could do as a private citizen to help us fulfill our mission.

"From that time forward we were in very frequent contact, at least weekly if not more often. He was very generous in donating funds to help us with purchases of needed supplies and equipment that were not in our budget. This was perhaps somewhat irregular, but the state comptroller and the legislative oversight committee did not find it difficult to look the other way."

"What will happen now that he's deceased?"

"The answer to that question, Mr. Adams, will have to await the probate and reading of the will. My attorneys, Berman & Berman in Portland...I'm sure you're familiar with the firm...tell me that the hearing will be held as soon as the statutory notice period has expired. I understand that will occur very soon."

"I understand. Then let me ask this: Do you know outside the will what business interests Mr. Cory had?"

"Why should you have a need to know that?"

"Because, Miss Boyles, as I'm sure you're aware, I am defending Esther Dubrowski against the charge that she murdered Richard Cory. In order to properly defend her, I'm trying to learn as much about his life as I can."

"So you can point your finger at someone else in order to try to create reasonable doubt in the minds of the jurors?"

"You seem to be well versed in criminal defense strategy, Dr. Smedley. Are you by chance trained in the law as well as being a physician?"

"Only the laws pertaining to juvenile delinquency, Mr. Adams. But you would be insulting our intelligence—Reba's and my own—if you were to claim some other purpose. And for that reason, even if I...we...were to have any knowledge of Richard Cory's business interests, we should not be inclined to share it with you."

"And the same would be true as to knowledge of his social friends?"

"Indeed it would, Mr. Adams. Your client has confessed to murdering Richard Cory. We'll not be parties to your threadbare effort to blame the crime on someone else. Richard Cory was beloved by all who knew him, excepting of course your client."

"If you won't name any of his friends or business interests, do you know anyone, anyone at all who might have a reason to bring about the death of Mister Cory? Perhaps a romantic rival?"

"No, Mr. Adams; as I said, everyone admired and loved Richard Cory. I daresay that even your client felt affection for him and that's why she waited until he was asleep so that he would not experience any pain or terror when she murdered him. Now, Mr. Adams, Miss Boyles and I have an institution to run so you'll have to excuse us. I will summon Edna to see you out." Smedley pushed the call buzzer on his desk. "I'm glad to have met you, even if it's under these unhappy circumstances."

Upon returning to his office Adams found an unstamped

envelope bearing the return address of the attorney general's criminal division stuck half-way through the mail slot in the front door. He opened the envelope which contained a letter from Horatio Christmas advising that he'd tried to call Adams all morning to inform him there was going to be an inspection at the Oakdale Hall premises at two o'clock that afternoon and that he was invited to attend. Adams called Christmas's office and informed the secretary that he appreciated the invitation and would be at Oakdale Hall at the appointed time. After gulping down a clam roll from the Red Rooster kitchen, he drove out to Oakdale Hall where he found Christmas, Enoch Matthews, Deputy Sheriff Isaacson and one other deputy who was introduced as 'Deputy Humphrey' waiting on the front porch.

"Quincy, I'm glad you were able to make it. We're going to do a little experiment. Depending how it turns out, it may favor either the prosecution or the defense. Whichever, I think it'd be something we both ought to know. And speaking of the defense how goes the preparation of your case? Are you still thinking of keeping out the confession, or does Mrs. Dubrowski plan to retract it."

"I do appreciate your collegiality in inviting me to witness the experiment—whatever it is—but I'm not yet in a position where I can disclose my trial strategy with respect to my client's so-called 'confession.'"

"Meaning, let me guess, that you do not yet have one?" Christmas held out his hand as Adams came up on the front porch. As Adams took his hand, he added, "Sorry that was most ungracious of me. You've a difficult enough job without my needling you."

"Oh I don't mind, Horatio. You're only putting into words what's been very much on my mind. If I do come up with something, you'll be among the first to know. But, let me ask you this: Who do you expect to call as a witness to prove up the so-called 'confession?'"

"Well, that may change before I submit my witness list, but as of now, probably Bascom Pommus. I actually used the fact that District Attorney Pommus might be called as a material witness as the reason for him not to try the case." He placed a hand on Matthews's shoulder, "Enoch, since he will not be a witness, will be sitting second-chair for the prosecution.

"Now come inside and let's do our little experiment. Deputy Isaacson are you and Deputy Humphrey ready?"

"Yes, Sir, Reverend Christmas, we've got everything ready to go."

Once inside, Adams took the opportunity to inspect the entrance hall and the music room where Cory's body was found. "Horatio, do you mind if I ask Deputy Isaacson a question?"

"No, please do. Ask whatever you wish."

"Thank you. Deputy Isaacson, you were here with Sheriff Dowdy when he first arrived?"

"Yes, Sir."

Is the room exactly as you found it?"

"I can't see anything that's different, except of course Mr. Cory's body has been removed." He paused, "Oh, and the brandy decanter's been removed along with the glass. Our office took those and turned them over to the district attorney's office after the first day of the coroner's inquest. I brought the other property we'd taken from the house as soon as Sheriff Dowdy called and told me to. Those articles I brought directly to the courtroom as you may have heard. But I turned the brandy decanter and glass over later that day."

"Thank you, Deputy Isaacson. Horatio, I assume that everything District Attorney Pommus received from the sheriff's office has been turned over to you?"

"Yes, as far as I know. All we received in addition to the decanter and glass and the gun were the letter from the Illinois prison secretary and the veterinary bill file in which it was found." Matthews paused for a moment. "Oh, also the box with the brooch, some sort of ledger and the deceased's clothing."

"What about the envelope?" Isaacson asked. "There was an envelope which contained some other papers. I don't know what, but there was manila envelope with some papers in it. I think it was in a drawer of the coffee table." He pointed to the table between the chair and the settee. "I remember Sheriff Dowdy looking inside it and then closing it back up."

Christmas's face darkened. "What about this envelope, Enoch? Did you turn over to me everything your office had?"

"Yes, Sir. As far as I know, Mr. Pommus gave me everything we got from the sheriff's office, and I turned it over to you."

"Deputy Isaacson, did you make an inventory of what you turned over?"

"Yes, Sir, Mr. Christmas, but it was not until the following day. But I'm sure that I listed a manila envelope as 'one sealed manila envelope, contents unknown.'"

"Enoch, did you make an inventory of what your office

received?"

"No, Sir, not that I know of. After your meeting with Mr. Pommus, he told me that everything that had been turned over to us was in the top drawer of the file cabinet in his office. He told me to take it to your office and that's exactly what I did. I remember the box with the gun, the decanter and glass and the file folder, the velvet box with the brooch inside, the ledger, the letter and of course his clothing, but that's all that was in the file drawer. I may have put the reference letter in the bill file, but I don't remember handling an envelope, manila or any other kind."

"I will see what our received inventory shows. If this envelope has gone missing, it must be found. I shall also want to speak with Sheriff Dowdy about its contents.

"Enoch, does Mr. Pommus lock the file cabinet when he's out of his office?"

"I don't know, Reverend Christmas; I've never been in his office when he wasn't there."

"Ever?"

"Maybe a few times, but not since the Richard Cory case started."

"How about a lock on his office door?"

"There is one, Sir, but I believe it's broken and has been for some time."

"So anyone could have gone to Mr. Pommus's office, removed the envelope and we'd have been none the wiser had Deputy Isaacson not spoken up."

"Well, Reverend Christmas, I know that Mr. Pommus has tried to get the building superintendent to fix the lock, but he says there's no money in the budget to pay for a locksmith to repair the lock or to install a new lock. However there's a working lock on the entrance to our suite of offices, and I know it works. I've been the first to arrive some mornings, and I'm often the last to leave at night so I've used my key many times. And, Sir, if I may add a thought of my own, I would trust every employee in the District Attorney's office without reservation. To my mind there's not even the slightest possibility that anyone in our office would purloin evidence in an active case, even if the defendant was a close relative."

"Well, Quincy, it looks like we've got a bit of a problem. I promise you that I will cause a most thorough investigation — by my office — and we'll get to the bottom of this."

"Thank you, Horatio. Since Deputy Isaacson spoke up, I've been hoping that you'd take that position. I gather you're as curious as I am to learn the contents of this envelope."

"That's true, Quincy, but let us solve one puzzle at a time. The reason I'm here is to test the truth of something your client said in her testimony."

"Namely?"

"Whether she could have heard the sound of a gun being fired in this room while she was in her quarters. She said, so I have it, that she heard nothing. She was listening to music on her phonograph."

"What reason would she have to lie about whether she heard a gunshot?"

"That at the moment is a conundrum. Before we spend any more intellectual capital on solving it, let's first find out whether she was telling the truth.

"What I propose is that you and I go up to her quarters along with Deputy Isaacson. He will act as our witness. I think we can both rely on his impartiality, can we not?"

"I would like to say yes without reservation. However, I cannot consent to doing so without consulting with my client. Instead, I propose that if either one of us disagrees, that we repeat whatever it is that you're going to do with witnesses from both sides."

"That's agreeable. I plan to post Enoch at the foot of the stairs. I will call down to him when we're ready up here, and he can signal Deputy Humphrey. Deputy Humphrey will then fire one round from the murder…from the alleged murder…weapon into the sack of pebbles he's brought with him for that purpose. And we shall listen from Mrs. Dubrowski's rooms to see whether the shot can be heard over the sound of the phonograph."

"How will we know what music to play and at what volume to play it?"

"My hope is that the recording will still be on the machine, and that the on/off switch is separate from the volume control. If that's the case, then we should get a reliable result. If not, then we'll have to make allowances for those variables. Agreed?"

"Well, let's see what happens."

Adams followed Christmas up the stairs with Isaacson leading the procession since he'd been in the house and knew where Dubrowski's quarters were located. The quarters proved to be a pleasant room situated on the second floor in the same wing as the music room below. It has a seating area, a bed, chest-of-drawers and an armoire. There's a bathroom through a door on one side of the room. In the seating area are a small sofa and a shaker-style rocking chair along with a cabinet-model phonograph.

"Deputy Isaacson, did you inspect the room the day you were here with Sheriff Dowdy?"

"I looked in here briefly, Reverend Christmas. I can't say that I inspected it, no Sir. But everything looks as I remember it, except that if I recall rightly, the bed was unmade."

"How about the phonograph and the recording?"

"I can't say for sure, Mr. Adams. They look the same, but I couldn't swear one way or the other."

"I remember that your client said she was listening to 'Pat' somebody playing 'tunes' by someone else...started with a 'c-h' sound. But that's all I remember."

"I'm afraid, Quincy, that I can't be of much help either. My knowledge of music is pretty much limited to hymns and I probably know less about them than a preacher ought to know."

Adams walked over and looked at the phonograph. There was a record on the turn-table. He bent over slightly to read the label. "Paderewski. Playing Chopin Etudes."

"Yes, Sir, I believe that's what she said."

"Quincy, why don't we proceed on that assumption? If it's incorrect, then perhaps your client will correct it, although she's under no duty to do so.

"Deputy Isaacson, do we dare hope that the on/off switch and volume control are separate?"

"Yes, Sir they are."

"Then turn the machine on and go tell Mr. Matthews to wait a minute and then give the signal. That'll give you enough time to get back here and enough time for the music to get going. Then if we don't hear a gunshot, the worst case will be that you and I, and for all I know Mr. Adams as well, will have had our first exposure to Mr. Paderewski and Mr. Chopin."

Adams stood silently for a few moments. "Deputy Isaacson, did my client say whether the door was open or closed?"

"No, not as I recall."

"Then how will we know..."

"Let us try both ways, Quincy. I'd guess, however, that it was open. It was certainly a warm night, and I should think that she would leave the door open to circulate the air coming in through the open window. Also, it occurs to me that she'd want to hear when her employer returned home in case he wanted anything before retiring. There is, after all, the brandy decanter."

"Yes, but there's nothing to suggest that Mr. Cory didn't serve himself."

"That's so, but in the interest of thoroughness, let's try the test both ways. I'll go tell Enoch that we're going to want two shots fired. Deputy Isaacson, go ahead and start the phonograph. I'll tell Enoch to wait one minute before each shot."

To the beginning chords of the first etude Christmas went to the head of the stairs and related his instructions to Matthews. He returned to the room and closed the door and then checked his watch. "Let's first try with the door closed. Deputy Isaacson have a seat in the rocking chair. I assume that's where Mrs. Dubrowski would have been."

Just as a minute passed there was a dull 'thud' from below. "Well, Deputy Isaacson, was that a gunshot?"

"Sure could 'a been, Reverend Christmas. Of course we were all listening for just such a sound and maybe that's why it was so noticeable."

"Did it sound to you like a door slamming?" Adams asked. "If Mr. Cory came home slightly the worse for drink, might he not have shut the door a bit harder than necessary? Do we know who Mr. Cory's dinner companion was? Is it possible that someone brought him home in an automobile and the engine backfired as they left?"

"Good cross-examination, Quincy. But let's wait a moment and listen for the second shot." Christmas opened the door to the hallway.

In a few seconds there was a second, sharper sound from the first floor. "Now I'd be willing to swear to that being a gunshot, Reverend Christmas, Mr. Adams. No mistaking that for a door slamming or a car back-firing."

"Quincy, you can certainly bring up those possibilities, but I'm convinced at this point that Pommus's theory is at least plausible. If someone else had shot Richard Cory, Mrs. Dubrowski surely would have heard something and gone to investigate such a distinctive sound.

"Thank you for your efforts, Deputy Isaacson. I want you to take custody of the phonograph and take care that none of the settings are disturbed. And please turn it off now; I think we've heard enough of Mr. Chopin for the present."

Chapter Sixteen

Camille Winters sat in front of Adams's desk, Flammonde to her right and Adams behind his desk. Her posture and facial expression bespoke the failure of her mission. Flammonde reached across the space between them and patted her shoulder. "It's okay, Camille, it was a long-shot from the outset. As you so rightly said, the description the jewelry store proprietor gave me could have fit more than a hundred women. And the clerk's information, while it narrowed the search down to one place, provided no certainty that she'd be there last night. Perhaps she wasn't feeling well or perhaps she went to see a motion picture or…"

"Perhaps her other suitor…assuming he exists…took her out that evening," Adams finished Flammonde's sentence.

"Yes, and that too, Quincy. But, Camille, why don't you walk us through your evening, from beginning to end? Try to remember as much detail as you can. Perhaps we can learn from our lack of success."

"Maybe so, Emil, but it seems as though we're running out of time to put any lessons to much use. Perhaps we ought to try some other avenues. One that I've been pondering…"

"Hold that thought for a while, Quincy. Let's hear what Camille has to say; we've time to discuss other options when she's done. Camille…"

"I was dressed as you instructed. In order to conceal my own hair, even with this new bobbed haircut I had to pile it on top of my head." She brushed back a few strands of blond hair from the side of her head. "That made the wig look lumpy on top, so I put a scarf over the top of my head and tied it under my chin. It's just as well that I did, because most of the other women wore scarves tied the same way so that at least as far as my costume I fit right in.

"I waited to go in until they were about to shut the door so as not to have to talk to anyone as I was going in. Also, it gave me an opportunity to watch for the brooch-woman. Emil your description of the interior was accurate, so I had no trouble finding the stairway. I took a seat in the very top row since I was looking for a woman with dark red hair and it would be easier to spot her from behind assuming that she wasn't wearing a wig. Also, that way I didn't have to keep turning my head to scan those seated behind me.

"There were all together less than a dozen women almost all of whom had various shades of brown hair, one had very dark, 'raven' hair and more than a couple were gray or going gray."

"Did anyone question you about your being there?"

"Fortunately, Quincy, they were more interested in introducing me to their sons and nephews. One woman, seated next to me—'seated' being a relative term as they were alternately sitting and standing every other minute or so—who I'm sure knew I was an imposter."

"But how? Your disguise was perfect. You said you fit…"

"You omitted one little detail, Emil. When I walked in, a man, I suppose he was some kind of usher or greeter, handed me what I assume was a Bible or hymnal. I'm still not sure which, since it was entirely in Hebrew. He said some greeting also in Hebrew. I just smiled and nodded my head and he seemed to accept that as an appropriate response. I took the book and went up the stairs to the women's balcony. When I was seated and the service began I opened it as the other women were doing; or so I thought. What you failed to tell me, Emil, is that Hebrew is read from right to left, not left to right.

"I opened my book as I would any book written in English. The woman next to me noticed. I think she was looking to see if I was wearing a wedding band. Whatever her purpose, she saw that I was leafing through the book from left to right. She nudged me with her elbow and showed me what page they were on and that the pages read from right to left.

"I smiled and thanked her. I told her that at my congregation back in Cincinnati—that's the first place I could think of, I have no idea why—we always began the service at the back of the book. The way she looked at me, I may as well have said I came from China or the South Pole."

"What happened then?" Adams asked.

"Well, the service went on for a good while. All in Hebrew of course, except for the sermon which consisted of Rabbi Klein shaking his finger at the congregation and telling them that the High Holy Days were coming up and they ought to start thinking about what they needed to do to be inscribed in the book of life for another year. All throughout the service, there was lots of standing up and sitting down sometimes all together, and sometimes when everyone, or nearly everyone sat down, some would still be standing and kind of rocking back and forth. Not only that, but it was hotter than blazes up there in that balcony. And the wig and scarf didn't make it any cooler. I could feel the perspiration running down the nape of my neck and down the back of my dress.

"Anyway, when the service was over the woman next to me introduced herself and then all the other women gathered around as women do and started introducing themselves. The first woman mentioned that I was from Cincinnati and that was all it took. They all seem to have cousins or brothers or sisters in Cincinnati and they asked me if I knew them. I gave my name as 'Camille Weinstein' and that set off another round of 'are you related to the Weinsteins in Cleveland? In Columbus? 'My sister-in-law was a Weinstein from the Omaha Weinsteins'…and on and on."

"How did you escape?" Despite the failure of the enterprise, Flammonde couldn't help smiling as he saw Camille's predicament in his mind's eye.

"I said I had an early train in the morning and needed to be back at my hotel. I said I was on my way to Canada, to the Maritimes. I didn't dare name a city for fear of setting off another round of 'do you knows?' When I mentioned hotel, several of the women offered to have their sons walk me back. 'Of course a proper young lady shouldn't be walking the streets at night' and so forth until I was tempted to show them the derringer and let them know that I was capable of taking care of myself. I almost slipped up and said I'd see if I could call a taxi, then fortunately I remembered what you told me, Emil, that Orthodox Jews don't ride in taxis or even use the telephone from sunset Friday until sunset on Saturday. I'm sure my taking the train on Saturday must have raised some eyebrows."

"Job well done, Camille. I hope it wasn't too trying."

"Not at all, Quincy. As you know, my mother died when I was five, and I was raised in a household full of men. So all in all it was not an unpleasant experience for me to be surrounded by a bunch of women all of whom wanted to be my mother or mother-in-law. Perhaps I ought to give marriage a try."

"Quincy, before Camille gave her report, you mentioned that you were pondering another 'avenue' as you described it."

"Wait, before you two start another debate about strategy, may I be excused?" Last night was the first time in my life that I didn't sleep in my own bed. So I didn't get a lot of sleep."

"Was the room…"

"Oh, no, Emil. The room was fine. It's just that I was so keyed up and at the same time feeling down because I hadn't been successful, that I didn't fall asleep until well after midnight. And then I had to get up early to get the first train back here." As if to emphasize the point

Camille started to yawn. "I'm sorry. Please excuse me. It's not that listening to the two of you isn't exciting, but…"

"No, Camille, go home; take the day off. I'll fill in for you downstairs, if needed. Take Monday off as well if you like. I'll make excuses to Aunt Dorothy."

"That won't be necessary, Quincy. I've already told Aunt Dorothy that you're filling in for me on Monday."

"Can you come in if I need you?"

"No. You two work on strategy; I'm going back to Portland and find the brooch-woman."

After Camille left Flammonde took out a cheroot. "She's a treasure, Quincy. You ought to take her on full-time."

"As a secretary or a wife?"

"Either, both."

"I doubt she'd have me Emil. I'm just a small-town lawyer living from retainer to retainer. What kind of employer—not to mention husband—would I make? If you were Camille, would you marry me?"

"You're definitely not my type, Quincy. But if you have no interest in taking your relationship with Miss Winters to the next level, when this business is over, will you object if I try to poach her away?"

"As a wife, or to join your business opportunity enterprise?"

"Dear me, no. Not a wife. My peripatetic existence has little room for permanent relationships."

"Then why do you do it? Whatever it is that you do. Do you think Camille's cut out for that type of existence? You heard her; last night's the first time she slept in a bed not her own."

"I do what I do because it's a calling, just like the military or the ministry. As for Camille, who knows? Maybe she'd be content living the life of a small-town wife: Marriage; children; church-work; the country club. On the other hand, maybe there's an adventuress inside yearning to spread her wings."

"Possibly, Emil. But truthfully you lost me at the point where you said what you do is a 'calling.' How can going about from place to place, virtually living out of a suitcase, and I dare say bereft of friends and family, for the sole purpose of making money for other people be a 'calling?'"

"What is that you do all day, Quincy? I mean when you're not trying to save Esther Dubrowski from having to spend the rest of her life in prison."

"You know what I do all day. I write wills and contracts and leases; I represent clients in litigation. It's what every sole practitioner does. You are...or have been...a lawyer; what did you do all day?"

"You see, Quincy, practicing law is a calling that's essentially the same as my calling. You spend your time protecting your clients from having their property taken away from them, whether it's through a meritless lawsuit or a contract that is a bad bargain. The next day you may spend your time taking away someone's property and giving it to your client who in your eyes and in the eyes of the law is more deserving of it, whether it's because the other party injured your client through negligence or by breaching a contract with your client. If you substitute the word 'money' for 'property' we do exactly the same thing: We both take other people's money and give it to our client, or we try to stop other people from taking away our client's money.

"We don't grow or manufacture anything; we have no stock of good for sale—Abraham Lincoln's famous dictum notwithstanding—essentially we add no value to the economic wealth of society; we are merely conduits in its redistribution."

"You think that lawyers have no social or economic utility whatsoever?"

"I'm not saying that at all, Quincy. Were it not for lawyers there would be no legal system, or at least none worthy of the name. And what would society do without a legal system to decide disputes between private parties or to stand between the government and the individual?"

"So essentially you think that lawyers are a necessary evil?"

"That's one way to put it. But enough of this philosophical business; let's get back to the business of saving Mrs. Dubrowski."

"I agree. Your reduction of the practice of law to an exercise in redistribution of wealth has given me much to ponder, too much in fact. You make lawyering sound like being in the legislature."

"Why do you think there are so many lawyers serving in the Congress and in the state legislatures? Before they even take their seats, they're already trained experts in redistributing wealth."

"Spoken like a true robber baron. But before you start defending robber barons and the rest of Wall Street, tell me with whom Richard Cory had dinner the night he died, and where did he have it? If we can learn where, and if he was a regular patron, maybe we can find out who he was with."

"I'm afraid that too is a blind alley. My associates have checked every fine dining establishment from Portland to Augusta to Rockland — not that there are so many—but came back empty-handed. The Portland

Regency Hotel said he was a regular patron, even had a favorite table and waiter, but he was not there that Saturday night. A couple of others knew Richard Cory, but none had him as a guest that night."

"So where does that leave us? Up Cobbosseecontee Stream without the proverbial paddle?"

"Ah, Quincy, Quincy. Don't despair. You keep wearing out the law books to find a way to keep our client's confession out. Between the redoubtable Miss Winters and my humble self, we will find the brooch-woman.

"There is, however, one other thing you could do besides that and preparing to create doubt by punching holes in Dr. Goodson's diagnosis of homicide."

"And that is?"

"Add the charming Dr. Smedley and the effervescent Miss Boyles to your witness list."

"Why? So Dr. Smedley can get up on the witness stand and deliver his own eulogy to the deceased in case any of the jurors missed Judge Gribble's in the newspapers?"

"I admit there's a risk of that happening. But I think it worth the risk. Even if the will's not yet admitted to probate, you can certainly ask him whether he and Reba Boyles have anything to gain from Richard Cory's death. The question's relevant, so Judge Beauchamp will have to let it in."

"True; I'm sure the judge will let it in. Indeed, I doubt that Reverend Christmas will even object. If I were at the prosecution's table I'd certainly want the jury to know that Richard Cory left his entire estate to eleemosynary purposes. Whatever doubts the jury may harbor about Richard Cory being destined for sainthood will surely be dispelled. I'm sorry, Emil. I can see no benefit to Esther Dubrowski by putting Richard Cory on trial."

"You don't need to put Richard Cory on trial. If Smedley and Boyles know the contents of the will, that's enough. Wouldn't having absolute control over a sizable estate be a possible motive for murder? It's them that you'd be putting on trial, not Richard Cory."

"I can certainly make the distinction now that you point it out. But is the jury going to be able to grasp the point?"

"That's the sort of conundrum that makes trials interesting, don't you think? It's what separates the real trial lawyers from the pretenders. It can't hurt to put them on the witness list; you don't have to call them if it doesn't feel right."

"But our witness list is due day after tomorrow. That means I'll also have to get out subpoenas for them and have them served. They'll be on the 'phone to Horatio Christmas five minutes after they're served."

"And won't that be an amusing conversation? If nothing else, it'll drive Christmas to distraction trying to figure out why you had them subpoenaed."

"Well he won't be driven to distraction for long. I figure it'll take him about an hour to draft a motion to quash the subpoenas and get Judge Beauchamp's docket clerk on the 'phone to set a hearing on Wednesday at which I'm going to have to tip my...our...hand or risk having the judge quash the subpoenas."

"You're undoubtedly right. But I don't think you'll have to go that far. After all, no one is supposed to know what's in the will. You can plead ignorance. Just tell the judge that you've got a right to know who benefits from Richard Cory's death since that someone may have had a strong motive to do away with Richard Cory. Maybe that someone found out that the deceased intended to change his will and he or she didn't want that to happen. They don't know what we know.

"Christmas'll pound on the counsel table and fuss about fishing expeditions and red herrings. Worst that can happen is the judge will let you question them outside the presence of the jury and then rule on whether to let the jury hear what they've got to say."

"Well, you've almost convinced me, but it's a huge risk. It could blow up in our faces. What if Christmas makes a point of the fact that Mrs. Dubrowski was a beneficiary under the will? That would...could...give her an additional motive for murdering her employer."

"Think that one through, Quincy. Remember, it's Christmas, not Pommus, that'll be trying the State's case. How will Christmas prove that Mrs. Dubrowski knew the contents of the will? But even if he could, in doing so, he destroys Pommus's theory of the case. If Mrs. Dubrowski knows that she is a legatee under the will, do you think the jury will believe that she was going to wait around until the will was probated and she received her legacy? The State's theory is that she killed Cory because he was on to her and she was going to steal the brooch to finance her get-away. The two theories cancel one another out. If you were Christmas, which horn of the dilemma would you pick?"

"All you need do is ask Smedley to state the contents of the will. If he denies knowing the will's contents, then how'd he know he's the executor? If he's fool enough to do that, you get out an instanter subpoena for the probate court clerk who will have to testify truthfully that the will was not sealed when Smedley gave it to him to be filed, and then you've caught Smedley in a big, fat lie. And juries hate liars, as you know."

"Then what do I need Reba Boyles for?"

"Largely for the effect she'll have on the jury. If you want to get the jury on your side, what better way than to have Reba Boyles on the witness stand bellowing at you like an enraged hippopotamus?"

"I'd simply ask her whether she was aware of the will's contents. If you invoke the Rule, she won't be in the courtroom when Smedley testifies, so she won't know what he said." Adams gave Flammonde an incredulous look. Ignoring it, Flammonde continued. "If she says 'yes' then you've got another person with motive. If she says 'no' then she's a liar and the jury'll know it. In fact, you're better off if she does deny having knowledge."

"You certainly have a colorful way of putting things. I hope the jury will react the same way. In addition to your business acumen and knowledge of the law you seem to be a keen student of human nature."

"I suppose that by matriculating at Brown rather than Harvard, you've managed to avoid taking any theoretical courses in psychology and that's why you still use the somewhat quaint term 'human nature.'"

"In my senior year at Brown I tried reading *Principles of Psychology,* you know, the treatise by Professor Will James. But after a chapter or two I gave it up as a lost cause. I also tried a couple of other works—at that time I was thinking I might want to become a clinical psychologist—but they were written in academician English. I could make out the words, and I even knew what most of them meant, but as far as understanding what the authors were saying or trying to say, they may just as well have been written in Hebrew or Mandarin Chinese."

"I agree. That's why 'human nature' is such a useful term. It ought to be a field of study all its own. Let the psychologists flounder around trying to apply deductive reasoning to explain human thought. I, for one am perfectly content to continue my intuitive reading of people. But again we digress; do you recall what new rabbit trail you want to try out?"

"I think so. Are you familiar with Richard Cory's automobile?"

"Yes, it's a Nineteen Sixteen Packard Twin Six Touring Model. It's pretty hard to miss: Gold-painted body; burgundy-colored hood. He bought it when they first came out; traded in his Hudson. Why do you ask?"

"Do you think you can get a look at it now? I'd like to know whether it has any recent-looking damage to the coach-work. When I went to interview Smedley and Boyles, I noticed there was some damage to the picket fence that cordons off the construction site. It looked like perhaps someone had failed to negotiate the turn in the road between the new building and the current one and had run into the fence. If it was Richard Cory that might explain why no one seems to know where he dined that night."

"No one that is, except for Smedley and Boyles. I can take a look, perhaps on the pretext of being interested in purchasing the machine now that Mr. Cory no longer has a use for it. However, I won't be able to testify."

"Don't worry about that. I expect that Reverend Christmas will not have a problem making one more trip to Oakdale Hall before the trial. I'd just like to know, before I trouble the good Reverend again, what we're likely to see if we go out there.

"Now, unless you want to fill in for Camille typing our pre-trial motions, witness list and subpoena applications, I need to get busy. Let's reconvene late Monday afternoon. You'll have had an opportunity to check out the automobile angle and perhaps Camille will be back with something to report."

Chapter Seventeen

Adams and Flammonde were again eating dinner—'dining' seems a bit elegant to describe the culinary experience—at the Red Rooster. Flammonde, a napkin tucked under his chin, was attacking a pile of steamers as Adams picked disinterestedly at his baked cod. Flammonde set down his shellfish fork and dunked a piece of bread in the broth. "I wonder what's keeping Camille. No 'phone call, nothing."

"Could be that she missed the train. Or maybe the train's running late. As for a 'phone call, I'm sure she would have called if she had anything to report. She has convinced me that she can take care of herself…"

"You don't sound convinced." Flammonde set the broth-laden bread down on the edge of his plate and looked at his watch. "Let's finish eating and then go over to the railroad station to wait for the last train."

Flammonde paid the check and they walked to the railroad station, a substantial brick building in the usual utilitarian design. They waited under the canopy on the passenger platform, Flammonde sitting on a bench smoking a cheroot and Adams pacing the length of the platform glancing at his watch each time he passed Flammonde. As Adams completed his tenth circuit he began to feel the faint vibration in the platform that signaled the arrival of the train. Soon enough the locomotive's powerful headlamp appeared from down the track and in another minute the train came to a stop with the combination baggage and mail car and the two passenger cars perfectly aligned with the platform.

The station porter came out of the freight office and wheeled his hand truck into position to receive the mail bags and small freight packages being unloaded from the mail-baggage car. Adams walked the length of the two passenger cars expecting to catch sight of Camille. There were only half a dozen passengers, none of them Camille, who collected their luggage and descended through the rear door of the first car. Adams greeted a couple of them and nodded to the rest, each of whom he had seen in Tilbury Town but did not know by name. Only one passenger, again not Camille, descended from the forward exit door of the second car. He was medium-height and rail-thin with a small, neatly trimmed mustache. He wore a well-cut brown suit and a matching derby hat. In one hand he carried a Gladstone bag and in the other what looked like a traveling salesman's sample case. He moved a few steps away from the train, set down his luggage and lighted a cigar. As he did, Flammonde got up from the bench and started walking past the baggage cart to the north end of the platform. The man picked up his luggage and followed after him.

As Adams turned to start after them three men pushed through the doors leading from the passenger waiting room and surrounded Adams. They were dressed as lumber jacks: Heavy steel-toed boots, faded blue denim work trousers and open-collared shirts. The two younger men each looked capable of up-rooting a good-size tree with his bare hands, and when they each grasped one of Adams's upper arms, he was sure they could. The third man, the eldest of the three, stood in front of Adams. "Billy, Fred, take it easy. Perhaps Mr. Adams has a good explanation for why your sister's not on the train like she promised..." he paused "... and while he's at it, explain what it is she's been doing down in Portland twice in the past few days." Obediently the pressure on Adams's biceps lessened, but not by much.

"She's been there on business for a client, Mr. Winters. I'm sorry I can't tell you more, but the attorney-client privilege forbids my doing so. I'm sure her work took longer than expected, and she simply missed the train. I can assure you that she's not in any danger."

"If there's no danger," Fred tightened his grip on Adams's bicep, "what was she doing shooting a derringer at man-size paper targets out at the farm yesterday afternoon? Camille doesn't like guns. 'Fore Billy 'n' me each got married and moved out, she'd make us clean our guns outside on the porch. Besides, where'd she get the derringer in the first place?"

"What client?" Now it was Billy's turn to crush Adams's other arm. "Better not be that woman killed Mr. Cory..."

Adams angrily tried to jerk first his left then his right arm loose from the grip of Camille's brothers. "What if it is Esther Dubrowski? You're not her judge or her jury. Doesn't she have the right to a fair trial? What if you were wrongly accused? You've got two brothers in the Army. What are they fighting for if it's not the Constitution and Bill of Rights? And what Camille's doing is just as important." His outburst produced a lessening of the grips on his arms and he was finally able to free himself.

Camille's father, his face inches from Adams's, asked, "And is it as dangerous as what Paul and Jesse are doing in the Army, Mr. Adams? I'm her father; she lives under my roof. I've got a right to know what you've gotten her into and whether she's in any danger or is likely to be."

His tête-à-tête with the man in the derby hat concluded, Flammonde started back toward Adams in time to hear Adam's outburst and the angry words of Camille's father that followed. He tapped Harley Winters on the shoulder. "Excuse me, Mr. Winters, could we have a word in private?"

"What business is it of yours, Mister…"

"Flammonde, Emil Flammonde, Mr. Winters. I'm a client of Mr. Adams, and for that reason I've spent a good deal of time lately in the office with your daughter. Now, before your sons do something to my attorney that they'll all three regret, could we have that private word?" Flammonde took Harley Winters's elbow hoping to put some space between the elder Winters and Adams.

Winters jerked his arm away. "I'm not going anywhere until I get answers to my questions. If you know where my daughter is, now is the time and place to say so. Anything you tell me you can say in front of my sons; I'd tell then anyway not a minute after we're done."

"Have it your way, Mr. Winters. Just ask your sons to release Mr. Adams, and let's all behave like the gentlemen I know each of you to be. All of us have no agenda other than Camille's welfare. Are we agreed?"

"Let him be boys and let's hear what Mr.…."

"Flammonde…Emil…"

"Mr. Flammonde has to say."

"First of all, Miss Winters is checked in to the Portland Regency Hotel, Room 304. I expect that as we speak, she's relaxing in a nice cool bath and reviewing in her mind the events of the day so that when she reports to Mr. Adams she'll not omit any of the details."

"How…?" all four men asked in unison.

"Please, gentlemen, keep your voices down." He motioned the men to gather in closer. "I know because from the time she set foot on this platform this morning and boarded the train for Portland, she's been in the constant company of my associate, the gentleman with whom I was speaking just a few minutes ago and who is now checking into the Palace Hotel no doubt ready for a good night's sleep, well-earned after keeping Miss Winters company all day.

"That scrawny man in the derby hat? "What's he good for? String some barbed-wire on him and he'd pass for a fence post."

"Are you Billy or Fred?" Flammonde asked.

"I'm Billy, if it matters. What does matter is whether that fella could earn his keep if he had to. Camille has to make any more of these trips, assumin' Pa will let her, me and Fred are going with her, not Mr. Fencepost. "

"You'd not want to tangle with Mr. Fencepost. Take my word on that if nothing else. I won't give you all of my associate's background, but I will tell you this: He's had years of law-enforcement experience. Rode with the Texas Rangers for eight years. A couple of years ago he and I found ourselves in Hong Kong on a business matter. We had about concluded our business—successfully, I might add—and allowed ourselves an indulgent dinner at one of the floating restaurants in the harbor. When dinner was over we were walking back up the pier hoping to find a rickshaw to take us back to our hotel. We were almost back to the wharf when we were set upon by a gang of street-toughs, five in all. They were no doubt looking for money to buy a night in their favorite opium den. I'm sure when they saw us they thought this was their lucky day, or night as it were, so they came at us expecting easy pickings: Overpower us, slit our throats, take our wallets and valuables, then toss us off the pier to provide a late-night dinner for the crabs and fish.

"Three of them came at my associate, Mr. Raymond. The first one came at him with a knife. He lunged at Mr. Raymond who side-stepped the attack. He took the thug's wrist turned the knife around and rammed it into the thug's middle and sliced it around a bit before pulling it out. He put his arm around the man's neck and turned him around just as the other two were coming at him. Well, the slashing had the desired effect: The thug's guts spilled out on the pier and the other two tripped over them and both went down in a pile at his feet. He stomped on the neck of one of them breaking it. He took the other one by the hair and wrapped a couple of strands of the first thug's guts around his neck and then tossed him off the pier pulling his dead friend along with him."

"What were you doing while this was going on," Adams couldn't help but ask.

"I was doing okay. I found a length of lumber and was making pretty good use of it. When the two who were attacking me saw what'd happened to the first three, they took off running probably vowing to give up opium and their life of crime, become Buddhist monks for good measure."

"Well I guess that beats any story I've ever heard…if it's true."

"Oh, I give you my word, Fred, every last detail's God's honest truth. I'd swear to it in court. In fact, I did have to swear to it. Seems one of the thugs — one of the two who got away — was the son of a merchant who had some influence with the local police. As you know, Hong Kong is a British Crown colony, so the Brits run things, or at least think they do. Anyway, there was a minor fuss and we had to give sworn statements to the U.S. consul who, after a few days, managed to get everybody settled down. He was mighty glad when we got on our ship for San Francisco. Even came down to the pier in person to see us off."

"Well sounds like your associate's pretty handy with his hands and feet, but I bet it's a good thing none of those Chinese fellows was packing a gun."

"Well, I don't think it'd have mattered, Mr. Winters. My associate's pretty good with a gun as well. I've seen him throw four quarters in the air, draw his revolver and shoot all four coins before they hit the ground. He used to do it with dimes, but he says he's not as quick as he used to be so now he needs bigger targets."

"Okay, then Mr. Flammonde. The boys and me will take your word that your man can handle himself when he has to. But that brings up a second question: How come Camille needs that kind of protectin'? And third, what's your interest in seeing that she has it?"

"I don't really know that she needs such heavy-duty protection, Mr. Winters. But if Mrs. Dubrowski didn't kill Richard Cory, someone else did. We don't know who or why. But whoever it is will probably not be pleased should he happen to learn of our poking around. I would not take risks with Camille's safety any more than I would if she were my own daughter. That's why yet another of my associates is also checked into the Regency Hotel, Room 306 I believe. He will be awake all night listening for any unusual sounds. He'll see that Camille gets on the morning train and back to Tilbury Town without mishap.

"As for my interest in this matter, I became involved because the Dubrowski case is taking so much of my lawyer's time that I really have no choice. I can't complete my business here until I have Quincy's undivided time and attention. I can't switch lawyers, even if I wanted to, since it would be a matter of 'reinventing the wheel' as the saying goes; too expensive and too time-consuming. Quincy believes Mrs. Dubrowski's innocent, and has convinced me as well. So having nothing better to do, I've become an interested by-stander helping out in whatever way I can. Camille's role is a vital one to Mrs. Dubrowski's defense. I of course am not in any better position to tell you what she's doing than Mr. Adams. But if I can help make her job easier or more productive, or most importantly assure her safety, I'm only too happy to do so.

"Now, gentlemen, Quincy and I must bid you a good evening. I trust you will rest easier knowing that Camille's safety is our foremost priority. I must also trust you to keep our conversation confidential, even from Camille. As you even more than I or even Quincy know, Camille is a very independent young woman. I'm sure she'd take a dim view of our providing security for her without her knowledge or consent." Harley Winters mumbled his agreement.

"Now, I'm sure that Quincy's eager to hear what my associate has to report regarding the success of Camille's mission. So we'll bid you a pleasant evening."

Mollified for the time being, the men of Clan Winters took their leave crowding into the cab of their Ford TT slat-sided truck parked in front of the station. Adams and Flammonde walked the short distance to the Palace Hotel where the night-clerk told them that Mr. Raymond was expecting them in Room 106. Raymond without his jacket and in his stocking feet looked like a tired traveling salesman, not someone who could have dispensed such lethal violence as Flammonde had described. After letting them in, Raymond returned to the bed, re-lighted his black Marsh-Wheeling Conestoga cigar and offered his bottle of bourbon around.

"Just to be sociable, Lamar." Flammonde took a substantial swig and then passed the bottle to Adams who started to decline but caught a look from Flammonde and took a genteel sip.

"I'm pleased to meet you, Mr. Raymond," Adams managed to croak, his throat aflame."

"Same here, Son." Raymond took another pull on the bottle. "Emil here says good things about you, except for the part about not liking good whisky."

"And he says some pretty amazing things about you, Mr. Raymond."

"Call me 'Lamar,' Son. All my friends do."

"Thank you, Lamar. I'm delighted to be on your list of friends. I don't mean to be nosy or to give offense, but may I ask you a question about your career?"

"Sure, Son. I know what you're gonna ask, but ask away." Raymond blew a series of smoke rings.

"Emil told us — Camille's father and two of her brothers and me — about what happened in Hong Kong. I'm just wondering how many men have you sent to their just rewards during your career. I hope my question doesn't offend you."

"No offense taken, Quincy. By the way, callin' you 'Quincy' okay with you?"

"Oh yes, Lamar, 'Quincy' it is. And do you mind if I have another round of that whisky?"

Raymond handed the bottle to Flammonde who passed it to Adams. "How about a stogie to go with it? Box is over there on the bureau; help yourself."

"Well, I don't know about that. I'm not much of a smoker. But Emil, I will try one of your cheroots if you don't mind."

"Don't mind at all. Cigars and good whisky, they sort of go together." Flammonde took the leather case out of the inside pocket of his suit jacket and handed it to Adams along with a box of matches.

"Go ahead and get lit up, Quincy and then I'll answer your question."

It took Adams a few moments to get the cheroot lit and to get over the coughing fit caused by his inhaling. "I'm sorry, Lamar, I didn't mean to interrupt."

"That's okay, Quincy. You know, folks have asked me that question from time to time. The answer is: I quit countin' corpses after the first two. Way I figure it, the Good Lord's keeping score, and when I've got my share, He'll let me know for sure. It's not something that brings joy to my heart, except the relief that naturally comes from seeing the other man lying there and not vice versa. I never put a man down didn't ask me to do it."

"Ask you…?"

Flammonde interjected, "There are lots of way that a man can ask to be put down, and Lamar's probably seen most of them. But you can count on one thing: Whenever Lamar took a life the world became a better place because of it.

"It's been quite a long day. Lamar, go ahead and tell us how Miss Winters's day went in Portland."

"Wait a moment. I'm sorry to interrupt again, but you accompanied Miss Winters, Camille, as she went about whatever it was that she was doing?"

"Well, I did in a way; she just didn't know it."

"You mean you followed her around all day? And she never knew it?"

"Easy, Quincy. Like I asked her father, do you think Camille would have agreed to a body-guard? Of course Lamar followed her. He's good at it; as good at that as he is in dealing with murderous thugs. Did you know what she was going to do in Portland? Neither did I. That's why I chose my words so carefully with Mr. Winters."

"I..." Between the bourbon and the cheroot, Adams was beginning to feel light-headed. "I noticed...that. I would have put...put it the same way if I'd had the chance."

"That being the case, I wasn't about to let her do whatever it was she intended to do without Lamar there to lend a hand if needed."

"I take it, Lamar, that your intervention was not necessary?"

"Right, Emil. She spent the day just going from one office building to another. She'd look at the building tenant directory, make some notes in a little spiral-bound notebook she had with her and then go up either in the elevator or taking the stairs. Then she'd come back down in anywhere from twenty minutes to almost an hour.

"Second building she went into, I managed to get on the elevator with her. I got out on the same floor she did, but I walked in the opposite direction from the one she took. I turned around just as she went into one of the offices; a law office it was. I've got the name written down if you want it. She didn't stay but a minute or two came back out and pressed the up button for the elevator. I ducked into the stairwell so she wouldn't spot me. It wasn't as though she was taking precautions. Heck, there could have been a herd of elephants following her and I don't think she'd have noticed. Anyway, I went up one more floor and looked for her, but she must have gone on to another floor. So I took the elevator back down to the street level and waited for her to come back out which she did in just a few minutes.

"While I was waiting for her to come back down, I took a look at the directory. There were several lawyers and law firms in the building. Same thing in the next two buildings. So it seems to me that she must have been calling on lawyers."

"I wonder what she was doing calling on law offices." Adams held out his hand for the bourbon bottle.

"Maybe she's job hunting, Counselor. I warned you that you need to do something to hang on to her."

"Camille would never leave me in the present circumstances, especially without giving notice." Doubting his own words, Adams leaned forward, put his elbows on his knees and rested his chin in his hands.

"I have an idea what she was doing, Counselor. But listen to the rest of what Lamar has to say before we jump to any conclusions."

"This routine went on until a bit after four o'clock. She came out of one of the buildings and walked over to the Regency. She had gone to the hotel when she first got to Portland and left a small travel valise with the bellman. Soon's she got her suitcase I got to a telephone and called Maurice," Raymond paused for a moment. "That's Maurice Morton, Quincy. He's the fellow keeping an eye on things on the third floor of the Regency."

"And what is Mr. Morton's special skill? Or do I not want to know?" Adams put out his cheroot and motioned for the bourbon bottle from which Flammonde had just finished taking another sociable sip.

"Maurice's a right interestin' fellow. Was a carny most of his life. Run away from home age fourteen. Started as a roustabout. Worked his way into the show from there. Did just about everything from a strong-man act to fire-eatin', sword swallowin' and knife throwin'. I guess about everything except a midget act or a hootchie-cootchie dancer. He was working in a forty-miler over in Pennsylvania some years back. Couple o' yokels from the next town over stuck up the manager's trailer and tried to make off with the cash box. It happened that the robbery occurred at the end of the first good night they'd had in weeks, and Maurice wasn't about to let them get away with the show's money. So he grabbed hold of the two of them, knocked their heads together real hard, took away their guns, made them take off all their clothes and run 'm off the grounds and all the way back into town."

"So why'd he get out of the carnival life and into the business-opportunity business?"

"The what?" Raymond caught a sharp look from Flammonde. "Oh yeah. The business-opportunity business. Well, Quincy, you'd be right surprised how much a good carny knows about people. I'd put a good carny like Maurice up against any alienist or psychologist you'd care to name when it comes to readin' people. As for getting out of the carnival life…"

"Wait, let me guess." Adams thought a moment. "Like the Catholic priesthood, it was 'either punch or Judy.' I'd guess Judy."

"Good guess, Quincy. He fell in love with a magician's assistant. She wouldn't leave the magician so Maurice pulled a disappearing act of his own. Tried college for a couple years but it didn't stick. Finally ended up working with us."

Raymond downed the last of the bourbon. "Say, Emil, there's another bottle in the top drawer of the bureau. You mind gettin' it and another cigar while you're up?"

"How did he learn what room Camille had taken?"

"Quincy, now you're asking one of those questions maybe you don't want to know the answer to."

"No, go ahead and tell him, Lamar. He's familiar with some of our methods for obtaining information."

"Okay, Emil. But this thing goes south, you own him. Well, Quincy, it's a dodge we've used before. Maurice flashes some kind of impressive-looking badge. Tells the clerk he's a special investigator and he's been assigned to keep tabs on that woman just checked in. Hints maybe she's a gangster's moll. Slips the desk clerk a couple of bucks and he gets a room as close to her as he can and tells the clerk to keep his lips buttoned he knows what's good for 'im."

Quincy put one hand over his eyes and shook his head. "Camille a gangster's moll?" Of all the...why didn't you just say she's a German spy?"

Raymond lit his fresh cigar and thumb-nailed the cork off the fresh bottle. "Say, Emil, the youngster's got a good idea there. We need to try that."

"Well, it'd better be pretty soon; everybody's saying the war'll be over before Thanksgiving." Flammonde took out another cheroot and handed one to Adams. "If we're going to get our business wrapped up before Thanksgiving, maybe you'd better tell us what happened next. Here, let Quincy and me help with that." Flammonde stretched out his hand for the bourbon.

"Forty-five minutes later, she comes out lookin' fresh-scrubbed and all. Got a...I don't know how to describe it...a happy...no, serene...no, pleased-with-herself...look on her face. Kind of a lilt in her walk. Anyway, she flounces back to the last building and goes into the lobby. A minute or two later she comes out arm-and-arm with another woman. About Camille's age, maybe a couple years older. Then the two of them go back to the Regency, stoppin' to window shop along the way, gigglin' and laughin' like a couple o' school-girls.

"They go into the bar, have a cocktail apiece and then to the restaurant for dinner; poached haddock for each with vegetables and a glass of wine each. They split the check. Then they hug and say goodbye. The other woman gets in a cab in front of the hotel. I figure Maurice has Camille covered—he's in the lobby smoking a cigar and reading the newspaper; lookin' like a gumshoe in a ten-cent novel—so I get in the next cab and follow the other woman. Her cab takes her to a boarding house, Miss Rosie's Hotel for Refined Young Ladies, on Forest between Cumberland and Congress. She goes in, and I have the cabbie take me to the train station just in time to catch the last train."

Flammonde passed the bottle to Adams who hesitated for a moment and then took a sizable swallow. He wiped his lips on his sleeve and asked, "Is she the woman we're looking for?"

"Well, if she isn't, then she's her sister. She's just as you described her, Emil: Tall, dark red hair worn in a chignon…at least that's what I think it's called…Gibson Girl figure…"

"That's great news, Emil. I wonder…"Adams stifled a yawn…"what made Camille think of checking law offices?" He handed the bottle back to Flammonde.

"Why don't you ask Camille in the morning? The big question is: how are we going to get the lady to admit that she's the 'brooch-woman' as Camille calls her?"

Why can't…can't Camille just ask her? Maybe you could get the jeweler or his sales clerk to identify her. Then we can get out a…a…"

Flammonde got up from his chair and helped Adams to his feet. "Quincy, you look a little tired. Maybe you ought to lie down for a few minutes. Lamar, give me a hand. You mind if Quincy takes your place on the bed for a few minutes?"

"Seems a good idea to me, Emil. There's still some bourbon left and you and me need to do some talkin'. Guess the counselor didn't realize how much he liked sour mash after all. You'd best take that cheroot out of his hand though before he drops it and burns a hole in the rug."

As Flammonde obliged, Raymond took Adams's other arm and led him to the bed. "Here, Son, let me help you out of your jacket. You just lay right down here and take a little nap. Me and Emil got some plannin' to do."

In a moment Adams was asleep. Raymond took another sip of bourbon and handed the bottle to Flammonde. "Kid seems pretty sharp, Emil. When are you planning on letting him in on what we're really doing? You know it'll be gettin' right cold up here pretty soon, and I'm like one of those 'first-of-Mayers' as Maurice calls them. I don't like the cold. I want to get back to someplace warm and hibernate until spring."

"I don't think just yet, Lamar. Junior's bright and got a kind of toughness about him, but I don't want to distract him with the trial coming up."

"Wouldn't it better suit our purposes if she…I mean

Dubrowski…is convicted? Then we could do what we need to do without having to worry about staying out of the spotlight of the murder case.

"What if she did kill Cory? For all we know, she may have been up to her eyeballs in Richard Cory's affairs. If by some miracle she walks, then aren't folks…and I'm talkin' about that Reverend Christmas in particular…going to want to find out who actually did kill Cory and why? And aren't they going to want to know why Mrs. Dubrowski confessed if she didn't do it? Do you think they'll just blame the whole mess on that clown Pommus? And while they're wondering about those things, don't you think they may bump into us once or twice?"

"I've been wrestling with those conundrums since the first day I hired Adams. And I don't know the answers, Lamar. But I do know this: I don't want Esther Dubrowski to suffer for this situation a day longer than she already has. It's my fault she's in this mess."

"What do you mean, 'your fault'? You didn't kill Cory."

"Neither did she. She is covering up for someone; that's a certainty. Maybe it's the 'brooch-woman', maybe someone else. We'll just have to bear down and complete our business before the jury has a chance to get the case.

"How's finding the brooch-woman going to fit into your…your…I started to say 'plan,' but I don't know that 'plan' is the right word. She going to just up and admit that she's the brooch-woman and that she's the one killed Cory? What was her motive? She didn't like the brooch?"

"Yes, I do think she'll admit to being the brooch-woman But no, I don't expect her to confess to shooting Richard Cory. To prove she did, you'd have to show that she's the one that had access to the gun. I rather like Camille's notion of a jealous boy-friend. But the boy-friend's got the same problem: How'd he know where the gun was kept?"

"Okay, Emil, I guess one or both of us are too tired to think straight. You going to try and take the kid home?"

"In his condition? Even if I could get him moving, if I brought him home, our landlady'd toss us both out first thing in the morning. Better let him sleep it off here. I expect the desk clerk'd be happy to rent you another room, Lamar.

"There's one loose end maybe you can tie up for us. See if you can get a close look at Cory's automobile. Quincy thinks there may be some damage to the coach-work, probably on the driver's side. Tell Mr. Silas that you heard it might be for sale, and you'd like to take a look at it. I've got to meet our man in Augusta. I'll need to borrow Quincy's Ford and get on up there and get back by morning. Will you get him up in the morning, so he and I can meet the first train? You may want to pour some coffee into him. I expect he'll be a little unsteady in the morning."

Chapter Eighteen

The moment the porter put the portable steps down on the platform Camille was off the train. Flammonde tipped his hat and took her valise. Not wanting to let her know what he already knew, he said, "I can tell from your smile that you had some success. I can't wait to hear all about it."

"But where's Quincy? I want him to hear it at the same..."she spotted Adams sitting on the bench his arms wrapped across his body as though he were cold "... time. Quincy Adams, what on earth happened to you? You look like you've been run over by a train rather than coming to meet one."

Adams stood and tried to get his eyes to focus. He ran his hand through his hair and tried to straighten his neck-tie. "Camille, I..."

"Never mind, Mr. Adams, I know a hang-over when I see one. Come on, Emil, you steer him over to the Red Rooster. I'd like some breakfast, and I expect he needs a few cups of coffee."

Flammonde took Adams's arm. "Do you think Aunt Dorothy'll serve him in his condition? Maybe I ought to take him home to shave and clean up. I've got his car parked out front. It won't take a minute."

"No, let's take him like he is. If Aunt Dorothy throws him out, it'll serve him right. Besides, I'm just about to burst with my news."

"Then you found her?"

"Oh no Emil; not a word until I've got my breakfast in front of me and your drinking companion...I assume he was with you last night...is sobered up enough to listen and to understand."

Once seated at the Red Rooster, Camille placed her napkin in her lap, sugared and creamed her coffee. "Her name is Cecilia Durbin. She's a receptionist-secretary in a Portland law firm."

"How'd you find her?" Adams lifted his coffee cup with his right hand using the left to steady his wrist.

"Something Emil said that Mr. Hirschorn mentioned in describing the woman who brought in the brooch for him to appraise. He said she was nicely dressed except that her cuffs were slightly frayed. Look at mine." Camille set down her coffee cup and held up her hands palms outward. "So are mine. And you know how they got that way?"

Flammonde put down the warm, buttered biscuit he was about to bite into. "From using a typewriter?"

"Right. See how my cuffs are starting to fray, and I haven't had to do all that much typing. Mr. Hirschorn, from what he told you, deduced that she most likely had to work for her living. He described her as refined, but he didn't suggest that she acted snooty like you'd expect a woman with too much time and money to act. Nor from the way Mr. Hirschorn described her reaction to him telling her the value of the brooch, did I figure her for a…" Camille lowered her voice, "a… kept-woman. A woman of that sort would certainly not have reacted as Cecilia Durbin did."

Adams set down his coffee cup without spilling too much. "How'd you find her?"

"I just started going into office buildings that looked like they might have lawyers in them. I'd walk in and ask whoever greeted me if they were hiring. I said I was an experienced legal secretary…which is only a slight embellishment on the truth. I said I lived in another town, but wanted to move to Portland. This was at least partly true. And it may be entirely true pretty soon." She gave Adams a side-ways look to make sure he knew he was not at the top of her list of favorite people at the moment. "Every office I went into the people were really nice. Of course most said they weren't hiring, but even those said I should let them know when I got settled in Portland and if a need came up, they'd get in touch with me.

"Those that expressed an interest, I'd try to get them to show me around their offices and describe what kind of practice they had. Of course I was *mainly*," she glared at Adams full-face this time in case he'd missed the point last time, "interested in seeing all of the clerical staff."

"And…and that's how you found her?"

"Listen, Emil, he can talk. Does that mean he's alive? Yes, Quincy, that's how I met her, more or less. The last office I went to, Berman & Berman, she was at the receptionist's desk pounding away at the typewriter with what looked like about six carbons plus the original. I introduced myself, using my real name, and went into my song and dance. She said she didn't know if they were hiring, but I should have a seat and she'd go ask Mr. Berman, 'Harrell Berman,' was who she said. Well she came back in a couple of minutes and said that Mr. Berman would like to meet me. She said he'd be out in a few minutes if I wouldn't mind waiting. I said I'd be happy to wait, if just to get off my feet for a while.

"Of course as soon as I saw her, I knew she was the brooch woman. I wanted to find out as much as I could about her so I asked how she liked her job and how long she'd been with the firm. I asked her how many lawyers and what kind of practice did they have? She told me she liked her job fine; she'd been there about two and a half years. She told me they did pretty much everything, even some criminal work. I could tell she wasn't any too fond of having the criminal clients hanging around her reception room. She told me that there were two other secretaries and that they rotated receptionist duties.

"Emil, either you or I must be living right; it can't be Quincy. Just think how lucky I was. What if it wasn't her turn to be receptionist?"

"Maybe there was an element of luck, Camille, but you made your luck and for that you deserve a great deal of credit. But tell us the rest."

Camille blushed slightly. "Well she asked me about myself. I told her I was from a small town in the Counties and had worked for a lawyer up there. She asked about my family. I told her that my mother had died when I was little and my father took off not long after. I told her I was taken in by the lawyer and his wife who sort of adopted and raised me. They'd had a child, but she'd died in infancy. She'd have been about my age. Well, I went on, my mother had left me a few acres of land that had been leased for timber for many years. The lawyer had taken care of it and held the money for me. Then when I became of age, he'd turned the money over to me and that's what I'm living on until I find a job. When he gave me the money, he and his wife sat me down at the dining room table and told me I'd best get out of there and see some of the rest of Maine, if not the world. So, I told her, that's what I'm doing in Portland. I said I was thinking about enrolling at Colby College...they admit women...but decided I wanted to work a while first. Besides, whatever they could teach me there, I could learn for myself at the Portland Public Library.

Adams, with his feelings hurting worse than his head, asked: "That's a great cover story, Camille, but did you manage get anything out of her?"

Camille stood and threw her napkin on the table. "Quincy Adams, you apologize right now. Apologize for getting stinking drunk and for being the meanest man I've ever known. If you don't, I may just move to Portland and take a job in the first law office that'll hire me. And I won't need a reference from you...you..." Tears beginning to well, Camille started to walk out, but Flammonde stood not exactly blocking her way, but not making it easy for her to walk out.

"Camille, don't be too hard on him. He was near sick with worry about you; not knowing where you were or whether you were in some kind of danger. If anyone's to blame it's me. I'm the one got him started drinkin'. Just to get his mind off fretting about you. He wanted to get in his automobile and drive down to Portland to look for you. I figured that a few drinks were as good a way as any to keep him occupied. And, truth be known, I was a bit worried myself so did my share of the drinking as well."

Camille paused and stared at first at Flammonde, then at Adams, weighing her hope that Flammonde was telling her the truth against her intuition that he was lying through his teeth. Unable to reach a satisfactory conclusion, she walked over to the counter, got a fresh cup of coffee and walked back to the table..

Adams managed a look of contrition, "I'm so, so sorry, Camille. I promise it won't happen again. But what Emil says is true; I was really concerned, especially when you didn't call."

"If you two hadn't been out pretending to be a couple of sailors on pay-day, you might have been around when I did try to call. I called the office and I tried to get you at Mrs. Norman's. Where were you…never mind, I don't want to know. Do you want to hear the rest?"

"Yes, please, Camille." Flammonde held her chair for her. "Here, Quincy, eat one of these biscuits. Food'll do you good."

"I suppose," Camille continued, "that my 'cover story' must have struck a responsive chord. She told me that she came from a similar background except it was her father who died and her mother who took off. She says she was raised by a couple in Boston. She'd graduated from The Girls' Latin School in Boston and went to Radcliffe College for a year, but her surrogate parents couldn't afford to send her after the first year so she didn't go back. Took a job at Filene's Department Store and hated it. Floor-walker leering at her all day, making her uncomfortable. But in spite of that she kept the job until she'd saved enough money to go to secretarial school where she learned typing and short-hand. That's how she got to be a legal secretary.

"About that time Mr. Berman came out and introduced himself. He apologized for keeping me waiting and I said that I didn't mind. He said that he was expecting a long-distance telephone call so he wouldn't have time to interview me that afternoon and he'd be tied up all day today. He asked if I could come in Wednesday. He told me that they had been discussing whether they needed to hire another secretary. They'd just gotten a substantial piece of new long-term business and were thinking they might need to bring in someone to help with the work-load."

"The Richard Cory Estate." Flammonde and Adams said at the same time. "That could be a problem," Flammonde continued. "If they ever found out that Camille worked…works for you, they're bound to think that you planted her in their office to find out what you could about the estate. Camille, did Berman ask you for whom you worked and where?"

"He did, but before I could answer, his long-distance call came in and he had to leave."

"That was a close call." Adams wiped his mouth to remove a small blob of blueberry jam that had escaped from his biscuit. "What would you have told him?"

"I…I don't know, Quincy. I know it was my own idea to undertake this masquerade, but honestly I feel guilty as heck about it."

"You shouldn't, Camille. You harmed no one, and you may have saved an innocent woman from having to spend the rest of her life in prison. Why don't we go up to Quincy's office and you can finish your report. I'm most curious to learn how you…" Flammonde caught himself before he asked how she'd managed to get Miss Durbin to go to dinner, "…the rest of your adventure."

Using her office key Winters opened the door. She and Flammonde waited in Adams's office as Adams dragged himself up the stairs and lurched his way to his desk. When he was seated, Camille handed him an envelope addressed to Adams and bearing the Attorney General's return address. "This was stuck in the mail slot, same as the last one. Maybe you'd better open it before I go on with my story."

"Wait, give me that." She reached across the desk and plucked the knife-like letter opener from Adams's hand. "You're just as apt to poke yourself as that envelope. Now give me the envelope and we'll see what new devilment Reverend Christmas is up to." She sliced the envelope open and extracted a single page. "It's dated yesterday. '*Dear Mr. Adams: I beg to inform you that Mr. Matthews has located the envelope that Deputy Isaacson mentioned while we were at Oakdale Hall. It appears that it somehow became wedged in the back of the file drawer in Bascom Pommus's office. Since Mr. Matthews was unaware of its existence, he did not know to look for it. Just yesterday he remembered that it was still missing. He asked Mr. Pommus for permission to go through the file cabinet a second time. Mr. Pommus readily agreed and upon searching again, Mr. Matthews located the envelope. Based on the sheriff's handwriting on the envelope and the fact that it was still sealed, Mr. Pommus is willing to swear that it is the same envelope as was turned over to him in the courtroom. With that assurance, I saw no reason not to open it and examine the contents. Unfortunately, the contents appear to have nothing to do with the case at hand. All that the envelope contains is some advertising brochures for several brands of automobiles. Mr. Cory must have acquired them prior to purchasing his Packard, placed them in the coffee table drawer and forgot about them. You are welcome to examine the envelope and it contents at your convenience. Very truly yours.'* And it's signed Horatio Christmas."

"That's odd," Adams rubbed the bridge of his nose with his thumb and forefinger. "The way Deputy Isaacson described the sheriff finding the envelope, looking in it and then putting it in his pocket, you'd think it was something that maybe had to do with Cory's death. You'd think that if it was nothing but some automobile advertisements he'd have just put them back in the drawer instead of slipping the envelope into his pocket.

"I saw that Christmas listed the envelope on his exhibit list, so I guess I'd better take a look at it even though it's probably a total waste of nearly a whole morning. Camille, go ahead and tell us the rest of your day. It seems like your sleuthing has been a lot more productive than anything I've done lately."

"Quincy, don't sell yourself short. I read your pre-trial motions and their damn good, I'd say first-rate."

"Thanks, Emil. But let's withhold the accolades until we hear what Judge Beauchamp has to say. Camille…"

"When Mr. Berman had to take his call and asked me to come back, he said that I should feel free to visit with Miss Durbin…he was pretty formal calling her 'Miss Durbin' instead of 'Cecilia.' I liked that; it shows that the clerical employees are respected just like the lawyers.

"After he'd left the reception area I said to Cecilia that I didn't want to interfere with her work; it looked like she had a lot to do before the end of the day. I said there's so much I want to know about Portland: Places to live…shopping…men…and so on. I said if she was free, I'd like to take her to dinner. Well she thought about it for a moment. I'm sure that's the first time she'd been asked out to dinner by another woman, just as I'm sure it's the first time I've ever asked anyone—woman or man—out to dinner. Well, she said she'd go, but only 'Dutch treat.' I didn't know what that meant until she explained it to me. I said I'd be glad to pay, but she insisted, so I finally said okay.

"We agreed to meet when she got off work at five o'clock, so I went back to the hotel and checked in."

"Back?" Flammonde asked.

"Oh, sorry. I forgot to mention that I took a suitcase with me in case I had to stay overnight. When I first got to Portland I went to the

Regency and left my suitcase with the bellman. So when I found Cecilia and arranged to meet her after work, I went back to the hotel and checked in. I didn't want to appear in a hurry to finish dinner, so I decided to spend the night and take the first train in the morning. When I got to my room I tried to call you here, but there was no answer. I knew it was useless to try and call my dad because he'd most likely be out with Billy and Fred either in the field or on the timber lease. I didn't want to call Alice or Evelyn, my sisters-in-law; they'd pester me to death wanting to know what I was doing in Portland and were the new fall fashions in the stores yet? Not that Billy or Fred ever take them anyplace worth getting dressed up for, but there's no harm in wishing.

"As I was saying, I went back to the hotel. I checked in, freshened up a bit and then went back to the lobby of Cecilia's building. She came down a couple of minutes after five and we walked back to the hotel. We had a drink in the hotel bar; first time I've ever done that. But Cecilia said it was okay; that two women could be together in a nice place like the Regency bar and have a drink or two without causing a scandal as long as they didn't get too noisy or hold hands. But a woman alone; that's something else. If a man, preferably your husband, didn't show up in fifteen minutes, you could expect that the house detective would drop over to have a word with you. Maybe someday a woman will be able go into a hotel bar without every man in the place thinking she's looking for male companionship, especially his, either for fun or for profit."

"Maybe that'll come next, Camille, right after women get the vote." Adams rubbed his eyes with his knuckles. "I mean no disrespect to you or to women in general. You know I'm in favor of women getting the vote and every other right that men have. But unescorted women in hotel bars…"

"Why don't we save the discussion of politics and social issues for another day, Quincy? Camille, is that okay with you?"

"Sorry, Emil, I know I can get on a soap-box when it comes to women's rights. To continue…say, I assume you don't care what we had to eat or drink, do you?"

"No, as long as you enjoyed it."

"We did Emil. During dinner I asked her where she lived. She gave me the name of an apartment hotel for single women. It's on Forest Avenue which I think is on the south side of town. Cecilia says it's a nice neighborhood and the apartments are pretty nice for the money. She thinks there is a vacancy if I want it, or if there isn't she's sure Miss

Rosie—that's the owner's name—will let me stay with Cecilia until there is a vacancy or I can find another place. I said that'd be swell as long as I could pay my fair share. She said that would be fine with her.

"I asked her about the eligible male situation. She said she had no trouble getting asked on dates, the problem was that the gentleman doing the asking wasn't always someone she'd want to say 'yes' to. In fact she said she'd just recently broken off a relationship and hadn't started dating again. From the way she said it I could tell that it wouldn't be a good idea to press the matter. Anyway, to change the subject we shared a few stories about being a legal secretary. Her stories were a lot more interesting than mine, except for the one I was living at that moment. We talked about clothes and make-up and that was about it, except that she admired my new hair style. The waiter brought the bill; she paid half and I paid half. I walked her to the front door; she got in a cab and that was it."

Camille paused for a moment as though trying to remember something else. Finally she spoke. "There's one other thing. It's probably just my imagination, but I ought to mention it all the same. I think I was possibly being followed. Several times I saw a man in a brown suit and derby hat. At least I think it was the same man. He didn't act suspicious or anything. But he kept turning up when I came out of several of the office buildings, and I thought I saw him again on the way back to the hotel with Cecilia. Is it possible that Reverend Christmas is having me followed?"

"I doubt it, Camille. Not Horatio Christmas. From Emil's description, as well as my own observation, I believe that he's a straight-arrow when it comes to ethics. And following the opposite side's lawyer's investigator around is as unethical as can be. It's the same as stealing his briefcase to get a look at his file. You work for me—even though Emil's paying you—so the attorney work-product privilege applies to you just as it does to me. So if anyone from the other side's following you, it would be at the behest of Pommus most likely, or possibly Sheriff Dowdy. But I wouldn't bet on him because I don't think that Deputy Isaacson would stand for it."

"Assuming he knows about it." Flammonde was enjoying Adams's dissembling as much as it was making Adams uncomfortable.

"True, but there doesn't seem to be much goes on in that office he doesn't know about. And I'm pretty sure he's no friend of Sheriff Dowdy's. I wouldn't be surprised if he didn't quit and run against him next election."

"I wouldn't be surprised either, Quincy. But no more politics. Camille, I take it that's all you've got to report?"

"All? I should think it was enough. After all I did find her..." Camille paused and briefly put her hands over her mouth. "What have I done? She's so sweet, and we became fast friends just that quickly. How can I go back and confront her about the brooch and Richard Cory?" This time the tears not only welled, but began flowing freely. "I...this is terrible...She'll hate me forever. Quincy, I hope that Esther Dubrowski's worth it. Emil, I still don't know and don't want to know what you're up to. But whatever it is, I hope it's worth making me miserable for the rest of my life."

"Camille, wait. You've done a remarkable job, and when this is over, I expect you and Miss Durbin will be able to carry on your friendship just as it was yesterday. Quincy and I will be the ones to confront Miss Durbin, although I think 'confront' is much too strong a word. Write out a note to Miss Durbin telling her that you've just gotten word that one of your foster parents has taken ill and you need to return home. Tell her to thank Mr. Berman and conclude by telling her that you'll be in touch soon.

"Quincy and I are off to Portland. We'll deliver the note to the bellman at the Regency and instruct him to take it to Miss Durbin saying only that you gave it to him as you were checking out."

"Emil, I don't know that we both ought to be meeting with her. Don't you think that two men would be intimidating, whereas one...myself...would be less so. I'll just be up-front about it: Tell her I'm Esther Dubrowski's lawyer and I'd like to ask her a few questions about her relationship with Richard Cory."

"And you think that will persuade her to 'spill her guts' as they say in the detective novels? Just like Smedley and Boyles did?"

"Thanks for the reminder, Emil. Just how would you get her to 'spill her guts'?"

"Well, Quincy, since you ask, I'd say 'Miss Durbin, I'm representing your mother and...'"

"Her what?" Adams sat back down.

"How do you..." Camille started to ask.

"'Elementary my dear friends, elementary,' if I may borrow a phrase from Sherlock Holmes. 'Durbin;' 'Dubrowski.' Father deceased; mother in the wind? Esther Dubrowski goes to the synagogue where she often sits with a younger woman, undoubtedly the same young woman described by Martin Hirschorn. And speaking of descriptions, do you not see a good bit of Esther in Cecilia: Height, skin tone, hair color, shape of the face. To my mind, if Esther had been given any chance at a decent life, she'd have looked twenty-five years ago and perhaps even today like Cecilia's twin sister.

"And as for a motive for confessing, what loving mother wouldn't do anything…even confess to murder…to protect her only child. Do you remember our discussion about the lavaliere and the Jews' reverence for life? What better return on her investment than to save her daughter? She'd killed once before to protect Cecilia, hadn't she?"

"Then you believe she…"

"No, no. Quincy. Not for a minute. What I do believe is that for some reason Esther Dubrowski thinks that Cecilia shot Richard Cory. And as she so trenchantly observed when you first met with her, what difference does it make to her whether she spends the rest of her life in prison in Maine or in Illinois?"

"What you say makes sense now that I think about it. But how can Cecilia help us now? It's too late to list her as a witness, although under the circumstances Judge Beauchamp would possibly consider allowing me to amend our witness list. But what good would she do? Mrs. Dubrowski would never allow me to put Cecilia on the stand. Even if I could, am I going to try to get her to confess to killing Cory? And if I just ask her about the brooch, what good'll that do? Her owning up to the brooch just possibly places her in Oakdale Hall at or near the time of the murder. Besides, if Christmas sees an opportunity to make a fool of Bascom Pommus he will tear Cecilia to shreds on cross.

"Think about it: 'Isn't it true, *Miss Durbin* that you and Richard Cory were having an'… he lowers his voice to a whisper…'affair? You had dinner together that night for what was to be the last time. He told you that he wanted to break off the affair, but you didn't. He said he'd met someone else and planned to marry her. To convince you, he even showed you the brooch that he purchased as an engagement gift for his intended bride. Or perhaps he offered it to you as a parting gift. In either case, you were furious, were you not? You stormed out of the restaurant in a rage, even then plotting your revenge. If you couldn't have Richard Cory, no other woman would have him either.

"'You made your way to Oakdale Hall; perhaps you even had an accomplice, *Miss Durbin*? You'd been to Oakdale Hall many times, so you knew where he kept his revolver and that you could get to it without being concerned about being heard by Mr. Silas,'…Christmas raises his voice so he's nearly shouting…the Civil War hero. *Deaf Silas* as you probably referred to him. Correct so far, *Miss Durbin*? You knew that Richard Cory had consumed some amount of alcohol and would likely be sound asleep. His falling asleep in the music room rather than his bedroom made it that much easier for you, did it not?

"'You entered the house, went into the music room, *murdered Richard Cory in his sleep.* And then'…Christmas gives her his wrath-of-God stare…'you unbuttoned his trousers one last time trying to find the brooch to keep as a *souvenir* of your night's dastardly work. Is there anything I've said that's not the God's honest truth, *Miss Durbin*? If so, please tell the jury now." Adams slumped forward, his elbows on the desk-top and his head in his hands. "Camille, do we have any aspirin? I've got a terrible headache."

Camille went out to her desk and returned with a bottle of Bayer's. "Shall I go down and get you a glass of water?"

"Yes, please. Thank you."

In a couple of minutes Camille returned with a pitcher of ice water and three glasses. She poured a glass for Adams who quickly downed it with two aspirin. "Thank you, Camille."

"I'm sorry, Quincy, I can't see Cecilia Durbin…Dubrowski…as a murderess." Camille poured a glass of water for Flammonde and one for herself.

"Your instinct may be right, Camille, but look how angry you get at Quincy whenever he gives offense. What is it that Shakespeare wrote: 'Hell hath no fury like a woman scorned'?"

"Actually, it was William Congreve in '*The Mourning Bride*'. The complete quotation is 'Heaven has no rage like love to hatred turned / Nor hell a fury like a woman scorned.' I had a minor in English literature to go along with my major in classics. I always knew that someday it'd be useful.

"But I agree with Camille, my moot court cross-examination notwithstanding. Remember what Mr. Hirschorn told you. She'd had the brooch for at least a week or two before Cory died. And remember her reaction? It doesn't seem to me that she reacted like a woman scorned. And what about what she told Camille? She said she was the one that broke off the relationship. In fact, the more I think about it, the more I'd love to see Christmas light into her on the stand. All I'd need to do is call Mr. Hirschorn in rebuttal."

"But if you did that wouldn't you be taking Mrs. Dubrowski out of the frying pan and putting her into the fire? If she's lucky, Christmas would dismiss the murder indictment and she'd be charged with obstruction of justice; an offense which is no small matter either when it comes to sentencing.

"More likely, the murder charge would stand; only Christmas would have a new theory to sell to the jury: she feared that Cory, a rejected suitor, would seek some awful revenge against which she needed to protect Cecilia. By the time the jury gets the case, they'll be so befuddled that whoever gets in the last word is who they'll go with. And you know who that is."

"I guess you're right about that. So I can't risk putting Cecilia on the stand. Then if I can't use her as a witness, what's the good in having found her? All we've accomplished is to make Camille feel miserable."

"I'll get over it Quincy. Maybe Emil's right: When this is over and her mother goes free…at least in Maine…Cecilia will forgive me. At least I hope so."

"I know I'm right, Camille. What we've got to do is convince Esther Dubrowski that her daughter's innocent and she can stop covering up for her. If we can do that, then finding Cecilia will have been worth the effort. As for Illinois, there may be hope on that front as well. I have asked my home office to make some inquiries, and I may have some good news in a day or two.

"In the meantime, I agree. Quincy, you'd best approach Cecilia on your own. While you're in Portland doing that, I need to meet with one of my associates."

"Where are you in finding out who 'Major F. Sharp' is?

"Don't worry about him, Quincy."

"I've got to worry about him; he's on Christmas's witness list."

"You needn't be concerned about him appearing as a witness. That's one subpoena that I'm pretty sure won't be served."

"How do you…" Adams paused, interrupted by the telephone.

As he started to lift the receiver Camille reached across the desk at took the instrument. "Quincy Adams Law Office. May I help you? I'm sorry, Mr. Adams is in with a client just now; may I take a message? Oh, certainly, can you hold a moment, I'll interrupt him." She put her hand over the mouthpiece.

"It's Judge Beauchamp's calendar clerk; she needs to talk with you immediately." She passed the instrument back to Adams.

"This is Quincy Adams." He listened for a moment. "Next Monday? But we weren't supposed to start jury select…and Judge Beauchamp hasn't ruled on our…Yes, ma'am. Pretrial conference on Friday, jury selection next Monday. Er…thank you for calling.

Adams put the receiver back in its cradle. "I assume you heard?"

"How come, Quincy? Do you think Christmas is behind it?"

"I don't think so, Emil. It's the judge's doing. He's concerned about this outbreak of influenza that's spreading this way from Massachusetts. Remember, there was something in the Portland paper in the last day or so. There have been outbreaks all over the East, and one was just reported at an Army training camp in Massachusetts, Camp Devens, and apparently some cases have been reported in Portsmouth. Judge doesn't want a courtroom full of people...especially jurors...coming down with it in the middle of trial so that he has to declare a mistrial."

"He's right to be concerned. From what little I've read, it's a right nasty bug. There have been several deaths reported, but I suspect they're mostly the elderly and those who are frail from some other illness. Still, it's not anything you'd want to catch."

"Well, I sure don't want to get it. Quincy, do you want me to go to Augusta and look at the contents of the envelope today?"

"It's probably a waste of time, Camille, but yeah, I think you'd best have a look at the envelope. And while you're there, check with the Sheriff's Office to see if they got all of our subpoenas served. It looks like Mr. Silas, Sheriff Dowdy, Smedley and Boyles will be our only witnesses. Our only witnesses other than our client and I don't think it'll be necessary to have her subpoenaed.

"And one more thing: If Deputy Isaacson is on duty, see if he can bend a couple of rules again. Tell him I'm bringing two people, in addition to myself, to see Mrs. Dubrowski tomorrow. I'd like for all three of us to meet with her, and I'd like to do it somewhere other than sitting on the floor in the cell block corridor.

"I guess there's one more thing: You'd better let him know, if he doesn't know already, that the trial date's been moved up. We may also need his help in serving new subpoenas. I'll have to stop at the clerk's office and get new ones issued. Maybe they'll let me bring them back with me if they can get them out before the end of the day. In fact, I think I'll drop by the judge's chambers and see if they can build a fire under the clerk's subpoena department, seeing as how needing new ones is on account of Judge Beauchamp.

"Let's meet back here in the morning. Camille, why don't you take my auto? I can take the train to Portland, do what I have to do and spend the night in Portland. I'll take the first train back here. Emil, will you check with your associate about the condition of Cory's automobile?"

"Wait just a minute, Mr. Adams. You can't go to Portland looking like you do. I'll take you to Mrs. Norman's so you can at least try to make yourself look presentable. Then I'll drop you at the station and head up to Augusta. While you're trying to get cleaned up I'll call my father and let him know I'm back from the wicked city and I'll be home in time to fix his dinner. I don't know if he was worried about me or was worried about missing his dinner two nights in a row. In either case I need to call him before he sets Billy and Fred—my brothers, Emil—on a rampage looking for me.

"Now, Camille…"

"Don't you 'now Camille' me, Mr. Flammonde. Go…go meet your associate. Come on, Mr. Adams or you'll miss the train."

Chapter Nineteen

Adams noted the gold leaf lettering "Berman & Berman" on the elegant-looking walnut double door to the firm's offices. Cecilia Durbin was again at the reception desk. "Good afternoon, Sir. May I help you?"

Adams recognized her from the descriptions supplied first by Flammonde and then corroborated by Camille's first-hand observation. But in keeping with the plan he'd worked out in his mind on the train down to Portland he replied, "Yes, please. I'd like to see Mr. Berman...Mr. Harrell Berman... if he can spare a few minutes."

"Whom shall I say..." Adams handed her his card. When she saw his name, she clasped her hand to her mouth and her eyes grew wide. She stared at her typewriter for nearly a minute. Finally, she laid the card down on her desk and turned to face him, her composure restored. "I assume, Mr. Adams, it's really me whom you wish to see. I've been expecting you for some time, alternately hoping that you would find me and at other times that you would not. Let me ask one of the other secretaries to take my place here, but it can be only for a few minutes. Then we can talk in the library, and if we need further conversation, it will have to be after I get off work at five o'clock.

In a couple of minutes she was back with another woman who gave Adams an unpleasant scowl and took Cecilia's place at the reception desk. "Thank you, Olive; we'll be just a few minutes. I really appreciate it. Mr. Adams, would you come this way, please?" She led him to the firm's law library which he noted with envy was nearly a match for Trout and Dickson's in Boston.

After they'd seated themselves at a small table that was relatively clear of books and note pads, Adams spoke first. "We've much to discuss, Miss Durbin, and I do not expect that we can conclude our business in a matter of minutes. Before coming here, I telephoned the synagogue and spoke with Mrs. Nachamovich. I asked her to make an appointment for me to see Rabbi Klein. I told her that I knew it was short notice, but the trial will be starting next Monday..."

"But I thought..."

"So did I, Miss Durbin, at least until earlier today. It seems that Judge Beauchamp has taken it upon himself to move up the trial date out of concern for the influenza...I believe it's called the 'Spanish Influenza'...outbreak that appears to be turning into a major epidemic and public health crisis of overwhelming proportion. Whether the epidemic will reach Southern Maine, of course no one can predict. But the judge doesn't want to take a chance on having a juror or witness come down with the disease causing a mistrial and infecting everyone else in the courtroom. In any case, Rabbi Klein has agreed to meet me in his study at five-thirty. I assumed that you'd prefer to wait until you'd gotten off from work, and I also assumed that Rabbi Klein's study would be a congenial environment for you, as well as for myself.

"If that is acceptable to you, I will leave you to your work and in the meantime, I will make a stop at the courthouse to get new subpoenas issued…and no, Miss Durbin, you are not on the witness list. Then I'm going to check into the Regency and perhaps have something to eat as I've not had an opportunity to do so yet today." Adams took a deep breath and then continued, "If you prefer, I could meet you at Miss Rosie's?"

"That offer is wholly unnecessary, Mr. Adams. If you found me at work, I must assume that you also know where I live. You needn't worry. I will not run out on you; I'll be at Rabbi Klein's study at five-thirty. And please, Mr. Adams, try not to insult my intelligence or threaten me again. You'll find me much more agreeable to be with and I expect much more amenable to whatever you have in mind for me." She stood, indicating the interview was over. Come, Mr. Adams, I'll see you out." She held out her hand, "Until five-thirty, Mr. Adams?"

Cecilia Durbin kept her word as Adams knew she would. Promptly at five-thirty Mrs. Nachamovich led them into the rabbi's study. He shook Adams's hand warmly and waited for Adams to introduce Cecilia Durbin. She extended her hand which Rabbi Klein took for a moment and indicated that they should be seated on the sofa. Mrs. Nachamovich had brought a pitcher of ice tea with three ice-filled glasses which she set on the coffee table.

"Thank you for making time for us, Rabbi Klein," Adams began.

"It is I who should be thanking you, Mr. Adams. First for bringing this charming young lady with you, an unexpected pleasure. Second, I welcome the interruption. I've been working on my sermon for *Rosh Hashanah*…the New Year according to the Hebrew calendar…and I find myself in my annual quandary: how to merge the teachings of *Torah* with the pace and complexity of life in the times in which we live. And how to do so in a fresh and meaningful way. But alas, this is what I chose to make my life's work, and by which means I earn my daily bread. So if God is listening, I'm not complaining.

"But what brings you here with…Miss Durbin, is it? I feel that I know you, Miss Durbin, but I cannot place you in my mind. You look familiar; but I don't think you're a member here."

"That's true, Rabbi Klein, I'm not a member but I do attend services from time to time."

"That you attend, Miss Durbin is all that matters. I'm especially glad to see young people taking an interest in their heritage. But why has Mr. Adams brought you? Do you have something to do with his case?"

"Yes, Rabbi Klein, Esther Dubrowski is my mother."

"*Ach, Gott in Himmel!* Esther is your mother? I should have known. Now I recognize you; you look just like her. There, Mr. Adams, there's another Yiddish expression for your glossary."

"Even I can figure that one out, Rabbi."

"So how can I be of help?"

"Let me explain, Rabbi, if I may. As I told you in our first meeting, I know just as certainly as I know my own name that Miss Durbin's mother is innocent of the charges against her. The question in my mind has always been: Why would she confess to a crime she didn't commit? The only reason has to be that she is protecting someone else, someone she cares about so much that she would spend the rest of her life in prison rather than let that person be endangered.

"Through much effort on the part of the persons assisting me…you recall that I am bound not to disclose their identity…"

"I'm sorry to interrupt, Mr. Adams, but is Camille Winters one of those persons?"

"Yes she is, Miss Durbin."

"I was afraid you'd say that. I was such a fool to have been taken in…"

"No you weren't Miss Durbin. Please let me tell the rest and perhaps your feelings will change. At least for your sake and for Camille's, next to seeing your mother free, that is my most fervent wish.

"Esther…Mrs. Dubrowski's reaction to being confronted with the brooch when she was on the witness stand at the coroner's inquest led me to think that she knew much more than she was willing to tell me. Indeed she made it clear that…thanks to Rabbi Klein's intervention…she would let me defend her, but she would not tell me anything to aid in her defense.

"So from the beginning I've been playing a game of blind man's bluff. I knew that the brooch must have something to do with the events at Oakdale Hall that night, so I made it my business to find the person for whom the brooch was intended. The fact that it is a piece of jewelry intended for a woman of course set me to looking for a woman. We knew that Mrs. Dubrowski sometimes attended services here, so I asked Rabbi Klein if he knew of anyone with whom Esther was friendly, thinking that a friend might be able to lead me to the 'brooch-woman' as we took to calling her.

"That proved to be a dead end. But as a result of my associate...not Camille... tracing the brooch to the jeweler who made it, we learned that it had been in the possession of a young woman matching your description. From the description we were given...and please don't ask me from whom we got the description...Camille came up with the idea that you might be a legal secretary. After that, it was simply a matter of visiting Portland law firms until we, that is, until Camille found you.

"We, Camille and I, had no idea that you were Esther's daughter. For all we knew, the woman for whom we were searching may have been in league with Richard Cory's murderer, or had even killed him herself. Of course as soon as Camille met you and got to know you, she dismissed that idea out of hand and convinced me to do so as well. This left but one possibility: That your mother mistakenly thought that you were somehow implicated so she was willing to do anything to protect you.

"We knew from your mother's testimony at the inquest that she had a daughter who would be about your age, but she'd told the coroner's jury that you and she were estranged. It was another of my colleagues who finally put things together and hit upon the truth. That happened only this morning and as a result, here we are.

"I should add that Camille, while she understands that you would be angry with her, is devastated by the idea of losing you as a friend. She was only doing what she did in the interest of defending your mother. She hopes that you will not let the way you met stand as an obstacle to your friendship. I would like to contribute my own opinion on that subject if you'll allow me to do so."

"Go ahead, Mr. Adams, it will do me no harm to listen." Cecilia picked up her glass of ice tea and took a sip.

"Two things come to mind: First, practicing any deception is wholly contrary to Camille's nature, and..."

"She certainly had me deceived, Mr. Adams. Is she really a legal secretary? Is anything she told me about herself true?"

"Yes, she's been my part-time secretary almost as long as I've been in practice in Tilbury Town. My law practice, at least until your mother's case came along, did not require the services of a full-time secretary. My office is located over the restaurant where Camille works when she's not helping me, so it's convenient for her. As to whatever else she may have told you, I leave it to you and Camille to sort out the facts from the fiction."

"Was there something else you wanted to say?"

"Only this: Camille's mother passed away when Camille was very young. She was raised by her father and four brothers. So she's been deprived of the companionship of a sister or close female cousin. There are very few young women in Tilbury Town that share Camille's interests or can match her intelligence. That's why she was immediately taken with you."

"He makes a persuasive case, Miss Durbin...may I call you 'Cecilia?'"

"Yes, of course Rabbi Klein. You too, Mr. Adams."

"What do you prefer, Miss Durbin? Camille told me that Mr. Berman calls you 'Miss Durbin.' Camille liked that because it shows that Mr. Berman has respect for all his people, support staff as well as lawyers. In fact, until this case, Camille and I were on a 'Mr. Adams' and 'Miss Winters' basis."

"Cecilia suits me fine. I'm satisfied, at least so far, that I'm not being patronized. Putting amenities aside, now that you've found me, what do you propose to do with me?"

"That depends on your answers to a few questions that I need to ask you."

"Well, then you'd best ask them and I will answer if I can."

"First, why did you not come forward as soon as your mother was arrested?"

"I suppose at least in that respect I'm also guilty of deceiving Camille as well as she is guilty of deceiving me. I told her that my father was dead and my mother had abandoned me when I was very young. I'd been taken in by a family in Boston. That's all true, except of course the part about my mother abandoning me.

"That night...when my mother finally shot my father...I assume you heard her testimony at the inquest. She said she took me and ran next door to the neighbor. As I remember it, that's what happened. When the police came and took her away, I stayed with the neighbor until my mother's trial. The neighbor, Mrs. Taub...I called her 'Aunt Pessie.' I'm sure as I think back her name was probably 'Bessie,' but as often happens with young children 'B' sounded to me like 'P' so she was my 'Aunt Pessie.' Anyway, Aunt Pessie begged my mother many times before the trial to let me tell what happened that night and maybe my mother wouldn't have to go to prison at all. But my mother refused. In part, she was too ashamed for people to know what a disgusting monster my father really was. But I think her overriding concern was that if I came forward and she had to go to prison anyway, I'd be taken away and put in an orphanage or sent to a foster home where the people would only care about the money the state would pay them to keep me.

"When my mother was convicted, she begged Aunt Pessie to find a good Jewish home for me, in a place as far from Chicago as she could find. She said I must get a new name and forget about her. As it happened, Aunt Pessie had a younger sister in Boston. She is married to a high school teacher. They are childless themselves, so they readily offered to take me in. They even came to Chicago so I could meet them in a place where I would feel comfortable and so that I would not have to take the train all the way to Boston by myself or in the company of someone I did not already know. They were so kind that I took to them almost immediately, so they took me back to Boston and raised me as their own."

"They are also named 'Durbin'?" Rabbi Klein asked.

"No, 'Durbin' is just a made-up name. It's close enough to 'Dubrowski' that I would always remember my mother's name…as though I could somehow forget. They did not adopt me because they, like me, hoped that my mother would be released from prison someday, and also out of concern that some busy-body child-welfare worker would start asking too many questions if they filed the papers for adoption. So since then and even now, I'm Cecilia Durbin. I will not bore you with the details of my up-bringing as I'm sure that Miss Winters…okay, Camille…has reported what I told her, all of which is true.

"When I was old enough to better understand what had happened to my parents, my mother began writing to me. She did not write to me directly because the prison officials censor all inmate mail except correspondence to or from a lawyer and she did not want anyone to learn my whereabouts. So she did what all prison inmates learn to do: She smuggled letters out either through other inmates being released or through visitors. I believe they refer to the practice as 'kiting', you know, like flying a kite. I could not write her back, but I would write to Aunt Pessie, and sometimes send my report cards or drawings I made in school. Aunt Pessie would visit my mother whenever she could and let my mother see the letters and other things. I even sent her a few of my school pictures. So in that way I maintained at least a tenuous relationship with my mother, neither of us ever giving up hope that we'd be re-united some day.

"As you know, my mother was granted parole after ten years. I was at the time still in high school. I went to The Girls' Latin School, the females-only equivalent of The Boston Latin School which is for boys only. Girls' Latin is just as rigorous academically as Boston Latin, so I couldn't miss school to go to her. So she came to Boston. She knew she was violating the terms of her parole, but she wanted to be with me so badly that she was willing to take the risk. And of course I wanted to be with her. But had I known the risk she was taking, I would have gone to her or waited until the Christmas holiday and gone then.

"She was required to report to her parole officer only bi-weekly, so she left the same day of her first or second parole office visit, thinking that she could come to Boston and we could be together for at least a few days. She assumed that she could make it back to Chicago well before her next scheduled visit to the parole office. She was warned that parole officers sometimes made surprise visits to a parolee's home or workplace, but through the prison grape-vine she also knew that the chances were small that she'd be subject to a visit if she were gone for only a few days.

"Of course what was a small chance turned into a one hundred percent chance. The day before she was to leave Boston, Aunt Pessie sent a telegram warning Mother that the parole officer had come looking for her. Mother had given Aunt Pessie as her next-of-kin although as far as I know we're not related. The parole officer was very angry, so Aunt Pessie said, because mother was not at work as she should have been. She had gotten a job as a maid at the Morrison Hotel. Anyway, Aunt Pessie said to the parole officer that perhaps Mother was sick. 'No', the parole officer said. He'd also tried her apartment but she wasn't there either. Aunt Pessie said, 'Maybe she…Mother…had gone to the doctor or out to the drug store to buy medicine.' But the parole officer was having none of it. He swore he'd find her and she'd be on the next bus back to prison just like…" Cecilia snapped her fingers sharply…"that.

"So Mother couldn't go back to Chicago, and staying in Boston was a risk as well. A paroled murderess…her description and photograph would be sent to every major city in the country. So there Mother was: Sitting in Boston, a wanted fugitive, relying on the kindness of two people who were strangers to her and who would be at risk should she be captured.

"When she'd been in Boston for about a month, she began trying to figure out a way to get back to Poland without a passport. With the war on, I have no idea how she would manage the trip, even with a genuine passport. She was reading the newspaper one morning...she learned to read and write English while in prison...and saw an advertisement for a housekeeper to live some place in Maine, Tilbury Town. It was so small and out-of-the-way, you could hardly find it on a map. She saw it as a solution to our problem. So she applied for the job. She remembered the reference letter they'd given her when she left the prison, but of course the original was in the personnel manager's office of the Morrison Hotel in Chicago."

"And she could hardly write and ask for another one?" Adams asked.

Cecilia smiled at that and took a long sip of tea. "My foster father knew a small-job printer who for a fee would print anything you wanted except U.S. currency. So Mother had a letter-head made up to look like the genuine thing. She remembered the wording of the letter, or at least near enough so that an English teacher could word it in what read like proper official language such that a bureaucrat would use.

"The letter did its job and Mother was hired by Richard Cory to be his live-in housekeeper. It's a good thing," Cecilia paused, took out a handkerchief from her hand-bag and dabbed her eyes, "or at least it was a good thing that Richard...I mean Mr. Cory...did not decide to check out her reference letter. Now I wish he had and I would not be sitting here nor would Mother sitting in the jail in Augusta."

"Perhaps some good will come of it yet, Cecilia."

"Thank you, Rabbi Klein. I hope you're right. But to cut short a long story, Mr. Adams, as soon as Mother was arrested, I made plans to go to her. But, as mothers do, she read my mind. She was able to kite a letter out of the jail. In the letter she said she would refuse to see me if I tried to visit her. She begged me to leave my job and go back to Boston, or to New York, or anyplace else that was not in Maine.

"I didn't know what to do. When I read the account of her confession in the newspaper, I must admit that for a brief moment even I considered the possibility that the confession was true. I knew of you from the newspaper stories, and while you have no reason to believe me, I'm telling you the truth: I thought many times about contacting you. But again, to be perfectly frank, I didn't know anything about you: What kind of lawyer you are...good or bad...whether Mother'd hired you or you were appointed by the judge, or whether you'd just taken the case for the publicity. Also, I had no idea…it honestly never occurred to me…that Mother might have thought that I killed Richard…Cory.

"I also thought about coming to consult you, Rabbi Klein. What would you have told me to do?"

Rabbi Klein stroked his chin for a few moments. "Back in the old country, Poland, Russia…in the ghettos and the *shtetls*…," he turned to Adams, "the ghettos are the Jewish quarters in the cities. *Shtetls* are the small villages. We did not have courts like in America. Even the *goyim*…the gentiles did not have courts. When they had a dispute they settled it with knives and clubs. When it was settled they'd embrace, get drunk and go out and find a Jew or two to beat up.

"Among the Jews it was an unwritten law: Don't bother the police or the bureaucrats and perhaps they won't bother us so much. And Jews, they fight among themselves just as much as their gentile neighbors, only with words, not knives and clubs. So in the ghettos and *shtetls* when there was a dispute between two merchants, or between family members, or when anyone had a problem they couldn't work out, it was to the *rebbe*…the rabbi…they would come to give them advice or to resolve the dispute.

"The rabbi would stroke his chin, or put his clasped hands to his forehead…whatever gesture he used to make it appear that he was in deep concentration or calling upon God for guidance…and finally after a good while he would speak. Sometimes, when the answer was an obvious one, he would give a straight-forward answer. But often, when the matter brought before him was truly complex or especially vexing, or if he just happened to be in an irascible mood, he would mutter some arcane passage from the *Torah,* or some inscrutable parable or aphorism from the commentaries or other texts. The contentious parties would nod their heads in understanding and either shake hands or embrace and then go off and solve the problem themselves rather than admit that neither had the slightest idea of what the *rebbe* was advising them.

"This is perhaps the greatest wisdom a rabbi can have: The ability to get people to figure out for themselves the answers to life's questions be they every-day ones or matters of the utmost importance. And that is what I must do in this matter, Cecilia. That you have struggled with this problem says that you are both a loving daughter and a keenly intelligent woman. These are not mutually exclusive."

"You asked Rabbi Klein not me, Cecilia, but may I venture an opinion?"

"I don't..."

"You should hear what he has to say, Cecilia. Perhaps lawyers are the sages, the wise men, of today. Perhaps Mr. Adams knows of some statute or precedent that he can call to mind and which will help you decide what is the right thing to do."

"Okay, Mr. Adams, what should I do?"

"You should come with me tomorrow to see your mother. Rabbi Klein, can I prevail upon you to come as well? Mrs. Dubrowski trusts you, and if you endorse my strategy, she will perhaps go along with it."

"Without knowing your strategy, I am reluctant to make such a commitment."

"I don't know whether Mr. Adams is allowed to make such a disclosure, Cecilia."

"In normal circumstances, I would not, Rabbi Klein. But in the present case, without the cooperation of you both, I have no strategy worthy of the name. My problem is the so-called 'confession' or to use your term 'statement.' If I can keep it out of evidence, the only other evidence is circumstantial and is so weak that the judge would have to instruct the jury to return a 'not guilty' verdict."

"You mean the judge can tell the jury to do that? Can he also tell them they must find the defendant guilty? That doesn't seem right; I thought it was up to the jury."

"Yes and no, Rabbi Klein. If the evidence is so weak that no rational jury could find the defendant guilty based on such evidence, then it is the duty of the court to tell the jury they must acquit. But at least in this country a judge cannot tell the jury they must convict. In England the judges have much more discretion to comment on the weight of the evidence so that as a practical matter they can almost tell the jury which way to find."

"What if the judge refuses to tell the jury to acquit?"

"That's why we have appellate courts: To make sure the trial judge gets it right. If he doesn't, the appeals court can itself do what the trial judge should have done, or in some circumstances the appellate court will send the case back for a new trial. However, sometimes the appellate courts make mistakes as well. That's why any lawsuit, civil or criminal, is always an uncertainty.

"An experienced lawyer knows this and will almost always suggest that his client at least consider settlement. In a civil case, accepting less money or paying more money, depending on which side you're on. In a criminal case, it means that the defendant will make a plea bargain, either plead guilty to a lesser offense, or agree to a reduced sentence. From the state's standpoint, unless it's a particularly egregious offense or a sensational case...such as *State v Dubrowski*...the prosecutor will welcome a plea bargain in order to move the case. If they had to try every case, they'd have to increase their staffs ten-fold and populous counties would have to add many more courts and judges just to keep up with the backlog."

"So there's no chance of a plea agreement in this case, Quincy?"

"I doubt it. Reverend Christmas rarely does plea bargains. He would not have come into the case other than to try it."

"But what is your strategy, Quincy. How will you keep the confession...statement... out of evidence? And how can we, Rabbi Klein and I, help with that?"

"I don't need you to help me keep it out, I need your help in the event it is allowed in. And frankly, I cannot think of any reason to keep it out."

What do you mean you cannot think of a reason?" Cecilia stood, angry at Quincy's apparent fecklessness. "Isn't the fact that it's a total fabrication by a frightened, helpless woman, enough reason to keep it out?"

"No, it's..."

"Cecilia, sit please. Quincy's here for our help, not our criticism. I think I see his quandary: If the jury hears your mother's statement, then they will be inclined to believe it unless she herself repudiates it and they understand why she said it in the first place. So she must testify and tell the jury why she confessed.

"Exactly, Rabbi Klein. Incidentally, I like your word 'statement' much better than I do 'confession'. Cecilia, we must convince your mother to tell the truth...why she said she shot Richard Cory when in fact she did not."

"Yes, but didn't she make the *statement* under oath? If she recants, won't she then be charged with perjury?"

"A possibility, but I doubt that Reverend Christmas will wish to see your mother at the defense table again. And Bascom Pommus won't have the stomach for it either."

"And what about me? Will Reverend Christmas not want to have a crack at me? After all, even my mother thought that I'd killed Richard Cory and surely someone must pay for such a terrible crime."

Adams made note of the sarcastic tone of Cecilia's characterization of Richard Cory's death as a 'terrible crime.' "Not if you can account for your whereabouts that night and early morning."

"That will be easy. I along with three other girls who live at Miss Rosie's took our bathing costumes and a picnic lunch and went to Peak's Island. We spent the day and as it turned out, the entire night on the island. They had a band and a dance pavilion so we stayed and danced and flirted with the boys until we missed the last ferry back to Portland. We took a room at the inn and took the first boat back the next morning.

"All three girls still live at Miss Rosie's so they will tell you I'm telling the truth. Also, one of the other girls knew one or two of the men; at least she acted like she did. So maybe you can find the men as well. One of the other girls may still have the hotel bill which we all chipped in our share to pay."

"So if your mother's convinced that you had nothing to do with Richard Cory's death, she will recant her statement…you see Rabbi Klein, now I am using your words."

"So she recants, Mr. Adams. What if the jury doesn't believe her recantation?"

"A fair question, Rabbi Klein. Perhaps you should do like Reverend Christmas: Give up your pulpit for a seat at the counsel table. It's a risk we must take. If the statement is admitted into evidence and we do nothing, she will be convicted no matter what else we do.

"I am going to try to at least raise the question of whether Richard Cory died by his own hand. The sheriff, Sheriff Dowdy, believes that to be the case and he is under subpoena to testify. If there's a doubt as to whether Richard Cory was murdered or took his own life, then the jury should acquit, although with the doctor's opinion that it wasn't suicide I don't think that the judge will instruct them to do so.

"My other tactic is to show that others may have had a motive to want Richard Cory dead."

"May I ask who?"

"I can't reveal that at the moment, Cecilia. But trust me; I have a couple of candidates in mind.

"So now do you understand why I want you to come with me tomorrow? Both of you?"

"Cecilia, this must be your choice. You must do what you think best, and I will follow your lead."

"Then we must go, Rabbi Klein. If there's even the smallest chance we can persuade Mother, we must take it. But I have one more question, Quincy: Even if Mother is acquitted, what will happen with Illinois? Won't she have to go back to finish her sentence? Then I too will have to go back to Illinois so that I can visit her as often as they will allow."

"All I can tell you at the moment is that we must deal with one problem at a time. One of my colleagues has undertaken to deal with Illinois. I frankly don't know what he's trying to do, but he told me this morning that he expects to have news by Thursday or Friday. So you'll come?"

"Yes, Quincy, we'll come."

"Can you be on the first train?"

"No, I will have to go in to work first and explain that I must take off the next couple of days to deal with a family emergency. And if Mr. Berman wants to know more, I will tell him the truth. I'm thoroughly sick of living a life of lies."

"Then we will take the mid-morning train and meet you at the jail."

"I'd rather you come to Tilbury Town, Rabbi Klein. I will meet you at the station and we can drive to Augusta in my automobile. It's a short trip as you know. The reason is that the arrangements at the jail are a bit complicated, and I want to be sure that everything's set before we get there. Also, it will give us a little more time to talk before we go in. There are a few more questions I want to ask you. In fact, Cecilia, would you care to have dinner?"You as well, Rabbi Klein."

"I..I..."

"You should go Cecilia. This is advice I can give with confidence. It will give you more of an opportunity to observe Mr. Adams and make up your own mind about him."

Won't you join us, Rabbi?"

"No, Cecilia, just the two of you should go. Besides, I've still got a sermon to finish. Indeed, since I'm going to be traveling tomorrow, I'd best try to get it finished tonight.

Chapter Twenty

Adams suggested that Cecilia pick the restaurant. She led him to a small restaurant on Fore Street that served Italian food, a passion they shared from living in Boston where the North End abounds in the cuisine native to the various regions of Italy. Adams was impressed when the proprietor greeted Cecilia with a hand-kiss and a *"Buonasera, Signorina Durbin!"* After a short wait, they were seated in a small booth. The table was covered with the requisite red and white checked tablecloth and decorated with a candle stuffed in the neck of a wicker-encased wine bottle with old wax dripping down the sides.

"Perhaps a cocktail before you order, *Signore*?"

Adams looked at Cecilia who answered for them. "No, Arturo, *grazie*; this is a business dinner."

"But *la Signorina* will at least have a bottle of *vino*?"

"Absolutely, Arturo." What is it they say: 'A day without *vino* is a day without sunshine'? Please, do you have a wine list?"

"Never mind, Quincy," Cecilia allowed herself a small smile which immediately reminded Quincy of Esther's smile as she was being led away from the courtroom after the O'Brien twins' escape from custody. "How's the *cannelloni* tonight, Arturo?"

"Squisito, Signorina, molto lodato!"

"Buonissimo, Arturo. *Cannelloni per due.* And bring a bottle of the Barolo Riserva if you have it."

"Si, Signorina; immediatamente!

"Did you just order dinner and wine?"

" I do hope you like cannelloni, Quincy."

" I guess I've been away from Boston longer than I thought. I think this is the first time I've been to a restaurant with a woman and she did the ordering."

"It's not as though we're on a date. If you want to go Dutch, that's fine with me."

"No, no. I invited you."

In a minute or two the wine appeared along with a small antipasto platter. Cecilia tasted the wine, somewhat to the amusement of Arturo, and declared it drinkable. Arturo poured a generous portion into each of the glasses, wiped the neck of the bottle and left it on the table. Quincy immediately began to transfer a sampling of everything on the antipasto platter to his small plate. Realizing that he was being rude, he stopped his fork in mid-air. "I'm sorry, please excuse my bad manners. After I left your office, I never did get to eat as I said I would. It took forever to get the subpoenas reissued in the clerk's office."

"Please go ahead. I know what you mean. Dealing with court clerks is by far the most frustrating part of my job. I'd rather type a twenty-page brief with six carbons than deal with a court clerk. Is it the same in Kennebec County?

"Once they get to know you, and if you don't ask them to do anything too taxing, I suppose they're okay. You probably ought to ask Camille...Oh, sorry, you're angry with Camille. Well, I'll ask her for you..."

"Let it be, Quincy. Camille and I will work things out or we won't. I've got a lot of thinking to do as I imagine Camille does. You've given me your opinion, now it's up to me...or I should say Camille and me."

"That would be my preference. It seems that I have a talent for making both of you angry at me. Do you mind if I ask some of my other questions?"

"Are you going to spoil my dinner?"

Quincy finished downing an *involtini de asparagi e pancetta* he'd been eating and took a sip of wine. "Probably. Good wine by the way. What's the cheese?" Quincy cut off a sizable piece and downed it. "Hmm, cheese is good too."

Cecilia helped herself to what remained of the cheese. "It's taleggio, I expect." She followed the cheese with a sip of wine. "Well, if I have to sing for my supper, let's get on with it."

"Some of my questions are going to be pretty nosy, I hope you..."

"You want to know about my relationship with Richard Cory, I assume."

"How and when did you meet?"

"At Berman & Berman almost two years ago. He came in to sign his will."

"And he asked you out?"

"Not right away, but a few weeks later. I didn't know whether to accept. I have never dated any of the lawyers in the office, but I wasn't sure about dating a client. The few who have asked me out all had the same skin disease."

"Skin disease?"

"You know that patch of pale skin where a wedding band

normally goes. Anyway, I asked Mr. Berman whether I should go out with Richard Cory. He neither encouraged nor discouraged me, saying only that my personal life was my personal life."

"I take it that you eventually accepted. What'd your mother say?"

"I didn't let Mother know, at least at first. I was sure she'd be dead-set against it."

"So why'd you finally stop saying 'no?'"

"I admit that I found Richard attractive. I assume that you knew him in Tilbury Town. I mean he was good-looking; he dressed well and when he spoke he sounded educated. Someone, one of the girls in the office as I recall, said he'd lived abroad which meant that he could probably talk about something other than this year's lobster harvest, the weather and the Boston Red Sox. He obviously had money, enough for Berman & Berman to prepare his will. But that wasn't, I assure you, as important to me as the other things; although it wasn't a draw-back either. Lastly, no one seemed to know whether his money was inherited, or he was in some business or other. That made him something of an enigma, a man-of-mystery, so to speak."

"That's disappointing. I…"

"What's disappointing? The *salumi*? It's home made. Arturo's mother will be devastated."

Quincy allowed himself a moment of satisfaction. Evidently Cecilia's icy reserve had melted enough for her to try a little humor. "No, no. The sausage is fine; a bit salty, but that's okay. What's disappointing is that you know nothing about Cory's financial affairs. One of my…my investigators has been trying every legal means — and even some dubious ones — to find out the source of Richard Cory's wealth, so far without success.

"Someone murdered Richard Cory, someone who was familiar with Oakdale Hall. Since it wasn't your mother or you, maybe it was someone with a business grudge…someone who thought, rightly or wrongly, that he'd been cheated by Richard Cory."

"You just said something that makes me curious. May I ask you a question?"

"And spoil my dinner as well as your own? I suppose; 'what's good for the goose…'"

"You said 'one of your investigators' has been trying to get a line on Richard's apparent wealth. Just how many investigators do you have, Quincy, and who's paying them? I know Mother's been pretty frugal and has managed to save most of her salary, but if you were not court-appointed and did not take Mother's case *pro bono*, she'd have been out of money long before now. So someone, other than Mother, has got a lot of money tied up in Mother's defense. I want to know who and why."

"I know part of the who but none of the why. The part of the who that I know is that he's a gentleman, although the two of his associates that I know about both have, shall I say, 'interesting' backgrounds. He tells me that he's in the business opportunity business which I gather has something to do with mergers and acquisitions. Apparently his firm has very deep pockets and he's not been reticent about dipping into them.

"He won't tell me his real interest in the case, other than he was in the process of checking Richard Cory out. I assume he was looking at Cory either as a potential investor or as an acquisition target when Cory was killed.

"Cecilia, I know it sounds bizarre, but he sought me out and he's the one who convinced me that your mother's innocent. He hired me and has paid me well. He's a lawyer by training, but does not practice. But even without his ever-ready wallet, he's been a great help just by acting more or less as my co-counsel. Apparently, he's tried quite a few cases, so his advice has been invaluable. Other than what Camille has done, most of the investigative work's been done by him or his associates. He's also paying Camille's salary. If not for him, your mother would have had a drunken stumble-bum court-appointed lawyer and by now she'd be starting to spend the rest of her life in prison.

"He's asked me to trust him, and I have. So far he's been true to his word, and I have no reason to think that he'll betray us in the end. I'm sure that's a less-than-illuminating explanation, but it's absolutely all that I know. I understand that you're uncomfortable; truthfully, so am I. But here we are; I've taken the king's shilling so to speak, and you must as well."

"When do I get to meet this benefactor?"

"Hopefully tomorrow, but it's up to him. He's very shy about meeting people. I'll do my best."

The arrival of the entrees gave Cecilia time to mull over what Quincy had told her. After they'd all but finished eating, Cecilia emptied her wine glass and asked, "Did he say why he hired you? Why didn't he bring in some luminary of the criminal defense bar, from Portland or even from Boston?"

"I suppose my feelings should be hurt, but it's a fair question.

Indeed I asked it myself, only to get another evasive answer. I suppose he has his reasons; perhaps one of them is that he thought a local lawyer'd be better than bringing in an outsider. Sometimes that can make a negative impression on a jury. Besides, don't you think I've done a good job so far?"

"Well, you did get a change of venue, although that rather ends your usefulness as a local lawyer. And at least you have a plan to counteract the confession…or I guess I should say 'statement'…even if your plan's a pretty shaky one. And most important of all, you did persuade Mother to let you defend her. I suppose we'll see how good you are come Monday."

"Thanks for the rousing vote of confidence, Cecilia." Adams followed suit and drained his wine glass as well. "Do you think I can handle the rest of the story of your romance with Richard Cory?"

"I suppose I deserved that, Quincy. I'm sorry I've been such a…" she lowered her voice"…bitch…since I met you. Rabbi Klein clearly thinks you're a good person and a good lawyer, and so far you've given me no reason to think otherwise. I suppose if I had a choice, I'd rather you were less a good person and more of a good lawyer."

"Do you think the two are mutually exclusive?"

"No, Quincy, I spend every day around lawyers, remember? Mother's fortunate to have you…and I suppose your associates as well.

"To continue," she paused as Arturo came to clear the entree plates. "Arturo, the cannelloni was *bellissimo,* just as you promised. Could you bring me a cappuccino? Quincy?"

"Yes, I'll have coffee, please."

"To continue," She began again, "He sent flowers, both to the office and to Miss Rosie's, and everyone kept asking 'Who's your new beau?' 'When do we get to meet him?' 'Is he from Portland?' And so on. You know how gossipy women can be." Adams let that last comment pass without reply.

"So I finally said 'yes.' He called for me in his Packard. You can imagine the scene: He parks at the curb and gets out of this enormous automobile. I was praying that he didn't have a chauffeur. When he came to the door, I thought every girl at Miss Rosie's was going to fall out of the windows staring at the car and trying to get a look at Richard. He took me to dinner at the Black Point Inn in Scarborough. I had a wonderful time and he was a perfect gentleman.

"How often would he ask you out?"

"More times than I accepted. As I think back on it, at first he'd call two, three times a week. But I wanted to take things slow. He could talk about all kinds of things: The arts and literature, politics, places in Europe that he'd been; he'd even been to the Orient and to Egypt, at least he said he had. He talked about everything but himself, which in my experience is unique for a man trying to impress a woman on a date. Also, he hardly asked anything about me. Of course if he had, I'd have told him my poor-little-orphan story and left it at that. I suppose that his reticence to talk about himself must have made me leery. It wasn't a conscious reaction, just woman's intuition.

"I tried to draw him out more about himself; at that time I was really becoming attracted to him. But he'd always laugh it off or change the subject with a story about some exotic place or another. He was a veritable Baron Munchhausen." Adams took a sip of coffee and tried not to look impressed.

"After a few months, things began to taper off a little. Instead of calling me two or three times a week, it was more like once a week and there were a couple of weeks when he didn't call at all."

"Did you wonder about that? Did you think he might have been seeing someone else?"

"To be honest, yes. I mean what girl wouldn't want to know if she had a rival? I asked him once or twice; he'd laugh and call me 'silly girl,' which of course made me want to claw his eyes out. All he'd say when I pressed him...a tear or two would usually do the job...he said that he'd been away on business, or on a hunting trip, or some other equally vague answer."

"Did you believe him? Do you think he was seeing someone else?"

"I honestly don't know. If I had to guess, I'd say he probably was. I do know that I didn't believe his gone-a-hunting story. The one time I was at Oakdale Hall, I didn't see any hunting trophies, or a gun case or anything else that you'd expect to see in a wealthy sporting hunter's home."

"So you've been to Oakdale Hall. I want to know about that, but let's finish the subject of other romantic interests first. How about you? Were you seeing anyone else?"

"I had a few dates, but no one serious. After all, I didn't want Richard to think that I just sat around waiting for him to call. I've learned that it doesn't take much for a man to start taking you for granted."

"Then there was no one..."

"That would have been jealous of Richard on account of me?

Jealous enough to kill Richard?

"I had maybe half a dozen men that asked me out and who didn't have the skin disease I mentioned earlier. Two of them have moved on to other conquests; I'm still occasionally dating a couple and the other two have become friends. I see them for lunch or perhaps for a drink, or a group of us might go to the beach for a clam-bake. I can't imagine any of them wanting to do away with Richard over my affections."

Adams thought, "The heck you can't, Cecilia."

"All the same, do you mind giving me their names tomorrow? I'd like to have them checked out…discreetly or course."

"Isn't it a bit late to be hunting for red herrings, Quincy? I thought you said that you already had a couple of other burnt offerings to lay on the altar of reasonable doubt."

"That's a pretty sophisticated metaphor; or is it an analogy?"

"Metaphor, I think. That's the problem with working with lawyers: You stay around them long enough and you start to think and sound like one."

"I suppose you're right…I mean about the timing. But I didn't realize that my zeal in representing your mother would be offensive…"

Cecilia reached across the table and put her hand over his. "Quincy, Quincy, don't act like a little boy who's just been scolded for being a little boy. Please, you've been cross-examining me all evening about my love life, not to mention my life in general. Can't I have my peevish moment now and then?" She gave him her best Mona Lisa smile and slowly took back her hand.

Now Quincy reached across the table and took both of her hands in his. "You can, but this time it's me who was being peevish." He looked at his hands covering hers as though his hands had acted on their own with no guidance from his conscious mind. He withdrew his right hand and made a pouring motion in Arturo's direction indicating that they were ready for coffee refills. "I'm afraid I've still got two or three voyeuristic-type questions to ask. But first, how about a small grappa?" Cecilia nodded and extricated her hands.

"*Favore, Arturo due grappa.*"

"*Si, Signorina, due grappa, presto.*"

"Tell me about your trip to Oakdale Hall. When was it?"

"First Saturday in May. I was of course interested in seeing the place, and the only reason I kept putting him off was I wasn't yet ready to face Mother. Finally, I got up enough nerve. Mother had told Richard early on that she is Jewish and that she wanted to attend worship services from time to time. She asked if she could have those Friday afternoons and Saturday mornings off.

"She told Richard that she had friends who belonged to the synagogue who would let her stay with them overnight and that she'd take the train back mid-morning on Saturday. I would meet her train in Portland and we'd have dinner together, go to services and then she'd come back with me to Miss Rosie's. Miss Rosie has an overnight guest room which was usually available and she'd let Mother have it at a very reasonable price, much less than what a decent hotel would have cost.

"I have to say that Richard was nice about it; in fact I'm pretty sure he treated Mother quite well. There were a few times when he had some dinner or other event planned at Oakdale Hall, but those times I would wait for her at the station and if she didn't show up, I knew she had to stay and look after the arrangements for whatever it was that Richard was having that weekend. Usually she'd make it the next week.

"Anyway, I told her that Friday night that I'd been dating Richard for a while and that he'd invited me to visit."

"And her reaction?"

"Was about what I expected; she was furious. First, she was angry that I was 'having an affair' as she put it with an older man, and a *goy*…a gentile. Second…

"Were you?"

"Was I what?"

"Having an affair."

"That, Mr. Adams, is none of your business. What do you take me for…a…?

"I'm sorry, Cecilia, I know the question's way out of line, but you can be sure that Christmas will have no compunctions about asking it. I'm really sorry, but I thought I had to ask. Do you want to leave now? Should I have Arturo call a taxi?"

"No, no and no. No I don't want to leave; no don't call a taxi; and no, I wasn't 'having an affair' if by that you mean was I *shtupping* …having sexual relations…with Richard.

"I consider myself a modern woman, but not quite that modern. Sure, when we were alone together and his hands would sometimes go where perhaps they shouldn't, was I perhaps slower than a proper young lady should have been in removing them? Yes; to that I plead guilty."

"For what it's worth, I have no difficulty in believing you,

Cecilia." Adams continued studying his fingernails lest his facial expression betray his skepticism. "So give me the rest of the story of your visit to Oakdale Hall."

"As I say, Mother was furious. She wanted me to have nothing to do with Richard for all the reasons you can imagine: He wasn't Jewish; he was older than me, although not *that* old; she was afraid that he'd find out she is my mother; nice girls don't spend the weekend in a country house with a single man and no chaperone; and last but by no means least, I think that Mother felt that something was not quite right about him. She never said so in so many words, except she did ask me what I knew about him."

"I still want to hear the rest, and there are a couple more questions I need to ask. It looks like we're the last customers; do you think we should leave?"

"No, it's okay. I've closed the place up before, Arturo won't mind. He's still got to supervise cleaning up, and when he's ready to lock up, he'll let me know."

"With Richard?"

"With Richard what?"

"Did you and Richard close the place up?"

"No, that's why I brought you here. He came one time and hated it. Said there was too much garlic and not enough pork in the sauce *Bolognese*.

"To get back to Oakdale Hall: Richard picked me up a little before noon on that Saturday and we drove back to Oakdale Hall. He introduced me to his housekeeper…I forget her name." Cecilia pouted her lips a little when Adams didn't react to her humor. "She had prepared a nice luncheon…chicken salad as I recall…which we ate *al fresco* on the terrace. Then he said he'd like to show me the grounds…on horseback. Of course I made the obvious objection that I hadn't brought a suitable costume for horseback riding and he said not to worry about that. He'd taken the liberty of purchasing a riding habit just for me and it was awaiting me in my room.

I have to admit I was impressed. He'd ordered everything: riding boots, skirt, ruffled blouse, velvet jacket and one of those silly-looking helmets…all from Bergdorf Goodman in New York no less. And it all fit perfectly."

"I don't know the store, but I assume it is expensive. I wonder what he'd have done if you'd said 'no'?"

"I'm sure Richard would have found someone else to dress up in them."

"Are you a horsewoman?"

"I'd never been on a horse before that day unless you count a pony ride at a carnival I was taken to outside Revere the first year I came to live in Boston. And I haven't been on one since."

"But you rode anyway?"

"Yes, between Richard and Deaf Silas, they managed to get me on the beast's back more or less where I was supposed to be. And off we went. We must have ridden for more than two hours, because the sun was going down when we got back. It seemed to me more like two days; my…"she lowered her voice even though no one else was in the dining room…"back-side was sore for a week."

"I can only imagine how you must have enjoyed sitting at your desk at work that week.

"What were the grounds like? I've seen the inside of the mansion, but not the estate grounds."

"Richard was a gentleman farmer. Probably at one time Oakdale was a working farm, but from what I could see there was only an acre or so planted in vegetables, a few acres in a row crop; I think it was corn. It was pretty early in the season to tell, and I didn't ask. And there was an acre at most of sunflowers. The rest of the land was a mixture of timber and pasture, and there is an abandoned quarry. There were several field roads probably cut for hauling timber from the woods and stone from the quarry."

"For a city girl you seem to know a great deal about farms and farming."

"The firm has a large real estate practice so my typing includes lots of contracts, deeds, leases…you know, the same stuff you deal with on a daily basis. When my work-load permits, I like to actually read what I've typed. And when I don't understand something, the lawyers are really nice about explaining it. So while I don't pitch hay or weed the vegetable garden, I have learned a good deal about land use in Maine.

"Did you spend the night?"

"In May?"

"You said you'd been there but once."

"Yes, I did. After the horseback ride we dressed for dinner and drove up to Augusta. That's the only time I've been to Augusta. There was a nice restaurant overlooking the river. We had dinner and drove back to Oakdale Hall. Mother was still up just as I expected. I gave Richard a long kiss, both to thank him for a delightful day and to spite

Mother, retired to my room and went to bed...*alone*. Next morning we had breakfast, on the terrace again, and Richard drove me back to Portland."

"Tell me about the brooch."

"Richard said that he'd ordered it custom-made for me by Cross, that's a jewelry store in Portland. He asked me to go to New York with him...he said he had some business there...and gave me the brooch as an inducement. I told him I wasn't ready to take our relationship to that level. I handed the brooch back to him, but he wouldn't take it. He said he understood, and that I should keep the brooch anyway as a token of his deep affection for me."

"He actually said 'deep affection'? Not 'love'?"

"Yes, Quincy. In fact, I think that if he had said 'love' I probably would have gone with him."

"Do you think he was in love with you and like some men couldn't bring himself to say the word?"

"Is that question really necessary?"

"I guess not, Cecilia. But the thought did enter my mind that maybe your breaking off the relationship really did send him into such a depressed state that he took his own life, Dr. Goodson's opinion notwithstanding."

"I suppose we'll never know the complete truth about Richard Cory, including whether he was actually in love with me. My instinct is that it wasn't love; it may have been infatuation, even lust, or maybe I was just another conquest. But I didn't think then nor do I think now that it was 'love' as I am and as I believe that you are using the word.

"When I was in my early teens...I matured early as a woman...and boys began to notice me, and vice versa, my foster mother was the one who had to give me the...the... lecture. She included one extra piece of advice: She told me never to accept an expensive piece of jewelry from a man unless it's an engagement ring and then a wedding band. After that, she said, 'if your husband can afford to buy you fine jewelry, you should accept it but know that he's not buying it for you, he's buying it for himself.'"

"I assume that you did return the brooch. May I ask why?"

"I hope you know the law better than you apparently know women. I asked you a while ago what kind of woman you think I am, and you didn't answer me directly. Perhaps you'd best do so; either that or pay the bill and have Arturo call the Regency and have the doorman send a taxi for me."

"I…I…you're right; I am a naïf when it comes to understanding women. So if I get it wrong, I don't mean to. I think you're beautiful, charming…but you've got a temper…you're very intelligent…"

"Why must a man begin describing a woman by saying she's 'beautiful' or 'homely' or 'she's charming' or 'she's a shrew'; 'she's promiscuous' or 'she's an ice-queen.' You've described my physical appearance…I should thank you for the compliment, I suppose… but you haven't said a word about me. Who am I, Quincy? I am a good person? Or am I a Jezebel? Do you think I'm the type of woman you'd take home to meet your mother, or am I the type woman who'd give herself to the first man that came along and offered to keep her in style?"

"Please, Cecilia, aside from having to ask some awkward questions…questions that I'd never ask a lady unless I were defending her mother against a murder charge and needed the answers…have I not been respectful? How else does a man tell a woman that he holds her in the highest esteem?

"Look, we've been brought together under the most difficult of circumstances. Next Monday I have to do everything I know how to do and then some to keep your mother from spending the rest of her life in prison. That's all that's on my mind at the moment. You yourself said this isn't a date, it's a business meeting. If it were a date, I would have spent the evening telling you the highlights of my life, some true and some made up, and asking discreet questions like: 'Do you play tennis?' 'Do you like motion pictures, the Boston Symphony?' I wouldn't be asking you if you've slept with other men."

"And…?"

"And yes, you're a woman I'd be proud to take home to meet my mother.

"What about the brooch? Did your mother ever see it?"

"Yes, right after Richard gave it to me and I tried to give it back."

"What did your mother say?"

"Give it back. She was adamant; she wouldn't even touch it."

"Did she give you a reason?"

"No; mothers don't have to give reasons, even to adult daughters.

"You obviously gave it back to him; when was that?"

"The Friday before he died."

"You were with him that Friday night?"

"Yes. We had dinner at that same restaurant in Scarborough where he'd taken me on our first date. I picked it, not Richard."

"Why?"

"I suppose I thought it would be symbolic; that's where our relationship began, and I felt it would be fitting to end it there."

"Why'd you break it off, if you don't mind my asking?"

"I should think that by now you would know the answer: I didn't love him, nor do I think he loved me. I was not interested in the type of relationship that he wanted, so there was no point in continuing as we were."

"And you told him that?"

"In just about those words."

"How'd he take it?"

"Graciously, as always. He was, as I said, always a gentleman…head to toe."

"Here comes Arturo with the bill. I think I'd better act like a gentleman and see you home. Did you say to call the Regency for a taxi?"

"Yes, Arturo has a very good relationship with the desk staff. They send him customers and he rewards them. So they'll be glad to do him a favor. There's always a taxi or two at the taxi-stand, at least until midnight. I'm going to powder my nose while you take care of the bill. It'll only take the taxi a couple of minutes to get here. We can wait outside."

Chapter Twenty-One

"Well, Counselor, how'd things go with Miss Durbin?" Flammonde folded his newspaper and put it aside as Adams took a seat at the table and Camille brought the coffee pot and a mug for Adams. "You certainly got back late enough."

"How do you…"

"One of my associates called me early this morning to report."

"Thank you, Camille." Adams took a welcome sip of coffee. "Can you join us? I'll give you a full report."

"In a few minutes, Quincy. I've still got two other tables, neither of which has their food yet."

"Well, let me just tell you this: Cecilia and Rabbi Klein are coming here on the mid-morning train and from here we're driving up to Augusta to see Cecilia's mother. Camille, I'd like for you to meet the train."

"So she's 'Cecilia' now? Why do you want me to meet the train?"

"Because I told her the truth about you. I couldn't help it. She asked, and I decided that there'd be no more lies between you. She was angry at first; she does have a temper just like someone else I know. But I think she understands and I'm convinced she wants to be friends just as much as you do. So will you come?"

Fifteen minutes later they were seated at a table at the back of the café. Camille had finished with her tables and cleared away the dishes and utensils. Aunt Dorothy was in the kitchen supervising the preparations for the lunch-time rush, and the bus boy was busy sweeping the floor. It took Adams nearly an hour to cover his initial meeting with Cecilia Durbin, their meeting with Rabbi Klein and their 'business-dinner' as Cecilia had described it.

Neither Camille nor Emil asked many questions and when he was through, Camille gave her report. "I asked Deputy Isaacson about making someplace available to you for your meeting with Mrs. Dubrowski. He asked me who else was coming, but I said I didn't know. That raised an eyebrow, so I told him that I thought one would be Rabbi Klein, but I had no idea who else might be along. I said that it might be me, but that you hadn't said whether it was me or someone else. That seemed to satisfy him, so I left it at that. He said he'd think of something and would meet you at the jail.

"He also knew the trial had been rescheduled and said he'd do his best with the new subpoenas and to give them to him when you arrive. He told me that of course Sheriff Dowdy'd been served, but Smedley and Boyles hadn't been served yet. He said he'll take the subpoenas for Smedley and Boyles himself when he gets the new ones from you. He didn't know about Mr. Silas. Another deputy has that one and also has the subpoenas for Pommus and Dr. Goodson. He said that when you get him the new ones he'll send the same man back out as soon as he comes back in.

"Before I left the courthouse to go to Christmas's office I asked Deputy Isaacson for one more favor: He gave me permission to go up to Oakdale Hall and get some clothes for our client. I don't know how you want her to appear, but I'm sure it isn't in a garment with the word 'prisoner' stenciled on it.

"So after I went to The Attorney General's office, I went to Oakdale Hall. Deputy Isaacson did have to send another deputy with me. When we got there, the deputy told me which her room was. I took just about everything in the closet, not that there was very much. I thought at least I'd give her…and…you the choice. I also took what little make-up there was, figuring that whatever else you were planning, you wouldn't want her looking to the jury like she's been in jail for a month. I packed everything in a suitcase I found in her closet; you can take it to her when you go there."

"Well, done, Camille. As usual, you're thinking ahead of the rest of us. If by some miracle Esther Dubrowski walks, you're the one deserves the credit."

"Thanks, Quincy. I do appreciate being appreciated for being something besides a pretty face who can also type. And speaking of pretty faces, I going to run home and clean up a bit before I go to meet the train."

"What about the envelope?"

"It contained just what Christmas's letter said: a bunch of automobile advertisements. I made a list. There was one thing that caught my eye, but now I can't remember what it was. I'll show you the list later and it'll probably come back to me. There was also something odd about Oakdale Hall. But I'll save that for later too."

"Camille, take my car, Emil and I can walk to the station; you can just meet us there."

As soon as Camille had left, Emil gave Quincy a bemused look. "Whoa, Counselor, who said anything about me going to the station?"

"Cecilia, Miss Durbin, was most insistent that she meet you."

"And she knows about me because?"

"Because, Emil, she's a very smart person. She figured out that her mother couldn't afford much of a defense and that I couldn't afford to take the case *pro bono*. So I had to tell her that someone else was helping not only with the lawyering, but also with the investigative work and the expenses."

"I suppose you also told her why I'm doing this?"

"Even less than you've told me. All I told her was that you're in the business opportunity business and are convinced that her mother's innocent."

"And she bought that?"

"I doubt it, but at least it kept the conversation going. I did tell her that I trusted you and that she'd have to do so as well."

"Did you tell her that she could meet me?"

"No, I told her that you were very shy and it would be up to you."

"Sounds like you handled it the best that you could, the best anyone could. However, I think I'd best stay in the background for now. If I meet her, all that will happen is that she'll ask a lot of questions...the same ones you've asked me...and all I'll be able to do is give evasive answers or no answers at all. Just tell her that I was unable to make it today, but that I look forward to meeting her at the appropriate time."

"What if she refuses to go up to Augusta because you won't meet her?"

"I doubt that'll happen. I expect that by now, she's pretty anxious to see her mother."

"I hope you're right.

"By the way, did you get a look at Cory's Packard?"

"Yes, and you're right; there's a small crease in the left front fender and a small streak of white paint. The automobile is kept in the stable with a canvas cover over it. I managed to get a quick look while Mr. Silas was not around. You're going to have to figure out how to get in the evidence. You'd be able to get it in through Mr. Silas, but if he doesn't know anything about it, you've got a problem. Also, who's to say when it happened?

"I could go out and visit with Mr. Silas. While I'm there, I could just ask him if I could take a quick look at the vehicle. When he shows it to me...assuming that he does...I could just point it out to him and ask him if he's seen the damage before."

"And when are you going to have time to do that?"

"I suppose I could go out there when I get back from the motion hearing in the morning."

"It seems to me that you're spreading yourself pretty thin, Counselor. Have you prepared your *voir dire* questions? Have you even thought about an opening statement?"

"You're right, Emil, but I don't have much choice. Not if I'm going to get in the evidence."

"What about the fence damage? You're only one knows about that, except for Richard Cory, and neither of you is going to be able to testify."

"I don't know, Emil, I don't know." Adams folded his arms on the table and rested his head on his forearms. "There's so much to do, so many loose ends. How am I ever going to pull it all together?"

"Don't let yourself get down, Quincy. You'll get it done. Ask Deputy Isaacson to look when he goes out to serve the subpoenas on Smedley and Boyles. If you have to, tell him why you want to know. He'll do the right thing. He'll have to report to Christmas what you asked him to do and what he found, but so what? I don't see how Christmas can change the facts...at least that one. When we first discussed this business about Cory's automobile you suggested that maybe the best way to handle it is to get Christmas involved."

"You're right, Emil: I don't have time to go see Mr. Silas and you're right about handing it off to Isaacson, even if he has to involve Christmas."

"Good. Now you'd best be heading to the station. I'll talk to you when you get back."

Adams arrived at the station a few minutes before Camille. When she walked through the waiting room doors out onto the platform Adams stared at her in slack-jawed amazement. She was dressed in a sleeve-less shift in pale straw-colored linen hemmed just below her calf. The only ornamentation was a thin belt wrapped several times around her waist. She wore open-toe pumps and a wide-brim straw hat.

"Do you approve?"

"I approve, Camille. You look...terrific. You look like you're meeting a boyfriend, not an elderly clergyman and the daughter of a client."

"Perhaps I am, Quincy."

"Perhaps what? Meeting a boyfriend? I'm sorry, Camille, I just don't get it."

"Evidently not, Quincy." Camille gave a small shrug of her

shoulders, walked to the edge of the platform and looked south down the track.

Adams put his hand over his eyes and shook his head. Finally he walked over to Camille. "Look, I'm really sorry. All I did was say how great you look. I thought women liked to hear that...especially when it's true."

"Thank you Quincy. That's very nice." She gave him a wistful smile and patted his cheek. You've got a lot on your mind. Concentrate on what you've got to do starting in about..." she paused and looked up at the station clock "...ten minutes or so, assuming the train's on time."

Not knowing what he'd done to offend, Adams couldn't think of anything else to say, so he turned and walked over to the passenger bench where he sat down heavily and into the midst of two six-year-olds playing Eddie Rickenbacker versus Manfred von Richtofen, the 'Red Baron.' In the middle of the air battle complete with the sounds of high-compression engines putting out their maximum horsepower, the rattle of the synchronized machine-guns and the whine of the air rushing past guy-wires and wing struts as the enemies chased one another around their imaginary French sky, Adams retreated into the recesses of his own mind which soon poured out a cacophony of thoughts surpassing in volume even the mortal combat of the two enemy aces. Adams stood, intending to walk to the far north end of the platform just as Captain Rickenbacker proclaimed victory, a claim which was being hotly disputed by the Red Baron. He stopped, snapped his fingers, and to the astonishment of the former enemy combatants who'd never seen such a sight, danced a small jig, did a pirouette for the finale and skipped over to Camille whose turn it was to look on in wide-eyed amazement.

Reaching her, Adams grasped her shoulders and gave her a chaste kiss on her lips. "Camille, I think I know a way to keep out the confession."

"How? By kissing Reverend Christmas hoping that he'll be so astonished that he'll forget to offer it?"

"Oh, I'm sorry. Here, take my handkerchief. I've gone and smudged your lip-stick."

"You'd better use it on yourself. I can handle my part." She fished around in her small clutch handbag for a tissue. The train'll be here in a minute; I can feel the vibration. Are you sure about the confession...I mean keeping it out?"

"No, not positive. Cecilia...Miss Durbin...said something last night that's been rolling around in the back of my mind ever since. I don't know that there's any law to support it, but it's at least worth a try. I'll have to spend the afternoon at the county law library when I finish at the jail."

"Assuming your client hasn't fired you for getting her daughter involved in this mess."

"She won't fire me; anyway, I can't imagine that Judge Beauchamp would let me withdraw on the day before trial. That'd mean at the least a postponement which is something he wants to avoid. But I will have to put Miss Durbin and Rabbi Klein on the train in Augusta rather than driving them back. It'll also mean that I won't be able to meet with Emil this evening. I'll have to fill him in when I get back from Portland after lunch on Friday."

When the porter handed Cecilia down the steps on to the platform she and Camille stood staring at one another as Quincy shook hands with Rabbi Klein and inquired as to whether he'd had a pleasant trip. Rabbi Klein replied yes, it was much more pleasant than his first journey to see his congregant.

While these pleasantries were being exchanged Camille and Cecilia stood motionless staring wordlessly at one another, neither one so much as blinking an eye. Cecilia was also 'dressed to the nines' as the expression goes. She was wearing a navy-blue straight skirt which also ended well above her ankles. Over the skirt she wore a sleeve-less blouse in blue and white polka-dot with a matching hat. Like Camille, she wore open-toe high-heel pumps and carried a matching handbag.

Even with their minds preoccupied, it took Adams and Rabbi Klein only a few seconds to figure out what was going on. Prudently they stepped aside so as not to interfere with whatever was going to happen next.

It is unclear as between Camille and Cecilia who blinked first. If it were a contest, the judges would have to call it a draw. Cecilia let a tiny smile form in one corner of her mouth and Camille did the same. In an instant there were mutual squeals and the two women were embracing like long-lost sisters. After a minute or so of laughing and animated conversation, they linked arms, gave Adams and Rabbi Klein a "well, what are you waiting for?" look and marched through the doors to the waiting room. Shaking their heads, Adams and the rabbi followed them and from there out to Adams's automobile.

The drive up to Augusta was unremarkable. Since Quincy didn't mention his inspiration regarding the confession, Camille said nothing as well. She did let Cecilia know that she'd brought Esther Dubrowski's wardrobe, so they discussed which dress would be best and whether to wear make-up. Anything to distract the mind, even for a few minutes, from how the meeting was going to play out and from the ordeal and anxiety that Monday would bring. By the time they'd reached the north side of Hallowell everyone had lapsed into silence, each lost in his and her own thoughts.

When they arrived at the county facilities Quincy took his briefcase and Esther Dubrowski's suitcase and led the party into the jail. He told the deputy manning the kiosk at the entrance whom they were there to see and were told in return that they were expected. The deputy told them to have a seat on the wooden bench outside his kiosk while he went to summon Deputy Isaacson. In a few minutes he returned along with Deputy Isaacson and a matron who was introduced as Maude Woods's replacement while Matron Woods was on leave recuperating from her ordeal at the hands of the O'Brien twins. Her being on leave had the additional benefit of sparing her from the ordeal of dealing with a phalanx of newspaper reporters from as far away as New York City, eager for their readers to have the inside story of the O'Brien twins desperate escape.

As before, they were led through the steel outer door and into the first-floor hallway where they were patted down for weapons and Adams's briefcase and the women's purses were given a cursory inspection. It took longer to examine the suitcase and its contents lest there be a hacksaw blade concealed in the paste-board lining. As he led them down the hallway, Deputy Isaacson explained, "I've arranged for you to use the watch commander's office…where you and I met, Mr. Adams…but I can only give you half an hour, maybe a few minutes more. It's small, as you know. Miss Winters said there'd be two additional visitors, not three. I don't think there'll be enough room to hold five of you."

"That's not a problem, Deputy Isaacson." Camille took Quincy's briefcase. "I have the new subpoenas to give you and I hope you can tell me what the arrangements will be in Portland when the trial begins."

"That's a good idea, Miss Winters. You and I can use Sheriff Dowdy's office. He's over in book-in. Seems we've got two more mouths to feed around here. One returning and one newcomer. The deputy who went down to Oakdale Hall to serve Mr. Silas made quite a catch. He got one of the O'Brien sisters and Mr. Silas. Apparently the girls have been hiding out at Oakdale Hall and the deputy walked in on them by accident. He managed to get a handcuff on one of them and then he put the other cuff on himself. He decided a bird in the hand is worth two in the bush, so the other one got away.

"Then he took Mr. Silas into custody charging him with aiding and abetting an escapee. Fortunately he had some spare handcuffs. He had to use one set on the O'Brien girl's legs otherwise she'd have kicked him all the way back here. As it is, he's got a pretty good black eye from a punch she landed with her free hand and a painful looking bite on his arm that was handcuffed to hers. He finally wrestled her into his car and handcuffed her to the metal ring that we had welded to the frame for just that purpose. Mr. Silas wasn't any trouble; said he had no idea she was an escapee and that he'd come along and let them get things straightened out here.

"Sheriff sent a few men back down to Oakdale Hall in case the other one's still hanging around, but I wouldn't bet on them finding her. As far as Mr. Silas goes, he may be telling the truth. Not for me to say. But I will say this: 'We won't have to send anybody out to serve him with the new subpoena and we won't have to worry about him not showing up for the trial.'"

"Matron Shuttlesworth here will go up and fetch Mrs. Dubrowski. Then she'll have to get over to book-in to search the O'Brien girl and be there when they take her photograph. The girl's going to have to remove most all of her clothing. I want to be sure that she's not mistreated while being questioned by the sheriff. If I have a photograph taken during book-in it's less likely that anyone'll mistreat her later."

"Are you…"

"No, no, Miss Winters, I'm not saying that mistreatment of prisoners happens in here. But what has been known to happen is that a prisoner can sometimes meet with an accident like slipping on a freshly-mopped floor and get awfully bruised up in some odd places.

"Now you folks…by the way, we weren't introduced…Miss…?"

"Cecilia Durbin; I'm here with Rabbi Klein."

"Well, pleased to meet you, I'm sure." Deputy Isaacson unlocked the door to the office and held it open. "Just go on in and make yourselves as comfortable as you can. Matron Shuttlesworth will have Mrs. Dubrowski down here in a minute. When Miss Winters and I have completed our business, we'll come back and let you out."

"Let us out?" Cecilia stopped as she was about to enter the office.

"I apologize. I was going to have Matron Shuttlesworth sit outside the door, but we're shorthanded and as I said she's needed elsewhere. Since the O'Brien twins escaped, we've become much more security conscious. You want a private meeting; this is the best I can do."

"Thank you for your efforts, Deputy Isaacson. You've been most accommodating and we very much appreciate it." Adams held out his hand for Isaacson to shake. "If you'd like, I'll certainly tell Sheriff Dowdy what a great help you've been"

"Thank you, Mr. Adams, but if it's all the same to you, I'd rather that you didn't say anything. In fact, I insist."

"Oh. Sorry, Mr. Isaacson. I wasn't thinking."

Esther Dubrowski was handcuffed with her hands in front. As the matron opened the door and stepped back for her to enter and she saw Cecilia she clasped her hands to her mouth let out a small scream. Her body sagged as though she'd fainted. Adams, who was standing closest to her, caught her by the shoulders and guided her to one of the chairs on the front side of the desk.

"Is she okay?" Matron Shuttlesworth squeezed by Adams to attend to her prisoner. "What happened?"

"It's nothing, Matron. Perhaps just the excitement." Rabbi Klein stepped adroitly between the matron and Esther.

"Do you think she's really okay?"

"Yes, yes. She will be all right. Perhaps if you could find, please, a glass of water that would be all that is needed. In addition to being a clergyman, I have medical training." Rabbi Klein turned around and bent his head close to Esther's as though he were examining her for some symptom discernible only to the medically-trained eye. He took her chin in his hand and turned her head away from the door. As he did, he whispered a few words to her in Yiddish and that seemed to restore her composure.

"I'll ask the guard at the front to bring the water. I have to go over to the book-in area. I'll have to lock the door, but the guard also has a key. I'll tell him to knock before he enters."

"Thank you, Matron. You've been most kind."

As soon as the door was locked Cecilia came from around the desk and knelt in front of her mother who clasped Cecilia's face in her manacled hands. Adams gestured to Rabbi Klein that he should take the chair behind the desk.

"Are you also a physician, Rabbi Klein?"

"No, Quincy. I said that I had 'medical training,' not that I'm a doctor. When you are a Jew growing up in Russia you learn how to speak to the authorities. One always tells the truth, but not necessarily the whole truth.

"I was born and raised in a small village two days' walk from Minsk…in the Ukraine. The land was then ruled by the Czar. When I was about twenty years old…you must understand that accurate birth records were not so common-place in those days…I was still living in the *shtetl*…the village…where I was born, working for my father in his dairy business and wondering what I should do with my life.

"One day the Czar's army recruiters came to the village. I think it must have been early in 1877 because that year's war was one of the Russo-Turkish wars. The recruiters rounded up all the young men and teen-age boys and they gave us a choice: Either volunteer for the army or be conscripted to serve as targets for live-fire training exercises. So I enlisted in the Czar's army. One afternoon during basic training they had a doctor and his assistant give us training in how to dress a wound, how to apply a tourniquet, make a splint for a broken limb, that sort of thing. So when I say that I have medical training, it's true. I would never lie to the authorities. But we reminisce too much. I think your client…my patient…has recovered so you'd best get to the point before the deputy brings our meeting to an end."

Adams touched Cecilia on the shoulder and motioned for her to take the other chair. He sat on the corner of the desk and started to give his prepared speech. As he was drawing a breath to begin speaking, Esther Dubrowski turned to him her eyes blazing with anger. "You have betrayed me, Mr. Adams. I do not want you as my lawyer any longer. And you, Rabbi Klein, you are a party to this betrayal? How could you do this? I don't have enough *tsuris*? All of you get out; leave me alone. I will go alone to Portland and plead guilty."

"Please, Mrs. Dubrowski, will you listen for a moment before you do yourself, and Cecilia a great injustice?"

"Yes, Mama, please. Listen to Quincy. Just listen for a few minutes to what he has to say."

"Oh, so he's 'Quincy.' First 'Richard,' now 'Quincy.' *Oy*, *Tzippi*, why have you come here? Why didn't you leave as I told you to do? What can this man possibly say to me that will make up for exposing you to this…this…?"

"Yes, please, Esther. Listen to Mr. Adams. He has worked very hard for you. Forgive me for being blunt, but no obscure parables come to my mind at the moment. Esther, your *tsuris*, as you properly call it, is of your own making. You need help in fixing things. Now listen to Quincy; see, I call him that too. He's a *mensch* and a good lawyer. Will you listen for your daughter's sake?"

"Please Mama?"

Esther started to speak when there was a knock on the door. In a moment the guard opened the door and handed a glass of water to Adams.

"Can you hold the glass, Mrs. Dubrowski? I mean with your hands…"

"Yes, yes. I can hold it. Thank you, Mr. Adams. Please tell me why I should follow your advice. I will listen to you until I've finished drinking the water in this glass. If you haven't made me understand that my daughter is in no danger by that time, you will please to summon back the matron to take me back to my cell. Do you understand? Do you accept these conditions?" She took a substantial swallow from the glass.

"Yes, Ma'am. I understand. May I begin?"

"Begin, Mr. Adams."

"Your daughter had absolutely nothing to do with the death of Richard Cory. You know he was alive as late as that Saturday night, and you found him dead the next morning, Sunday. This is true, is it not?"

"Yes, it is true. Go on."

"That entire time…from Saturday afternoon until what, Cecilia, ten o'clock or so on Sunday morning?"

"Yes, about then."

"Mrs. Dubrowski, Cecilia was on Peak's Island with three other girls…women…that also live at Miss Rosie's. They can testify and there are probably others who can confirm that's where she was." Adams stood up. "If you do not believe me, ask your daughter. If you don't believe her, then I suggest that you finish your glass of water."

"*Tzippi*, this is true?"

"Yes, Mama, what Mr. Adams said is true." Cecilia's eyes were glistening. "I don't know why you thought that I…"

"I didn't know what to think, *Tzippi*." Esther leaned forward and handed the nearly-empty glass to Adams. "I thought that Mr. Cory had taken you out that night. When he came home, I was in my room as I testified at the inquest. I had the window and the door open because it was so warm. When he first came home I was sure that I heard conversation. One voice…it was very soft…sounded like a woman, a young woman. Later, I heard a gunshot…I still remember what a gunshot sounds like…and I ran to the window overlooking the front porch. I didn't dare go downstairs for fear that whoever fired the gun might still be in the house.

"A short time went by and I was still standing at the window. I heard the front door slam closed. I saw a woman run down the front steps and down the drive. She was wearing a cloak, which I thought odd because it was so warm that night. I couldn't see her face or tell anything more about her. Then in another minute or two, I hear automobile start and drive off. I wait a few minutes more and then I go downstairs to the music room."

"You thought it was me, Mama?"

"Who else should I think?"

"What did you see when you got to the music room, Mrs. Dubrowski?"

"I saw him…Mr. Cory…sitting in his chair in front of the fire place. He was just sitting there as though he'd fallen asleep. This he has done many times, times when he has too much drink. So I went over to him and started to ask him if he was all right. That's when I saw that he'd been shot. Then I saw the gun in his hand."

"Did you see the brooch?"

"The brooch, Mr. Adams? Do you mean that *tchotchke* that he bought for Cecilia and I told her she must not accept it?"

"*Tchot*…what Mrs. Dubrowski?"

"That means a cheap ornament, Quincy, a trinket. There, another word for your Yiddish vocabulary."

"Thank you Rabbi Klein. You'll have to help me with the spelling later."

Adams turned back to his client. "Yes, Ma'am, that's the one."

"Yes, it was in Mr. Cory's left hand. As soon as I saw it, what else could I think? It must have been Cecilia that I saw from the house running."

"I take it that's why you waited until morning to call the sheriff's office?"

"Yes. I was trying to think of a way to contact Cecilia, but I was afraid that if I waited too long it would look suspicious. I didn't know what to do with the…the brooch. I think throw it away; maybe hide in my room. All night I'm thinking what to do; cannot decide. Then when I hear sheriff coming, I stuff it between the seat cushion and the arm of the chair; decide what to do with it after sheriff leave."

"Did you know about the gun, the revolver?"

"No, I'd never seen it before. I don't even know whether it belonged to Mr. Cory."

"I think we're almost out of time, Mrs. Dubrowski. Now that

you know Cecilia's innocent, will you let me defend you properly?"

"What must I do?"

"Unless I can keep your statement at the inquest out of evidence at the trial, you'll have to testify. You'll have to tell the jury that you made up the story to protect your daughter, and you'll have to explain why you did it."

"And they will believe me? After I've just admitted that barely a month ago I lied under oath? After they find out that I've been convicted of murder once before? And that I'm a prison escapee? Please Mr. Adams, I am not an educated woman, as you know. But that doesn't mean that I am stupid. Rabbi, is it possible that a jury, twelve *goyim,* will believe me?"

"I don't know, Esther. Everything you just mentioned will certainly be brought up against you. But so what? If Cecilia's not at risk, and I trust Mr. Adams on this, what have you got to lose? All I can tell you is that if I were you, I'd follow Mr. Adams's advice."

"And I remember an old saying, Rabbi Klein: 'If the rabbi's wife had a beard, she'd be the rabbi.' I appreciate your advice; I mean this with all my heart. And I want to thank you for bringing Mr. Adams to me. I also think it may have been you that is responsible for bringing my *Tzippi* to me. For this you also have my thanks.

"Mr. Adams, there's still water left in the glass. You are a very persuasive lawyer. Let me think overnight; no, make it over the weekend. I will give you my decision when I see you on Monday."

Before Adams started the automobile to drive them to the train station, he turned to Cecilia, "What do you think she'll do?"

"I honestly don't know, Quincy. I think you've won her over; at the least you convinced her that I didn't shoot Richard. Your daring her to finish the glass of water was very brave on your part. For a moment I thought she was going to do it. The fact that she didn't makes me think she'll come around by Monday."

"Rabbi Klein?"

"Esther Dubrowski is a very complicated person. She is weighing her options. I agree with Cecilia that you've convinced her that Cecilia is not involved. But in doing so, you've made her decision much more difficult. When she thought a trial might put Cecilia at risk, her decision was informed by that fact alone.

"Now that she no longer has to worry about Cecilia, all she has to think about is where she wants to spend the rest of her life: In a prison in Maine or a prison in Illinois? She senses, and rightly so, that Cecilia will never again allow herself to be separated from her mother, at least insofar as prison regulations will allow them to be together. Cecilia has made for herself a life here: She has friends, a good job, a Jewish community that will help her in any way it can. She has nothing in Chicago. Her 'Aunt Pessie'…such a name…is gone…what is there for her in Illinois?

"Mind you, *Tzippi*…may I call you that among friends?"

"Yes, of course, Rabbi Klein. It's been a long time since anyone's called me that, even Mother."

"Is that a nick-name? I wondered about it when your mother called you that." Adams turned so that his arm was over the back of the front seat and he could see Cecilia's face.

"My Hebrew name is '*Zipporah.*' It means a 'bird' doesn't it Rabbi Klein?"

"Yes, a bird. But let me finish what I was about to say before I interrupted myself. I'm not the Chamber of Commerce; I'm not trying to persuade you to stay in Portland, *Tzippi*. All I'm saying is that your wishes will most likely determine what your mother does. But I think you know that without me telling you."

"I…I…I" Cecilia could no longer hold back the tears. "If only I'd turned Richard Cory down and not gone out with him…none of this would have happened. What a vain, stupid girl I am. Can God forgive me, Rabbi Klein…even if I can't forgive myself?"

Chapter Twenty-Two

"Can you spare one of those cheroots?" Adams wearily set down his briefcase, small suitcase and a box from David Schwartz Clothing Store in Portland. "I suppose it's too early for a dose of Lamar's bourbon."

Flammonde took out his cigar case and passed it to Adams. "I take it the motion hearing went badly."

"A major setback, at the least." Adams took Flammonde's match box and lit his cheroot. "The judge granted all our motions."

"And that's a disaster? I thought they were brilliant."

"No, that part is good; the problem is that he granted Christmas's motion as well."

"Tell me about yours."

"Well, Judge Beauchamp was totally prepared, so there wasn't much argument. There were only two of the four that Christmas put up any kind of fight about. The first is the one that requires him to wear a conventional collar and tie and be referred to as 'Mr. Christmas' not 'Reverend Christmas.' But the judge went with me on that one as well as the other three."

"So you've got 'Mr. Christmas' not 'Reverend Christmas.' Which of the others did he put up a fuss about?"

"Who does the *voir dire* questioning. I didn't want Christmas up there selling the jury his case, first thing they get to hear after '*oyez, oyez*,' or whatever the bailiff says down there at the beginning of court. Judge sort of split the difference on that one: Judge'll do the questioning, using questions submitted by each side. Our list is due by noon tomorrow, so I need to get to work on it."

"That doesn't seem too bad. He's going to ask all the questions each side gives him? It'll take you two weeks just to pick the jury."

"Not necessarily. Judge said he'd work over the weekend on the list of questions, eliminating the redundant ones and perhaps combining others and changing the wording as he thinks necessary so that they don't comment on the weight of the evidence. Said he'd give us the list Monday morning and give us ten minutes to suggest changes that he's likely not to make anyway."

"What about the other two?"

"Christmas can't bring up her prior conviction unless she takes the stand. Has to tell his witnesses, Pommus in particular, to not mention it either."

"Will she?"

"Take the stand?"

"Yes."

"Probably, unless I can keep the confession out. With the judge granting Christmas's motion, I won't have a choice."

"What's the last one?"

"That's the biggest of all: Christmas can't talk about the confession in *voir dire*, or in his opening statement and he has to gag his witnesses as well. No mention of the confession unless I bring it up first, or until the judge admits it in evidence."

"And he'll hear whether to admit it outside the jury's presence?"

"Yes. So now all I have to do is keep it out."

"And you have a plan to do that?"

"Maybe. It still needs some work. Also," Adams reached into his briefcase and pulled out a list of names and addresses and handed it to Flammonde. "Here's the jury list. Will you get Lamar and Maurice to check out as many as they can?"

"Well, Lamar's available, but Maurice's over on Peak's Island checking out Miss Durbin's story. I'll give the first half of the list to Lamar and get him started. I'll tell him to leave the other half for Maurice at the hotel."

"Maybe you ought to split the list in thirds and leave the last third for whoever gets through first."

"So that no good deed goes…"

"…unpunished. No, it's just I doubt that we'll get more than two-thirds through the *venire*. We've each got six peremptory challenges. And with the judge doing the *voir dire* we're not likely to have very many challenges for cause."

"Tell me the bad part. I don't think I saw Christmas's motion."

"He's only managed to gut reasonable doubt. Sheriff Dowdy can't testify that in his opinion Richard Cory committed suicide."

"That's not so good, Counselor. Why won't the judge let him give his opinion?"

"Essentially because he doesn't know what he's talking about. Christmas made the point that the sheriff has no medical training, forensic or otherwise. He hasn't investigated enough cases so that he can testify based on his own experience. His opinion is based on his own say-so, without any data or reasoning to support it. When you said that Christmas knows the law of evidence, you understated it. All I could do was just sit there and watch my case for reasonable doubt keel over and die before my eyes."

"So if you don't keep the confession out, your only shot is for the jury to be willing to disregard it. And because the judge is handling the *voir dire* you can't get the prospective jurors committed to keeping an open mind as to whether they'd disregard the confession if it gets in. So you've got no way to challenge a juror for cause based on the confession. What's the expression: 'hoisted on your own petard?'"

"Well, at least Christmas doesn't get to talk about it either."

"True, and for that reason I think you got the long end of that particular stick. At least they won't have made up their minds beforehand, which they likely would do if Christmas gets to pummel Mrs. Dubrowski over the head with it in his opening statement.

"Of course once he hears her story, he'll try to sell the jury on the notion that your client plotted to get Cory to marry her gold-digging daughter. Then, after a year or two, they'd murder Cory and live happily ever after on Cory's wealth. Only Cory got suspicious and found out about your client so she had to do away with him. Even though they'd missed their opportunity with Cory, at least Esther and Cecilia would be free to find a new victim."

"Cecilia's no gold-digger, Emil."

"If he gets the opportunity, Christmas'll make her out to be a calculating gold-digger holding out for the big prize and not just a cheap toy from a Cracker-Jack box. And as for your client..."

"That's outrageous, Emil. You take that back. Maybe if you'd go to the trouble of meeting her, you'd have a different opinion."

"No doubt I would, Quincy, and so would the jury. But they're not going to have that opportunity."

"Well how can you make that kind of judgment about her?"

"Take it easy, Counselor. Save your righteous indignation for your closing argument. When the trial's over, I look forward to meeting your client as well as her daughter whom I should think is as lovely a person inside as she is on the outside. I'm just playing devil's advocate here. If I'm distracting you, I'll shut up or even leave if you think you'd be better off without my heckling."

"No, you're right as usual. I'm just venting my frustration. I've never put this much effort into a case with the prospect of such a poor return. You're right about lawyers: All we're good at and for is redistribution of wealth. When it comes down to a situation where real values and lives are at stake we're...I'm...totally useless." Adams planted his elbows on his desk and lowered his head into his cupped hands.

"This case is like a soup sandwich: No matter which way I pick it up, something falls out. When it's over I'm going to shut this dump down and either go back to patents and trade-marks, or better yet find a job in a mill or factory where I can actually do something useful and not have to engage in mortal combat with everyone with whom I come in contact: Clients, opposing lawyers, judges, clerks, lying witnesses, you name it."

"Quincy, it's time you took a break. Give me the jury list; I'll divvy it up later. Let's go over to the Palace and get Lamar and a bottle of his bourbon. Then we can get in your auto and drive to someplace quiet along the river. We can get drunk, smoke cigars, and, if the mood strikes you, go for a swim in the river."

"No. Emil. Thanks, but I'd better work. I've got so much to…"

"Quincy, what you need is not to work for a few hours. Besides, I've got some good news for your client about Illinois, and I'll only tell you if you do as I suggest."

"Since you put it that way…"

"Good, come along, Counselor."

While Emil was rousting Lamar and his bourbon bottle, and stopping at the Palace tobacco and news counter for a supply of twenty-five cent Cuban cigars, Quincy got Aunt Dorothy to pack a basket of sandwiches, Saratoga chips, iced lemonade and three slices of blueberry pie. Camille had promised Aunt Dorothy that she'd work the dinner shift so Quincy left her a note telling her that he and Emil would be back around dinner time and that they'd meet her at the Red Rooster.

By the time they arrived back, the dinner trade had slacked off. The only patrons remaining were Camille's father, brothers and sisters-in-law. Harley had invited them to dinner…and picked the Red Rooster as the restaurant…a statement that Camille could not fail to notice.

The bourbon consumption during their picnic had been restrained so Camille found nothing in Quincy's or Emil's manner or appearance at which to take offense. When they were seated at their usual rear table Aunt Dorothy put on a fresh pot of coffee and offered them what was left of the evening's desserts on the house.

Camille folded her used apron and placed it in the laundry bin. She poured herself a cup of coffee and took a seat at the table, her back to her family. That gesture caused no small measure of relief to Quincy and Emil who were dreading another confrontation with the Clan Winters.

"It appears," Quincy began, "that Emil may have a solution to our client's dilemma. Why don't you tell it, Emil?"

"I assume that you've heard of Clarence Darrow?"

"Isn't he the lawyer that defended those brothers that were charged with blowing up a newspaper office in California? Then he was charged with trying to bribe the jury?" I read that someone called him 'The lawyer for the damned.' He's in Chicago isn't he?"

"Yes to all that, Camille. He's also by many people's estimate the greatest trial lawyer in this country, maybe the greatest ever."

Camille paused for a moment, processing what Emil had just said. "Quincy, are you telling me that Darrow's going to take over your case? After all you've done? Emil, you should be ashamed after talking Quincy into taking the Dubrowski case in the first place now you want to replace him with some supposedly high-powered lawyer from Chicago who's suspected of bribing the jury in some other sensational case. Quincy Adams, you don't have to sit second chair to Clarence Darrow or anybody. Don't you dare let some slick lawyer from Chicago…or anywhere else…hijack your case. I'm going down to Portland in the morning and tell Cecilia to tell her mother to refuse to accept Mister 'Lawyer for the damned' and to tell the judge that she wants you.

"On second thought, maybe I won't. If you don't have enough backbone to stand up to Mr. Flammonde, Mrs. Dubrowski's probably better off without you."

"I think you should go to Portland tomorrow or at least call Cecilia." Adams tried to put a soothing hand on Camille's arm but she drew it away. "Only don't tell her that I'm being replaced; tell her that Clarence Darrow is going to represent her mother *pro bono* in seeking a pardon from the Illinois governor based on the fact that her trial was a farce and she'd never have been convicted if she'd had a competent lawyer…even a Quincy Adams. Mr. Darrow's been studying the record…it still exists…and he feels there's a good chance of winning. He will tell the governor, off the record of course, that if he can't see fit to grant the pardon, Mrs. Dubrowski will file a petition for a writ of habeas corpus in the federal court based on constitutional grounds and get the conviction overturned that way, even if Darrow has to take the case all the way to the United States Supreme Court. The habeas corpus route, if it succeeds, will make new law and will embarrass the entire Illinois criminal justice system."

"Quincy, Emil, can you forgive me? I can't believe I've made such a fool of myself. Emil, I'm so sorry for thinking that you'd do something as low as what I've accused you of. And Quincy, if you won't fire me, I promise never to doubt you again. Please excuse me, I need a cigarette. I'll be back in a minute or two. That'll give you time to decide whether to fire me."

Camille's exit did not go unnoticed at the front of the restaurant. In a moment Billy followed by Fred came to the back table. Quincy started to rise and hold out his hand, but Billy's hand firmly planted on Quincy's shoulder kept him in his seat. "Don't need to stand on our account. We're just checkin' be sure Cam's okay. Looked to us like she got up in a pretty big hurry, like she's upset about something."

"Yeah," added Fred. "We thought dad made it clear to you fellows that we didn't appreciate you putting Camille in harm's way."

"Nor has Mr. Adams done so, Mr. Winters."

"I don't recall askin' you, Mr...."

"Flammonde, Emil Flammonde, Mr. Winters. No you didn't ask me. Had you done so, and in a civil manner, either I or Mr. Adams would have told you that Miss Winters merely stepped out to 'powder her nose' as the ladies say, and she'll be back in a minute. Your concern, while perhaps admirable, is wholly gratuitous."

"Grat...what?" Fred asked.

"Gratuitous, not called-for, if you prefer. Now please go back to your table. You don't want to spoil a cordial family dinner with an unnecessary altercation. Do, however, tell your father that he's raised an exceptionally clever and resourceful daughter. Please add that without her efforts Mrs. Dubrowski's defense may well have been doomed."

"You tellin' us that because of Camille that murderin' Polack-woman's gonna' get off?"

"Now just a..." Quincy tried to stand but Billy's hand kept him in his seat.

Billy turned to Fred, "That ain't right Fred. She ain't guilty 'till she's had a trial. An' bein' a Polack don't make her guilty either. If Cam's workin' so hard for her maybe she didn't do it."

"You're right, Billy. She didn't do it."

"Oh, Cam, you're back. Fred 'n' me were just wishing Quincy good luck with the trial."

"Well thanks for your support, Billy. For a moment there Fred sounded like he was wishing something else. Tell pop that I plan to stay in Portland from Sunday night until the trial's over. I hope Alice and Evelyn don't mind taking care of pop while I'm away. I sure appreciate their doing it."

"I'm sorry for eavesdropping on your conversation with Billy and Fred. I promise you they're not nearly as ignorant as they behave at times. It was good to hear that at least Billy's got some sense."

"Did you say you're coming down to Portland and staying for the trial? Emil, can you afford that?"

"It won't be too expensive. I'm going to stay in the guest room at Miss Rosie's. I want to be there for Cecilia and to help in the trial any way I can."

"Actually, I was going to suggest that you do just what you said, Camille. You can stay at the Regency if you prefer and I'm happy to pay your salary as well."

"Thanks, Emil, but Miss Rosie's will do just fine. I expect that Cecilia's going to need me around. She's pretty nervous, especially since she's decided to blame herself for her mother's predicament."

"Well, I'm glad we've got that settled. Is Cecilia going to attend the trial? I may want you at the counsel table with me. I think it'd look good to have a woman seated there alongside the defendant, even if you don't get to address the court. So if you're with me, you can't be sitting with Cecilia. And I'd really like someone to be there with her, especially when Christmas lets loose with his accusations. Which would you rather do?"

"How about if I sit with Cecilia?"

"Does that mean you're ready to be introduced to her?"

"I don't see any other way. I can't just sit down beside her and strike up a conversation. I do that and she's liable to do like Little Miss Muffet. 'How do you do, Miss? I understand it's your mother who's on trial for murder. How do you think it'll come out?'"

"Just tell her the same thing you told Rabbi Klein: I'm a client who only wants his lawyer back and is willing to help any way he can."

"She's more likely to peg you as a newspaper reporter. What if I tell her Sunday night and introduce you Monday morning?"

"I think that's the best plan, Emil. Now, I need to get my prospective juror questions typed up. I've got them written out in long-hand, but I'd rather have them typed-up and professional-looking for the judge. Camille, I don't suppose…"

"Your typing won't make them look any more professional, so I guess I'd better do it. But how are you going to get them to the judge before noon tomorrow?"

"You two leave that to me. I'll have my associate drop them off at the judge's chambers since he's going to Portland anyway. But before I leave, Camille, you said there was something odd about the envelope contents and something not right at Oakdale Hall. Do you want to tell us now just in case there's anything needs following up?"

"What I saw at Oakdale Hall...or actually what I didn't see...has an explanation now that I know the O'Brien twins were hiding out there. I didn't see any dust, any cob-webs, anything that would say that no one's been living there for a month. I expect that the twins were keeping the place clean in exchange for room and board."

"You're most likely right, Camille. The more interesting questions are: How'd they get there? And did Mr. Silas know they were fugitives?" As I told you, one of our client's conditions for representing her was that I also take on the twins' cases. And I think I mentioned how our client took the news that they'd escaped."

"I don't want to distract you from what you've got to do tonight, but..."

"But what, Emil..."

"I hope your client doesn't end up getting charged with aiding and abetting their escape. If she did, I expect it won't take much persuadin' by Sheriff Dowdy to get the one he's got in custody to give up Mrs. Dubrowski."

"Talk about 'no good deed goes unpunished'...

"And speaking about talking, which one does he have: The talker or the non-talker?"

"I don't know; let's just hope it's the non-talker or that the talker stays as tough as she's been so far.

"Now we really need...I mean Camille really needs to get to work on these questions."

"What about the envelope?"

"It can keep."

"No, that's okay, Quincy. It'll just take a minute to tell, and I doubt that anything'll come of it."

"If you want to tell it now, Camille, it's up to you. Maybe you should have another cup of coffee. I'd hate for you to fall asleep at your typewriter."

Camille brought the coffee pot back to the table and poured a fresh round for Quincy and Emil as well as herself. "It was exactly what Christmas's letter said: There were just a bunch of automobile brochures. But what struck me as odd is that one of the brochures was for a Ford Model TT, a truck like my dad's got. It didn't go into production until this year. My dad got what the dealer said was one of only a dozen allocated by Ford to Maine. Dad says he was lucky to get it. He says that he saw the first advertising about the end of winter, maybe late March.

"I think you," she nodded to Flammonde, "said Richard Cory had the Packard since it came out in 1916. And Quincy said that Cecilia told him that Cory picked her up on their first date in the Packard."

"Were all of the other brochures new or old?"

"Emil, if you mean were they for models that have been on the market for longer than a year, the answer is: I think so. That's why the Ford truck stood out, that and the fact that I recognized it because Dad was so proud of getting one."

"Maybe Cory was looking into getting one too and just happened to put the brochure in with the others he already had."

"That's possible, Quincy. But why would he be interested in buying a truck? Oakdale Hall is no longer a working farm. He had the farm wagon and two draft horses. I doubt that 'hayrides' are nearly as much fun in a truck as they are in an old-fashion wagon."

"I suppose you're right, Emil. But what other explanation is there?"

"How about this one: Sheriff Dowdy didn't like what he saw in the envelope when he opened it that morning. That explains why he didn't just leave it. He didn't want anyone else looking in it, so he took custody of it.

"I'd speculate he must have seen that Deputy Isaacson noticed him putting the envelope in his pocket, so he had to account for it somehow."

"Do you think he switched the contents of the envelope for a hand-full of automobile advertising brochures?"

"Camille, what other explanation fits the facts?"

"But why'd he turn the envelope over to Pommus's office?"

"Same reason he took it in the first place. Once he had it, he had to do something with it. He couldn't just let it disappear. He never counted on Dr. Goodson opening a can of worms by debunking the suicide theory."

"Do you think he made the switch before he turned it over?" Adams drained his coffee cup.

"No, either he didn't have time or in his anger at Pommus he just plain forgot. I think he made the switch after the envelope was turned over to Pommus. I think he broke into Pommus's office and took it back, intending that it disappear...so to speak...while in Pommus's custody so that Pommus would have to take the blame. He gets rid of a pesky piece of evidence that maybe argues against suicide and at the same time puts the blame on his hated rival.

"It could have worked, except that Deputy Isaacson brought it up in front of you and Christmas. What I think happened is that Sheriff Dowdy got into Pommus's office that night and replaced the original envelope with a look-alike containing whatever he could get his hands on in a hurry that wasn't strips of newspaper or a wad of money. He probably had the brochures lying around somewhere in his office or at home. He took the imposter envelope filled it and sneaked it back into Pommus's file cabinet."

"And that's why Enoch Matthews didn't find it the first time but found it when he looked the second time."

"Right, Camille."

"But what's he trying to hide? Why does he want Richard Cory's death to be a suicide?"

"Quincy, I think I'd better find out the answers to those questions by Monday morning or Tuesday at the latest, assuming it takes all day Monday to seat the jury and maybe get through opening statements. Hopefully I'll have some interestin' questions for you to put to Sheriff Dowdy, much better than him giving his half-assed...excuse me, Camille, I didn't mean to be so coarse...opinion that the deceased died by his own hand."

"No offense taken, Emil. Believe me; I've heard that and much worse at home. Actually," Camille smiled, "I think the imagery's kind of funny."

Chapter Twenty-Three

They finished their final pretrial conference in the judge's chambers. As Adams had predicted, the judge allowed Adams to "make a record" stating his objections to the *voir dire* questions but declined to make any changes. Since the state has no right of appeal in criminal cases, Christmas contented himself with advancing a couple of tepid suggestions which the judge also proceeded to ignore. Perhaps as a result of being forced to wear a conventional collar and tie, or perhaps because he realized that he'd underestimated Adams, Christmas was polite, yet Adams could sense that the former spirit of collegiality Christmas had fostered since their first meeting was gone.

Outwardly, Adams looked like what he was: A young lawyer in a freshly-pressed and brushed conservative dark suit over a new conservative white shirt with a new heavily-starched white collar and new conservative dark tie. Inside the trial lawyer's uniform, his mind was pulling him in two different directions. Although not a Catholic, he made the ritual obsecration to St. Thomas More, the patron saint of trial lawyers: "Please don't let me make a fool of myself." That out of the way, he vowed to himself that on this outing it was he who would be the hunter and Christmas the rabbit.

As he'd driven down from Tilbury Town to Portland the prior evening, he recalled the sense of purpose that he'd recognized occasionally in other trial lawyers and that was spoken of by the notable Harvard Law alumni trial lawyers that from time to time gave guest lectures and seminars on trial practice. He wanted to win this case so badly that the desire caused knots in his gut and bile to rise in his throat.

There was still more than half an hour until court was scheduled to convene. The jury panel, those that had accepted it as their civic duty to respond to their summonses, were milling about in the hallway and on the grand marble double-stairway. There they awaited the bailiff's call to enter the courtroom in the order in which their names had been drawn at random from the Cumberland County jury wheel. Those that happened to know one another stood chatting in small groups. Others who felt inconvenienced but had come anyway were standing about looking bemused and others, who had been summoned on prior occasions, tried to read their newspapers or other reading material they'd brought with them. Anyone who has been summoned to jury duty more than once knows to bring a supply of reading material to fill the frequent periods of time when nothing appears to be happening and the hands of the clock seem to tick off eons rather than minutes and hours.

Adams entered the courtroom lugging his two briefcases, one he'd had since graduation and the other he'd found gathering dust in a corner of his office when he moved in. Camille had more than once urged him to get rid of it as it had brought the previous occupant nothing but misfortune. He set the briefcases down beside the front counsel table, the one on the far side away from the jury box. The Cumberland County Supreme Judicial Court courtroom was even larger than the one in Augusta. Like the courtroom in Augusta, it had two sets of counsel tables inside the bar, two on each side. The bench took up the entire front of the courtroom. The room was paneled in dark wood. Lighting was provided by generous windows and elaborate light fixtures in the ceiling. The spectator benches, Adams estimated, could easily handle at least a hundred and fifty.

The first rows had been cordoned off for the jury panel and there were already a few spectators seated in the back rows. Adams could understand people from Tilbury Town coming down to observe the trial. He wondered, however, what motivated strangers, who presumably knew none of the principals and had no stake in the trial's outcome, to give up their normal pursuits to spend the day, perhaps many days, as passive participants in an event that had no immediate effect on their lives.

One of the celebrity lecturers at Harvard had likened the excitement of observing a trial to watching paint dry. Since Maine had abolished capital punishment some thirty-six years ago, there would be none of the drama of sentencing a guilty defendant to be "hung by the neck until you are dead." Adams thought of his legal pads full of questions for the witnesses and concluded that none of them was likely to produce any sensational testimony, other than perhaps Richard Cory's state of dishabille. Was it morbid curiosity such as attends a train wreck with mangled bodies strewn up and down the right-of-way? Is it the same curiosity that causes people to skim the newspaper headlines and turn immediately to the so-called "agony-columns?" Or is it the same curiosity that propels people into carnival tents to gape at immensely obese women and two-headed animals? Or was it simply boredom with the quotidian pace of life? Adams shook his head and pushed these musings out of his mind.

While Adams was pondering these conundrums, Emil, Camille

and Cecilia came in and quietly took seats in the first row of benches that were not roped-off for the jury panel. As Quincy was beginning to unload one of his briefcases and arrange the contents on the counsel table, Camille came through the low-rise swinging door in the bar that separates the judge's bench and the counsel tables from the spectator galleries. As Quincy was reaching into the briefcase for more files she touched him on the shoulder. "We're here, Quincy."

Quincy jerked his head up barely missing the corner of the table. "I take it the introduction went well?"

"Yes. You know how charming and persuasive Emil can be," Camille paused, "even when he's telling the most outrageous lies."

"How do you know he was lying?"

"Quincy," she paused, "his lips were moving."

"I expect you're right, Camille, but at least he's gotten Cecilia here and hopefully with her feelings under control."

"Don't be concerned about Cecilia; she'll be fine, with or without Emil. Although having him with her probably is a good idea especially if Christmas gets going strong in his opening statement and if Pommus gets to testify about the confession."

"Did she tell you how she left things with her boss?"

"Yes. She told him everything. Of course he knew about the case; what lawyer in this part of the world doesn't? But he was really nice about it. He's letting her take a leave of absence from her job — with pay — pending the outcome of the trial. If Mrs. Dubrowski's acquitted, Cecilia can come back as soon as she's ready. But if things go the other way, since the firm is handling the Cory estate he'll have to terminate her because of the scandal that would erupt if it became known that she is the daughter of the woman who murdered Richard Cory."

"I suppose Mr. Berman's got to think of his firm's reputation first, not to mention the sizable piece of business that the estate represents. And it's decent of him to continue her salary. But still, I think that's a pretty hard-nosed attitude."

A bailiff came through one of the doors behind the judge's bench. "Mr. Adams, we have your client here in a holding cell. She says she'd like to speak with you before I bring her in and we seat the jury panel. If you'll follow me, Sir, I'll show you the way back.

"Also, one of your witnesses, a hard-of-hearing older gent, wants to speak with you real bad. I'm not supposed to kite messages, but my daddy and two uncles were in the Seventeenth Maine and served with him during the Civil War. It just don't seem right turning down a veteran like that. He's still over at the jail, so either you'll have to see him there, or wait 'till the testimony starts and I can bring him over.

"Thank you, Sheriff…"

"Joseph — Joe — Witherspoon."

"…Witherspoon. I think Mr. Silas will have to wait a bit. I really do need to see my client. Is it all right if my assistant, Miss Winters, comes with me?"

"Not unless she's a lawyer, Mr. Adams. Sorry, but I've bent all the regulations I intend to bend today. Since she's not a lawyer, she'd have to be searched. That'd mean I'd have to get a matron over here from the jail to do it and there might not be enough time. Once Judge Beauchamp decides it's time to get goin' he can get mighty impatient if things and people aren't in their proper places and ready to go."

"That's okay, Mr. Adams. I got the research on the jury panel this morning from your investigator. Why don't I go over it and see what he's come up with?"

"Good idea, Miss Winters. I'll be back as soon as I can."

Adams's heart was pounding as the bailiff led him through the door and to the holding cell. When he saw his client dressed in civilian clothes, an ankle-length soft pleated skirt with a fitted matching jacket over a crisp-looking white blouse, his hopes rose. "Good morning, Mrs. Dubrowski. If I may say so, you look very nice."

"Thank you Mr. Adams. I decided that since this is going to be my last opportunity to dress in clothing of my own choosing, I would attempt to look my best."

"Then you've…"

"Yes, Mr. Adams. Although I thank you for everything you've done, I've made my decision."

"And that is?"

"To plead guilty here. My daughter is here and this is where I want to stay. At least I will have her close by. I hope that eventually she'll marry and have children. And when they're old enough, if I live that long, they too can come visit their *bubbe* in the prison."

"I feared that would be your decision, Mrs. Dubrowski. But there is a new development in your case in Illinois. Will you let me tell you about it and keep an open mind?"

She stood grasping the cell bars and said nothing for what seemed to Adams like an hour. She turned and sat down on the metal bench bolted to the floor. "Yes, Mr. Adams, I owe you this much. I will listen and keep my mind open as you ask."

"Thank you, Mrs. Dubrowski. I believe what I'm about to tell you will make a difference. Have you heard of the famous lawyer Clarence Darrow?"

"Yes, I think so. I remember when I was still in Illinois. They would allow us to read the newspapers and I remember reading of his ability to win hopeless cases. He was very popular among the inmates. We would sometimes during rest periods talk about him wondering how our cases might have turned out if he'd been our lawyer. But what has he to do with me?"

"He wants to re-open your case in Illinois. He will petition the governor to grant you a full pardon based on the fact that you should never have been charged, much less tried and convicted, because you acted in self-defense and in defense of Cecilia."

"And this is possible, Mr. Adams?"

"Yes, it is possible, although by no means is there an absolute guarantee, Mrs. Dubrowski. But Mr. Darrow thinks there's a very good chance of succeeding, otherwise he'd not have taken the case."

"Why would he take my case, Mr. Adams? Surely he has been told that I have very little money."

"Mr. Darrow has also enjoyed considerable financial success along with his success in the courtroom. He has many clients who can afford to pay him and do pay him very well. He says that he will take your case *pro bono*."

"*Pro…*"

"*Pro bono;* it's a Latin expression. It's short for *pro bono publico*. It means 'for the public good.' All lawyers have a duty, when justice demands it, to assist those who cannot afford a competent lawyer. It serves justice and therefore it is in the public interest. Unfortunately, too many lawyers ignore their responsibility. But for you, it means that you have a real chance of freedom after the eighteen years you've spent in prison, ten in Illinois and eight at Oakdale Hall."

Esther Dubrowski sat for a while looking at the blank wall. Then she stood and paced back and forth the short length of the cell. She turned and stood facing the bars, tears glistening. "You have persuaded me once again, Mr. Adams. I can only hope that you are as good at persuading the judge and the jury. I will let you defend me on one condition."

"And that is?

"You must also promise to defend the O'Brien sisters, as you promised me before. One of them, I suppose you know, has been recaptured and the other one soon will be. I will pay your fee, as much money as I have."

"How do you…"

"Because of what they call the 'prison telegraph.' Anything that goes on, in a jail or in a prison, does not remain secret for very long. I knew…everyone in the women's cell block and the men's as well…knew within minutes that one of the girls had been recaptured. We also found out that as soon as she was processed she was taken to the Industrial School."

"Without a hearing?"

"No. She had a hearing if you could call it that. The judge…the judge who was going to hear my case…"

"You mean Judge Gribble?"

"Yes, that's the one. " She turned her head and spat at the floor. "That *mamser*. He came to the sheriff's office, signed the paper and the sheriff himself took her to Winthrop Hill. The sheriff said he didn't want the responsibility for keeping her in his jail.

"They — the twins — somehow read each other's minds. The other sister will come to free her and so she too will be captured."

"What is it about the Industrial School that makes you so concerned?"

"Unless you promise me that you will be also their lawyer, Mr. Adams, I will not tell you."

"Yes, yes, of course I promise, Mrs. Dubrowski. Unless representing them somehow conflicts with my representing you or another client, not that I have that many…"

"Judge is ready for me to bring in the jury panel, Mr. Adams."

"Oh, thank you Deputy Witherspoon." Adams turned to his client, "Mrs. Dubrowski, they're ready for you in the courtroom. They want us to be seated at the counsel table when the jury panel comes in. We'll finish this conversation later."

"Sir, if you'll stand back, I'll open the cell and escort your client to the courtroom." As he inserted the key in the lock he looked at Esther and asked her, "Do I need to handcuff you, Ma'am?"

Esther smiled at the deputy, "No, Sir, that won't be necessary. I'm not going anywhere until the judge tells me that I can."

While Adams was speaking with his client, Christmas and Matthews had set up shop at the front counsel table on the jury's side of the courtroom. As Adams and Mrs. Dubrowski entered the courtroom Adams saw in Christmas that same look that had given Adams a chill at their first meeting. It was impossible to describe, but it made Adams think that it must be how a butcher looks when approaching a lamb about to be slaughtered. The two opposing sides had exchanged pseudo-pleasantries at the in-chambers conference, so there was no need of further conversation. From now on they would speak to one another only by addressing the court.

Adams sat down next to his client and leaned toward her. "Don't let Christmas intimidate you, Mrs. Dubrowski."

"I am not afraid of him, Mr. Adams. It's he who is afraid of you."

"Afraid of me? Why would he…how can you tell?"

"It's a skill I learned in prison. I learned to read English and I learned to read people. Such knowledge is something you must have to survive inside. You need to be able to tell whether someone means to be your friend or to do you harm in some way. Either a matron or another prisoner. If you do not learn to tell the difference, things can go very badly for you."

Camille, who had been seated at the second row counsel table came up behind Quincy and gently tapped him on the shoulder. "Mr. Adams, here is what I have so far on the jury panel. The investigators divided the list and worked as many names as they could. I put a red check-mark beside those names that I thought would merit special notice. I still have a couple of pages to go. Should I stay at the second table?"

Adams took the pages and put them on the table. "Thank you, Cam…Miss Winters. First I'd like you to meet our client. Mrs. Dubrowski, this is my assistant Camille Winters."

"I am so glad to meet you, Miss Winters. When they brought me down from Augusta yesterday afternoon Rabbi Klein was able to visit me for just a few minutes. He told me how hard you've been working on my case. He said that you are the person who finally found Cecilia."

"I hope you're not…"

"No, no, Miss Winters. I admit that I was not pleased when I first saw Cecilia in that office at the jail in Augusta as I'm sure Mr. Adams has told you. But now I know it was the right thing to do so I am most grateful to you."

"Miss Winters, please ask the bailiff if he can squeeze one more chair at this table. I'd rather have you here. If you need to tell me something during the trial, it wouldn't look good for you to have to get up and tap me on the shoulder every time." Just as this had been accomplished the bailiff advised that a second bailiff was about to begin seating the jury panel. This necessitated everyone on both sides of the aisle turning their chairs around and moving to the front side of the second tier tables so that they could see and be seen by the prospective jurors as they filed in to the courtroom and took their assigned seats.

Seating the panel took some time owing to the fact that the prospective jurors had been doing nothing for nearly an hour and were as if by tacit agreement collectively taking their own time in responding to the bailiff's roll call. When the seating was completed, the chief bailiff retired to the judge's chambers to inform the clerk that all was in readiness.

Trial court judges soon learn that court cannot begin without them. What judges do when they are supposed to be on their benches dispensing justice—but are not—is a question that vexes all trial lawyers. Whatever the cause, Judge Beauchamp had taken the lesson to heart and kept those in the courtroom fidgeting in their seats for nearly the next half-hour. So when the bailiff finally intoned "all rise" more than a few thought briefly about staying put in their seats.

When everyone had resumed their seats, Judge Beauchamp got down to business in a hurry. "Gentlemen, you've been summoned here as prospective jurors in a criminal case in which the defendant is accused of murder." This last word was spoken slowly and an octave or so below the judge's normal voice. "This is the most serious charge the state can bring against a person, except for treason in wartime." Adams didn't much care for the judge placing Esther Dubrowski just a cut above a German sympathizer working to undermine the war effort. He started to rise, but then decided that all he could do would be to ask the court for a mistrial, which he almost certainly wouldn't get. Better, he thought, to pick your battles, especially battles with the judge.

"This alleged murder," again the dragging out of each syllable, "is alleged to have taken place just outside Tilbury Town which, I'm sure most of you know, is in Kennebec County, not Cumberland County. The case was moved here, I'll tell you frankly, out of concern that because of the prominence of the deceased the defendant might not receive a fair trial in Kennebec County. I'm telling you this because there will be no cause for such concern in this court. The defendant and the state for that matter are both entitled to a..." pause, "...fair trial. And I mean for them to have just that." Adams made a mental note that the judge had used the word "deceased" and not "victim".

"What's going to happen now is that I'm going to ask you some questions in order to determine whether it's appropriate for each of you to serve on the jury in this case. What I'll do first is ask you a series of questions that go to whether you're legally qualified to sit on a jury. If your answer is 'yes' to any of these questions or if you're not sure, when I'm through the bailiff, Mr. Witherspoon, will have you form a line to come up here and tell us about it.

"Now remember, you don't have to raise your hand or answer out; just wait until I'm through and join the line, if there is one. The first question is: Are you a citizen of a country other than the United States? Next, is your principal residence anywhere but Cumberland County? Third, have you ever been convicted of a felony or are you presently under indictment for a felony? A felony is a crime for which you can be sent to prison for longer than a year. Last, are you not able to read and to understand the English language? Now I realize that last question's down-right silly, but the law says I've got to ask it anyway." As expected, this last question elicited a few snickers, a few incredulous looks and what the judge was searching for: A couple of blank stares.

These questions produced a short queue, including the couple of blank stares who finally came forward when the bailiff read out their names. Judge Beauchamp quickly worked through the list and excused each one without objection from either side.

The next batch of questions produced a larger cohort composed of those who said they knew or knew of Richard Cory, or had read about the case in the newspapers, or who were in law enforcement or had a family member who was, or who had been the victim of a crime or had a family member who was a crime victim. When pressed by the judge, most agreed that their knowledge or experience would not prevent them from sitting as a fair and impartial juror, so they returned to their seats. A handful had figured out that if they admitted to a prejudice they would be excused. If their story had a ring of plausibility to it, Judge Beauchamp sustained the defense's challenges for cause and excused them.

Another question, one of those requested by the prosecution, produced a surprisingly large queue comprised of those who on account of religious or secular humanistic scruples did not believe that any man had the right to sit in judgment of his fellow man. Of this group, those who could convince the judge that their beliefs were genuine were excused to go on their way. Those who were unable to overcome his honor's skepticism returned to their seats as Adams made notes to not to use his peremptory challenges on any of this group. One prospect who objected to serving because women were not allowed to serve even though it was a woman who was on trial was sent back to his seat over Christmas's heated objection and with Adams's silent prayer that this one would survive Christmas's peremptory challenges and would end up as the jury foreman.

When Judge Beauchamp explained that an indictment is not evidence of guilt but is merely an accusation, there were an incredulous few who under the judge's questioning allowed that they now understood the presumption of innocence, or at least professed to do so. A single prospect who could not be persuaded that circumstantial evidence was sufficient to convict was excused on the state's challenge for cause. Finally there were two others who said that if the accused declined to testify that would indicate to them that she had something to hide so she was probably guilty. They stuck by their views despite near badgering questions from the judge and thus were excused on the defense's challenges for cause.

Once the *voir dire* was completed the judge declared a ten-minute recess and excused the panel so that the lawyers could exercise their peremptory challenges, that is, each side could challenge up to six prospective jurors and excuse them for no cause at all. Christmas and Matthews retired to the jury room to strike their list and Adams remained at the counsel table with Camille and Mrs. Dubrowski. Flammonde had a duplicate list which he'd been using to keep track of the veniremen who had been excused for cause. He had also made his own list of particularly interesting prospects based on the investigations done by Raymond and Morton. Before sitting down with Adams, Camille had conferred briefly with Flammonde and gotten his choices for peremptory challenges. These she gave to Adams who matched it against his own list and Camille's. Four names that showed up on at least two of the list were struck. Adams used one of his remaining two challenges on one prospect who said he had met Richard Cory several times and had followed the newspaper accounts closely. He said he could decide the case based on the evidence and not on anything else, but Adams was not convinced. The last challenge he offered to his client and then to Camille, both of whom declined. He finally ended up using it on a state employee who seems to Adams a bit too eager to serve.

At the end of the allotted ten minutes, the bailiff collected each side's list of strikes and took them back to the clerk who then went down the master list and circled the first twelve names that had not been excused, successfully challenged for cause or peremptorily stricken by either side. These twelve became the jury. The clerk read off the names and they were guided in turn by the bailiff to take their seats in the jury box. As soon the jurors were seated, by counting the number of excused, excused for cause and the twelve jurors, both Adams and Christmas realized that they'd had one common peremptory challenge; the bane of a trial lawyer's life. Each wondered to himself: "What did I miss that the other side picked up on?"

As Adams and Christmas were each trying to figure out why they'd struck a juror who the other side thought they themselves ought to strike, the bailiff again intoned "all rise," and Judge Beauchamp resumed the bench. He looked the jury over and glanced at his watch with satisfaction. He had the clerk swear in the jury and then he excused everyone for lunch, admonishing the jury not to discuss the case until they were told to begin their deliberations. He thanked those potential jurors who had not been selected for their valuable service and excused them from having to return.

Chapter Twenty-Four

"Gentlemen of the jury," Christmas paused and eyed each juror as though he could read their inner-most thoughts, "as Judge Beauchamp has already told you this is a murder case. Now although there are different types of murders, they all result in one thing: The death of one human being at the hands of another. We read in the newspapers about a drunken motorist running over and killing an innocent pedestrian; that's one type of murder. Perhaps you've heard of a tavern brawl getting out of hand when one man breaks a bar stool over the head of another man resulting in death. Or two men fight for the hand of a lady and in the heat of combat one pulls a knife and stabs the other. You've heard stories no doubt of a wife killing an unfaithful husband in a rage over his betrayal, or for that matter a man killing an unfaithful wife and her lover. Although, so I'm told, in the State of Texas that is not even a crime. Yes, gentlemen, in Maine these are all murder and they have one other thing in common: The perpetrator acts without first giving much thought to the consequences. That's because their capacity to think things through has been impaired either by alcohol, or by rage, jealousy or passion. They are driven by emotion rather than reason.

Now there are two other homicides, one person taking the life of another, that we also call murder: The armed robber who forces the terrified shopkeeper to empty his cash register and then shoots the shopkeeper to keep him from identifying the robber should he be arrested. That's one, and here is another: Where one person deliberately takes a handgun and shoots a sleeping person through the head, for whatever his or her reasons may have been, or indeed, as I'll mention later, perhaps for no reason at all. Those two kinds of murder have these things in common: First, they are crimes of planning, calculation if you will; second, until the very last instant he…" Christmas paused, "…or she could have said to herself, 'I do not have to pull the trigger.' And third, unlike the crime-of-passion killer who may or may not care whether he is caught, the murderess who plans her crime does not plan to be caught at all. Gentlemen of the jury," Christmas turned and pointed his finger at the defendant, "this is what is referred to as 'cold-blooded murder'…"

"Objection, Your Honor, that's…"

"Sustained. Gentlemen of the jury, 'cold-blooded murder' is not a legal term; it is one invented by the press and," he glared for a moment at Christmas, "Mr. Christmas knows better than to use it. Remember my instructions: What the lawyers say is not evidence. Nor is what they tell you necessarily the law. I will instruct you on the law at the proper time. Accordingly, you will disregard the prosecutor's last remark." Yes, Adams thought, like the jury can disregard a skunk in the jury box. The skunk may be gone, but the stench remains.

Unlike Pommus, Christmas was incapable of being or even appearing to be contrite. He continued his one-eyed stare boring into each juror. "Another thing I'd like to speak with you about before we start the evidence, Gentlemen of the Jury, is something we do *not* have to prove. We believe that Judge Beauchamp will instruct you that the State must prove each element of the offense charged beyond a reasonable doubt. That is the law, and it's a burden the State must undertake in every criminal prosecution. However, one thing we do *not* have to prove is motive. No, gentlemen, we do not have to prove to you *why*..." Christmas paused to give the jury time to think about what he was telling them..."the defendant Esther Dubrowski shot Richard Cory to death as he slept in his own home, a home, gentlemen, that he'd provided for the defendant for some eight years. Just as we do not have to prove why the drunken driver got drunk the night he killed that pedestrian, just as we do not have to prove that the robber who shot the shopkeeper did so to prevent the shopkeeper from identifying the robber in a police line-up, we have no duty to prove to you why the defendant in this case...the woman who sits here before you...decided one calm summer night to put a bullet through Richard Cory's head.

"Now the last thing I want to speak with you about before we get to the evidence is this business of the burden of proof. I mentioned a few minutes ago that the State must prove the elements of the crime with which a grand jury has charged the defendant..."

"Your Honor, I..."

"Overruled, Mr. Adams. What Mr. Christmas says is true, Gentlemen of the Jury. A grand jury in Kennebec County did charge the defendant Esther Dubrowski with the crime of murder. However, as I have already told you — and I trust that you will obey my instructions — an indictment is no more than an accusation. It carries no weight. So you will not consider it for any purpose except that the State must prove what is alleged in the indictment. In other words, if the State were to prove beyond a reasonable doubt that the defendant shot John Smith and not Richard Cory, it would be your duty to acquit because the indictment charges that the defendant shot Richard Cory. So too, and you might not like doing this, but if the State were to prove that Esther

Dubrowski took the life of Richard Cory by stabbing him in the heart with a butcher knife, again it would be your duty to acquit because the indictment alleges that the defendant killed Richard Cory by shooting him with a gun.

"Now, Mr. Christmas, would you like to complete your opening statement? It appears to me that you are making what amounts to a closing argument."

"Yes, Your Honor. As I was about to say, the State must prove its case 'beyond a reasonable doubt.' Gentlemen, that doesn't mean beyond *any* doubt whatsoever, or as some writers of popular fiction would say 'beyond a shadow of a doubt.' The only way the State could meet that burden of proof would be if each of you personally witnessed the commission of the crime...excuse me...the *alleged* crime. And obviously if you saw the crime occur, you'd be witnesses and not jurors." Christmas allowed himself a folksy smile. "All a reasonable doubt amounts to...again, as Judge Beauchamp has said, he will explain the law to you...but to my mind reasonable doubt means simply a doubt based on a reason. And that reason must be based on the evidence, or lack thereof. You may not convict the defendant simply because you feel sympathy for one-eyed state's attorneys, nor should you acquit just because the defendant is a woman.

"With that, gentlemen, I conclude the State's opening statement, confident that when you've heard the evidence, and Judge Beauchamp has instructed you on the law, you will, consistent with your jurors' oath to a true verdict render, find the defendant Esther Dubrowski guilty of the murder of Richard Cory. Thank you for your attention."

"Mr. Adams, do you have an idea how long your opening statement will be? If it'll take a while, then perhaps we should give the jury a ten-minute break."

"Actually, Your Honor," Adams rose to address the court, "I'd like to reserve my opening statement until after the State has rested its case."

"Very well, then. Gentlemen of the Jury, we will stand in recess for ten minutes. Please follow our bailiff. He will take you back to the jury room where there are convenience facilities. When we return, Mr. Christmas, you will call your first witness."

"All rise."

After the judge had left the bench, Adams turned to the spectator gallery. Flammonde nodded his head in approval. Last night he and Adams had debated whether Adams should reserve his opening statement or give it immediately in order to counteract what they anticipated Christmas would say in his. They had accurately predicted what Christmas would talk about, given that he couldn't mention the confession or Dubrowski's criminal record. They agreed that Christmas would test the judge early on, but they were pleasantly surprised at Judge Beauchamp's firm reaction to being tested. It was Judge Beauchamp's keeping Christmas on such a tight leash that in the end persuaded Adams to defer his opening statement, that and the fact that neither he nor Flammonde could come up with anything that didn't sound vapid at best, and at worst promised to put the jury to sleep.

"You may call your first witness, Mr. Christmas."

"Your Honor, the State calls Sheriff George Dowdy."

Sheriff Dowdy was summoned from the witness room and took the stand. After he was sworn and had taken his seat Christmas quickly led him through the preliminaries: His name, place of residence, his occupation. Christmas asked the sheriff whether his office had received a call that Sunday morning, August fourth. This question called for a hearsay response, but Adams let it go, figuring to save his objections for when they counted. Neither the rules of trial procedure nor the judge may impose any limit on the number of objections that a side can make. The jury, however, sets their own limits as to how much popping up and interrupting that they will allow a lawyer before they will start to punish the lawyer's client for the lawyer's butting in to prevent the witness telling what he knows.

Knowing this was probably what Adams was thinking, Christmas pressed forward. "Who received the call, Sheriff Dowdy?"

"The dispatcher who was on duty that morning. Do you want the name?"

"No, Sheriff, I don't think that will be necessary. And the dispatcher called you?"

"Yes, Sir."

"What were you told?" This of course was also hearsay and Adams's objection would no doubt have been sustained, but Adams wanted the jury to know that Mrs. Dubrowski had called the sheriff's office to report her employer's death. The fact that she did so would seem, Adams thought, to work in her favor.

Sheriff Dowdy paused, waiting for Adams to object. Seeing that Adams was sitting, his pencil poised waiting for the sheriff's answer, the sheriff continued. "I was told that the housekeeper, a Missus..." Dowdy paused again to emphasize that he'd learned his lesson and would not be caught in another lapse in his recall "…Dubrowski, called to report that the owner of Oakdale Hall, Richard Cory, had been shot sometime in the night and appeared to be deceased."

"Well, as a result of that 'phone call what, if anything, did you do?"

"I was well-acquainted with Richard Cory." Dowdy sat up a little straighter in his seat. "Knew him from his good works…helpin' out and all up at the Industrial School in Hallowell. Also knew he was well-known and highly-respected there in Tilbury Town. Anyhow, I told the dispatcher to call in every man who wasn't already on duty and have them assemble in my office as fast as they could get there. I got to my office within a few minutes and briefed my men on the dispatcher's call. We then loaded up two vehicles, turned on the red lights and sirens and headed out for Oakdale Hall fast as the machines would get us there."

Christmas quickly led the sheriff through his description of what he observed at Oakdale Hall, Adams taking a covert look now and again at the jury as Christmas worked through the details of finding the body. The jury appeared interested, but not hanging on every word. A few jurors nodded affirmatively when the sheriff said that there were no signs of forced entry or a struggle or evidence pointing to a burglary gone wrong apparently jumping to the conclusion—as Christmas intended—that Cory knew his murderer or that he was murdered in his sleep by someone in the household or who had free access to the premises. When Christmas asked the sheriff to identify the revolver found in Cory's hand as the murder weapon Adams was on his feet so fast that he knocked over his chair. "Objection, Your Honor. Assumes facts not in evidence. Indeed it assumes the very question the jury will be called upon to answer!"

"Sustained! Gentlemen of the jury you are instructed in the strongest possible terms to disregard Mr. Christmas's description of State's Exhibit Number One, the revolver, as the 'murder weapon.' Mr. Adams is correct. It is for you—not Mr. Christmas or Sheriff Dowdy—to determine whether the deceased's death was in fact 'murder' as I will define that term for you and whether State's Exhibit Number One was the weapon that fired the bullet that took the deceased's life, if in fact he did die from a bullet wound. As for you Mr. Christmas, you will not take such liberties in my courtroom again. Understood?" Another skunk in the jury box thought Adams. Esther Dubrowski, in disregard of Adams's instructions to her, gave his arm a reassuring pat.

"Yes, Your Honor. May I approach the witness?" Without

waiting for the judge to reply Christmas stood in front of the witness box and handed the revolver to the sheriff. "Now, Sheriff Dowdy, let me re-phrase the question: Is this the revolver that you found in Richard Cory's lifeless hand when you went to Oakdale Hall on the morning of August fourth?"

"Yes, Sir, it appears to be. This is a Smith & Wesson Model Seventeen six-shot, single-action revolver, same as I took from the hand of the deceased on August fourth. The last three digits of the serial number, eight-one-eight, are the same. I made a mental note at the time. The only difference is that the revolver I recovered on that Sunday had one spent casing and five live rounds in the cylinder, but this one's got only one live round and the rest of the cylinder's empty."

"Pardon me for interrupting, Mr. Christmas, but Sheriff Dowdy, would you please remove the live round and hand it to our bailiff, Mr. Witherspoon? I don't want anything untoward to happen while the weapon's in my courtroom."

"Yes, Sir." Dowdy removed the live round and handed to Witherspoon.

"Mr. Christmas, you may proceed."

"Thank you, Your Honor. Sheriff Dowdy, although you were not present on either occasion, do you know whether some tests were performed using the revolver subsequent to your taking it into your possession?"

"Yes, so my deputies have reported to me."

"And as far as you know, that would account for there being only one live round left?" Adams started to rise to object to the sheriff's second-hand knowledge as hearsay, but decided to let it go. Christmas would get the two experiments in through Doctor Goodson and Deputy Isaacson, and Adams was prepared to score a few cross-examination points when the experiments were put in evidence.

"Sus…" Judge Beauchamp started to sustain Adams's objection even before he'd made it and then caught himself. "Go ahead and answer the question, Sheriff Dowdy."

"Yes, Sir. My understanding is that two rounds were fired in each of the experiments. That's four, plus one left in the gun and one in Richard Cory's head; that accounts for all six rounds."

"Was the defendant, Esther Dubrowski, present when you were at Oakdale Hall?"

"Yes."

"Did you have any conversation with her at that time?"

"Yes."

"Before I ask you about what was said, Sheriff Dowdy, let me ask you how did she appear?"

"Well, she was dressed in…I don't know…a woman's dress. Weren't no blood or anything on it. Is that what you mean?"

"Not exactly, Sheriff Dowdy, but thank you for that information. What I meant was can you describe her demeanor? Did she appear distraught? Nervous? Upset? Had she been crying? That's what I mean."

"No, she was just as calm as could be. Just as though we'd come out to meet Mr. Cory to ask for a donation to our widows' and orphans' fund. You see…"

"Yes, thank you, Sheriff Dowdy. Now let's get to what was said. First, what did you say to her?"

"I asked her who she was, of course, and she told me her name and that she was Mr. Cory's housekeeper.

"I asked her to tell me what she knew about how Mr. Cory came to be shot dead in his own parlor. She said that she'd come downstairs that morning to make breakfast for herself and coffee for Mr. Cory because he'd want some when he awoke. She said she noticed the door to the parlor…I think they call it a 'music room'…was open and went to look in case Mr. Cory was already up. Said she always kept that door closed, but sometimes when Mr. Cory retired after she did, he'd leave it open.

"Well, she said that she went to the door and looked into the room. She said that's when she first saw Mr. Cory sitting in an armchair by the fireplace. She said it happened sometimes that Mr. Cory would fall asleep there and sleep through the night. She said she thought that's what he was doin', sleeping. She said she went to make coffee and came back a few minutes later to see if he was still asleep. She said she called his name softly a couple of times and when he didn't respond or even stir like a sleeping person might she went over to him. That's when she saw the bullet wound in his head and…"

"She said she saw 'the bullet wound in his head'? Are you quoting her exactly?"

"Yes, that's my recollection."

"So obviously she knew what a bullet wound looked like, wouldn't you say?"

"You could say that, yes, Sir."

"What else did she say on that occasion?"

"That Mr. Cory must have come home late, because she didn't

hear him come in. I asked her if she'd heard any disturbance, loud voices, or even any voices at all. She said no; she'd been in her room upstairs listening to music on her Victrola and then she'd gone to sleep."

"Did you make a search of the premises?"

"Yes, Sir, actually two."

"Tell us about those, but first did you ask permission to search the house?"

"For one of the searches, yes."

"Which one was that?"

"That was the second one."

"Tell us about the first one."

"That was right when we got there. I asked the defendant whether there was anyone else on the premises and she said no, except for the stable hand, Mr. Silas, who is hard of hearing and was probably out in the stable or somewhere on the property. But just to be sure, I had some of my men search the house and the immediate grounds in case there was an intruder still about."

"May we understand that they found no one?"

"Yes, Sir, that's correct."

"Then tell us about the second search."

"I asked if we could look around; maybe find a suicide note, some paper might be a reason for Mr. Cory to take his own life. She seemed pretty reluctant at first, but then I told her I'd go get a warrant and in the meantime we'd have to lock the place up and not let her or anyone else in until we'd made the search. So she kind of shrugged her shoulders and said okay."

"Where was the defendant while you made the second search?"

"She said she'd go up and wait in her room until we were through, and I told her no, that wouldn't be a good idea. I asked her to sit on a bench there in the front hall, so she did."

"Was she doing anything?"

"Well, I wasn't keeping an eye on her the whole time, but the few times I did come out there in the hall, she was just sitting there biting her lower lip and sort of wringing her hands."

"In other words, in contrast to her demeanor earlier, she appeared upset, maybe nervous?"

"Yes, Sir, I'd say so: Both nervous and upset."

"Like maybe she had something to hide?"

"Objection, Your Honor; calls for speculation as to the defendant's state of mind."

"Your Honor, it's part of the *res gestae…*"

"Overruled. Sheriff Dowdy, you may answer Mr. Christmas's question."

"Yes, Sir, like she maybe had something to hide.

"Then, when Dr. Goodson arrived and he and I and most of my men were there in the parlor she kept lookin' in every couple minutes or so, tryin' real hard to see what was goin' on."

"Objection, Your Honor. That's sheer speculation on the part of the witness. I request that you instruct the jury to disregard the Sheriff's opinion as to why Mrs. Dubrowski was looking in the parlor, if indeed she was."

"Overruled. Sheriff Dowdy is an experienced law officer. He can give his opinion based on his first-hand observation. The jury may consider it or not, as they see fit. Proceed, Mr. Christmas."

"Thank you, Your Honor. Now Sheriff Dowdy, back to the second search: Did you find a suicide note or a paper indicating why Mr. Cory'd want to take his own life?"

"No, Sir."

"Well, did you find anything that might in any way be connected to Mr. Cory's death?"

Adams was on his feet instantly. "Objection, Your Honor. Mr. Christmas's question is calculated to elicit an answer that will violate the court's pre-trial ruling."

"Counsel, approach the bench. Gentlemen of the Jury, we'll stand in recess for ten minutes. There's a matter I need to take up with the attorneys. Please retire to the jury room."

After the jury had left the courtroom the judge nodded to Adams. "Mr. Adams, what's your objection?"

"It's two objections, Your Honor. First, the question's an invitation for the sheriff to talk about the reference letter from the Illinois prison official. Even if he doesn't get to go into the contents of the letter, that's going to raise the question in the minds of the jurors as to what's in the letter. It's a question that'll never go away even if the defendant doesn't testify. It's another skunk in the jury box, Your Honor."

"Now just a minute…"

"Wait your turn, Mr. Christmas. And you, Mr. Adams, you can forget those kind of expressions in this courtroom. I won't have you disparaging opposing counsel. Clear?

"Yes, Your Honor."

"Good; what's your second reason?"

"The question calls for speculation. It allows the witness to speculate as to what is or isn't related to the death of Richard Cory. Mr. Christmas is asking the sheriff to speculate as to whether the letter, or for that matter anything else, is connected to the death of Richard Cory."

"Mr. Christmas?"

"Perhaps Mr. Adams is correct, Your Honor. I will waive my motion *in limine* and not object to Mr. Adams asking the sheriff whether he thinks Richard Cory committed suicide."

"Well, Mr. Adams?"

"I am usually glad to take yes for an answer, Your Honor. But in this instance, I think not, at least not without knowing with certainty whether the sheriff has changed his opinion in light of supervening events. From his testimony in the last few minutes, it is reasonable to assume that he has."

"Your Honor, if Sheriff Dowdy's changed his opinion, Mr. Adams can use his prior testimony to impeach him."

"Mr. Adams?"

"Your Honor, I'd just as soon Sheriff Dowdy kept his opinion to himself."

"In that case, Gentlemen, I will sustain Mr. Adams's objection. Sheriff Dowdy, you will not answer Mr. Christmas's last question. Do you understand?"

"Yes, Sir."

"May I ask Sheriff Dowdy what items he removed from Oakdale Hall?"

"Your Honor…"

"No, Mr. Christmas, you may not. You may ask him to identify specific items — except for the letter — as they may come up. But that's it. No mention of the letter unless the defendant takes the stand. Mr. Witherspoon, please bring the jury back in."

When the jurors were back in their seats, Christmas continued, "Just a couple more questions, Sheriff Dowdy. First, what became of the remains of the deceased?"

"Soon's Doc Goodson finished with him…"

"Wait a moment, Sheriff. Who is Dr. Goodson? You mentioned him a few minutes ago before our short recess."

"He's sort of the unofficial medical examiner for Kennebec County. Lives and practices there in Tilbury Town. I had one of my men go to his home and bring him out there to Oakdale Hall."

"Why did you do that Sheriff Dowdy?"

"I suppose just in the interest of being thorough. My office takes pride in being thorough in its investigations."

"There wasn't any doubt that Richard Cory was deceased when you got to Oakdale Hall, was there?"

"No, no doubt about that. I checked for a pulse; there wasn't one. Also, the body was pretty cold. I just wanted Doc Goodson's opinion as to whether Mr. Cory'd taken his own life, or someone else took it from him."

"We'll hear from Dr. Goodson presently. What did you do after Dr. Goodson finished whatever it was that he was doing?"

"He examined the body. When he was done I called Ulysses Davis, the undertaker there in Tilbury Town to ask him to take custody of the remains until after the coroner's inquest. Mrs. Davis...she answered the telephone...said that Mr. Davis was taking care of another funeral, I believe up in Augusta and she'd send him right out soon as he returned. I cautioned her not to say anything to anyone and to tell Mr. Davis to keep it to himself.

"I also sent one of my men to get a hold of Ebeneezer Ingersoll, he's the county coroner, let him know what was going on. I also told the deputy to tell him I thought we ought to have a formal inquest. After that, it was just a matter of waiting for Mr. Davis. I left some of my men there to do that and I went with the rest back to the office."

"Thank you, Sheriff Dowdy. Pass the witness, Your Honor."

"Mr. Adams, your witness."

"Thank you, Your Honor. Sheriff Dowdy, how long have you been sheriff of Kennebec County?"

"Since January, nineteen-oh-one; so almost eighteen years."

"And were you in law enforcement prior to that?"

"Yes, I was a police officer in Augusta for five years before that."

"So all told, you have almost twenty-three years in law enforcement. I bet you've arrested lots of folks during that time, haven't you?"

"Yes, Sir. I've had my share; too many to recall at this point."

"I'm sure that's true, Sheriff Dowdy. Let me ask you..."

"Your Honor," Christmas was on his feet, "in the interest of time, the State will stipulate—as Your Honor has already noted—that Sheriff Dowdy's a highly experienced law officer."

"I'm not sure, Mr. Christmas, that the point Mr. Adams is trying to make is merely that. You may continue, Mr. Adams."

"Thank you, Your Honor. Sheriff Dowdy, would some of the

arrests you've made have been at the scene where the crime was supposedly committed?"

"Yes, Sir."

"And I assume that you're familiar with the process of applying to the court for an arrest warrant? You have to convince the district attorney, and he in turn has to convince a judge that there's probable cause to arrest the person when you don't arrest them at the scene."

"Yes, Sir."

"Done that lots of times, I suppose?"

"Yes, Sir, done that lots of times. Just ask Mr....the district attorney."

"Let's go back for a minute to those cases where you'd arrest someone at the scene. What would cause you to arrest someone at the scene?"

"Oh, could be any of several things."

"What if the person acted nervous or distraught? Say he or she were wringing his or her hands and biting his or her lower lip. Would that cause you to take that person into custody?"

"It might, I just can't say."

"How about if that person kept trying to look over your shoulder, so to speak; see what's going on?"

"I don't know; it sort of just depends."

"What if that person didn't want to let you search the premises? Would you arrest him or her?"

"Depends; if we did search and found something incriminating, sure we would. Otherwise, I can't say."

"Now in the present case you didn't arrest my client, Esther Dubrowski, at the scene did you?"

"No, Sir, I didn't."

"Didn't go later that day or the next day and ask a judge for a warrant to arrest Mrs. Dubrowski, did you?"

"No, Sir."

"Thank you, Sheriff Dowdy. Now let me ask you a couple of questions about the wound in Mr. Cory's head. I'm sure Dr. Goodson will describe it in great detail, so I'd like for you to clear up just one point: There was no doubt in your mind that what you saw was a gunshot wound, is that correct?"

"Yes, Sir, definitely a gunshot wound."

"Any of your men see it besides yourself?"

"I reckon all of 'em musta looked at it while we were there."

"I see; any of them ask: 'What's that hole in Mr. Cory's head?'"

"Not that I know of."

"Well, if one of them had…had asked you what it was…what would you have said?"

"Objection, Judge. Calls for speculation on the part of the witness."

"Sustained. Mr. Adams, you'll have to try another way."

Adams paused for a few seconds. "Okay, Sheriff Dowdy, let me put it this way: There was this dead man sitting there in his armchair; he had a small, dark hole in his right temple. Have I got it right so far?"

"Yes, Sir."

"And there's this black powder-like stuff sort of spreading out from the hole in several directions. Right?"

"Yup, several directions."

"And there's a gun, a revolver, in this dead fellow's hand. That's how you found him?"

"I suppose so."

"I object to the answer, Your Honor, as non-responsive. Was it how you found him, or not? Do you not recall, Sheriff Dowdy?"

Judge Beauchamp turned to the sheriff. "Mr. Sheriff?"

"Er, yes, that's how we found him."

"So what I'd like to know, Sheriff Dowdy, is whether, given his appearance — being dead and all, the gun, the revolver, in his hand — and given the description of the wound, was it a surprise to you that Mrs. Dubrowski told your dispatcher that Mr. Cory'd been shot?"

"I suppose not, no Sir."

"Indeed, if Mrs. Dubrowski'd said the wound was anything other than a gunshot wound, you'd of found it mighty curious, wouldn't you?"

"Objection, calls for speculation."

"Sustained. Any further questions of this witness, Mr. Adams?"

"Yes, Your Honor, just a few. May I request State's Exhibit number six from the prosecution, Your Honor?"

"Mr. Christmas, do you have Exhibit number six?"

"I do, Your Honor."

"Do you plan to object to Mr. Adams offering it and asking this witness questions about it?"

"No, Your Honor, the State was going to offer this exhibit later, so if Mr. Adams wants to ask about it now, we don't object." Enoch Matthews rooted around in his exhibit box and found the envelope which he handed to Adams.

"May I approach the witness, Your Honor?"

"Yes, Counsel."

"Sheriff Dowdy, I hand you what has previously marked for identification as 'State's Exhibit Six' and ask you if you recognize it?"

"Yes, Sir, that's my handwriting and initials I wrote on there on the outside."

"Is Mr. Adams offering the exhibit, Your Honor?"

"Mr. Adams?"

"Yes, Your Honor, the defense offers State's Exhibit number six."

"No objection, Your Honor."

"Then State's Exhibit number six is admitted."

"Did you remove this envelope and its contents from Oakdale Hall on last August fourth incident to your investigation into the death of Richard Cory?"

"Yes."

"Where'd you find it? Was it in a desk, a cabinet, lying on a table?"

"It was in a drawer in the coffee table right where Mr. Cory was sitting...I mean where his body was found."

"I notice that the envelope is open, Sheriff Dowdy. Was it open when you first noticed it?"

"Yes, Sir, it was."

"Was it still open when you removed it from Oakdale Hall on August four, nineteen eighteen?"

"No, it wasn't."

"Then it was sealed?"

"Yes, it was sealed."

"And you know that because?"

"I sealed it."

"Why did you seal it, Sir?"

"To preserve the contents from tampering. So if you or the prosecutor asked me about it, I could testify that the contents are the same as when I sealed it."

"That's very professional of you, Sheriff Dowdy."

"Well, it's what we've learned to do; preserve the chain of custody."

"But this envelope hasn't been in your custody since August the fourth, has it?"

"No, it hasn't."

"Did you remove it from Oakdale Hall yourself, Sheriff Dowdy?"

"Yes, Sir."

"When did the envelope leave your custody?"

"On Monday, August fifth, the next day."

"Where'd it go? I assume you turned it over to someone?"

"Yes, I turned it over to Bascom Pommus, the Kennebec County district attorney during the coroner's inquest."

"Was it sealed at that time?"

"Yes, it was."

"Do you know who opened it?"

"Not first hand, but I understand that it was eventually turned over to Mr. Christmas and he opened it or had someone in his office open it."

"Your Honor, the State will stipulate that the envelope was opened in my office at my request and in my presence by Mr. Matthews, assistant district attorney for Kennebec County."

"Is that agreeable, Mr. Adams?"

"Yes it is, Your Honor."

"Very well, then, Gentlemen of the Jury you've heard Mr. Christmas's offer of stipulation, so I won't repeat it. You are instructed that you may consider the stipulation for evidence purposes with the same effect as though it had been in the form of sworn testimony from a witness."

"Mr. Adams, any further questions?"

"Yes, Your Honor. Sheriff Dowdy, now would you please open the envelope and examine the contents?"

The sheriff opened the envelope and spent a full minute shuffling through the automobile advertisements. "I've looked at them, Sir."

"Thank you, Sheriff Dowdy. Now can you tell the jury whether the contents as you've examined them just now are the same contents that you sealed in the envelope on August fourth?"

"Yes, Sir, just the same."

"Would you be so kind as to hold the contents up so that the gentlemen of the jury can see for themselves what we're talking about here?"

"Like this?" Sheriff Dowdy fanned half the advertisements out in each hand and held them up for the jury.

"Yes, that's it; thank you."

"They appear to me to be advertisements for different motorcars and one for a truck. That the way you see them?"

"Yup; I mean yes, Sir. Sorry."

"That's okay, Sheriff Dowdy; I don't get addressed as 'Sir' very much up in Tilbury Town. But those advertisements: Were any of them addressed to Mr. Cory, say like they came in the mail?"

Dowdy glanced through the stack on the back sides of each piece. "No, none of them looks like it came in the mail, unless it was in a separate envelope that got thrown away."

"They all look to me like maybe they were cut out of magazines or newspapers, or maybe something anyone could just go in a dealer's showroom and pick up from the salesman. Would you agree?"

"Objection; calls for speculation."

"Sustained. Move along, Mr. Adams."

"Yes, Your Honor. Just a couple of more questions. Sheriff Dowdy, did Mr. Cory own an automobile that you know of?"

"Yes, Sir, I've seen him driving it. In fact I rode in it as grand marshal of the Tilbury Town Fourth of July parade last year. It's a Packard sedan. Big automobile and I'd say right expensive."

"I imagine so, Sheriff Dowdy. Do you know what model year it is?"

"No, but I know he owned it I'd say as much as a year before I rode in it."

"So do you know why he'd have a bunch of advertisements for automobiles, mostly Fords, Chevrolets and if I saw rightly, one for a Ford truck, the new Model TT?"

"Objection, Your Honor. Calls again for speculation."

"I'll overrule the objection to the question as asked, Mr. Christmas. The witness can answer if he has actual knowledge. Sheriff Dowdy, do you understand? If you know why Mr. Cory had an envelope containing automobile advertisements in a drawer in a table in his parlor, you can answer, but you cannot guess."

"Yes, Sir, I understand. And no, I don't know why he had an envelope containing automobile advertisements...and one truck advertisement...in a table drawer in his parlor; it'd just be a guess on my part."

"Without telling us what, Sheriff Dowdy, did you have a guess on August fourth as to what he...Mr. Cory...was doing with those advertisements in the table drawer in his parlor?"

"Ob...oh never mind."

"Do you have an objection to the question, Mr. Christmas?"

"No, Your honor, just seems to me like a lot of the jury's and the court's time being wasted on this subject."

"I object to Mr. Christmas's side-bar comment, Your Honor."

"Sustained. Mr. Christmas, the jury and I will decide for ourselves whether Mr. Adams is wasting anyone's time. That said, Mr. Adams, I should also observe that it's increasingly difficult for me to see where you're going with this line of questions."

"Yes, Your Honor. If Sheriff Dowdy'll answer my pending question, I'll wrap up with just one more question. Do you recall my question, Sheriff Dowdy?"

"You wanted to know if I had a guess on August fourth as to why Mr. Cory had these advertisements, is that right?"

"Close enough, Sheriff; did you have a guess?"

"Nope, don't reckon I did."

"Thank you, Sir. Now just one last question: If I recall your testimony rightly, you're the one found the envelope; you're the one sealed it and wrote on it; you're the one transported it back to your office. Have I got that right, Sir?"

"Yup, I put it in my pocket and took it back to my office."

"Did you show it to anyone?"

"Mr. Adams, is that your 'one last question'?"

"I apologize, Your Honor. That's the next-to-last."

"Very, well, Mr. Adams, but I intend to hold you to that."

"Yes, Your Honor. Sheriff Dowdy, do you recall the question?"

"Yes, and the answer's no; I didn't show it to anyone."

Thank you, Sir. I appreciate your patience. Here's my last question: Why'd you go to all that trouble for an envelope full of automobile advertisements if you had no idea why Richard Cory had them? If you had no idea why he had them, how could you know they had anything to do with his death?"

"I...I...I don't know, I just did, Counselor."

"Thank you, Sheriff Dowdy. I pass the witness, Your Honor."

"Sheriff, will it disrupt the working of your office a great deal if we have you come back in the morning in case Mr. Christmas has any further questions for you?"

"That won't be necessary, Your Honor. The State has no redirect for this witness. As far as we're concerned, he may be excused to return to his duties."

"We have no objection to Sheriff Dowdy being excused, Your

Honor, provided that he agrees to return if needed."

"Is that acceptable, Sheriff?"

"Yes, Sir. Just call my office. The dispatcher always knows where I am."

"Very well, then. Sheriff, you're excused subject to recall. Do not discuss the case or your testimony with anyone except the attorneys, and then only if you wish to do so.

"We'll stand in recess until nine o'clock in the morning. Gentlemen of the Jury, you are not to discuss the case with anyone, which includes family. You are not to read anything about the case in the newspaper, and if someone tries to discuss the case with you, you must report that person to the bailiff in the morning. Have a good evening."

"All rise."

Chapter Twenty-Five

"Congratulations, Counselor." Flammonde handed Adams a cigar. "Try one of these: Cuban leaf, hand-rolled in Florida."

"Same here, Quincy. From where I sat, looked to me like the jury wasn't taken in by any of Christmas's flummery. Judge wasn't either. Want a pull?" Raymond offered the freshly-opened bourbon bottle."

"Just a sip, Lamar. I don't want what happened to me last time to happen again, at least until the trial is over. While I was sleeping on your bed, I had a dream and now I can't seem to put it out of my mind. You and Emil were arguing about something and Emil said something about he was the one got Esther Dubrowski into this mess. I don't remember the rest, just that part."

"That was some dream, Quincy. Did I say how I did it: Got her 'into this mess'?"

"Not that I remember, Emil. If you'll recall, I was pretty blotto at that point." Adams leaned toward Flammonde who had struck a wooden match and held it in Adams's direction. Adams rotated the cigar to be sure it was properly lighted. "Thank you, Emil." Adams took a satisfying puff on the cigar. "Say, this is pretty good. No offense to your Marsh-Wheelings, Lamar, but I think I like these a good deal more."

"Cigars are like women, Quincy, to each his own The Marsh-Wheelings are an acquired taste. I've got a question; been thinking about it ever since Christmas offered to let the sheriff give his suicide opinion. Why didn't you take him up on it? You said after the judge excluded it at the pretrial that keeping it out gutted your case for reasonable doubt."

"Well, I thought so at the time, and my not accepting Christmas's offer may be a mistake. But two thoughts occurred to me when he made the offer: One, I thought he made the offer a little too eagerly; he wanted me to accept it. Except for the fact it was the sheriff on the stand, it really didn't relate to my objection. He was just horse-trading; trying to get something he really wants in exchange for something he really doesn't care about. "Christmas wants that letter to get in too much for my liking. It's his only shot at motive. Remember what he said in his opening statement about not having to prove motive? He is worried about it. I was looking at the jury when he said it, and unless I'm badly misreading them — or at least two or three of them — they're going to need a motive to convict, at least on circumstantial evidence."

Nodding appreciatively, Flammonde asked," What's your other reason? You suppose he got the sheriff to change his opinion?"

"I'd say that's a good possibility. I started to ask if I could ask the sheriff his opinion outside the jury's presence."

"Why didn't you?"

"Lamar, even if the sheriff stuck by his opinion, it wouldn't amount to anything compared to the doctor's testimony. Time the doctor gets through, nobody on that jury's going to buy suicide anyway."

"If Christmas thinks he needs to prove motive, he's worried about the confession getting in." Flammonde took a sip from the bourbon bottle and offered it to Adams.

"No thanks, Emil. That's what I'm thinking too."

"Why do you suppose he's worried?"

"I wish I knew, Lamar. At some point he's going to call Pommus, and I guess we'll find out then."

"How's your client doing?" Lamar took out one of his Marsh-Wheelings and proceeded to fire it up.

"Okay, I suppose; at least Camille thinks she's holding up pretty well. Camille says she stiffened up when I started talking about the envelope. Then when the sheriff held up the automobile advertisements, she put her hand over her mouth as though she was trying to keep from laughing out loud. Anyway, that's what Camille thought. I was busy concentrating on the sheriff so I missed what Mrs. Dubrowski was doing."

"She have anything to say about it—the envelope—after the judge recessed for the day?"

"We didn't have much chance to talk. They wanted to get her back to the jail before feeding time so she wouldn't have to miss her meal, although I don't imagine that she was particularly hungry. But I did ask her if she'd seen the envelope before today. She said no, but I don't believe her. I started to press her on it, but by then the deputy was getting real antsy, so I had to let it go."

"Well, now we know it was Sheriff Dowdy made the switch."

"I expect you're right, Emil." Lamar passed the bottle to Emil. "If somebody else'd made the switch, Dowdy wouldn't have said the contents are the same. At least now we know where to look, maybe find what was really in there."

"Maybe Pommus made the switch, or maybe even Christmas."

"Possible, Quincy, but not likely." Flammonde took another sip and passed the bottle to Adams who hesitated a moment and then took a sip before passing it back to Flammonde. "That would mean the sheriff is covering up for someone. Given the enmity between the sheriff and the district attorney, I can't imagine it'd be Pommus. In fact, I can almost see Dowdy making the switch and then blaming it on Pommus."

"You don't think Christmas made the switch? Why would he do that and why would the sheriff back his play?"

"Good questions, Lamar. Unless Christmas is up to his eyeball in some really bad business, it wouldn't make sense. If whatever was in the envelope originally had anything to do with Cory's death, he'd likely have turned it over to me. Now I've heard of prosecutors *losing* evidence that hurts their case, but whatever else Christmas may be, I can't see him doing something like that."

"Yeah, and the fact that the envelope was sealed—as least so Christmas says—means he didn't know what was in there until he opened it."

"You're right, Emil. In order to pull that off, Matthews would have to be in on it along with the sheriff and Christmas and Lord knows who else." Lamar flicked the ash off his cigar and shook his head.

Adams, noticing that his own ash was getting long reached over and flicked it into Lamar's ash tray. "Well, now that we've decided that it was the sheriff made the switch in order to hide something, all we need to do is find out what he doesn't want made public. Emil, any ideas on how we...you're...going to do that?"

"Maybe you don't want to know that, Quincy."

"You're probably right, Lamar, but just speaking hypothetically, how would you go about it?"

"Well, if I were Emil and I was ram-roddin' this outfit, I'd have already sent Maurice up to Augusta where, if Maurice is doin' his job, about now he'd be in a bar downin' Irish whisky—that's his drink—and raisin' a ruckus. Maybe get too friendly with another fella's girl, maybe start up a three-card Monte game; that'll do it every time. Start messing with a man's girl friend that can get risky sometimes; might have to hurt someone so's not to get hurt yourself."

"Do what every time?"

"Get yourself thrown in jail, Son. How else you expect he's gonna find out what the High Sheriff's hidin'?"

"He gets thrown in jail, based on my limited observation, isn't he going end up in a cell? With a locked steel door? And guards? Maybe a bunch of other prisoners take umbrage at him getting a free pass to roam around the jail while they gotta just sit there?"

"Don't forget Maurice's background, Quincy. Among his many talents he did an escape act for years. Some say he's as good as Houdini. He can pick his way out of a pair of handcuffs, hands behind his back, in about eight seconds. Seen him do it. He'll find what we're looking for and be back here in time for breakfast.

"As far as any jealous cell-mates: Couple packs of cigarettes, that'll keep 'em happy. If one of 'em gets pushy, Maurice's got this wrestling hold put a man to sleep in twenty seconds. Want me to show it to you?"

"Thanks, Lamar; I'll take your word for it. Just one other thing bothering me though: How's he going to know what *it* is when he finds it?"

"That's going to involve you and your client. You'll have to talk her into telling what she knows."

"Thanks, Emil. I suppose you've forgotten what you learned in law school about misprision of felony."

"I wouldn't worry too much about that, Quincy. If what's in that envelope is as bad as it's likely to be, won't be many folks thinkin' in those terms. Besides, all you've got to say is that whatever it is got shoved through your mail slot; you don't have to say you discussed it with your client. You just hand it over to Christmas...or better yet the judge...and let them run with it."

"That's a great comfort, Lamar. Would you mind passing the bottle again? I need to get some sleep. And now, thanks to the polymathic Maurice, I've got a whole new nightmare to keep me company.

"Gentlemen," Adams ground out the stub of his cigar and handed the bottle back to Lamar, "I'm off to my room. I want to look over my notes on Dr. Goodson before the bourbon makes that a useless endeavor. Good night."

"Have a good night, Quincy." Emil stood and shook Adams's hand. "You're doing a great job; Clarence Darrow couldn't have done better today."

After Adams left, Lamar took a pull on his cigar. "Poly...mathic?"

"Let the kid be, Lamar. Remember his background: Major in classics, minor in English literature; he's bound to let loose a 'polymathic' or some such once in a while. Just hope he doesn't do it with the judge or in front of the jury."

"Any idea what it means?"

"Not a one, Lamar; mind passin' th' bottle?"

"What's he gonna' do with the doctor?"

"Not much, I expect. He's puttin' all his eggs in the confession basket. 'Course he's still got Smedley and Boyles and Cory's will. Jury takes a dislike to Smedley and Boyles, they just might disregard the confession…"

"And the fact she's an escaped convict…a murderer at that."

"Funny thing about juries, Lamar. You've been in the law-enforcement business longer than I have. My experience, they get it right most of the time."

"I don't know, Emil, some folks I worked with down in Texas, they didn't want to take the chance a jury'd get it wrong, 'specially the accused was a Mexican or a colored fella. Some of those county sheriffs wouldn't worry about what a jury'd do; took care of that end themselves. That's why I got out."

"Which is why you're sittin' in a hotel room in Portland, Maine 'stead of whatever else you'd be doin' down in Lubbock or wherever it was."

"Speakin' o' Maine, what are we doin' here, Emil? I mean besides helpin' out some nice folks didn't mean to get mixed up with us in the first place? We don't start earnin' our keep pretty soon, boss's gonna ship both of us off to Lubbock."

"It pretty much comes down to this: Quincy walks Esther Dubrowski, which means someone else killed Cory; that is unless you believe he pulled the trigger himself."

"Maybe, Emil, but just 'cause jury finds her not guilty that don't mean she isn't or that Christmas'll give up thinkin' she is. All it means is that young Quincy did a better job than Christmas. What's that you said one time? 'A trial's a contest to see who has the best lawyer?' Christmas may just pack up his briefcase and head back up to Augusta, leave it to Pommus and the sheriff to handle things from then on."

"I don't think so, Lamar. You see how fast Christmas got rid of Dowdy once Quincy got through with him. He knows something's not *kosher*…well, maybe that's the wrong word…something's not *right* about that envelope. And if he thinks that, he's gotta be thinkin' something's wrong with Dowdy.

"Maurice finds what was really in that envelope and it puts Dowdy in the middle of things, I expect he'll roll over on the rest of them to save his own fat ass."

"And if he doesn't…I mean if Maurice doesn't get lucky…"

"We'll deal with that problem when it happens. We've also got our man in Augusta; he may come up with something."

"Emil, if this isn't the toughest job we've ever had, I don't want to see the one that is. We've been chasing our tails up here for months."

"Stick with it, Lamar, I got a feeling that Richard Cory's turning in his grave about now."

Chapter Twenty-Six

"Quincy Adams, your suit smells like a cheap cigar."

"And a cheerful 'good morning' to you as well, Miss Winters. Actually, it was an expensive cigar, at least so Emil said."

"How was the bourbon? Was that expensive too?"

"I suppose; I didn't ask. Does my suit really smell?"

"Like a cold chimney after a rainstorm.

"Here's Mrs. Dubrowski. After court take your suit down to the hotel bell captain; he'll get it brushed and aired out for you. Really, Quincy. Good morning, Mrs. Dubrowski. Cecilia sends her love. She thinks things went really well yesterday. So do I."

"And what does Mr. Adams think?"

"I'm pleased at how things went. I'm glad I didn't bite on Mr. Christmas's offer to let the sheriff give his opinion about whether Richard Cory took his own life."

"But you said that would be good for us...for me."

"Possibly, but I think...it's very complicated, Mrs. Dubrowski, I..."

"I am not stupid person, Mr. Adams; is jury going to say I am guilty?"

"No, Esther...Mrs. Dubrowski. I think first of all that the sheriff would now say that he's changed his mind; it wasn't suicide after all. Second, I don't think the jury cares in the least what Sheriff Dowdy says. I did make him look pretty bad yesterday. It's all going to come down to the confession...or as Rabbi Klein prefers to call it, the 'statement:' If I can keep it out, the prosecution's finished and you're a free woman, at least in Maine; if the statement gets admitted and the jury hears it, then it'll come down to whether the jury believes you."

"Yes, this you have said."

"That's why Christmas wants so much to get the G. Miller letter into evidence. He's worried that unless he can give the jury some believable reason for you to have killed your employer, the jury is more likely to believe you when you tell them the statement's false and why you made it up."

"You are correct, Mr. Adams; this business is very complicated. But it's best that the jury doesn't get to hear the confession...the statement. Is that not so?"

"Yes, Mrs. Dubrowski. And I expect we'll have the answer to

that question this afternoon. That's probably when Christmas is going to put District Attorney Pommus on the stand. But first, we'll have to hear from Dr. Goodson."

"All rise!"

"Good morning. Counsel, are you ready to proceed?"

"The State is ready, Your Honor."

"As is the defense, Your Honor."

"Very well, then Mr. Witherspoon, you may bring in the jury."

Once the jury was seated and wished a good morning by the judge, Christmas rose, "May it please the court, the State calls Dr. Philip Goodson."

Christmas took some time leading Dr. Goodson through his education and background in order to be sure the jury was duly impressed. After Christmas led the doctor through his having been summoned by the sheriff and his arrival at Oakdale Hall, he asked the doctor whether he had in fact examined the body of Richard Cory there at Oakdale Hall. Dr. Goodson described how the body looked...the wound, the state of rigor and lividity... and how he'd checked for any signs of life. Through all of this, as expected, the jury sat intently taking in every word.

"Dr. Goodson, you've now told us that you did an examination of the deceased there at Oakdale Hall. Did you have a further occasion to examine the body of the deceased?"

"Yes, I did."

"When and where did that subsequent examination occur?"

"In the embalming room at Davis & Son funeral home in Tilbury Town on the morning of August sixth."

"Was anyone else present?"

"Yes, Sir. Should I just go ahead and say who?"

"Yes, Doctor, please do."

"Well, there was District Attorney Pommus; a deputy from the sheriff's office, Mr. Davis, his assistant Adolphus Presley. Then there was Eb Ingersoll...he's the coroner...and the six men who made up the coroner's jury. Well, before we got through, it was down to five. One of the jurors became...um...indisposed."

"Thank you Dr. Goodson. Now what was the purpose of this second examination?"

"So I could show the coroner and the coroner's jury what I meant when I testified the previous day at the inquest about the skin area surrounding the entry wound. A couple of the jurors wanted to see for themselves what I was talking about, so Eb recessed the inquest until Tuesday morning. Then had Mr. Davis come in the courtroom and arranged with him for everyone to come out to his place to see first-hand what I was talking about."

"And what was it in particular that you were talking about, Dr. Goodson?"

"The presence of a star-like pattern of gunshot residue...powder and ash...on the skin around the bullet wound in Richard Cory's head."

"Why was that important?"

"Because to me it said loud and clear that Richard Cory didn't shoot himself; someone else pulled the trigger."

"Was there also a demonstration of what you were talking about done there in Mr. Davis's basement?"

"Yes, Sir, there was."

"May Mr. Matthews approach the witness, Your Honor?"

"Go ahead, Mr. Matthews." Matthews approached the witness stand with a paste-board box from which he removed the flour sack used in the test at the mortuary.

"Dr. Goodson," do you recognize the object that Mr. Matthews is holding up there?"

"Yes, I do."

"Please tell the court and jury what it is."

"It appears to be the flour sack we obtained from Daisy—Mrs. Ulysses—Davis that was used to show the coroner's jury what I was talking about: The difference between the gunshot residue from a contact wound...that is one where the barrel of the gun is held pressed against the skin of the victim...and the residue pattern where the gun is fired with the business-end of the barrel a short distance from the victim's skin.

"Yes, this is the same flour sack. I wrote my initials, 'PG', in pencil in the lower right-hand corner."

"Your Honor, we offer State's Exhibit Three in evidence."

"Mr. Adams?"

"No objection Your Honor."

"State's Exhibit Three is admitted without objection."

"Now, Dr. Goodson, with Mr. Matthews holding the exhibit up so that the jurors can see it, would you please explain what it is we're looking at?"

Dr. Goodson took out his fountain pen to use as a pointer and with it showed the jury the difference between the two residue patterns and explained how they occurred. With little prompting from Christmas, the doctor explained the significance of the fact that in the instance at hand, the residue pattern made it extremely unlikely that Richard Cory was the one who fired the weapon. Christmas then walked the doctor through the absence of a suicide note and the absence of any gunshot residue on Richard Cory's hand.

"So if I understand your testimony, Dr. Goodson, you're of the opinion, for the reasons that you've just given, that Richard Cory did not take his own life by placing the barrel of the revolver next to or in very close proximity to his right temple and pulling the trigger?"

"That's correct."

"Is there even one bit of physical evidence that you saw that would lead a medical man...someone with your training and experience...to conclude that Richard Cory shot himself sometime between the late hours of August third and the early morning hours of August fourth?"

"No Sir, nothing at all."

"Thank you, Dr. Goodson. I pass the witness."

"Mr. Adams, any cross-examination?"

"Yes, if the court please. Just a few questions.

"Dr. Goodson, based on your examination of the deceased on the morning of August fourth, you concluded that the wound to Mr. Cory's right temple was inflicted peri-mortem...that is about the time of his death?"

"Yes, that's so."

"Did you conduct an autopsy on the body of Richard Cory?"

"No, I did not."

"Have you ever done an autopsy, Dr. Goodson?"

"I assisted or participated in many, many such procedures during my medical school tenure and during my internship and residency."

"Would you please explain to the jury what an autopsy is and what the purpose of an autopsy is?"

"An autopsy is an examination and dissection of the body after death to determine the cause of death. Usually it involves surgically opening the body cavities and inspecting the major organs...the heart, lungs, liver, sometimes the brain...for signs of disease. Sometimes you examine the major blood vessels, the aorta, the carotid arteries, sometimes the stomach and bowels. If there's external evidence of trauma, say a gunshot or knife wound, or it is reported, for example, that the deceased fell off a ladder, then you'd want to examine the site of the trauma, look for a skull fracture, broken neck. Is that clear, or do you want more?"

"No, that's fine, Dr. Goodson. Now I think I heard you say that the purpose of an autopsy is to determine the cause of death. Did I hear you correctly?"

"Yes, you did."

"If I recall your other testimony rightly, you said that you did not conduct an autopsy on the body of Richard Cory."

"Again, that's correct."

"Then I have just one more question relating to your testimony on direct examination by Mr. Christmas: You did *not* say that Richard Cory died from the gunshot wound that you saw, is that correct, Dr. Goodson."

"Yes, Mr. Adams. Mr. Christmas didn't ask me that question."

"Had he asked you that question, Dr. Goodson, you would not have been able to give him a categorical—that is a yes or no—answer. Is that correct, Dr. Goodson?"

"Yes, Mr. Adams, that's correct."

"And that's because you didn't perform an autopsy?"

"Didn't do one; wasn't asked to."

"Would you have done so if asked?"

"Yes, I would."

"Now, Dr. Goodson, let me sort of switch topics on you if I may. Based on your examination of the deceased Richard Cory at his residence—Oakdale Hall—on the morning of August fourth, did you form an opinion as to whether Mr. Cory died where you found him?"

"No, I did not."

"If asked, could you have expressed such an opinion with any degree of professional certainty? I mean an opinion that you could give a good medical reason for."

No, Sir, I could not."

"In other words, Dr. Goodson, Mr. Cory could have met his death…whether by gunshot wound to the head or some other means…anyplace, and not necessarily his own parlor."

"That's true, Mr. Adams. However, although Mr. Cory was slim of build, he was muscular. I would estimate that at his death he weighed a hundred forty pounds, give or take. And that would be…no humor intended…what you'd call 'dead weight,' that is it would have taken a very strong individual or even two people to carry the corpse from where Mr. Cory died to where he was found."

"So it's possible that if Richard Cory met his death somewhere other than his parlor that might account for Mrs. Dubrowski saying to Sheriff Dowdy that she didn't hear any kind of disturbance or gunshot."

"I object, Your Honor. The question calls for speculation on the part of this witness."

"I tend to agree, with Mr. Christmas on that one, Mr. Adams. Gentlemen of the jury, you must form your own inferences and conclusions from the evidence.

"Thank you, Dr. Goodson. Pass the witness, Your Honor."

"Redirect, Mr. Christmas?"

"Yes, Your Honor.

"Dr. Goodson, did you have occasion to treat and examine Richard Cory at any time prior to August fourth, that is while he was still alive?"

"Yes I did. It was back in early May of this year. He came in as a result of an accident that occurred…as he told me…while horseback riding. I reintegrated a separated shoulder."

"You say you examined him at that time?"

"Yes, I did. Someone comes in from a riding mishap, you've got to think broken bones, possible concussion. So I persuaded Mr. Cory to allow me to give him a thorough examination."

"Did you note any other disease or adverse condition present?"

"No, aside from a slightly separated shoulder, Mr. Cory was in perfectly good health as far as I could tell."

"Thank you, Dr. Goodson. The State has no further questions."

"Mr. Adams?"

"Just this, Your Honor: Dr. Goodson, is it possible that Mr. Cory may have had some other serious medical condition that had not yet progressed to the point where it presented any clinically-observable symptoms?"

"Yes, Mr. Adams, that's possible. However I feel sure that if Mr. Cory had, just as an example, a fatal heart attack on August fourth I'd have recognized some symptom or another back in May."

"Thank you, Doctor. That's all I have for Dr. Goodson, Your Honor."

"Counsel, any objection to Dr. Goodson being excused?"

"No, Your Honor, the defense has no objection, as long as he remains subject to recall."

"The State has no objection, Your Honor."

"Dr. Goodson, you are excused subject to recall. Please leave your telephone number with our bailiff in case you need to be recalled. Also, you are still under the Rule; in other words, you should not discuss your testimony or anything about the case except you may speak with an attorney for either side if you wish to do so."

"Gentlemen of the Jury, this is a good point to stop and to take our lunch recess. Please be back in the jury room by one fifteen. And bear in mind the instructions I gave you yesterday: Do not discuss the case among yourselves or with anyone else. And if someone tries to discuss the case with you, please report the incident to our bailiff."

"All rise."

"You've hardly touched your lunch, Mr. Adams. Is something wrong?"

Adams wrapped his ham and cheese sandwich, all but the two bites he'd taken, back in the wax paper it came in when Camille brought it in along with chicken salad sandwiches for herself and Mrs. Dubrowski. Adams laid the sandwich next to where he sat on the steel bench. Camille had persuaded the bailiff that since she was still presumed innocent it would be unfair that Mrs. Dubrowski be forced to go without lunch. And when she pointed out that the logistics of providing personnel and transport from the courthouse to the jail and back would be both costly and time-consuming, the bailiff relented and permitted her to bring in lunch for all three to the holding cell behind the courtroom.

"I'm just not hungry, I suppose, Mrs. Dubrowski."

"That's not right, Mr. Adams. Miss Winters went to a great deal of trouble to bring you…us…lunch, the least you could do would be to eat. Your mother, I'm sure taught you better…"

"I know. It's just…"

"Just that you're now worried about the case, Mr. Adams? I thought, from what little I know that you got a very important admission out of Dr. Goodson. Now, since Mr. Cory could have been shot somewhere else, this experiment you told me about is meaningless. Is that not so?"

"Yes, as long as you don't have to testify."

"So you're worried that I'll have to testify…that the judge will allow my statement to be heard by the jury?"

"Yes, Mrs. Dubrowski, that's true."

"But you have from the beginning had concerns about this; have you not eaten for a month? Why *mitn derinnem* are you so worried that you cannot eat?"

"Mitten? I'm sorry, Mrs. Dubrowski, I haven't learned that one yet."

"I'm sorry, Mr. Adams. I still think first in Yiddish. Why suddenly are you so worried?" Has something happened?"

"I guess it's because in just a little while Christmas is going to put Pommus on the stand. All through the weeks of research and preparation, until now I've been able to look at the confession...statement...as something I'll have to deal with in the future. And now the future's here; the admissibility of the statement is no longer an abstract question. It's the moment of truth...when we find out whether I'm a lawyer or just an empty suit." Adams slumped down placing his elbows on his knees.

"You're no empty suit, Quincy Adams." Camille pushed aside Adams's sandwich and sat down next to him putting her arm across his shoulders and pulling him toward her. "You stop that! Since the trial started, as my father would say: 'You've been whipping Christmas like a rented mule.' And you'll whip him on the confession too."

After about a minute Adams stood letting Camille's arm fall to her side. "Ladies, I apologize for feeling sorry for myself. I shouldn't let my private fears become yours. It's just that...and I know, Mrs. Dubrowski, that the outcome of the case means so much more to you and to Cecilia...but when you put everything you have into a case, if it doesn't go your way, well it's pretty hard."

"Miss Winters is right, Mr. Adams, you will beat this man Christmas like...like a rented mule; whatever means this expression. But don't worry about me, Mr. Adams, whatever the outcome, I'll manage. Just knowing that you and Miss Winters and Rabbi Klein have tried so hard and that you care so much is enough for me. And that I now have my daughter back, I can deal with whatever Maine and Illinois have in store for me."

"Counsel, you about ready? It's almost ten after, and Judge'll be wantin' to get started."

"Yes, thank you, Mr. Witherspoon; we're ready to go."

Chapter Twenty-Seven

"The State calls Bascom Pommus, Your Honor."

Upon entering the courtroom, Pommus instantly observed the reporters for both the Portland and Augusta papers sitting in the front row of the spectator gallery. He gave the spectator galley his best politician's smile and turned to face Judge Beauchamp. The judge nodded to the clerk who rose to administer the witness oath.

"Your Honor, since Mr. Pommus is an officer of the court, it is not necessary that he be sworn."

Pommus turned to Christmas, "That's okay, Rev...I mean Mr. Christmas. I don't mind being sworn. Even though I'm an officer of the court, I'm here as a citizen doing my civic duty to come before the court," Pommus turned to the jury box, "and these twelve good gentlemen of the jury and give my evidence in this case, a case which is so important to the people of Kennebec County."

"And as an officer of the court, Mr. Pommus, you ought to know and to obey its rules. I don't know much about how they do things up in Kennebec County, but you are one gratuitous comment away from wearing out your welcome in Cumberland County. Please raise your right hand, Mr. Pommus, and I'll administer the oath."

Once Pommus was seated in the witness box, Christmas elicited from Pommus his name and that he was during the week beginning August four, nineteen eighteen, and is still today the district attorney in and for Kennebec County, Maine. Christmas expeditiously established that Pommus in said capacity had filed the paper work for the coroner's inquest into the death of Richard Cory and that Pommus had represented the People of the State of Maine in that proceeding. During the course of the proceeding, District Attorney Pommus had selected the jury that was impaneled to hear the evidence and as the People's attorney, Pommus had presented the evidence. Adams was torn between trying to concentrate on Christmas's questions and Pommus's answers while at the same time thinking about his own questions for Pommus. Even with all that going on in his head, Adams noted that Christmas was phrasing his questions even more meticulously than he usually did. Evidently Christmas was aware of Pommus's propensity to be a loose cannon and Christmas was probably thankful that Judge Beauchamp had seized the initiative in tamping down the flames of Pommus's ardor for self-promotion.

"There are some events that occurred during the course of the inquest, Mr. Pommus. One such event was the inspection of the deceased's body in the morning of the second day. The jury's heard that testimony and we'll ask you about some of the other matters that occurred in just a bit. But just now, I'd like to ask you whether the coroner's jury reached a verdict in regard to the death of Richard Cory?"

"Yes the jury…"

"Objection, Your Honor. May we approach?"

"Yes. Mr. Christmas, please approach as well."

"Okay, go ahead, Mr. Adams, what's your…"

"Excuse me, Your Honor, could we have the jury retired for the purpose of my objection?"

"Are you anticipating that Mr. Christmas is going to go straight to the alleged confession? Seems to me he intends on beating around the bush a while 'fore he gets there, Mr. Adams. What about it, Mr. Christmas?"

"No, Your Honor, now I'm only going to establish what the verdict is. Save having to call the Kennebec County Clerk to prove it up.

"And you wish to object to that, Mr. Adams? Are you going to make Mr. Christmas bring the clerk down here based on a best-evidence objection?"

"No, Sir; my objection goes to the admissibility of the verdict no matter how the State tries to prove it up."

"Well then, I hate chasing the jury out of the courtroom while you lawyers wrangle and I decide. They go back there thinking all sorts of strange thoughts about what we're doing out here and generally punish one side or the other if they think something fishy's going on."

"May I make a suggestion, Your Honor?"

"I suppose, Mr. Adams, but make it quick; jury's already thinking about conspiracies."

"Why not excuse the jury for the rest of the day? That way I can make my objections to both the verdict and to the alleged confession at the same time. The alleged confession's going to require that I take Mr. Pommus on *voir dire* for the purpose of my objection, and then I've got some argument to present to the court. All in all, I'd say that we'll take up a good bit of the afternoon with the jury twiddling their thumbs back there in the jury room. Maybe if you let them go home they won't be so irritated."

"What do you think about that, Mr. Christmas?"

"Well, my expectation was to finish up the State's case this afternoon. But if Mr. Adams is going to take a while to make his objections…"

"And the court to rule on them, Mr. Christmas?'

"I don't think that part will take very long, Your Honor, with all due respect to Mr. Adams."

"You may be right, Mr. Christmas, but maybe not. I want to hear what Mr. Adams has to say, and your response, and I don't want any of us to feel like he's being rushed. Then are we all agreed to let the jury go home for the rest of the day?"

"Defense agrees, Your Honor."

"As does the prosecution."

"Gentlemen of the Jury: there are some legal issues that have come up that I need to rule on. These are questions of law, and do not concern your duty as fact-finders. Insofar as any rulings I make on questions of law may affect your duties as jurors, they will be reflected in my instructions to you.

"As these matters are likely to take a while, the Court, with the agreement of counsel for both sides, has decided to excuse you for the remainder of the day. So please exit through the jury room, and be very mindful of my instructions about not discussing the case. And I should add, odd as it may seem, that anyone else wants to hear a bit of legal wrangling is welcome to stay, everyone that is except you jurors. Your instructions are to go about your business and put this case out of your minds until five minutes before nine o'clock tomorrow morning when I'll expect you to be back in the jury room. Good day to you all."

"All rise."

After the jurors had made their way back to the jury room, Judge Beauchamp rose and stretched. "Gentlemen let us take a fifteen-minute break and then I'll hear Mr. Adams on why the verdict of the coroner's jury is inadmissible.

"Mr. Pommus, you may return to the witness room and be available when the bailiff calls for you."

"Yes, Your Honor. I'll be ready."

"All rise."

"Why did the jury leave, Mr. Adams?"

"Because now we're going to make our arguments on the admissibility of the verdict of the coroner's jury and whether the jury should be allowed to hear your confession… I mean your statement. I don't care about the coroner's jury verdict, but it's an argument I'm fairly sure I can win. That will give me more credibility with the judge when I make the argument against admitting your statement."

"Maybe Christmas is trying to offer it to get you to object knowing that the judge will rule with you on that one, hoping that the judge will split the difference; give you one and give Christmas one."

"That's a thought I've had myself, Miss Winters. But that'd mean the judge is keeping score: One for the prosecution, one for the defense, or vice versa. Sometimes it seems that way, but I think this judge is calling them the way he sees them. The best thing I've done in this case so far is get the trial moved out of Judge Gribble's court. I can only imagine what he'd done with my arguments."

"Can I get you a glass of water or anything? Mrs. Dubrowski, anything?"

"Yes. Thank you, Miss Winters. All of this is so much to take in that my mouth is dry. Are you sure, Mr. Adams?"

"Yes, Mrs. Dubrowski. Thank you both for asking, but if I drank anything right now I'd probably choke."

Camille went over to the bailiff and asked where she might find some water for Mrs. Dubrowski. The bailiff pointed her in the right direction and in a minute she was back with a glass of water which she gave to Mrs. Dubrowski who took a few sips, smiled and handed it back to Camille. "Thank you, Miss Winters."

"You're welcome. I'm glad to see you smiling."

"Yes. I was just thinking back to when Mr. Adams gave me a glass of water. I didn't finish that one either. Later I will tell you the story."

Chapter Twenty-Eight

After twenty minutes the bailiff intoned "All rise."

"You may proceed with your objection to the admissibility of the coroner's jury's verdict, Mr. Adams. I take it that you do not need Mr. Pommus's testimony for the purpose of this objection?"

"That's correct. Indeed, without waiving our objection, we will stipulate that the verdict of the coroner's jury was one of homicide."

"Mr. Christmas, do you accept Mr. Adams's conditional offer to stipulate?"

"Yes, Your Honor."

"Thank you both. Let the record reflect that the parties have stipulated that the verdict of the coroner's jury in the matter of the death of Richard Cory was one of homicide.

"Now, Mr. Adams, tell me why the jury shouldn't hear that."

"May it please the Court. The coroner's inquest is an *ex parte* proceeding. The State presents only such evidence as the district or county attorney is pleased to present. Mrs. Dubrowski, the defendant, had no standing, much less opportunity, to cross-examine the witnesses called by the state. Nor did she have standing or opportunity to call any witnesses in her own behalf."

"Can't the coroner summon witnesses, Mr. Adams? Doesn't he have subpoena power? Would he not have called any additional witnesses if requested to do so?"

"Yes he does, Your Honor, but as a practical matter only those witnesses that the State's representative wants to call are in fact subpoenaed."

"That was not the case in this matter as I understand it, Your Honor. If you will recall Dr. Goodson's testimony, the coroner, Ebeneezer Ingersoll, recessed the inquest until the following morning at the request of the jury so that they could examine the body first-hand."

"Thank you for reminding us, Mr. Christmas, but I think we'll proceed in a more productive fashion if you wait your turn to speak. I'm sure Mr. Adams will accord you the same courtesy. But Mr. Christmas does have a point, Mr. Adams. How do you respond to it?"

"With the crux of my argument, Your Honor: The coroner's proceeding is wholly irrelevant. It is not *res judicata*...not binding on this court or the defendant...as to the cause of death. It carries no more weight than the indictment. This jury must still determine whether

Richard Cory died from a gunshot wound and whether it was inflicted by someone other than himself, and if so whether that someone was my client Esther Dubrowski.

"What the coroner's jury found, no matter how conscientiously they and the coroner went about their jobs, does not conclusively establish a single thing in regard to the offense charged in the indictment. My client was not represented by counsel, she was not given the opportunity to object to evidence…in fact she was not present in the courtroom except when she herself was on the witness stand…she was afforded no opportunity to cross-examine witnesses or to call witnesses who might have had a different point of view as to the means of Richard Cory's death. Since the inquest verdict is not *res judicata*, it is, as I said, irrelevant." Adams sat down and asked Camille if he could borrow her handkerchief.

"Mr. Christmas, your response?"

"My response, Your Honor, is first of all, that Mr. Adams opened up the subject in his cross-examination of Dr. Goodson. It was the defense that raised the issue of whether Richard Cory met his death as a result of a gunshot wound to his brain, or improbable as it may be, from some catastrophic disease which as late as three months or so prior to his death had manifested no symptoms which so learned and capable a physician as Dr. Goodson was able to detect in the course of, to use his words, a 'thorough examination.'

"Second, the manner in which the inquest was conducted belies Mr. Adams's argument. The coroner was as diligent and fair-minded as any I've ever seen or known about. He let the jury examine the corpse to their satisfaction, he allowed them to witness the experiment that resulted in State's Exhibit Six, which I might add was admitted without objection on the part of the defense.

"Third and last, Your Honor, the coroner's jury did in fact hear conflicting testimony. Sheriff Dowdy was strongly of the opinion that Richard Cory took his own life. Indeed, I waived my objection to his giving that same opinion before this jury, but Mr. Adams chose not to ask him. In sum, the coroner's jury heard detailed evidence and conflicting opinions. They were properly instructed by the coroner. They reached a verdict of homicide and we respectfully submit that this jury ought to know that since it would undoubtedly aid them in their deliberations."

"Mr. Adams?"

"In response, Your Honor, I wish to make three brief points:

First, allowing the coroner's jury verdict into evidence would undoubtedly aid the jury in their deliberations; it virtually directs the jury to find that Richard Cory's death was in fact a homicide—a fact which is a crucial element of the State's case against Mrs. Dubrowski. Thus allowing the verdict into evidence would infringe upon the defendant's right to a trial by jury as well as her right to confront the witnesses against her.

"Second, if the coroner's jury had returned a verdict of suicide, or death from unknown cause, and yet my client had made her purported confession, would the State have declined to prosecute Mrs. Dubrowski? I think not. If the inquest verdict had been other than homicide, would the prosecution have objected to my offering it into evidence? I think they would and on the very same grounds as our objection.

"And finally, as for my 'opening up' the subject, I submit with all due respect that it is the State who opened the door when it sought and obtained an indictment and put my client on trial for the murder of Richard Cory.

"Thank you, Your Honor; the defense closes on its objection."

"I will take the objection under advisement. Are you ready to proceed with your objection to the alleged confession? I think I'd like to hear that before I rule on the objection to the coroner's verdict."

"Yes, Your Honor, the defense is ready to proceed on the alleged confession."

"Is the State ready as well, Mr. Christmas?"

"It is, Your Honor."

"Then the defense would like to call District Attorney Bascom Pommus on *voir dire* for the purpose of our objection. Also, Your Honor, we request leave to treat Mr. Pommus as a hostile witness."

"Permission granted. However, for the purpose of the defense's objection, before we get Mr. Pommus on the stand can we agree, gentlemen, on the substance of the alleged confession? I've jotted something down; tell me what you think:'Mrs. Dubrowski admitted while under oath and in response to questions asked by Mr. Pommus in his capacity as district attorney in and for Kennebec County, Maine while he was representing the People in the coroner's inquest into the death of Richard Cory, that in the late hours of August third or early morning hours of August fourth she took Richard Cory's twenty-two caliber revolver from a desk drawer where she knew it to be kept, and with the revolver fired a bullet into the head of Richard Cory while he slept in his parlor?'

"I'd rather not quibble about the exact words Mrs. Dubrowski is alleged to have used if we can avoid it. Of course if the exact words become material, I will not hold either of you to the agreement. Is that acceptable, counsel?"

"It is to the State, Your Honor."

"And to the defense as well, Your Honor."

"Good, thank you both. Mr. Witherspoon will you please ask Mr. Pommus to rejoin us?"

Adams sat down at the counsel table while the bailiff went to fetch Pommus. "Well, Mrs. Dubrowski, it's time. In the next hour or so, you'll know whether you're a free woman in the State of Maine. Do you have any suggestions? You too, Miss Winters, any thoughts?"

"I thought your argument on the coroner's jury verdict was great, Mr. Adams. If you were using it to get the judge on your...I mean our...side, I think you accomplished your purpose."

"Thank you, Cam...Miss Winters. However, it didn't seem to me that Christmas put up much of a fight. He knows the judge far better than I've been able to read him from just this one case. Maybe there's something to my speculation about the judge keeping score and now it's Christmas's turn to win one."

"You yourself said there wasn't, Mr. Adams. But even if there were something to it, which one is he going to give you, and which one is he going to give Christmas?"

"Fair question, Miss Winters. Mrs. Dubrowski, do you have anything you'd like to add?"

"I don't know about this 'keeping score' business. Such thoughts can make you *mesheggeneh*...crazy. But I do know that this man Christmas is afraid of you. The judge, he seems to respect you. He seems to know the law, not like that *mamser* in Augusta, *kine-hora*. Phooey." Esther Dubrowski turned her head as though to spit on the ground. "I'm sorry, Mr. Adams, Miss Winters.'*Kine-hora*' is an expression to ward off the evil eye. You say it when you mention the name of a bad person, and you spit on the ground. This part I only pretend to do, but it is enough."

As soon as Pommus had taken his seat in the witness box, Judge Beauchamp reminded him, "You're still under oath, Mr. Pommus. Do you understand that?"

"Yes, Your Honor."

"Good. Mr. Adams you may proceed with your *voir dire* examination of Mr. Pommus and you may treat him as an adverse witness."

"But I'm not…"

"Quiet, Mr. Pommus. I've ruled that Mr. Adams may treat you as an adverse witness, and you have no standing to challenge my ruling. Mr. Christmas, do you object to Mr. Adams treating Mr. Pommus as an adverse witness?"

"No, Your Honor. No objection. I may have to ask leave to do so as well."

"Now that'll be interesting. We'll cross that bridge when we come to it. Please proceed, Mr. Adams."

"Thank you, Your Honor. Mr. Pommus, my understanding is that the inquest lasted the better part of two days; began Monday morning and ended Tuesday afternoon. Is that correct?"

"Yes it is."

"The first day was taken up with selecting the jury and taking the testimony of Sheriff Dowdy and Dr. Goodson, correct?"

"Correct."

"Then on Tuesday morning, the inquest resumed at the premises of Davis & Son Mortuary in Tilbury Town?"

"Yes, some of the jurors wanted to examine the body themselves to better understand Dr. Goodson's testimony."

"Yes, thank you, Mr. Pommus. We heard the details of what occurred during Dr. Goodson's testimony, including the experiment and one of the jurors becoming indisposed."

"Can I tell my side, Your Honor?"

"No, Mr. Pommus, you may answer the questions put to you by counsel, and if I have any you can answer those too."

"But it was just something that I ate…"

"Mr. Pommus! Enough! Mr. Adams, please continue."

Adams looked down as though studying his notes in order to let his grin melt away before resuming. Along with everyone else in Tilbury Town he'd heard about the district attorney's own indisposition and had decided against bringing it up. As usual, Christmas sat poker-faced. "Yes, Your Honor. Mr. Pommus, I am told that you were somewhat tardy in returning to court for the afternoon session on Tuesday. Is that so?"

"Yes it is. As I explained to Coroner Ingersoll and to the jury: I was in communication by long-distance telephone with the prison officials in Illinois confirming your client's status as a convicted murderess and fugitive."

"Yes, thank you for adding that. I was about to ask you why you were late.

"What witnesses did you call during the inquest?"

"There was the sheriff, Sheriff Dowdy, and Dr. Goodson; that was on Monday. On Tuesday, well, Dr. Goodson did a lot of explaining and showing the jury the gunshot wound. That was at Davis & Son. Then there was the experiment with firing the gun. I think the deputy showed the jury the gunshot residue on his hand; but I don't think he was sworn. Then too Ulysses Davis and his apprentice, Adolphus Presley, explained how they'd kept the body and that no one had tampered with it overnight."

"Excuse me; were Mr. Davis and Mr. Presley sworn as witnesses?"

"I believe Mr. Davis was; I'm not sure about his apprentice. The clerk would have a record of who was sworn."

"Then when you returned to court on Tuesday afternoon, what witnesses did you call?"

"The stable hand, Mr. Silas, and the defendant in this case, Esther Dubrowski."

"Was Mrs. Dubrowski the last witness?"

"Yes, she was."

"At any point in the proceeding did you invoke the Rule? And to be sure we're talking about the same 'rule,' I am referring to the rule that excludes all witnesses from the courtroom while any other witness is testifying and that prohibits any witness from discussing his or her testimony with anyone other than a lawyer in the case. Are we clear on that, Mr. Pommus?"

"Yes, Mr. Adams, I know what rule you mean. I've been trying lawsuits since…"

"That'll do, Mr. Pommus. The Court is satisfied that you and Mr. Adams are talking about the same rule. Did you invoke it, or not?"

"Yes I did, Your Honor."

"May I continue, Your Honor?"

"Please do, Mr. Adams and do try to move along."

"Thank you, Your Honor; I'll do my best.

"Do you always invoke the Rule in coroner's inquests, Mr. Pommus?"

"We don't have that many in Kennebec County, at least since I've been the district attorney."

"Regardless of how many, Mr. Pommus, my question is: Do you

always invoke the Rule?"

"I don't remember."

"I don't wish to argue with you, Mr. Pommus, but if you don't have that many coroner's inquests in Kennebec County, how is it that you don't remember whether you invoke the Rule in each one?"

"Well, I don't make it a practice, Mr. Adams. Whether I invoked the Rule in each and every case during my tenure as district attorney or as an assistant prior to that, I just don't remember."

"So you don't make it a practice?"

"Correct."

"Tell the Court why you did it in this case, Mr. Pommus."

"Because of who the deceased is...was, for one reason. I wanted to make sure that there'd be no criticism of the way my office handled the matter.

"Second, but most importantly, I had my doubts as to whether Richard Cory took his own life."

"You mean that you didn't trust Sheriff Dowdy's opinion that it was clearly suicide? Is that the reason for the altercation between you and him in the courtroom?"

"That's two questions, Mr. Adams."

"Sorry, Your Honor. Please answer the first one, Mr. Pommus."

"Yes, I had my doubts as to Sheriff Dowdy's opinion. As for the altercation, you'll have to ask Sheriff Dowdy; he's the one started it. I was just doing my job, the job the good citizens of Kennebec County elected me to do and pay me to do."

"Why did you doubt the sheriff's opinion?"

"You knew Richard Cory, Mr. Adams. He was rich; some say richer than a king. He was a handsome man, at least the ladies all thought so. He had his estate...Oakdale Hall...big fancy car, the finest clothes, robust good health. He had a world of friends: Did you see the flowers at the funeral? Just about everybody in town was there to pay their last respects. Whatever a man could want in life, Richard Cory had."

"So because Richard Cory led a life of privilege, as well as all the other things you mentioned, you doubted that Richard Cory took his own life?"

"Yes, that is exactly what I thought and still think today."

"Do you know whether any witness violated the Rule?"

"Not to my knowledge."

"I take it that Mrs. Dubrowski was not present during the testimony of any other witness. Is that correct?"

"Yes; she was not in the courtroom during the testimony of any other witness, nor was she present at the funeral parlor."

"To go back for just a moment, Mr. Pommus: From the very outset, you doubted that Richard Cory took his own life."

"Yes."

"Did you suspect anyone in particular of being the murderer or murderess from the very outset as well?"

"Actually, my suspicion fell on the defendant almost immediately."

"How so, Mr. Pommus?"

"Two things: First, she was a stranger, a foreigner. She had no friends in Tilbury Town; no one knew anything about her."

"How do you know that, Mr. Pommus?"

"When the war in Europe started and there was talk of America possibly entering the war and talk of German spies and such, as part of my duties as district attorney I made it a point to learn as much as I discreetly could about the fairly small number of people in Kennebec County that weren't born there or had family or some other roots in the area. Anyone with a foreign-sounding name...especially a German-sounding one...fell into that group."

"What is the second reason, Mr. Pommus?

"I figured out right away that if Richard Cory didn't shoot himself, it had to be someone either in the household or that had frequent access to the house and knew the routine as well as where Richard Cory kept his revolver."

"Then to sum up your testimony on this point, Mr. Pommus, you suspected the defendant Esther Dubrowski from the beginning, and that's why you invoked the Rule?"

"Yes, I would agree with that."

"Why did you not just have the sheriff bring her to your office for questioning?"

"She could have refused to go, then where would the investigation be? I wanted her where I could have her put under oath so that she would feel compelled to speak the truth."

"Did you, Coroner Ingersoll, the clerk Martha Parsons, Sheriff Dowdy, any member of the jury, or for that matter anyone else present tell Mrs. Dubrowski that she did not have to testify if in doing so she might incriminate herself?"

"For the reason I've already said, I did not; nor did anyone else to my knowledge."

"Did you or anyone else to your knowledge warn Mrs. Dubrowski that anything she said could be used against her should she later be charged with a crime?"

"I did not have to, Mr. Adams. She was not in custody at the time. And giving her that warning would have defeated the purpose of the interrogation."

"Did you or anyone else to your knowledge inform Mrs. Dubrowski that she had the right to have an attorney to advise her during questioning?"

"No, because she was not then charged with a crime."

"Prior to Mrs. Dubrowski taking the witness stand, did you form an opinion as to whether it was she and no one else that had shot Richard Cory in the head thereby causing his death?"

"As I've already testified, Mr. Adams, I had my suspicions from the very beginning. After my telephone conversations with Mr. Miller there in Illinois, I knew for certain she was the one who did it. After all, she'd already committed murder once and was a fugitive from justice. What more proof did anyone need?"

"Then why'd you put her on the witness stand?"

"Because that's my job, Mr. Adams. To make certain that anyone who commits murder in Kennebec County gets the swiftest and surest justice possible. What better, more conclusive evidence of guilt could I have presented to a jury?"

"Would you have sought an indictment without the confession?"

"Objection; calls for speculation."

"You're right, Mr. Christmas, but I'll let the witness answer if he knows. Since this is a *voir dire* examination, I'll allow some latitude. You may be sure that in making my decision I'll consider only the legally relevant testimony. You may answer, Mr. Pommus."

"I probably would have, yes. But before doing so, I would have carefully reviewed all the evidence and then made my decision."

"Would your review of the evidence have included further investigation of the inconsistency between Mrs. Dubrowski's testimony as to where she got the revolver and the testimony of Mr. Silas as to where the weapon was usually kept?"

"I don't recall such an inconsistency, Mr. Adams. In any event, even if I'd have noted it, it would not have made a difference. In my long experience, Mr. Adams, people do not confess to crimes they did not commit…especially a heinous crime such as murder."

"Mr. Adams, I tend to agree with Mr. Pommus on that point; usually people do not confess to crimes they did not commit. Are you suggesting that Mrs. Dubrowski's confession is false?"

"I am indeed, Your Honor."

"May I be heard on this point?"

"Yes; go ahead Mr. Christmas."

"Whether a confession is accurate in each and every detail, Your Honor, is irrelevant. Either it's legally admissible, or it's not. If it's admitted, then the defendant can take the stand and repudiate it if she wishes to do so."

"I think Mr. Christmas may be right, Mr. Adams. I'm mighty curious as to why your client would confess to a murder she didn't commit, but I haven't yet decided whether the truth or falsity of the confession…or as Mr. Christmas says ' the confession is accurate in each and every detail'…has any bearing on its admissibility. That's a point I need to think about. Do you have any further questions for Mr. Pommus on your *voir dire*?"

"No, Your Honor; I pass the witness. However, since Mr. Pommus does not seem to recall the testimony of the stable hand, Mr. Silas, it will be necessary that I also call Mr. Silas on *voir dire* in order to establish that the revolver was kept in a chest in the stable. Perhaps the court could ask the bailiff to call and have him sent over."

"Mr. Christmas, in the interest of time will you stipulate that if Mr. Silas were to be called as a witness he would testify that the revolver was kept in a chest in the stable?"

" Yes, Your Honor, in the interest of saving time, the State will so stipulate without prejudice to our position that the truth of the confession—or its accuracy in each and every detail—is irrelevant to its admissibility."

"And I assume that you will as well, Mr. Adams?"

"Yes, Your Honor."

"Very well. Thank you Mr. Christmas and Mr. Adams. The record will reflect that the parties have stipulated that if," Judge Beauchamp paused and looked at his witness list, "Ellsworth Henry Silas were called as a witness he would and could testify…I assume from personal knowledge, Mr. Adams…"

"Yes, Your Honor, from personal knowledge."

"…that the revolver which the State contends was used to take the life of the deceased Richard Cory as alleged in the indictment was kept in a chest in the stable.

"Mr. Christmas, you may proceed with your examination of Mr. Pommus and if necessary you may treat him as an adverse witness."

"Thank you, Your Honor."

"Mr. Pommus, I understand that you did not tell Mrs. Dubrowski that she did not have to testify; but did you tell her that she did have to testify?"

"No, Sir. I just called her as a witness."

"Did you threaten her in any way if she declined to testify? Did you offer her any inducement?"

"No, Sir; I didn't have to; she took the stand willingly."

"Objection, Your Honor; Mr. Pommus is merely speculating as to Mrs. Dubrowski's state of mind."

"Sustained."

"That's my point, Your Honor. Any coercion was in the mind of the defendant; it was not as a result of any threat or inducement on the part of Mr. Pommus."

"You can make that point in your argument, Mr. Christmas; now move along."

"As far as you were concerned, Mrs. Dubrowski was free to leave at any time?"

"Yes."

"She wasn't under subpoena?"

"No."

"Did you offer her leniency…either from you or the court…if she confessed?"

"No, I did not."

"Did you threaten her in any way in order to get her to confess?"

"No."

"Did you refuse to allow her to consult with an attorney?"

"She never asked to."

"I take it that means you did not refuse."

"That's correct."

"Is there any reason that you know of to suggest that the defendant's confession was other than freely and voluntarily given?"

"No, Sir."

"Then she was under no compulsion other than a guilty conscience?"

"Absolutely none."

"Thank you, Mr. Pommus. I'll pass the witness."

"Mr. Adams, anything further for Mr. Pommus?"

"Yes, Your Honor, just a couple of questions. Mr. Pommus, you testified in response to a question from Mr. Christmas that Mrs. Dubrowski was free to leave at any time. My question is: Did you tell Mrs. Dubrowski that she was free to leave at any time?"

"No, I did not."

"In fact, when the inquest recessed on Monday afternoon, Mrs. Dubrowski was instructed by the bailiff, at the request of the coroner, to return the following day. Do you recall that?"

"Yes, I do."

"Then I have no further questions for Mr. Pommus, Your Honor."

"Very well then; I take it you have some argument to present?"

"Yes, Your Honor."

"Mr. Pommus, you are excused from the witness stand; please return to the witness waiting room for now in case you're needed again in today's proceedings. You will also return tomorrow morning, in the event I admit the alleged confession."

"Well, Adams thought, "at least he hasn't made up his mind yet."

Chapter Twenty-Nine

As soon as Pommus had left the courtroom, the judge nodded to Adams. "Please proceed, Mr. Adams."

"May it please the Court. The alleged confession was extracted from the defendant under compulsion in violation of her rights under the United States Constitution, Amendment Five, and the Maine Constitution, Article One, section six."

"Counsel, the Court is quite familiar with the constitutional provisions you cite. But you heard Mr. Pommus's testimony; indeed much of it was elicited by you. The defendant was not in custody; she was not even under subpoena. A coroner's inquest is at best a quasi-judicial proceeding which, as you have so ably pointed out, is without any binding effect. I do not believe that the coroner...I believe his name is Ebeneezer Ingersoll...could have held Mrs. Dubrowski in contempt should she have declined to testify or even simply ignored a subpoena had there been one. Where is the compulsion?"

"The compulsion was in the mind of the defendant, Your Honor. She is foreign-born, English is not her native language and she has no formal education. How was she to know her rights? From her so-called 'trial' in Illinois?" Proceedings conducted when she was a terrified young woman, almost still a child, without the slightest capacity to understand what was happening to her?

"In the present case, an officer of the law, the sheriff, tells her she must appear and give evidence. She is administered a solemn oath by a magistrate of the law, an oath which places her under a duty to speak 'the truth, the whole truth and nothing but the truth...so help her God.' She is told by that magistrate that she must not discuss her testimony with anyone other than the district attorney. Would not this admonition alone have deterred even a well-educated person, fluent in the English language from seeking the advice of her own attorney?

"Then after sitting all day in a tiny room, having no idea what was going on a few feet away in the courtroom, another officer, the bailiff, comes and tells her that she must return in the morning to give her testimony and not to discuss the case with anyone.

"Thinking that the bailiff's injunction compels her to forgo consulting a lawyer and to return as directed, Mrs. Dubrowski returns and is eventually put on the witness stand where District Attorney Pommus confronts her with her past, her status as a fugitive, and ultimately pries from her a purported confession. A confession, which I should add, was demonstrably false and its falsity well-known to the district attorney.

"I raise this last point because, Your Honor, it establishes that Mr. Pommus had already concluded in his mind that Mrs. Dubrowski was guilty of the murder of Richard Cory, and never mind the facts. That is important—I would say crucial—to Mrs. Dubrowski's position. Once Mrs. Dubrowski came under such suspicion...in the mind of Mr. Pommus not merely suspicion but absolute certainty of guilt...his sole reason for putting her on the stand was to extract a confession. At that moment, we submit, Mrs. Dubrowski was entitled to all the protections afforded a person in these circumstances under the constitutional provisions I have cited."

"I understand what you're saying, Mr. Adams, but is compulsion in the mind of Mrs. Dubrowski sufficient? It seems to me that any person who confesses to a crime is under some form of compulsion. Why else would they do so? Even the most ignorant among us has some awareness that a civilized society must have rules...laws if you will...that prohibit certain behavior that is deemed inimical to society. And those persons know that violating those rules...laws...will have adverse consequences to themselves.

"So if a person knows that if he or she commits a crime, which if discovered, could result in imprisonment or in some jurisdictions even death, why would a person in that circumstance confess if not under some compulsion of the mind that drives that person to do so? Perhaps that compulsion is remorse; perhaps it is fear of the afterlife; or in some cases a sense of pride of accomplishment or in other cases merely indifference to the consequences. Would you exclude all confessions because they are induced by some internal compulsion that arises in the mind of the perpetrator?"

"I think the difference, Your Honor, is that in the circumstances you describe, the compulsion is, to use your word, 'internal.' Here, the compulsion was *external* applied by the district attorney, a representative of the state."

"I understand your argument based on principle, Counsel. Do you have any authority to support your external compulsion argument?"

"I have but one case, Your Honor. However, I believe it to be very much in point and dispositive of the issue. The case to which I refer is *State v Gilman,* 51 Me. 206 (Supreme Judicial Court of Maine, Western District, 1862)."

"Eighteen Sixty-two, Counsel? Is it still good law?"

"I have not found anything later, Your Honor, which questions or overrules *Gilman*."

"Well then, Mr. Adams, what does *Gilman* teach us about confessions?"

"In *Gilman*, the defendant was charged with murder and just as in the present case, he made damning admissions while giving testimony at a coroner's inquest into the death of the deceased with whose murder the defendant was later charged, tried and convicted."

"You say 'damning admissions,' Mr. Adams. I take it these were something short of a full confession to the *corpus delicti* and the defendant's culpability?"

"That's true, Your Honor, but for our purposes, the distinction is immaterial."

"What happened to Gilman?"

"He was convicted, and his exceptions to the admission of his statement were overruled on appeal resulting in the affirmation of the judgment on the verdict."

"That would not seem to bode well for your client, Mr. Adams. You have conceded that the case cannot be distinguished on the basis of the difference between an incriminating statement and a full confession. Do you have some other distinction in mind that will persuade me to treat your client's alleged confession differently?"

"I certainly believe so, Your Honor. Just as in the case at hand, Gilman was under suspicion of being the culprit at the time he testified and so far as the record discloses, just as Mrs. Dubrowski, Gilman was without counsel. The difference between *Gilman* and the case at hand is that prior to his giving his testimony, Gilman was advised of his right to decline to testify. This warning was appended to the record of his testimony and signed by him.

"The opinion is a lengthy one, Your Honor. It states in great detail the arguments of Gilman's counsel and discusses the facts and the court's reasoning in many of the cases cited by Gilman's defense. With this in mind, I would like to quote only the penultimate paragraph from the court's unanimous opinion written by Justice Rice. The paragraph is found at page two twenty-six:

'*Great care should undoubtedly be taken to protect the rights of the accused. His secret should not be extorted from him by the exercise of any inquisitorial power. He should be fully informed of his legal rights, when called upon or admitted to testify as a witness in a matter in which his guilt is involved. No officious party should be permitted to extract confessions from him, by operating upon his hopes or his fears. But his voluntary statements, declarations or confessions, like his voluntary actions, wherever or whenever made, are legitimate and proper matters for judicial consideration, so far as they bear upon and tend to illustrate the question of guilt or innocence.'*

"I would say, Your Honor, that the second, third and forth sentences correctly state the law. The U.S. and Maine constitutions give an individual the right not to be compelled to give evidence against himself. Great care must be taken, according to Justice Rice, to protect that right. These protections are carefully spelled out in the following three sentences: The state may not use its inquisitorial power to extract a confession; the accused—even though he does not know he stands accused—must be fully informed of his right not to testify; and no government official should be allowed to extract a confession by playing upon the accused's hopes or fears.

"None of these protections were afforded to Mrs. Dubrowski: No one told her she did not have to testify; not knowing her rights, she allowed herself, by taking the witness stand, to be subjected to the state's inquisitorial power; and lastly, an *officious party*, the district attorney, used her fear of her past to lever a confession out of her. What occurred in that Kennebec County courtroom on the sixth of August was exactly what the *Gilman* Court said must not occur.

"Thank you, Your Honor." Adams sat down and Camille silently handed him her handkerchief with which she had just finished wiping her eyes.

"I assume you wish to be heard, Mr. Christmas."

"Yes, Your Honor, the State of Maine wishes to be heard."

"Then we'll stand in recess for fifteen minutes."

"All rise."

As soon as the judge left the bench, Adams turned to the spectator gallery. Cecilia too was dabbing a handkerchief to her eyes; Flammonde merely nodded his head in approval. Retaking his seat Adams turned to his client, "Were you able to follow what I said and the judge's questions?"

"As best I could, Mr. Adams. It is not easy to understand when you talk about this law and that law and some other case that happens in eighteen sixty-two. This other case is different from my case; I was not given warning. If they give me warning, maybe I not testify."

"That's the point I made to the judge; because Gilman was warned, his statement *could* be used against him in his trial. In our case since you were not warned, your statement cannot be used against you. But why do you say 'maybe' you would not testify?"

"As soon as I see *tchotchke*...brooch...I know what I must do."

"But," Camille, who was sitting to Esther Dubrowski's right, leaned toward Dubrowski and Adams, "If you had been warned and had declined to testify, you would never have seen the brooch."

Esther Dubrowski thought about it for a moment. "This is so, Miss Winters; then Mr. Pommus would have had me arrested and sent back to Illinois. I would be sitting there in the prison with no Mr. Adams and no Mr. Darrow to be my lawyers. And Cecilia would have to either forget about me or move back to Chicago where she knows no one. So I think Mr. Pommus although he did not intend to, has done to me great favor."

"I hope so, Mrs. Dubrowski; it all depends on whether this judge throws out your...statement."

"He will, Quincy...Mr. Adams. I know he will."

"Thanks for the vote of confidence, Miss Winters. Maybe he will, provided that Christmas doesn't talk him out of it."

"What can this Christmas say, Mr. Adams? The law is the law; is this not so?"

"I wish that were true, Mrs. Dubrowski. However, for good or ill, our laws are made and enforced by men. As I explained up in Augusta, sometimes these men...even judges... get things wrong although most try their best to do the right thing. But sometimes judges do not want to go where the law says they must go; so to reach the result they want, they bend the law so that it sometimes becomes twisted and even broken.

"This is why I want Judge Beauchamp to know that your statement is false. If he has doubts, this may influence his thinking. If he is certain that your statement is true...that you did shoot Richard Cory to death...then he is more likely to be persuaded by Christmas's argument."

"All rise."

"Mr. Christmas, let us hear from the State."

"May it please the Court. The language in *Gilman* quoted by Mr. Adams is *obiter dictum*...language not necessary to the decision. It is not the court's holding. The holding in *Gilman* is that a statement made under oath at a coroner's inquest by one suspected of causing the death at issue is admissible. Our office, Your Honor, is not unfamiliar with the *Gilman* case. As the Court has noted, the case is more than fifty years old. Our research has not disclosed a single reported case in Maine in which a higher court has sustained a defendant's exceptions to the admissibility

≈ 281 ≈

of his statement on the grounds urged here by Mr. Adams.

"There is no better evidence upon which to base a conviction than the evidence which comes from a defendant's own lips. With a confession there is no risk that physical evidence will be misinterpreted; there is no concern that a so-called 'eye-witness' is mistaken or lying. A confession is but one of that class of statements which the law of evidence calls 'admissions against interest.' The law presumes that a statement in the nature of a confession would not be made unless it was true. A confession is so reliable that it can be admitted even though not made under oath.

"This being so, the rule for which Mr. Adams so earnestly pleads is as a practical matter unworkable. The Court may take judicial notice that most crimes are solved through the defendant confessing his guilt. As this Court well knows, more than nine out of ten defendants who appear before you plead guilty. They do this because they have already confessed their crimes to an officer of the law.

"The 'Adams Rule'—if I may call it that—would paralyze this process. Under the 'Adams Rule' a police officer, or deputy sheriff, or district attorney, as soon as a person came under suspicion, would have to warn that person that he or she need not make any statement. And who's to say when a person comes under suspicion? Is there a bright-line rule that an average officer can learn and follow? Must the suspicion be only in the mind of the interrogator, or is the rule that if anyone with an official connection to the case has suspicions the warning must be given? Law officers are trained to keep an open mind and follow the evidence. But at the same time, they are trained…or quickly learn…to be suspicious of everyone in the course of an investigation. Conscientious law enforcement officials will never obtain a confession; only those who are willing to say—whether truthfully or untruthfully—that no suspicion fell upon the defendant until after he'd confessed to the crime would be able to obtain confessions.

"And will the 'Adams Rule' stop with just telling a suspect that he does not have to give a statement, or will the next step be to require that a suspect also be advised that any statement may be used to his disadvantage in any judicial proceeding? Under the Sixth Amendment to the United States Constitution, and under the very same Article One, section six of our own constitution cited in *Gilman*, a person accused of a crime has a right to legal counsel. Must a person be advised of this right as well? What if…as is often the case…a person is indigent? Must the state provide him with a lawyer merely so that he can be interrogated? If that person does request a lawyer, must questioning be postponed until the person consults with counsel? And, while I do not speak from personal knowledge, I cannot imagine any lawyer advising his client to confess to a crime. In short, Your Honor, there is no end to the mischief that will result from accepting Mr. Adams's argument.

"I respectfully conclude with this thought: In all other circumstances, an individual is presumed to know the law. It is no defense in a criminal case for the defendant to claim that he or she did not know the law. The same is true, so I am made to understand, in civil cases. So I say this, Your Honor: Just as ignorance of the law is no defense, neither may it be used as a weapon. Mrs. Dubrowski, regardless of her circumstances, is in the eyes of the law as learned in the law as you, Mr. Adams or myself. If she wanted the advice of a lawyer, it was her duty to ask for one, and to defer answering questions until she had obtained a lawyer's services. Similarly, she was presumed to know that she was not required to give evidence against herself and that such evidence could be used against her in a criminal prosecution brought against her based on her confession. The State of Maine respectfully submits that there is no principled argument, and certainly no authority that compels this Court to exclude the defendant's confession."

"Thank you, Mr. Christmas. Mr. Adams, a brief response?"

"Thank you, Your Honor. The crux of the State's argument, as I understand it, is that confessions are inherently reliable and therefore they must be admissible. But what if the confession, as in the present case, is demonstrably unreliable?"

"Unreliable, Mr. Adams?"

"Yes, Your Honor, unreliable. Unreliable both because it is patently false and because of the circumstances under which it was obtained. If a confession is inherently reliable...as Mr. Christmas says...then why would Mrs. Dubrowski lie about an important detail—where she got the revolver—knowing that her testimony could be easily contradicted, as it in fact was?

"My point is this: If Mrs. Dubrowski had confessed after being beaten by a sheriff's deputy...and I'm speaking only hypothetically...the truth of the confession would not be presumed and there'd be no question of its being admitted. If she'd been kept in a locked room and deprived of food and water or the use of the facilities all the while being subjected to intense questioning, the Court would not hesitate to exclude such a confession. In each instance the confession would be deemed unreliable as a matter of law. In other words, a coerced confession is presumably unreliable as a matter of law. In the present case, that presumption is reinforced by the fact that a critical detail is false.

"But is the test simply one of physical coercion? If a confession is beaten out of a person or obtained by means of the threat of immediate violence it's not admissible; but if that confession is obtained through intimidation…so-called 'brow-beating'…anything short of actual physical violence…is it admissible? There can be no serious doubt that under the circumstances described by District Attorney Pommus, Mrs. Dubrowski was as much deprived of her free will as if she'd been beaten into confessing; accordingly, her statement is unreliable and therefore should be excluded.

"Thank you, Your Honor. The defense closes."

"Thank you both, Counsel, for a spirited and enlightening argument. The Court will take both matters under advisement and inform the parties of its ruling in the morning at nine o'clock. We are in recess until then."

"All rise."

"It looks like we won't know anything until tomorrow morning, Mrs. Dubrowski. But perhaps that's good for us. The judge at least wants to think about what to do; maybe he'll even read the *Gilman* case. But you should try and get some rest; don't stay awake all night worrying. It's in the judge's hands now and there's nothing more that we can do but wait and cross our fingers."

"Do not be concerned for me, Mr. Adams. I sleep well tonight. I already know how judge will decide: You have won. Go; have a nice dinner, you and Miss Winters. Take Cecilia with you; Cecilia and her new friend who sits next to her all day in the back of the court."

"Mrs. Dubrowski is right, Mr. Adams. You have won. Let's have dinner. I'll go catch Cecilia and Mr. Flammonde in the hall before they get away."

"Thank you both for being so confident of the outcome; I wish I could be. I don't know how hungry I am, but dinner and perhaps a cocktail or two might not be a bad idea."

"Pardon me, Mr. Adams. Before you and your client leave for the day, could we have a word? I've already made arrangements with the sheriff's office to hold off taking Mrs. Dubrowski back until we're through; they'll also hold her supper."

"Of course, Mr. Christmas. Is it all right if we stay here, or do we need to go back to the jury room?"

"I think that here will do, Mr. Adams. Obviously I'm ready to propose an agreed disposition of this case that I think you and your client will find attractive."

"What means this 'agreed disposition' if I may ask?"

"Mrs. Dubrowski, even though these discussions are privileged, you should not speak unless Mr. Adams tells you it is all right to do so. But with his permission I will answer your question."

"Go ahead, Mr. Christmas."

"An 'agreed disposition' means a plea bargain: You would plead guilty in exchange for a reduced sentence."

"Why now should I plead guilty? Please ask him that, Mr. Adams."

"It depends, Mrs. Dubrowski. Let's hear what Mr. Christmas has to offer; then we can discuss it and you can decide."

"My offer…which is open until nine o'clock tomorrow morning…is that if Mrs. Dubrowski changes her plea to guilty, we will recommend a sentence not to exceed whatever her remaining sentence is in Illinois and we will agree that both sentences can be served concurrently. In other words, it will be the same as though Mrs. Dubrowski had not confessed. District Attorney Pommus found out about her fugitive status without any help from Mrs. Dubrowski, so it is inevitable that she would have to go back to Illinois to serve the remainder of her sentence anyway. My proposal in essence nullifies her confession."

"You say 'recommend' a sentence; does that mean that Judge Beauchamp does not have to go along with your recommendation?"

"Theoretically, yes; that's what it means. However, as a practical matter if judges do not go along with such agreements, we'd never be able to get one done. Judge Beauchamp knows this and has always gone along with recommendations from our office in the past. Moreover, in this case, it will remove any concern, no matter how remote, about being reversed on appeal.

"You made a very good argument, Mr. Adams, but I cannot see this judge tossing out a confession in a murder case, especially this case. But so long as there's even the slightest possibility that he could get reversed on appeal, I think that will provide whatever additional leverage we would need."

"In fact, to 'sweeten' the offer so to speak, if the judge doesn't buy in, I'll agree to allow you to withdraw Mrs. Dubrowski's guilty plea."

"I have a couple of additional questions. What if Mrs.

Dubrowski is again paroled in Illinois? What would happen to her sentence from Maine?" As you probably know, her Illinois conviction was the product of a farce, not a trial. What if that conviction gets set aside, or her sentence is commuted to time served or she receives a full pardon? What will happen to her Maine conviction?"

"I will not attempt to deceive you, Mr. Adams, Mrs. Dubrowski. The governor has unfettered discretion to grant or withhold a pardon, and the parole board is an agency under the governor's office. Technically the governor approves every parole as well as every pardon. For this reason, I cannot guarantee what would happen in Maine should Mrs. Dubrowski's Illinois sentence be truncated in any manner. I cannot bind the governor, nor for that matter any successor to that office or to the office of Attorney General. I can and would make the strongest possible recommendation and make it a part of the official file, but that is the best I can do."

"Thank you for your candor, Mr. Christmas. Mrs. Dubrowski and I will discuss your proposal and I will respond by your deadline. Please leave me a telephone number or some other means to contact you should I have need to do so this evening."

After Christmas had gone, Adams sat down and turned his chair so that he and Dubrowski were sitting face to face. "It looks like my dinner is off. Unless you have any questions, I suggest that you go back to the jail and have your dinner. I will make arrangements to meet with you after you've had your dinner to discuss what we should do, and you can think about it over night if you wish."

"This what you say is not necessary, Mr. Adams. I give you now my decision. I have told you that this man Christmas fears you. Now you must say that I am right. I have changed my mind about how to plead enough times already; I do not need to consider doing so again. You will tell Mr. Christmas in the morning that I will not change my plea. This is my final decision. Now go and have nice dinner; I will see you in the morning. Please give to Cecilia my love. And this other man…this Flammonde…who is with Cecilia, he is your other client, yes? Please tell him 'thank you' for all he has done."

Reuben Bright

Because he was a butcher and thereby
Did earn an honest living(and did right)
I would not have you think that Reuben Bright
Was any more a brute than you or I;
For when they told him that his wife must die,
He stared at them, and shook with grief and fright,
And cried like a great baby half the night,
And made the women cry to see him cry.

And after she was dead, and he had paid
The singers and the sexton and the rest,

He packed a lot of things that she had made
Most mournfully away in an old chest

Of hers, and put some chopped-up cedar boughs
In with them, and tore down the slaughterhouse.

Edwin Arlington Robinson
American (1869-1935)

Chapter Thirty

Adams had enjoyed the dinner, both the food and the beverages. As they were leaving the courthouse he had suggested Arturo's. But sharp looks from both Camille and Cecilia had prompted Flammonde to tactfully suggest seafood at a restaurant on the harbor side of Commercial Street overlooking the water. Inevitably, the conversation centered first on Pommus's surprising testimony and then the arguments and what the judge was likely to do. That he'd ordered Pommus to return in the morning was dismissed as not indicative of anything except that the judge wanted to keep the case moving in the event he decided to admit the statement.

Flammonde was unable to believe Pommus had initially suspected that Cory had died by anyone's hand other than Cory's own, let alone the hand of Esther Dubrowski. Flammonde postulated that but for the animus between Pommus and the sheriff, it was likely that the sheriff's opinion would not have been challenged. The more intriguing question, Flammonde suggested, was why Pommus had asked Dr. Goodson whether Cory'd shot himself. Was it Pommus's irresistible impulse to ask one more question than he ought to, especially if he didn't already know the answer? As for Pommus's checking out people without ties to the area, especially those with German-sounding names, Flammonde allowed that was no more than Pommus's self-serving fabrication.

Adams, reluctant to look a gift-horse in the mouth, suggested that they all raise their glasses in thanks to District Attorney Pommus for his invaluable — if inadvertent — aid to Esther Dubrowski's defense.

Each of the judge's questions was disassembled looking for clues as to how he might rule. Each of Christmas's arguments was subjected to every hypothetical fact pattern anyone could think of in an effort to expose fallacies. There was much speculation as to why the judge didn't ask Christmas any questions. Was that a good omen? Or did it mean that the judge was intimidated by Christmas's flood-gates argument…that Adams's reading of *Gilman* would 'open the flood-gates' with criminals claiming all sorts of pretrial constitutional rights thereby bringing the criminal justice system to its knees with new burdens? By the end of the dinner, the consensus was that Quincy had turned each question to his advantage and that the flood-gates argument would be to no avail.

The only pall cast over the evening was when Adams realized

the unintended result of his questioning Pommus regarding the sheriff's suicide opinion. As they were preparing to leave Camille mentioned that Enoch Matthews had been furiously taking notes. It took Adams only a moment's thought to realize that Matthews must have been writing down the questions and answers verbatim and why. "Well, I guess that I gave Christmas a big fat Christmas present; I opened the door and now Dowdy's going to get to testify that his suicide opinion was wrong."

Flammonde gave Adams a reassuring pat on the back. "Don't worry about that, Quincy. Getting that information out of Pommus is far more important. And as you observed last night, who's going to believe Dowdy anyway?"

It was agreed that Camille and Cecilia would take a taxi back to Miss Rosie's and that Adams and Flammonde would walk back to their hotel. As they walked back up the gentle rise toward the hotel, each enjoying a last cigar of the day, Flammonde took a manila envelope from the inner pocket of his suit. "Here's what Mrs. Dubrowski needs to look at, see if she can identify."

"What is it?" Adams started to open the unsealed flap.

"Don't bother with it now, Quincy. What's in there's bound to make you sick. It did me, and I've seen a lot in my time."

"Now you've got my curiosity aroused, Emil."

"If you won't listen to my advice, then at least wait until you're back in your room and next to the water closet."

"It's that bad?"

"Worse."

"Where'd Maurice find it?"

"He didn't; he never saw the inside of the jail."

"Then…"

"They came from another source."

"Your 'man in Augusta?'"

"You could say that."

"He has access to the sheriff's office?"

"I'd rather not say just yet, Quincy. Remember misprision of felony?"

"What happened to Maurice? Is he okay?"

"He's okay. It's just that his plan developed a little hitch."

"What happened?"

"Just like Lamar said, Maurice went into a bar; had a round or two. Flashes a wad of cash. Two, three fellas there at the bar invite him to shoot some craps there in the back room. Well invitin' Maurice to shoot craps is like invitin' a hungry lion to share your lunch; time he gets done, there ain't going to be much left for you. In due course Maurice had cleaned the locals out and as you'd expect, they took great exception to Maurice leavin' with their hard-earned dough. Things started to get a bit testy; the rubes accusin' Maurice of cheatin' 'n' all. As often occurs in those situations, someone throws a punch and then the melee's on. Didn't last long, though. Seems the proprietor produced a sawed-off shotgun from behind the bar and when he racked a round into the chamber, it immediately got everyone's attention and they calmed down. Then he called the cops."

"Isn't that what the plan was?"

"Yes, it was. But remember your Robert Burns, 'The best laid plans of mice and men....' And don't tell me that's also Congreve."

"No, Burns is right. But what happened?"

Well, looks like the City of Augusta's got some house cleanin' to do along with Kennebec County. Two of Augusta's finest show up right quick and take Maurice into custody...that also bein' just as planned. They put cuffs on Maurice—just like we're hopin'—and take him into their automobile like they're going to take him to the lockup. So far, so good. But that's when things get off track. Instead of takin' Maurice to the lockup, they took him to the edge of town, cleaned out his wallet and told him to get out of Augusta and never come back, he knows what's good for him. Well Maurice handed them back their handcuffs and took off just like they said to."

"Then how'd..."

"Maurice got to a 'phone; called our man in Augusta who came and picked him up. My man gave him the envelope and some money and took him to the train station. Maurice slept in the station and caught the first train this morning. So he didn't quite make it back before breakfast like Lamar said he would."

"So Maurice's okay?"

"Yeah, he can take care of himself, just like I told you."

"Then I guess 'all's well that ends well.' And that *is* Shakespeare."

"Actually, it turned out better than if Maurice done the job himself."

"Meaning?"

"That, I'll have to explain to you later."

"When is 'later,' Emil?"

"As soon as your client identifies the contents of that envelope as being what was in Richard Cory's cocktail table drawer."

"And if she can't?"

"Then I will pay any balance due on your fee and disappear from your life."

"If it comes to that I shall be very sorry to see you go. It's been an interesting few weeks. But what about Mrs. Dubrowski's difficulties in Illinois?"

"There's news on that front as well. I wanted you to hear it first; that's why I didn't bring it up at dinner. Mr. Darrow reports that the governor is willing to commute Mrs. Dubrowski's sentence to time served and to grant her a full pardon on the fugitive charge. You'll need to give her that information and get her to sign a letter agreeing to the terms."

"That makes one down and one to go. But I'm still worried about that remaining one. Christmas doesn't seem all that concerned about what Judge Beauchamp's going to do. He may be right; it'll take a big dose of judicial courage to throw out the confession of a murderess."

"She's a murderess only if he allows the jury to hear the confession, and even then they may believe her as to why she confessed. If the jury buys her reason, they'll acquit for sure. I recommend that you put off looking at the contents of the envelope until in the morning; get a good night's sleep. Tomorrow's gonna be a big day whatever happens."

"I guess you're right, Emil. Thanks for dinner…and for everything else. I'll get to court early so that I can meet with Mrs. Dubrowski and we can look in the envelope together. Good night to you as well."

It took a while for Adams to realize that someone was pounding on the door to his hotel room. Despite all the things clanking around in his mind, the pre-prandial martini cocktail and two glasses of sauvignon blanc with dinner had the desired effect of putting Adams to sleep almost as soon as his head hit the pillow. He threw on his ratty plaid bathrobe and opened the door a crack taking care to leave to the security chain fastened.

"What's the matter, Emil? Is the hotel on fire?"

"No, but you need to come down to my room for a few minutes. Lamar's there; so's Maurice. They've got an interestin' tale to tell that I think you'd best hear direct from them."

"Give me a minute to put some clothes on and I'll be right there."

"No need for that Quincy; Lamar and Maurice don't stand on ceremony."

As Flammonde was introducing Quincy to Maurice, Quincy noticed Lamar sitting in a chair his shirt off and a bloody bandage around his upper left arm. Adams released Maurice's hand and went over to Lamar. "Lamar, what happened to you?"

"Old age, Son. Try not to let it happen to you."

"I'll try my best, Lamar. But I meant what happened to you that resulted in your sitting there with a big bandage on your arm?"

"Oh, that. Just a scratch; don't reckon it'll even need stitches. Wouldn't have got even that, weren't for old age.

"Had a bit of a run in with a couple fellas outside Miss Rosie's. When y'all were leaving the courthouse this afternoon, Emil told me where you were going and suggested that Maurice and I grab a quick dinner and head over to Miss Rosie's; make sure the ladies got home safely. So I got a hold of Maurice and we ate at a little place on Forest right close to Miss Rosie's. Nice dinner, by the way. Didn't you think so, Maurice?"

"It was Lamar; but go on tell Mr. Adams the interesting part."

"As things turned out, it's a good thing we did. Not eat dinner; I mean hangin' out making sure Miss Winters and Miss Durbin were safe."

"You mean that someone tried to attack them?"

"Well, they didn't get very far. When we got close to Miss Rosie's Maurice and I split up; I took the front and he went around back. It was pretty near dark by then, so no one saw him. Anyway, Maurice makes his way 'round to the east side...there's a narrow alley leadin' from the back to the street in front...and sees these two gents sort of lurkin' behind a bush there toward the front." Raymond stood up. "Maurice, why don't you tell the rest; I feel a compelling need for a sip of sour mash and a cigar."

"Sure, Lamar; you just take it easy. Why don't you just lay down on the bed and Emil'll fetch you a cigar and your whiskey. We drinkin' out of glasses tonight or just passin' the bottle?

Quincy is it okay if I call you 'Quincy?' Seeing how..."

"That's fine, Maurice; go ahead."

"As Lamar was saying, I saw these two yahoos hiding there in the bushes. I went up behind them real quiet-like and tapped one of them on the shoulder. I guess I surprised him pretty bad; he jumped about two feet in the air and wet his trousers 'fore he even hit the ground. Time he'd landed Lamar'd come up from the front and we had the two of them sort of pinned between us. Neither the two of them nor Lamar and me wanted to make too much noise; 'cause if we did we might all four end up in the slammer.

"With me and Lamar pressing up against them and them with their backs to the wall of the house, it was pretty close quarters, especially with that one fella smellin' like the men's restroom in a train station. Then Lamar asks 'em 'You gents wouldn't happen to be a pair of Peepin' Toms, would you? We...' Lamar meanin' him and me...'we're also of the same persuasion and this is kind of our favorite spot. So we'd be obliged if you gents would just take off and maybe come back some other night.

"Seems that calling a fella a 'Peeping Tom' if he ain't one is apt to get a man mighty riled up. And that's what happened; th' one didn't wet himself pushed Lamar away and pulled out a sheath knife. He managed to get in one swing...sort of grazed Lamar's arm where you see the bandage...before Lamar could get him under control. At the same time, not thinkin' too hard on what I was about to do, I kneed the other one in the groin which made my trousers wet in the knee and the other fella's wet all the way down his leg.

"I grabbed my man by the hair, punched him a time or two then clapped my open hands to his ears; that sort of makes a man want to sit down and think things over for a bit. Lamar, he did that stuff he likes to do with the edges of his hands and his elbows and such. So it wasn't much of a tussle after that.

"We persuaded them to join us in an old tool shed I had spotted around back; give them an opportunity to convince us they weren't what Lamar said they were. They were only too anxious to do that, but were mighty reluctant to say what they were really up to. I carry this little thing with me when I go out sometimes." Maurice reached in his pocket and took out a folding blackjack which he slapped lightly in his palm. "Most of the time don't have to use it; I just slap my palm once or twice and they get the message. These clowns, they needed a more realistic demonstration. Thumped mister wet-pants once on the knee and tickled the other one's ribs a couple times; after that, they started jabberin' almost faster than me ' n' Lamar could take it all in.

"Seems they're a couple of local street-toughs, or at least that's what they try to pass themselves off to be. They got hired to make the acquaintance of a certain young lady thought to reside at Miss Rosie's. Tall, pretty, dark red hair; you know who I mean. Their job was to kind of rub up against her both at the same time, maybe flash the knife to convince her not to scream. And if they were so inclined, grab a pinch or two here and there. Just enough to get her pretty upset. Then the knife guy was supposed to put the knife up against her cheek and make like he was going to cut her up a little so's she'd know they were serious. Then they were supposed to give her this letter."

Maurice reached over and took an envelope off the top of the chest-of-drawers. He opened the envelope and took out a single page of unlined paper. "Here's what it says: *'Tell the old lady that if she does not change her plea to guilty, we'll carve up your face just like Christmas's.'* And of course it's unsigned."

"How'd they know to come after Cecilia?" Adams read the letter which Maurice handed to him.

"Mighty good question, Quincy." It took a couple more lessons from 'Blackie' here to get 'em to tell us who'd hired them. Turns out some mug works as a bartender up at the north end of Commercial Street is their go-between. Somebody needs the services of a pair like Jackie and Dennis — that's their names — they ask around; word gets back to Mikey — he's the bartender — and Mikey checks 'em out. If they're not the cops he gets word back to them that want to hire someone to do some kind of job, they need to drop by the bar; pay him a visit, maybe down a pint. Arrangements get made, money changes hands and Jackie and Dennis get their assignment.

"We tell Jackie and Dennis maybe they need to consider a career change and to look for something somewhere south of Maine. By now they're real quick learners and eager as can be to oblige. We truss them up with some rope we find there in the shed so they can't get loose any time soon. One of the things you learn from doing an escape act…I suppose Emil here told you where I come from…is that you can also tie knots that nobody can get out of. When we're done I tell Lamar, 'you go take care of that scratch, and I'll pay a call on Mikey.'

"I find the tavern okay; just north of Franklin. I step up to the bar and order a Black Bush. I offer to buy Mikey a round and ask has he got a minute to chat? Mikey says 'sure;' pours himself one of the same. We knock glasses and he asks me 'What do you want to talk about? You don't look like a fella with woman troubles.' So I says 'I want to talk about Jackie and Dennis…and by the way you'd best keep your hands where I can see them. 'Course he says right off 'I don't know any Jackie and the only Dennis I know is a cousin on my sainted mother's side lives in Buffalo, New York.'

"So I show him Dennis's knife; it's even got his initials "D.M.' carved in the handle. And I ask him, 'Now Mikey, why would a dyin' man lie about who is best friend is?' He gets all pale and his eyes kind o' bulge out. I figure he thinks Jackie and Dennis are pretty tough guys — not too bright — but can take care of themselves. So he thinks right away I gotta' be tellin' the truth; no way Dennis'd give up his knife 'less someone pried it out of his dead hand.

"I give it about thirty seconds to sink in and then order up another round, remindin' Mikey to keep his hands where I can see them. We toast the late, lamented Dennis Morrissy and then Mikey asks what do I want with him? I tell him I want to know who paid him to sic Jackie and Dennis on the red-head. He says he don't make it a habit givin' out the names of his customers. And I tell him it's indeed a pleasure to meet a businessman with such high ethical standards. None the less — here I kind of lean over the bar; I take Dennis's knife and put the point on Mikey's left hand, not too hard but just enough to draw a little blood...and I tell Mikey either he starts tellin' me everything he knows about who hired him, or he's going to have to make his livin' from now on as a one-handed bartender.

"Mikey, he's a much quicker learner than Jackie or Dennis. So he tells me he doesn't know much. He contracted his first job for this customer maybe a couple years ago, he thinks. They spoke only on the 'phone."

"I thought you said he checks out his potential clients, be sure they're not setting him up."

"That's right, Quincy. But as Mikey told it, when the customer called the first time he said that since the idea came from the customer it would be entrapment and he couldn't be prosecuted. The money came along with instructions by letter. The money overcame any misgivings about with whom he was dealing. Mikey says the money came in a box — no return address of course — post-marked Augusta. Mikey figures whoever sent the money and instructions was either already in Augusta or was taking the train up to Augusta to make it even harder to trace."

Quincy sat down in a straight-back chair and took a pull on the bourbon which Lamar had passed to him as Maurice was talking. "When was he contacted about this job?"

"He said it was just yesterday and the money and instructions were in his mail box this morning. No postmark, so his client must have just dropped it off last night after he closed up."

"That still doesn't answer my question, Maurice. How'd they

find out about Cecilia?"

Flammonde stood and scratched his back against the edge of the armoire. "That one's on me, I suspect. Whoever it is must have seen Cecilia with me in the courthouse and knew I'd been spendin' a lot of time with you. Saw Cecilia with me, noticed the resemblance between Cecilia and her mother and put two and two together, just like I did."

"What about the first job? If we can find out who it was that got worked over, maybe we can figure out a connection."

"We already know who that was, Quincy. As soon as I can, I'm going to pay a call on the first victim; assuming I can still find him. His name is Reuben Bright. He owned a butcher shop in Tilbury Town. His wife died...this was right about the time that you opened your office...they say from a heart attack. But the way I figure it her heart attack...if that's what it was...was caused by Lamar's and Maurice's new friends Jackie and Dennis. Right afterward Bright shut down his shop and just disappeared."

"I remember that. He didn't just shut it; he had the whole place torn down. Maurice, was there a message that Jackie and Dennis were supposed to convey to Reuben Bright like they were going to give to Cecilia?"

"As best Mikey could remember—and I pressed down a bit with the tip of the knife to jog his memory—is that Bright hadn't paid some money he owed and that if he didn't pay up he'd not only lose his contract but everything else he had. 'Everything' must have included the wife, I suppose."

"Emil, even if you can't find Reuben Bright, try Tom Hardwicke at the bank; he'd be the one most likely to know about Bright's business, especially if it involved a long-term contract of some kind."

"Good idea, Quincy, if he'll talk to me without a subpoena. You know bankers can be closed-mouthed when they want to be."

"Emil, Tom Hardwicke can barely keep his mouth closed when he chews his food. You'd almost have to do Maurice's knife trick to shut him up. But say, where are you going to get a subpoena anyway?"

"I'm coming to that Quincy. Let Maurice finish."

"There's not much more to tell, Quincy. Mikey asked if he could keep Dennis's knife as a souvenir. I told him sure; I'll mail it to you here at the bar. Do it first thing in the morning. Then I had one for the road and headed back here."

"You're not really going to mail it to him, are you?"

`"No. I don't have to go into my 'Mento the Mind-Reader' act to predict where Mikey's goin' and I don't reckon the folks in charge there gonna let him keep any sharp objects around."

"So I gather you're going to turn the letter and the knife over to the police? What about Jackie and Dennis? They're not actually going to get away are they?"

"Unless someone finds them first and calls the cops, I expect that in a day or so they'll work their way loose and show up at Mikey's place. Maybe Jackie's britches'll dry out by then. Either way, by then the police will have the whole story and they'll haul in the lot of 'em and charge 'em with aggravated assault and extortion. If Emil can find Reuben Bright, the D.A. might even make a murder charge stick. Although in Kennebec County, who knows what'll stick?"

"Quincy, have you decided what you're going to do about the letter?"

"There's no decision to make; I must tell my client. Emil, I think you knew what I'd say before you brought me here. I must say that I deeply appreciate your integrity in letting me know; but at the same time, a tiny part of me wishes maybe you hadn't. That said, it might help if I could convince Mrs. Dubrowski that Cecilia is safe and can come to no harm on account of this threat."

"Of that I can assure you. We've brought in some additional people and they're watching over her even as we speak."

"That's right now, Emil. But what about a week from now? A month or a year from now? Even if Mikey, Jackie and Dennis are in custody, whoever's behind this seems capable of unlimited evil and possessed of considerable resources. What's to keep him from hiring some other thugs to finish what Jackie and Dennis started but failed to do?"

"I could try to tell you that once the trial's over there'd no longer be any need to threaten Mrs. Dubrowski, but I can't quite convince myself that the person behind this would not do something to Cecilia just for vengeance. So I think you'd best go and get the envelope and bring it back here. Maybe it's time we introduce you to the 'business opportunity business.' Lamar, Maurice, are you okay with that?"

"Fine with me, Emil."

"Okay with me," Maurice echoed.

Chapter Thirty-One

Taking time to change into the trousers of his alternate suit, Adams returned to Emil's room with the envelope. "Have you looked inside yet, Quincy?"

"Not yet. From what you said earlier, I may need a swig from the bottle when I do. So I thought I'd best wait until I got back here. Is it okay if I pull this chair up and spread whatever it is that I'm about to look at on the bed? Won't bother you, Lamar?"

"No; go right ahead. And here's the bottle; you'll be needin' it soon enough. Only thing: If you feel like you're gonna be sick, please use the bathroom and not my leg."

"Okay, what have we got?" Adams opened the envelope and removed a thick bundle of photographs which he began to spread out on the bed. After less than a dozen, he put the rest back in the envelope and handed the envelope back to Flammonde. "Mind handing me the bottle again, Lamar? I'm sorry, Emil. Unless I have to, I'd rather not look at the rest. Maybe it's my straight-laced upbringing, but these are the most disgusting things I've seen in my life. When I was in college at Brown some fellows in the dorm would occasionally show around some French post-cards. Those were pretty salacious; but these…these…I don't know what to call these."

Flammonde took the envelope back From Adams's shaking hand. "The word 'pornography' comes to mind; but even that doesn't seem to do them justice. Just for curiosity's sake which one do you think is the worst?"

"Of the ones I've seen, second place is a coin-toss between Cory sodomizing that little girl…she can't be more than eleven or twelve…and the one where Reba Boyles is sitting naked in a chair with another naked little girl in her lap. But Smedley and the sheriff sodomizing yet another little girl both at the same time, I guess that one takes the grand prize. What in the world could make people do something like this? Are the other pictures just as bad? Worse? Emil, can I have one of your cheroots? Maybe that'll keep me from throwin' up."

"Take it easy, Quincy. We've all had about the same reaction." Flammonde handed Adams a cheroot and struck a match which he held so that Adams could light up. "Fact is, what you're seeing, bad as these pictures are, is not the worst part. Lamar, Maurice and I have been tryin' to get enough evidence on these perverts for months. You ever hear of the 'White Slave Traffic Act of Nineteen Ten?' Also known as the 'Mann Act?'"

"Yeah, I recall we debated its constitutionality in my Con Law class. But what does this bunch...or for that matter you three...have to do with the Mann Act?"

Flammonde took out his wallet and handed Adams a card on which the seal of the U.S. Department of Justice was embossed. The card read: "*Emil Flammonde, Special Agent, Bureau of Investigation, United States Department of Justice, Washington, D.C.*"

"Lamar, Maurice, I assume you both carry the same credential?"

"Yes we do, Quincy." Maurice reached for his wallet. "Need to see mine?"

"No; thanks anyway, Maurice." Adams ground the cheroot out in the ash tray and stood up. "What I really need to see...or hear...is one goddamn good reason why I shouldn't get up, go back to my room and try to figure out how to tell my client in the morning that the federal government has been using us as a couple of stalking horses to trap a gang of white-slavers. But now they're through with us, Mrs. Dubrowski, what happens to you, to Cecilia and to me from here on is no concern of the government's.

"I've got just two questions: One is Clarence Darrow's taking on Mrs. Dubrowski's case in Illinois just a story you made up? The second is: Last week, when I passed out in Lamar's bed, I didn't just dream that you said you're the one got Mrs. Dubrowski into this jackpot in the first place, did I?"

"Now cool down a minute, Son."

"I'm not your son, Lamar."

"If you were, Quincy, I'd be sorely tempted to reach over and slap you up-side the head to get your attention. Now you just sit back down and let Emil have the floor for a few minutes."

"Okay, I'm sitting. And I'd have another cheroot; maybe help calm my nerves. Also while you're at it, maybe you'd best pass the bourbon again."

"You think that's a good idea, Quincy? I mean the bourbon. Time we get through talking, you'll have to be in court in just a few hours. Mrs. Dubrowski doesn't need you to be there with a hang-over so's you can't think straight."

"I'll deal with that when the time comes. What does it matter to you anyway?"

"A great deal, Quincy. To answer your first question: Yes,

Clarence Darrow has taken the case. I had to go all the way to the Attorney General to get it done. Took a telephone call from him personally to persuade Darrow to take it on. And the offer from the governor, that's genuine as well.

"The answer to your second question is part of why it matters a great deal. It's true; you weren't dreaming. I got Mrs. Dubrowski into this 'jackpot' — to use your term — albeit quite unintentionally."

"How?"

"When I'm working under cover, I sometimes use the name 'Major F. Sharp.'"

"So that's why you told me not to worry about Christmas calling 'Major F. Sharp' as a witness. But what were you doing writing to the Illinois Prison Bureau?"

"Remember, Quincy, this was before Richard Cory was murdered. As I told you, I was trying to gather information on Cory. I admit I was less than candid about why I was doing it. I got Mrs. Dubrowski's name from one of the local merchants. I checked with Washington to see if they had any information on her: Immigration status, anything that might give me some leverage. You'd be surprised at the records your government keeps. After about a month they get back to me with the information that there's an 'E. Dubrowski' wanted on a parole violation charge in Illinois; conviction's for murder. Washington gave me the contact information and told me to write direct.

"Seems they're right busy just now chasing spies, subversives, saboteurs and what have you. The attorney general, Mr. Palmer, put his protégé — fellow name of Hoover — in charge of huntin' spies and subversives...mostly anybody he and Palmer thought might be a communist. And Mr. Hoover — a man with a lean and hungry look if I've ever known one — grabbed up just about all the manpower in the Justice Department and got 'em workin' for him. Anyway, so's not to draw attention to myself, I wrote the letter to G. Miller as Major F. Sharp and asked for the reply to be sent to me care of general delivery in Augusta. And you know what happened from there.

"I had no way to anticipate that Cory'd get his brains blown out while I was waitin' to hear back from Illinois. All I knew at the time I sent the letter was that Cory might be mixed up in a gang of white-slave traffickers operating somewhere in Maine. For all I knew, Esther Dubrowski, his housekeeper, was mixed up in it too. Then when I got the report back from Washington, I was convinced she was. I mean a convicted murderer? Why not a white-slaver too? You know how the mind can come up with some pretty weird ideas when it doesn't have any real facts to work with.

"To borrow a phrase from Lamar, we'd been up here for more'n two months chasing our tails without any break in the case. Now suddenly Cory turns up dead. So Lamar, Maurice and me, we huddle and decide I better go to the inquest. Either something will turn up, or we shut this one down and go back to Washington, our tails 'tween our legs. So I go there thinking that maybe the housekeeper's the one did it. Then the sheriff gets up there doin' his best to sell it as a suicide. Makes me start to think: 'What's goin' on here, Emil?' I start wondering maybe Dowdy's in it too and doesn't want anyone kickin' over any rocks. Soon's I hear what Doc Goodson's got to say, then I know 'Something's rotten in the state of Denmark.' That Shakespeare or somebody else?"

"No, Shakespeare's right; *Hamlet*, Act One I think. You got 'lean and hungry look' right too. That's *Julius Caesar*; I forget which act. But go ahead..."

"Well, as you know, next day, Doc Goodson puts on his dog-and-pony show at the mortuary and all the while Pommus is bustin' his tail trying to make Dowdy look bad by finding out on his own who done it. 'Course Dowdy's the one puts Pommus on the scent of Mrs. Dubrowski in the first place. Why else would Dowdy have taken the letter as evidence? After all, it was just an innocuous-looking employment reference letter. He take it because it was misfiled?"

"Must have been his back-up plan in case nobody bought the suicide story."

Maurice nodded his head in agreement. "I agree with Lamar, Emil. Looks like we may get the chance to ask the sheriff about it in the next day or so, things go our way."

As Raymond and Morton were making their comments, Flammonde stood and paced around the room. "The rest of the story you pretty much know. I suppose no one, Dowdy included, thought that Pommus would be creative enough to call long-distance to check on Dubrowski's reference. Maybe he's smarter than we give him credit for. Be that as it may, as soon as I saw Dubrowski up there on the stand, I started to have my doubts about whether she did it. Then when she confessed but made up where she got the revolver, I was convinced...just as I told you the first time I came to your office...that she didn't do it.

"That meant I couldn't leave her to her fate. Fact is, Quincy, I've been paying your fees and most of the expenses out of my own pocket.

No insult intended, but being on the government payroll don't make you rich unless you got your hand out, which I do not. You were available and the best I could afford. But Mrs. Dubrowski couldn't have gotten better representation than you've given her if I was a millionaire. I mean that sincerely...regardless of what you do from here on.

"So I hired you and persuaded Lamar and Maurice that we needed to stay, see how things played out. Three of us, we've been partners for a good while, so they didn't take much persuading. Now, it's up to you; will you hang with us a while longer, see if we can't put Smedley, Boyles and company out of business and into prison for good?"

"How do you know Cory, Smedley, Boyles and Dowdy are a white-slave ring?"

"We, the three of us, have been working Mann Act cases almost exclusively since   nineteen fourteen when the Department began to get serious about it. We've taken down brothels in New Orleans, Galveston, San Francisco and St. Louis in just the past two years. Time to time we'd come across girls, young girls, some barely into puberty would only say that they came 'from up north.' No city, no state; just 'from up north.' All of them scared to death of lawmen. They were taught to be. They'd been trained...mostly by being beaten, starved and sexually abused...to lie about anything and everything, even their names and where they come from. Some of them even got turned into dope addicts...keep 'em in line that way. Those we were sure were under-age got handed over to the state child-welfare agencies in whichever state we happened to be in. That's all we could do. The states were supposed to see that they were put in good, safe foster homes; maybe they'd have a chance at a normal life."

"At least that's what we keep telling ourselves." Lamar eased himself off the bed as he spoke. He went to the armoire and got out his shirt. "Damn, this is an almost-new shirt. Look at this slit in the sleeve not to mention my suit jacket." He put the shirt on and continued, "Those that were on dope, we could get some them into state hospitals; not that sending them there did all that much good. The ones wasn't addicts, the local cops would take in; charge them with misdemeanor prostitution maybe they get thirty days in the county slammer. After that, they'd go right back to the life. Not a damn thing we could do about it."

"What got us up to Maine," Maurice continued the narrative, "is an anonymous letter sent to Washington. Accused Richard Cory of

Tilbury Town of making young girls disappear. Normally, letter like that would get shoved into a desk drawer and forgotten. Sometimes, if things were kind of slow around the office that day, somebody'd maybe write the local authorities but then there wouldn't be any follow up.

"This time, though, we happened to be in D.C. to give the bosses a report consisting mostly of what they wanted to hear. We, Emil, Lamar and me are sitting around waiting our turn and we start talking about this 'up north' thing keeps coming up. Well a secretary…she's th' one deals with civilian letters; passes 'em on to whoever she thinks might want 'em…hears us talking and says 'hey, you guys, ain't Maine up north somewhere?' So Emil says 'yeah, I think it's up somewhere around the North Pole. Why do you want to know?' So she looks at him kinda' funny, hands Emil the letter and we end up here last week in May fightin' off swarms of black flies and tryin' to get a handle on this thing."

"When did you get on to Smedley and Boyles?"

"Not until I saw the will. It got me to wonderin' why Cory'd want to leave everything to that pair."

"You thinkin' maybe they killed Cory," Lamar asked.

"You suggested as much to me, Emil, when I was looking for someone else besides Mrs. Dubrowski might have a reason to want Cory dead. You know, some kind of falling out among thieves?"

"Could be, Quincy. Maybe Cory was getting weak-kneed and wanted out; threatened to roll over on the rest of them. Maybe they thought Cory was getting too big a cut; wanted all the action for themselves."

"You think Cory was the big boss, Emil?"

"Can't say yet, Maurice; but it does look that way."

"In my meeting with Smedley, from the way he described Cory's involvement with the school it's hard to say. Cory may have sought them out as Smedley told me or since Smedley and Boyles were up there first it's possible they brought him into the gang. Maybe out of the goodness of his heart he offers to help financially and next thing he knows he's in the white-slave trafficking business."

"I doubt that, Quincy. All the time we been doing this Mann Act thing, never once arrested someone said that he just got up one mornin' and decided to open a whorehouse or go in business buyin' and sellin' little girls."

"I agree with Lamar on that one. Where do you think Cory's money came from? Except for Oakdale Hall, there's not a single piece of real estate that's in Richard Cory's name or in any other name can be traced back to him in any one of eleven states we've checked. The Oakdale Hall estate—the mansion and the land—were in the same family since Maine was still part of Massachusetts. Cory bought it from the last family-member's estate. Paid cash for it; no mortgage.

"Just about every factory in this part of the world has a war materiel contract with the U.S. Government. Every one of those contracts has ownership disclosure requirements and provides audit rights to the War Department. Those guys do a thorough job, and Richard Cory's name hasn't turned up once."

"Have you found out anything about Smedley and Boyles?" Adams ground out the stub of his cheroot.

"Enough to know they're part of it." Maurice picked up the envelope containing the pictures. "Even before we got these, I called Washington; raised some hell. Must have gotten someone's attention, because they got back to me real quick-like. Another team…doin' same thing we do…already had a file on Boyles. Years ago, before Smedley and Boyles came up here she ran a whorehouse in Brooklyn. Got shut down a couple times; probably she wasn't payin' off the right folks: Cops, politicians, both. Anyways, after they shut her down the last time she just disappeared. Interestin' thing, according to her file, she had it pretty tough at least 'fore she got in the prostitution business. Evidently she was raped when she was around thirteen, fourteen. Got knocked up and had a child, a boy. Had to make a livin' however she could. Started out as a maid in a whorehouse. Lived there and that's how she raised her kid. Worked her way up 'till she ran the place. Can't say she owned it; owners were probably some of those foreign gangsters. You know, call themselves 'The Black hand' or some such nonsense. Want to guess who her son is?"

"That's sick, Maurice. I think I'll go throw up now. Watching his own mother…one who gave him life…sitting there being photographed naked while sexually abusing a child? How depraved can you get?"

"Look at the numbers, Quincy." Lamar yawned. "These all-nighters ain't as much fun as they used to be. Boyles is what, about sixty? How old does Smedley look, forty-six, forty seven? I had to guess, I'd say momma Boyles is the head honcho"

"Obviously the sheriff's part of it. What's his role?"

"That's easy enough to figure. The High Sheriff's the one gets 'em into the system. Picks up a runaway trots her by Judge Gribble and hands her over to Smedley and Boyles. Then Cory handled the sale when they're ready to put her on the market."

"Why did he keep the pictures? Why not throw them away? Burn 'em?"

"Be my guess," Lamar started to take another pull on the nearly-empty bourbon bottle but instead corked it and set it on the bedside table, "sheriff kept 'em for the same reason Cory did: To blackmail Smedley and Boyles, should the need arise."

"The photographs, Emil; can you tell me where you got them? You mentioned something about the way you got them was better than if Maurice had been successful."

"You ever hear of the *Weeks* Case, Quincy? U.S. Supreme Court, about four years ago?"

"I might have read something in the Boston paper; something about the Fourth Amendment? In my practice I don't have much need to keep up with U.S. Supreme Court opinions."

"*Weeks* says that evidence seized in an illegal federal search can't be used in federal court. So if I'd found the pictures or anything else incriminating, we'd likely not have been able to use it. Couldn't use it or anything else it led us to; be fruit of the poison tree."

"But you can use it if someone other than a federal officer hands it to you like on a silver platter?"

"As long as we don't tell him what to look for or where to look."

"Emil, I gather that 'your man in Augusta' has access to the sheriff's office?"

"You could gather that Quincy, if you're of a mind to, assumin' he got the envelope from the sheriff's office. And that's not something I'd be askin' I didn't have to."

"Just out of curiosity, can you tell me now who it is, 'your man in Augusta'?"

"I'm surprised you haven't figured that out by now, Quincy. You know that deputy, th' fella's been so helpful?"

"You mean Walter Isaacson? How do...did...you know he wasn't in it along with the sheriff?"

"He applied for a job with the U.S. Marshal Service about a year ago. They checked him out but didn't hire him on account of a hiring freeze. When we came up here, we asked them they had anybody reliable up in Kennebec County. They put us in touch with him. So besides bein' a deputy sheriff, he's been helpin' us out from time to time."

"Doesn't that make him a federal officer?"

"Not as long as we don't put him on the payroll; don't tell him what to do, how to do it."

"Well this beats anything I've ever heard of."

"You sure gotta admit it beats writing timber leases or patent applications."

"I suppose you're right Maurice…it's just…I don't know…I don't know what to do. This whole thing's out of control."

"No, but it'll get out of control, Quincy, you don't do something about it."

"What do you want me to do?"

"Be our 'silver platter,' Quincy. We need Mrs. Dubrowski to say…if it's true…that those pictures originally came from Oakdale Hall. On account of the *Weeks* Case we need a search warrant for Oakdale Hall. She'll need to sign an affidavit. The U.S. Attorney's already got the warrant drawn and he can take it to the judge as soon as he can attach the affidavit."

"We need to get something ties Cory and Smedley and Boyles together."

"Don't the photographs do that, Lamar? I mean how much more graphic can you get?"

"Ain't enough, Quincy. We need to tie them together financially and tie all of 'em to interstate transportation of the girls. Most we could maybe get on the photographs alone might be some kind of state sodomy charges."

"Lamar and me, while you were in court kickin' Christmas's back-side harder 'n' it's ever been kicked before, and Emil here was keepin' an eye on things, we were looking through a bundle of photographs of girls. Weren't any of 'em French post-cards either. When we'd take down one of the houses we had photographs made of all the young girls. Brought a bunch of the pictures up here with us. Figured we'd show a few around, see if anybody recognized any of them. Hadn't made much progress that way though. So today we were tryin' to see if we could match any of them to the girls in the Cory picture album. We maybe got one, two matches, but it's really hard to tell. We find something in searchin' Cory's place ties him to Smedley and Boyles, that should be enough to get a subpoena for the reform school records, maybe put some names to faces. We track down a few of these girls, that'd be enough to get indictments and convictions on Mann Act charges."

"I'm going to have to tell Mrs. Dubrowski about the threat. Are you sure Cecilia's safe? I can't lie to my client."

"There are two deputy U.S. Marshals sitting on Miss Rosie's already. Nobody's getting near Cecilia she don't want 'em to. She'll never have to testify in anything, so nobody's going to want to shut her up for that reason."

"Perhaps so, Emil. But what about her mother? Isn't she going to have to testify same as her affidavit?"

"As I stand here I don't see it. Cory's dead, so she won't be needed to prosecute him. She doesn't know Smedley, Boyles or the sheriff; at least we don't think so. But if something comes up we don't yet know about and we need her, we'll provide protection until the case is over and even after if necessary.

"From what you've told me about her, Quincy, I don't think you'll have too hard a selling job. Why is Mrs. Dubrowski so concerned about the O'Brien twins? It has to be because they've told her some things. My guess: She's seen the pictures and put two and two together while she was in jail up in Augusta. I think she's going to be eager to do her part once she knows help's coming."

"Speaking of the O'Brien twins, what's going to happen to them? I'm especially worried about the one who's back in custody."

"We've been working on that too, Quincy. Soon as we arrest Smedley and Boyles, and the sheriff and anyone else we can get a warrant for, our boss in Washington's going to call the Maine Attorney General let him know what's going on; suggest that he go to court; get a special master appointed or whatever he needs to do to take control up there until things get sorted out."

"Won't that mean having to go to court in Kennebec County? What if Gribble's in this too?"

"That thought hadn't escaped our attention, Quincy. He wasn't in any of the pictures, but it's hard to see him not being in it. That's why we need the search warrant so badly. As for the school, if the state can't or won't act immediately, the U.S. Attorney General will ask the federal judge up here to issue a writ of habeas corpus for every inmate at the school. That'll put them in federal custody so the U.S. Marshal Service can take over running the school until everything gets sorted out and the State of Maine can figure out what it wants to do and how to go about it.

"Far as the O'Brien girl that's still loose, she hasn't gone far. We'll find her, be sure she's safe."

"That'll be a big help too. I'm going to have to get over to the courthouse early so I can talk to Mrs. Dubrowski before court starts. Let me have the pictures back. I'm going to try to get a couple hours sleep."

"I better hang on to them just in case; give them to you in the morning. I'll meet you downstairs for breakfast, say seven o'clock?"

Chapter Thirty-Two

Flammonde's prediction that it would not take much to persuade Esther Dubrowski to cooperate was largely but not entirely correct. Once assured that Cecilia was safe she invoked some Yiddish imprecations on Jackie, Dennis and Mikey and refused to consider changing her plea. She admitted that she had known immediately that the automobile advertisements that Sheriff Dowdy, that *zaftig mamser*, had shown to the jury were not the original contents of the envelope. She had not mentioned this to Adams because he'd done such an effective job of making the sheriff out to be a liar that she didn't think Adams would want to be bothered with what had originally been in the envelope.

She also admitted that she was ashamed of herself for not having done something sooner. She had discovered the envelope in the table drawer while doing the annual spring cleaning in early April. Her first impulse was to quit her employment but she'd decided that having no place to go made leaving not a viable alternative. She had thought many times about doing something, but didn't know to whom she should turn, and…the most shameful part…she was afraid that bringing down the law on Cory would expose her own outstanding debt to society. The thought of Cecilia being romantically involved with such a man made her sick but all she could do was discourage Cecilia without revealing her awful secret. But had she known the entire story…about the commercial aspect…she would have certainly done something. At least that's what she tearfully tried to convince herself she would have done.

She had looked at the envelope contents that one time and had not looked at all of the pictures. Of the ones she'd seen she was positive that she recognized several, including the ones Adams had found the most offensive. She readily agreed to sign whatever affidavit was required.

Where Esther Dubrowski went her separate way was in regard to the commutation offer from the Illinois Governor. It was unacceptable; either she wanted a full pardon or a new trial with Mr. Adams as her lawyer. Adams's feeble protest that he was not admitted in Illinois was rejected out of hand; she had no doubt he would be admitted. His pointing out that if she rejected the offer and the governor balked, it might take years for the case to work its way through the federal court system. Even then, Adams tried to persuade her, there was a chance it wouldn't be successful. His entreaties were met with a stubborn set of the jaw and shake of the head. "Tell Mr. Darrow that he must be firm; the governor will give in. Come, Mr. Adams, now it's time for Judge Beauchamp to give his decision. Then I will sign paper for Mr. Flammonde. As for this," she took the letter Adams had brought for her to sign accepting the commutation, tore it in two and handed it back to Adams "Please thank Mr. Darrow for me and tell him what he must do."

Adams and his client had just enough time to be seated before the command to "all rise" was given. As he stood he turned his head toward Christmas and mouthed "no deal, sorry." And as the judge was sitting down Adams managed to turn the other way and nod to Flammonde as a signal that Mrs. Dubrowski recognized the photographs and would sign the affidavit.

"Are the parties ready to proceed in *State v Dubrowski*?"

Adams and Christmas rose as one and gave their respective announcements of "ready." Evidently the courthouse grapevine had worked with its usual efficiency; the public gallery was filled with lawyers and assorted courthouse habitués. The *Daily Kennebec Journal* and *Portland Press Herald* reporters were in their regular places, notebooks out and pencils poised. The interest generated by the case and especially by the argument over admitting the confession was the last thing Adams wanted. Would the certainty of extensive publicity nudge the court to rule in the State's favor?

An accepted wisdom among the criminal defense bar is that trial judges would much rather not make controversial rulings in favor of the defense because the State has no right of appeal. Avoid being labeled "soft on criminals" and let the appellate courts make the controversial rulings is the cornerstone of prudent trial bench judging.

Judge Beauchamp took several typewritten sheets from a folder. "Dammit," Adams mumbled to himself. "He's written an opinion. Only reason he'd do that is he wants the appellate court to know exactly why he's going to admit the confession. That way whatever inferences that may be drawn from the facts, he can make sure the higher court knows he found them against the defendant."

Adams gave a side-ways look at the prosecution table. Christmas was sitting there, his hands folded in front of him, a serene half-smile on his face. No paper, no writing implements; Christmas didn't need to write anything. He knew how the judge was going to rule; probably drafted the opinion himself. Adams lay down his own pencil. He asked himself, "What's the point of writing anything down?" He folded his hands and tried to look as serene as Christmas. Smiling was out of the question.

"Now before the Court," Judge Beauchamp began, "are two motions by the defendant Esther Dubrowski: The first is her motion to exclude the verdict of the coroner's jury in the inquest over the body of the deceased, one Richard Cory, late of Kennebec County, Maine. The second of defendant's motions is to exclude her sworn testimony at the aforesaid inquest to the effect that she in the late hours of August third, or early morning hours of August fourth, nineteen eighteen took a revolver from a desk drawer in the Cory residence and with it shot Richard Cory in the head as he slept thereby causing his death." Beauchamp paused for a few seconds to allow the murmur in the public gallery die down. He did not like to use his gavel; gavels are for judges that can't control their courtrooms.

"Both motions," he continued, "were presented orally outside the presence of the jury by and through defendant's counsel, Mr. Quincy Adams. The said motions are each opposed by the State represented by Mr. Horatio Christmas. Outside the presence of the jury the Court heard oral argument from each side on each of the motions. The record will also reflect that the jury is sequestered during the instant proceedings as well.

"The court has considered thoroughly the able arguments from both sides and has carefully read the authority cited by Mr. Adams in support of his second motion as well as the argument of Mr. Christmas as to why the Court should not apply to the case at hand the peculiar...excuse me...I meant *particular* language of the *Gilman* case so earnestly pressed upon the Court by Mr. Adams."

Adams's heart had stopped beating on the word 'peculiar' and had barely started again even after the judge corrected himself. "But 'pressed upon the Court?' Why didn't he just come out and say I made an ass of myself?" Adams thought. "Well at least he called it 'language' in the *Gilman* case and not '*obiter dictum*;' maybe that's a good sign."

"In giving my decision, I will discuss the two motions together because I find them to be interrelated; the common factor being that they both involve the defendant's testimony. According to State's Exhibit number four, a copy of the coroner's instruction to the jury in the aforesaid inquest written in the coroner's own hand, said exhibit having been admitted by agreement at the beginning of the trial for consideration only by the Court, the coroner charged the jury that in reaching their verdict they could but were not bound to consider Mrs. Dubrowski's statement the substance of which I recited earlier. Because the coroner's jury also heard Dr. Goodson's testimony that in his professional opinion Richard Cory's death was a homicide, they could have reached their verdict based on his testimony alone and disregarded Mrs. Dubrowski's testimony entirely. However, I cannot make that assumption; on the contrary, I must presume that the coroner's jury followed Coroner Ingersoll's instruction and did consider Mrs. Dubrowski's self-incriminating statement in reaching their verdict.

"There is much to commend Mr. Adams's argument that the verdict of the coroner's jury is not *res judicata* in this case. For those of you in the gallery who are not lawyers, *res judicata* is a Latin phrase that simply means that the judgment or verdict of the coroner's inquest would be binding on the jury in the present case."

Adams gripped the edge of the counsel table to keep from standing up and saying something that would get him held in contempt. "My argument," he thought, "has 'much to commend' it. But evidently it's not enough to persuade His Honor. Do judges feel better if they pat you on the back while they're sticking a knife in your gut?"

"In most circumstances," His Honor continued, "I would be compelled to accept Mr. Adams's argument. Here, however, a different rule applies. In the present case, as I have said, the verdict of the coroner's jury was presumptively based, at least in part, on Mrs. Dubrowski's own testimony. In this unique circumstance, I hold that if Mrs. Dubrowski's testimony at the coroner's inquest is admissible as bearing on her guilt in the present case, it also makes the verdict of the coroner's jury admissible against her. It seems to me that the verdict of the coroner's jury is an official act just like any other official act. If the issue in the present case happened to be whether Mrs. Dubrowski was married to a certain individual, I have no doubt that a marriage license which was issued to her and that individual on their joint application would be admissible as some evidence that she did in fact marry that individual."

"Well, that's that," Adams whispered. "Who is he deceiving by saying 'if I allow?'"

"Did you wish to address the Court, Mr. Adams?"

"No, Your Honor. I was attempting to explain Your Honor's ruling to my client."

"Please try not to interrupt the Court again, Mr. Adams. You'll have ample opportunity to discuss the Court's rulings with your client when the Court is through announcing those rulings."

"Yes, Your Honor. My apologies to the Court."

"Turning now to the admissibility of the self-incriminating statement," the judge paused and rubbed the bridge of his nose between his thumb and forefinger, "Mr. Adams is in effect asking the Court to accept as the law in Maine what Mr. Christmas rightly points out is *obiter dictum* in the *Gilman* case. In other words, to exclude the statement I must go where no Maine appellate court has gone before. Such a step is contrary to the principle of *stare decisis* which is the very foundation of our common law system which has supplied the rule of law in Maine since colonial times.

"Moreover, as Mr. Christmas further points out, excluding a confession made under oath and in open court on the basis that the defendant was not advised of her right to remain silent portends many such claims of denial of constitutional rights such that, according to Mr. Christmas, law enforcement officers will be hamstrung in the performance of their duties to apprehend and prosecute those who break our laws. Some of these offenders may indeed escape their just deserts, no matter how egregious their transgression.

When the judge shifted from "self-incriminating statement" to "confession" Adams felt like he'd swallowed a live five-pound lobster whole and the creature was tearing at his insides trying to get out. Sensing his distress, Esther Dubrowski placed her hand over his and squeezed hard. With her other hand she also found Camille's hand and held it.

"This Court takes judicial notice of the fact that almost all defendants who appear before this Court do so in order to plead guilty. Were it not so, the burden on this Court and its sister courts throughout the state would be enormous.

"And this Court has no doubt that most of these defendants have already confessed their crimes to an officer of the law, either an arresting officer or one who interrogates them once they are arrested."

"These are valid concerns and weigh heavily upon the Court. Lastly, I am also troubled by the fact that Mr. Adams in his rebuttal yesterday had no answer to Mr. Christmas's argument that every person is presumed to know the law and therefore no official…police officer, prosecutor or magistrate…should be compelled to advise each person suspected of a crime that he…or…she has the right to remain silent and that any statement can be used against him or her in later proceedings. I can only assume that Mr. Adams had no effective rejoinder because the Court too has been greatly vexed by this issue even though I've had much more time to reach a conclusion than I allowed Mr. Adams."

"How ironic," Adams thought. "Because I had a duty to speak and did not, Esther Dubrowski forfeits her right not to speak. But then, what the devil was I supposed to say? Now I know how a condemned man must feel as he sits in his cell and listens to the sounds of his gallows being erected. I wonder how many times Christmas has used that 'ignorance of the law is not a weapon' argument?"

"There is language in *Gilman*," the judge continued, "that is not *obiter dictum* and which informs this Court's decision in the present case. At page two hundred twenty-three, Justice Rice says 'The true test of admissibility in this class of cases is, was the statement offered in evidence made *voluntarily, without compulsion?*' I must digress from the text to observe that the printed opinion places the words '*voluntarily, without compulsion*' in italics, presumably to emphasize their importance. Then Judge Rice goes on to say 'If this proposition be answered in the affirmative, then the statement is clearly admissible in principle; but if not *voluntary*,' again he italicizes the word 'voluntary,' if obtained by any degree of *coercion*,' the word '*coercion*' is also italicized, 'then it must be rejected, as well by the rules of common law as by constitutional provision.' Thus, in order for this Court to determine the admissibility of Mrs. Dubrowski's confession, I must determine whether it was voluntary or coerced. This is obviously a fact-intensive inquiry and each case, including the present one, turns on its own particular facts.

"At the outset, I must determine whether to apply an ordinary-person standard, or do age, gender, education and other factors unique to each individual have a part in the inquiry? Justice Rice gives no guidance on this point; however I think these factors must play a part, albeit not necessarily a decisive one.

"I will not reiterate the evidence in detail. In summary, it is undisputed that Mrs. Dubrowski is a person of limited education and cannot be assumed to be so well-acquainted with her rights that she would have known that she could ignore the instructions given her by the coroner or any other official. Having been called to the witness stand and administered the witness oath, unless she was so informed, how could she have known that she could have declined to testify? She was without counsel, and could, as Mr. Adams suggests, have construed the admonition not to discuss the case with anyone as a bar to her obtaining the advice of counsel.

"On the other hand, she was never placed in custody; never subjected to physical coercion, active or passive. Yet it also could readily be said that these factors were but a part of District Attorney Pommus's plan to obtain her confession by lulling her into a false sense of security. It is one thing to have a witness unexpectedly blurt out a self-incriminating statement where that person was not already under suspicion and was not put on the stand for the purpose of obtaining a confession. It is quite another to place a person already under suspicion on the witness stand for the very purpose of having her incriminate herself under the compulsion of the witness oath.

"Another factor has influenced the Court's thinking in this matter. As Justice Rice points out, and as Mr. Christmas so eloquently emphasized yesterday, a voluntary confession is inherently reliable. It follows then that an involuntary confession is inherently unreliable. But what if the reliability of the confession is called into question — not because it was involuntary — but because it is not plausible? In other words, would we be here today if Mrs. Dubrowski had confessed to stabbing Richard Cory to death with a butcher knife?

"Mr. Adams makes a compelling argument. Indeed, Mr. Adams, I find it decisive. Why, I must ask myself, would Mrs. Dubrowski confess to a crime she didn't commit unless it was involuntary?

"Based on the evidence adduced in the hearing outside the presence of the jury, the Court finds that the defendant's self-incriminating testimony given at the coroner's inquest was involuntary. Accordingly, I grant both of the defense motions; neither the verdict of the coroner's jury nor the testimony given by the defendant in the inquest shall be admitted in evidence in this case.

"Now, having so ruled, I feel bound to express some further thoughts which I suppose must be classified as *obiter dictum*. First, Mr. Christmas, law enforcement authorities need fear my decision today no more than they need fear the United States Constitution or our own Maine Constitution. Those accused of crimes may still voluntarily confess, whether out of remorse, or to seek Divine forgiveness, or in the hope of more lenient treatment by the state because they have taken responsibility for their conduct. They will still be able to do so, and the vast majority will continue to do so.

"But when a suspect is taken into custody to be interrogated, the constitutions, both state and federal, demand that proper warning be given. This is perhaps the proper answer to your argument that each person is presumed to know his rights. These constitutional provisions impose no duties of obedience on the public; they are restraints that operate only upon the government acting through its agents. The criminal laws, on the other hand, operate as constraints upon individual conduct. An individual may be presumed to know her duties under the law, but not necessarily her rights. Thus the constitutions place the burden on the agents of the state to respect those individual rights and if necessary to inform the individual that she has those rights.

"Mr. Bailiff, please ask District Attorney Pommus to come in and stand inside the bar. I have one more comment that should be made in his presence. While we're waiting, let me ask Mr. Christmas, do you plan on calling any more witnesses?"

"I think not, Your Honor. The State rests,"

"Mr. Adams?"

"Your Honor, the State having rested, the defendant moves for a directed verdict of acquittal."

"Mr. Christmas?"

"The State does not oppose Mr. Adams's motion."

"Very well. The defendant's motion for directed verdict of acquittal is granted. As soon as we're through speaking with Mr. Pommus, we will call the jury in and I will so instruct them. And perhaps we can all avoid the influenza outbreak."

When Pommus had entered the courtroom and stood before the bench the judge began. "Mr. Pommus, the Court has a few remarks that are directed to you. Before I say them, I think you should know that I have excluded Mrs. Dubrowski's so-called 'confession' and since the State has rested its case, I have granted the defendant's motion for a directed verdict of acquittal."

"But Your Honor, what…"

"Please, Mr. Pommus. I said the Court has some remarks to direct to you. You'll have an opportunity to respond in another forum. Are we clear?"

"Yes, Your Honor."

"The Court finds your conduct in representing the State of Maine in the inquest over the body of Richard Cory held in Augusta, Kennebec County, on the fifth and sixth of this past August, and your subsequent actions in seeking the arrest and indictment of Esther Dubrowski and in prosecuting this case to the point when you were recused, to be reprehensible. It is the duty of every prosecutor to seek justice and not merely convictions.

"Evidently you allowed your personal prejudices against Mrs. Dubrowski to get in the way of your judgment and your duty as a state official. As a result of your single-minded determination to persecute…yes I said 'persecute'…an innocent person, nothing has been done in the way of bringing the real culprit to justice. Not only have you trampled on the rights of Mrs. Dubrowski, you have failed in your duty to the people of Kennebec County.

"You are indeed fortunate that Mr. Christmas assumed the duty to prosecute this case. Had you appeared as counsel in this Court, you would find yourself charged with contempt. However, do not permit yourself to indulge in any feeling of relief. It is the Court's intention to forward a transcript of your testimony and my ruling to the State Bar of Maine in order that it may undertake such disciplinary proceedings as it may see fit. Now, Mr. Pommus you are excused. Mr. Bailiff, please bring in the jury."

Chapter Thirty-Three

It was late that afternoon. Adams was sitting in the Portland Regency Hotel bar with Cecilia and Camille. Other than congratulatory hugs when court adjourned they'd not had an opportunity to speak at length. As soon as the hearing at which Judge Beauchamp released Esther Dubrowski on her own recognizance pending the governor's action on the Illinois fugitive warrant had concluded, Adams had answered the reporters' questions for a while. The impromptu press conference — Adams's first — had ended when Flammonde, standing just beyond the cluster of the curious and those determined to shake Adams's hand so that perhaps some of the glory would rub off on themselves, had held up his hands, the left palm open and the right making a writing motion, to signal that they needed to tend to the affidavit. The signing took place in the jury room which the bailiff had made available to them. After Flammonde had shown Esther Dubrowski his credentials and given her a sixty-second version of what Adams had been told last night Camille served as the notary public to administer the oath and attest to the affiant's signature.

It was necessary for Esther Dubrowski to look at the photographs and to initial on the back those that she recognized. Adams and Flammonde had begged Camille to sit at the other end of the long table, but she insisted that if they and Mrs. Dubrowski could look at the photographs she could as well. Like Adams, she'd seen a few so-called 'French post-cards' which had she discovered hidden in her brother's dresser drawer while foraging for contraband cigarettes.

"Do you think that Flammonde will keep his word?"

"About what? He has in everything so far."

"Letting Mother go with him when they raid the school. I'm really worried that she may be in harm's way if she does."

"I think Emil would listen to your concerns, but I don't know that your concerns would be enough for him to renege on a promise he made to your mother."

"Yes, but she did more or less have a gun to his head by refusing to sign the affidavit until he agreed. Please excuse the clumsy metaphor, Cecilia."

"That's all right, Camille; when you and Quincy told me what she'd done I had the same thought. Quincy, what if you went and talked to the judge? He'd listen to you. He's the one that released her instead of keeping her in the jail until they hear about Illinois. He could change his mind, couldn't he? After all, you did persuade him to rule in Mother's favor."

"I doubt that I'd even get in to see him. His clerk would ask why I want to talk to the judge, seeing's how the case is over and so on. I'd tell her; I couldn't lie about it. She'd go in and tell the judge and he'd say what's done is done. Anyway, there are two good reasons not to interfere. One is that your mother's right; she's probably the only person the O'Brien girl will trust. The other reason is that she'll be safe with Emil and his colleagues. They'll protect her like the Secret Service protects the President."

"Which President do you mean, Quincy? Lincoln or McKinley?"

"That wasn't their job, Cecilia. The Secret Service wasn't put in charge of protecting the President until after McKinley was assassinated."

"I'm sorry I was being so...so sarcastic. But still, what if Boyles and Smedley put up some kind of fight?"

Camille lit a fresh cigarette. "Cecilia, Emil mentioned that possibility, but your mother was adamant: Either she goes or nobody goes."

"If she's going, I want to go as well. I won't get in the way; I just want to be there and know she's safe."

"And if Cecilia's going, so am I."

"And if you two are going, I guess I am too. We can make it a picnic outing with sandwiches and potato salad. Anyone else you can think of might want to come along?"

"Now you're being sarcastic, Quincy."

"I apologize, Camille. I know when I'm out-gunned. I'll talk to Flammonde when he gets back here. They ought to be about through with the federal judge."

"What's next for the Law Office of Quincy Adams?"

"Maybe I can answer that Miss Winters."

"Excuse me for butting in to your conversation, Ladies, Mr. Adams. The ladies I know, but we've not met. I'm Harrell Berman, Mr. Adams, managing partner of Berman & Berman."

After Adams had risen and shaken Berman's outstretched hand, Berman asked, "May I join you for a moment?" Not waiting for a response, Berman took the fourth seat at the table. As soon as he did, the waiter came over to inquire whether he could bring Mr. Berman something from the bar. Berman ordered a scotch and soda for himself and a fresh round for the others. After the waiter had gone to turn in the order Berman continued. "Let me say first of all, Mr. Adams, congratulations for a brilliant piece of lawyering. Aside from our vested interest in the outcome," he leaned across the table and patted Cecilia's arm, "you did a truly outstanding job in representing your client. The legal profession was ennobled by your efforts."

"You're too kind, Mr. Berman. I did what any conscientious lawyer would have done. And don't forget Judge Beauchamp or for that matter Horatio Christmas. He's as passionate about winning as any lawyer I've seen, but he discharged his duties in keeping with the highest standards of a prosecutor."

"Unlike a certain other prosecutor we know," Camille added. "I wonder what'll happen to Pommus."

"Since I'm on the State Bar Ethics Committee, in fairness to Mr. Pommus, I shouldn't be discussing it. I will say, however, I look forward to reading the materials being forwarded by Judge Beauchamp.

"And speaking of his honor, yes, Mr. Adams, he's deserving of credit as well. Frankly, I was surprised that he didn't do what trial judges usually do with difficult cases; they 'kick 'em upstairs' so to speak. Let the appellate court get the bad press for letting a criminal go free.' That he did not do so reinforces the notion that you did a remarkable job."

As soon as the waiter had brought the fresh round, Berman raised his glass, "To Mr. Adams and Miss Winters for an outstanding job."

Adams responded, "Let's not leave out our brave client, Mrs. Dubrowski...or, last but not least, her daughter who has been such a great help as well." At Cecilia's inclusion Adams thought he saw just the slightest narrowing of Camille's eyes and pursing of her lips as she clinked her glass with the others.

"I invited myself to join you, Mr. Adams, because I have a proposition to make to you and Miss Winters. Berman & Berman have been considering for some time establishing an office in Kennebec County, in Augusta to be specific. The additional work resulting from the Cory estate makes such an office economically viable for at least the next year or two. By then we should have enough of a presence in Kennebec County that we will attract a self-sustaining clientele. Indeed a number of our Portland-based and out-of-state clients have interests from time to time that need representation in Augusta, especially when the legislature is in session.

"In short, we'd like for you to join the firm and head our new Kennebec County office. And of course the invitation extends to Miss Winters. Not that there's anything wrong with Tilbury Town, but we would want to establish the office in Augusta. An Augusta office would be more in keeping with our firm's image. Of course we'd buy out your existing lease, buy your library, pay your moving expenses and provide a housing allowance until you found a suitable permanent residence. The same holds for you as well, Miss Winters."

"That's a generous offer, Mr. Berman, but I have a question: Will Dr. Smedley and Miss Boyles approve of my doing work on the Cory estate? When I interviewed them they made it clear that they thought Mrs. Dubrowski was guilty and I was some kind of shyster for defending her. Given the way the trial ended, I doubt they've experienced a change of heart. Also, my having had them subpoenaed as trial witnesses cannot have served to endear me to them."

"For reasons that I am not at liberty to divulge at present, you have my assurance that the co-trustees will not object to having you as the estate's attorney."

"Obviously, Mr. Berman, you anticipate that Smedley and Boyles will at some point, quite soon I imagine, be removed as the executors and trustees. Do you think they possibly had a hand in Richard Cory's death? I'm sure you figured out that I was going to use that possibility in order to sow the seed of reasonable doubt in the minds of the jurors had my motion to exclude my client's statement not succeeded."

"That I cannot say. Indeed, there's nothing that I *can* say. Think how unseemly it would look for a member of the Ethics Committee to be accused of so egregious an ethical lapse as to betray a client confidence. I'm afraid you'll have to take my assurance at face value and let events take their course.

'I don't need an answer at this moment, Mr. Adams, Miss Winters. Take your time and get back to me when you've reached a decision with which you both are comfortable.

"And Miss Durban...or should I now call you 'Miss Dubrowski'...when may we expect your return? I don't want to rush you; it's just we need to decide whether to hire a temporary typist until you do return. If it will be a matter of a few days, we can get by. But if it will be more than a week, we'll need to hire someone. Not to replace you, but to fill in during your absence."

"I'd like to wait until my mother's business with the State of

Illinois is settled. I hope that will be in the next couple of days. Would it be alright if I let you know on Monday?"

"That seems reasonable. Monday will do fine. Again, Mr. Adams, Miss Winters, congratulations. Now if you'll excuse me, I'll settle the bill, take care of the waiter at the bar and leave the three of you to continue savoring the moment."

"That's a lot to absorb over one drink. Do you think he was offended by my smoking...in public?"

"I don't think so. A few people in the office smoke; in fact he smokes a pipe. He doesn't mind as long as no one lights up in any of the open areas; you know, the reception room, the hallway. But what I want to know is: Does he really think that Smedley and Boyles killed or had Richard killed?"

"Camille and I don't know the man at all. You've worked with him long enough to have some kind of opinion, Cecilia. What do you think?"

"Well, he can be awfully closed-mouth about things. He won't discuss client business at all outside his private office. Obviously we...the secretaries...learn things, but he's constantly reminding us about attorney-client confidences. So even if I knew whatever it is that he knows or suspects...which I don't...I'd have to keep my mouth shut as well. I do know this: He doesn't like either one, Smedley or Boyles. But if he knew that they were involved in white-slavery, he'd find a way to put a stop to it."

"Do you think he's the one sent the anonymous letter to the Justice Department that got this whole business started?"

"I had that thought too, Camille, but I just can't see Mr. Berman disclosing client confidences."

"But there is something called the 'crime-fraud exception' to the rule. I remember talking about it in legal ethics class. If a client tells you he committed a crime, there's nothing you can do about it. But if a client tells you he's *going to* commit a crime or commit fraud, you can report it unless the client promises not to do what he told you he was going to do. I suppose if Smedley and Boyles told Berman that they were in the white-slave business and planned to continue, he could report that."

"I can't see him continuing to represent them if he knew they were criminals. I know he's fired clients for a lot less than that, and for reasons besides not paying their bills."

"Must be a real luxury. If I quit representing clients just because they weren't paying, I'd have a lot fewer clients."

"Forgive me for stating the obvious, Quincy. But if you got rid of some of them you'd have more time to spend finding new clients and doing work for the paying clients."

"Fair enough, Camille. I'll try to take your advice to heart. In the meantime, what'd you think of Berman's offer?'

"I don't know. I'd like to think about it."

"Me too. Cecilia, what do you think? Would we fit in?"

"I'm with you and Camille; I'd like to think about it."

"I wonder what's keeping Emil. I thought he'd be through with the judge by now." Camille ground out the stub of her cigarette.

"Look," Cecilia pointed toward the door. "Isn't that the man who was sitting in the courtroom the whole time?"

"Yes, that's Lamar Raymond. He's one of Emil's associates." Adams waived to Lamar who was standing in the doorway, his eyes adjusting to the dim light.

"Quincy Adams, that's the man I thought was following me the day I spent hunting for Cecilia. So he *was* following me. Did you know it?"

"Not until later. It was Emil's idea. Just another layer of protection that you no doubt would have refused. Lamar, over here." Adams waived again.

"Ladies, this is Mr. Lamar Raymond, Special Agent, Department of Investigations, U.S. Department of Justice. Lamar, meet Miss Cecilia Durbin and I believe you know Miss Camille Winters, at least sort of."

"Pleased to meet both you ladies. May I?" Lamar pulled back the chair recently vacated by Harrell Berman.

"Of course, Mr. Raymond. We'd love for you to join us." Camille gave him her most dazzling smile. "It's so much friendlier than lurking about hiding behind lampposts, don't you think?"

"Bourbon, straight up," Lamar said to the waiter who had appeared the moment Lamar sat down. "Another round for you folks?"

"I think I'll pass this round Lamar. Ladies?"

"No, I'd better not," Cecilia declined.

"Yes, I'll have another," Camille said as she reached for another cigarette.

"My apologies, Ma'am. Both for followin' you and for being so clumsy about it. I keep tellin' Quincy here that he don't ever want to get old."

"That's okay, Mr. Raymond. You're forgiven. I'm sure you and Mr. Flammonde meant well." Camille smiled again, but her eyes remained cold. "I'm just thankful that nothing untoward happened."

"If it had, Camille, be assured that Lamar could have handled it. Why…"

"Let's save those stories for another time, Quincy. We finally got the search warrant for Oakdale Hall.

"What took so long?"

"You had many dealings with federal judges?"

"When I was handling patent cases back in Boston I heard rumors they existed. Lived in some kind of judicial Olympus and every once in a while they'd hurl down a decision like a bolt of lightning. But that's as close as I ever got to meeting one."

"For us, they're the only game in town. We gotta use 'em; play by their rules. Them knowin' they're the only game in town and that they get to make up the rules sometimes makes it pretty tough."

"Maybe that's the way they're supposed to be, Lamar."

"I suppose you're right, Quincy, but that don't mean they gotta keep you waitin' forever and then keep you there lookin' at the toes of your shoes while they ask a bunch of nit-picky questions."

"At least you can be sure that when they're done with their 'nit-picky questions' you'll be ready when some fool defense lawyer asks you the same ones on the witness stand. But anyway, congratulations. When are you going to execute the warrant?"

"We'll be going out tonight and takin' Mrs. Dubrowski with us, kind of show us around."

"If my mother's going, then so am I."

"And if Cecilia goes, so do I. Besides, you spent a whole day watching me; it's only fair that I get to watch you."

"I don't know, Miss Winters…"

"Better make it a table for three, Lamar. Where they go, I go. In fact all three of us can go in my car."

"That's up to you folks. Don't guess we can stop you. But you're liable to get right bored just sittin' out there in the car. We can't let you go in the house or poking around the barn or the grounds. Any defense lawyer'd jump on that like a chicken on a June bug. Any evidence we found they'd ask: 'How do you know some civilian, say Miss Durbin for example, didn't plant it so's you federal fellas would find it.' Gonna be hard enough just keepin' track of your ma, Miss Durbin."

"Lamar's got a point. Sounds like we'd be wasting our time just sitting there. Maybe we ought to wait until they turn up something and get the warrant to arrest Smedley and Boyles. By the way, Lamar, where are the fat lady and her puppet?"

They went back up to the school in Hallowell. Weren't anything we could do to stop them. They're in Cory's car. Boyles drivin' and sonny-boy ridin' shotgun. We got two men keepin' pretty close tabs on 'em; they start to rabbit, our folks will sit on 'em 'till the cavalry arrives."

"Where are you getting all these men, Mr. Raymond?"

"Well, to be honest, Miss Durbin, we had to pull the two off of watchin' out for you. Emil, he put in an urgent call to Washington...ask for some help. Closest they could find somebody wasn't out chasin' German spies was Richmond, Virginia. They're on their way, but not likely to get here until late tomorrow night, next morning."

"Do you think that it's safe to leave Cecilia without protection?"

"I'd say Miss Durbin's safe, Miss Winters. The locals have got Jackie, Dennis and Mikey locked up; bail set pretty high. So there's no risk from them. Anyway, I was them I'd think two, three times before decidin' to finish the job they got hired for. Desk sergeant told me they had to air out the paddy wagon after they got done bringin' Jackie in. I don't mean to be so crude, but..."

"That's okay, Mr. Raymond. With what Camille and I have listened to lately, our sensibilities are virtually numb."

"Still, Cecilia, I'd feel a lot better if someone is looking out for you. I'll stay with you...if you'll have me...but all I've to protect us with is this two-shot derringer that Mr. Flammonde gave me, and as I've said before, I'm not exactly Annie Oakley. Would you consider coming up and staying at my family place? We've got plenty of room, and I know my dad would be happy to have you. I'll get him to call my brothers Fred and Billy. Between the three of them I think they could hold off an entire German division."

"Where are you keeping my mother, Mr. Raymond?"

"I think Emil made arrangements at the hotel up in Tilbury Town. Emil's got a room on one side and Maurice...that's Maurice Morton, he's with Emil and me...has the other side. So she couldn't be in safer hands."

"Camille, that's such a gracious offer. Of course I'll come as long as you're sure your father won't be too inconvenienced. Besides, that will put us both closer to whatever's going on and I'd really like to see Tilbury Town and Quincy's office and the Red Rooster. Mr. Raymond, do you have time to come back to Miss Rosie's with us so that Camille and I can get our things?"

Chapter Thirty-Four

The Red Rooster breakfast crowd made it nearly impossible for Adams, Winters and Durbin to eat more than a bite of food at a time or to converse among themselves. Before they'd entered the restaurant they'd agreed that if necessary they would simply introduce Cecilia as "Cecilia Durbin from Portland and that she too had been helping with the case." The banker, "Just-call-me-Tom" Hardwicke, had started things off and in doing so made Adams uncomfortable by loudly proclaiming Adams to be the finest lawyer in Maine. Adams had a hard time deciding whether Hardwicke was working up to reminding him his loan was overdue, or was just angling for an introduction to Cecilia. By the time the banker left there was a good-size crowd around the table, a replay of the post-trial press conference.

At his customary table near the front Harley Winters was also holding court. All who paused to say hello and suggest how proud Harley must be of Camille, were told that while Harley didn't know all the details — "you know, lawyer confidential stuff" — Adams had told him that it was really Camille who'd done all the hard work.

It was past ten-thirty when Flammonde finally joined them. Before reporting the results of the search warrant he answered Cecilia's questions about how her mother was doing. "She's fine. We didn't get her back to the hotel until after mid-night, but she was up bright and early this morning. She enjoyed the hotel; first time she'd ever been in one except for her brief stint as a maid back in Chicago when she was first paroled.

"When I left to come over here she, Maurice and Lamar were finishing a nice leisurely breakfast. Maurice is tellin' her stories from his carnival days, and she's teachin' Lamar to speak Yiddish. But teachin' Yiddish to a cowboy from Texas must be kinda' like teachin' a horse to sing grand opera; don't reckon the lesson's gonna take. Your mother's still trying to figure out how to say 'y'all' in Yiddish. Anyway, I'm glad your ma is having a good time for a change."

"How'd the search go?" Adams asked at the same time Camille asked "What happens next?"

"Search was a total bust; we turned up nothing that would tie Cory, or Smedley or Boyles to violating the Mann Act. I thought for sure we'd find a ledger of some kind, some financial records. Mrs. Dubrowski showed us every nook and cranny in the place, so if there is anything it's not in the house or the barn.

"As to what happens next, I expect that Lamar, Maurice and I will be pullin' up stakes and headin' for someplace warmer. Fact is, it'll be hotter 'n Hades in Washington when we get back and report that we may have broken up the gang but there won't be anybody goin' to prison…at least to a federal prison.

"So I guess this is kind of a farewell party. Before we leave we'll stop by, pay our respects to Reverend Christmas. While we're there maybe give him a set of copies of those photos although I doubt the photographs alone will be enough to prosecute Smedley and Boyles or the sheriff."

"Why not?" Camille looked horrified. "Isn't sexual abuse of a child a crime? What about…" she lowered her voice to a whisper, "…sodomy?"

"They both are, Camille. But how's Christmas going to prove when the photographs were taken? Maybe the statute of limitations has run."

"Besides that," Adams interjected, "How is Christmas going to prove that the children in the photographs are really children? They may look like they are, but that's probably not enough. One of them would have to come forward and testify."

"That's outrageous. No wonder Mother is so concerned about those twin girls, the…"

"O'Brien twins." Camille supplied the name. "At least Christmas ought to be able to get Smedley and Boyles fired."

"That's not exactly the way it'll happen. Smedley and Boyles will be allowed to resign 'for personal reasons.' That way some bureaucrats up in Augusta won't end up with their tails in a crack because they didn't know what was goin' on down there at Hallowell.

"Christmas wants to push harder he could check the job application and references they gave before they were hired. It would probably be the first time anybody actually did any checking. Whoever done the hirin' thought 'anybody wants that job, they can have it.' My guess is that Smedley submitted his application and when he was hired said he needed to bring along his long-time executive assistant. Just forgot to mention that his assistant's experience was running whorehouses in Brooklyn. Turns out the application's a bunch of lies and the references fake, Christmas might be able to get 'em on fraud."

"What about the sheriff; he's in the pictures too."

"He is, Cecilia. If it were up to me, I think I might show a couple of those photographs to the *Daily Kennebec Journal* and let the editors do the work. They won't be able to publish the pictures, but they'll sure as heck editorialize about them enough.

"By the way, there's good news of a sort from Illinois." Flammonde reached in the breast pocket of his jacket and produced a telegram. "Here, Cecilia, tell your ma that Mr. Darrow fussed about it for a minute or two but ended up agreeing with Mrs. Dubrowski: Either a new trial or a full pardon. And he thinks like she does that the governor will fold rather than risk exposing what a rotten system they've got there in Chicago."

"I doubt that it's much better anywhere else. If you can't afford a lawyer, forget about getting a fair deal from the system."

"You're right, Quincy, but do you think it'll ever be any different? The taxpayers all of a sudden not going to mind payin' for competent defense of everybody accused of a crime and can't afford their own lawyer?

"And speakin' of paying for competent defense, you need to get me a final bill. I'd like to pay you before I leave town."

"Forget that, Emil. I should be paying you. You've taught me more about the practice of law in the last month than I learned in three years of law school and three years at Trout & Dickson, not to mention how much new business will come in on account of this case."

"That's mighty gracious of you, Counselor."

"I just wish the outcome had been better for you and Lamar and Maurice."

"Maybe it will be after all, Quincy. Emil, you said you were looking for a ledger of some kind?"

"Yeah, that or some bank records. Anything that would tie the three of them together and to the interstate transportation. What do you have in mind, Camille?"

"What about...wait. Quincy, are your briefcases upstairs?"

"Yes, but..."

"Never mind. Emil, don't move. I'll be back in a minute. I need to get the exhibit list out of Quincy's briefcase. Quincy, do you remember which one it's in?"

"Not mine; the other one. The one you want to get rid of."

Camille returned in less than five minutes clutching a manila folder to her chest. "Look at exhibit seven, Emil."

"It says: 'One accounting ledger taken from Oakdale Hall on August four, nineteen eighteen by Luther Housewright, Deputy Sheriff

Kennebec County, Maine.' Camille, thanks to you, we may not be leaving as soon as we thought. Your daddy gonna' cause trouble if I give you a big hug?"

"Thanks anyway, Emil, but there's no point in getting my dad all riled up."

"Well then, just consider yourself hugged. Quincy, what happened to the exhibits after the trial?"

"I assume the clerk has them unless she's already sent them back to the clerk in Augusta."

"Quincy, you mind goin' back down to Portland givin' us a hand? Might be easier to pry the exhibits out of the clerk's hands if you ask to see them. I think we'd best take Mrs. Dubrowski with us to see if she can recognize the ledger."

"Won't the fact that the deputy sheriff took it from Oakdale Hall be enough?"

"Maybe, Cecilia. But it'd be better if she could say that she saw Cory writin' in it or readin' something in it. That way there'd be no doubt it was his, and nobody'd be able to argue that it didn't belong to Cory. Don't worry about your ma; Lamar and Maurice'll still be lookin' after her."

"There is something I wish you and Camille would do for me while we're in Portland. Would you mind takin' Quincy's auto and drivin' up to Hallowell and letting the two deputy marshals know what's goin' on and to make extra sure that Smedley and Boyles don't rabbit on us?"

"Cecilia, will you go?" Cecilia nodded. "Yes; we'll go. But how are we going to know who we're looking for?"

"They're in a Ford Model T just like Quincy's. Two big fellas; one's got a handle-bar mustache. Both of 'em probably smokin' cigars. One with the mustache, he'll probably be on the passenger side. From what I've seen, Hallowell isn't very big. Just drive around until you spot them. After you talk with them why don't you ladies take in the sights in Augusta? We'll send Quincy and Mrs. Dubrowski up there by train as soon as they're done at the courthouse in Portland and you can pick them up at the railroad station. Probably they'll be on the late-afternoon train."

"I've got a question, Mr. Flammonde. What's this ledger going to tell you? Won't it be just a bunch of numbers? Remember, except for Smedley, Boyles and the sheriff, I knew Richard Cory better than anyone, even better perhaps than my mother knew him. And obviously I didn't know him at all. The thought of his hands pawing on me makes my skin crawl." Cecilia wrapped her arms around her chest and shuddered. "But the point is, whatever's in that ledger is bound to be in some kind of code. Richard...excuse me, I can't help still calling him 'Richard'...enjoyed being the man of mystery. Always making up riddles and guessing games, never talking about himself in any meaningful way. What I'm saying is, I suppose, that you're going to need all the help you can get in deciphering whatever's in that ledger."

"And you want to help?"

"More than anything in the world, after seeing my mother free from this nightmare. Also, maybe it will help me bury some of my guilt for my role in this thing. And last but not least, maybe I'd like to even things up a little between me and Richard even though he'll never know it."

"Okay, Miss Durbin, you're in."

"Call me Cecilia, Emil."

"What about you, Camille?"

"I'd much rather be doing that than driving around looking for two fat men with cigars and guns."

Chapter Thirty-Five

Reluctantly the clerk unpacked the exhibit box which she had already sealed intending to deposit it with the Railway Express agent at the train depot for transport back to Augusta. That was the extent of her willingness to cooperate without instructions from Judge Beauchamp who was at the time on the bench hearing a divorce case. She finally relented to the extent of allowing one person to examine the exhibits there in the clerk's office. Camille and Cecilia conferred for a moment then Cecilia dashed out returning twenty minutes later with an identical ledger purchased from a near-by stationer's shop. Taking turns with each page Camille and Cecilia soon made a replica of the exhibit. Calling upon his reservoir of good-will among the bailiffs, Adams obtained the use of the jury room where Camille and Quincy, Cecilia and Esther, and Flammonde, Raymond and Morton sat around the jury table trying to reach a verdict on what the rows of numbers comprising the ledger entries meant.

"This first column, with the three rows of numbers looks like they could be dates. The far left side is where you usually put the date in an account journal." Flammonde took out his cheroots and offered them around with only Lamar as a taker.

"That's true, but the first row has more numbers over twelve than numbers twelve or under." Camille took out a cigarette. Seeing no one recoil at the sight she calmly lighted up. "And the second row has only numbers twelve and under."

"And what do you make of the third row? It's just a series of numbers starting with one and going up to ten. All of the numbers are repeated four and five, and in a couple instances as many as six times. If we can't even get past the first column, this is going to take forever. Emil, maybe you should give the army cryptographers a crack at this."

"To do that, Quincy, we'd have to wait until the war's over."

"We may be here until then anyway; somebody doesn't come up with a solution pretty soon." Lamar walked over to one of the windows and opened it a few inches to let the tobacco smoke out.

"May I look?"

"Of course, Mrs. Dubrowski." Flammonde took the ledger which was in front of Camille and passed it along the table to Esther.

After studying the column for a minute, Esther Dubrowski looked up. "These are dates; at least the first two rows going down the page are dates. The month and day are written in European way; the day is first and then the month. This is way I learn to write date in old country. So first entry, one followed by a five, is May first. The last one," she turned over to the last page, "is May eleventh."

"But what about the years, Mrs. Dubrowski?"

"Maybe they're not calendar years. What if they're chronological years?" Morton came over to the table from the window where he'd been looking out at the setting sun.

"Like the one stands for the first year they started?"

"Yes, like that, Camille." Morton sat down next to Camille.

"But wouldn't we have to know what year they started? We know that Smedley and Boyles came in nineteen ought five; at least that's what they told me. And they said they met Cory a couple of years later during the legislative session."

"What if we worked backwards, Quincy?" Flammonde set his cheroot down in the nearly-full ash tray. "Mrs. Dubrowski, do you recall anything that happened at Oakdale Hall on May eleventh of this year?"

"Was that when Cecilia…" she hesitated unwilling to complete the thought.

"No, Mama; that was the first weekend in May." Cecilia turned to her mother. "It's okay. Quincy knows; I told him."

"Knows what?" Emil asked.

"That I spent the night at Oakdale Hall."

"And now that you all know, I will also tell you that I stayed up all night to be sure that *Tzippi*…Cecilia…remained undisturbed in her room."

"A precaution, Mother, that was wholly unnecessary."

"You say not needed. Did I not see you kissing him?"

"Ladies, please. This is not getting us closer to solving the code."

"I'm sorry, Emil. I did not mean to interfere. You have child? A joy but also such *tsuris*…"

"So the eleventh of May was the week after Cecilia was at Oakdale Hall. Do you remember anything that occurred?"

"Please remember, Mrs. Dubrowski." Adams turned to his client imploring her. "Remember Dr. Goodson's testimony about treating Cory for a separated shoulder in early May? When did that happen?"

"This was maybe the eleventh or the next day. He had one of those, those cart rides."

"Do you mean 'hay rides?' At least that's what Mr. Silas called them. Mr. Silas said he would hitch up the hay wagon then Cory and some of his friends would load a large hamper of food and liquor into the wagon and go on a picnic somewhere on the grounds."

"Yes, Quincy; that is when his shoulder is hurt. He comes back in much pain. I ask him: what has happened? Should I call doctor? He tells me no; he will be better in morning. I make for him ice pack; he takes and goes to his bedroom. But in morning he says is not better. I make new ice pack; he tells me tie around his shoulder so he can drive to doctor. I do this and he goes; comes back says feels much better. Doctor has made well. Has arm in…how you call bandage around neck…holds arm bend at elbow up close to side?"

Lamar answered first. "You mean a 'sling' Ma'am?"

"Yes, Lamar; a sling his arm is in."

"Who else was on the hay ride that time?" Flammonde stood behind his chair arching his back.

"Always the same ones: Smedley, Boyles, the judge, the sheriff."

"Kind of an odd group for a picnic, Mrs. Dubrowski." Flammonde started pacing. "I'm thinking maybe it wasn't a picnic, at least not one that any of us would want to go on. Did you pack the hamper?"

"No, I never pack. Sheriff always brings. It is strapped onto the shelf on back of automobile. The others, they ride with him."

"Do you know where they'd go on these outings?" Flammonde stopped pacing and gripped the back of his chair."

"I do not know myself. Mr. Cory would always come back with *shmutz*…dirt… on his boots and sometimes on his trousers. And his shirts, *oy gevald,* such a smell. You know, from sweating. One time I ask Mr. Silas: 'Where do they go on these picnics? What do they do?' And he tells me he does not know; he says he thinks possibly to the quarry they go. So I ask him, 'Mr. Silas, what is there at this quarry?' He makes like this with his shoulders." She shrugs her shoulders not knowing the word 'shrugged.' "Again he says he doesn't know. All he has seen is big hole in ground with filthy green water in the bottom. And back from the edge, there is wooden shack. He says there is a railroad track…you know wooden logs with metal rails…that goes from the shack to the edge of the hole. Not big track like for train to Portland." Esther held her hands about two feet apart to illustrate. "I never go on picnic, but if I did I would not want to go to such a place."

"Can we get back for a minute to the ledger?" Adams traced his finger up the column of figures starting at the end. "If this year's the tenth year, then they must have started in ought nine. That would fit the time line from when Smedley and Boyles came and then Cory."

"Or that's the first year for which they kept records," Maurice volunteered.

"Even if this isn't all, there must be over sixty entries."

"My guess is that each entry represents a girl they turned into a prostitute and then sold to someone else."

"I'm sure you're right, Lamar. But we still haven't tied Cory to Smedley or Boyles, or to the sheriff or the judge, much less to interstate commerce."

"I realize that, Quincy. Any suggestions as to how we do that?" Flammonde sat down heavily in his chair.

"Let's take another look at the ledger. Try working on the next column. Each one's a letter followed by a one- or two-digit number."

"Read off the letters, Quincy, and I'll write them down," Camille volunteered. "Maybe they spell a word or a name."

"Give it a try, but it looks to me like there's too many consonants and only two vowels, *A* and *O*. And what do you do with the repeating letters?"

"And what about the numbers" They must relate to the letters somehow."

"Surely they do, Lamar, but how? Quincy, read just the first six."

"Okay: *K, K, A, C, C* and *Y*. If we're reading the date column correctly, the first three were in nineteen oh nine, the next two in nineteen ten and the sixth in nineteen eleven."

"I guess you're right, Quincy." Camille put down her pencil and reached for another cigarette. Just as she started to light it, she put out the match. "Wait; what if the letters stand for counties: Kennebec, Kennebec, Androscoggin, Cumberland, Cumberland and York? The *O's* must be Oxford County and the *W's* for Washington.

"Yes and the numerals are case numbers. Look," Cecilia pulled the ledger from in front of Adams and put it between herself and Camille. "So the first entry in the first column is May first, nineteen oh nine; and the second column lists case number three from Kennebec County. In the same year there was case from Androscoggin County, case number one. Then in nineteen ten there were two from Cumberland County and in nineteen eleven the first one's from York County.

"There's a way we can check if we hurry. Let me write down the tenth year entries for Cumberland County. Then Cecilia and I can check to see if the numbers match up. Let's go, Cecilia."

While Camille and Cecilia were dashing out to catch the clerk before she closed her office, the rest tackled the remaining columns. "This next column," Adams pointed to the row, "must be the buyer's initials. See how they repeat. Each set of initials repeats several times through the years."

Morton leaned over Adams's shoulder. "What about the ones with no initials, just a dash?"

"Who knows? Maybe those didn't get sold." Adams ran his hands through his hair.

"You're right. Look at the last column." Flammonde ran his finger down the last column. Those are the sale prices, probably in thousands of dollars. Look how the amounts keep going up; run around ten thousand the first year and now they're getting' twenty and up.

"Emil, maybe I can send a telegram to Washington listing the initials and see if they have any names that match."

"That's probably the best we can do, Maurice. But why don't you wait a few minutes. Let's see what Cecilia and Camille come up with. If they're right, we're going to have to see the judge to get a warrant for the school records."

"What do you want me to do? Hypnotize him into signing the warrant?"

"I don't know, Maurice. I suppose I just want some company when I go see a federal judge who's likely home by now tucking into a plate of roast loin of lawyer. But your idea isn't a bad one"

"Emil, what if we got Christmas to go out and grab the records on behalf of the State of Maine? Would that give you a *Weeks* problem? They are state records; wouldn't the attorney general be entitled to see them without having to get a warrant? Or what about going to Judge Beauchamp? You surely could trust him. Then you could have deputy Isaacson serve the warrant. Wouldn't the warrant be directed to any sheriff or deputy sheriff in the State of Maine? It would still be a federal search since you instigated it, but with a warrant based on probable cause it would be a good search."

"Mrs. Dubrowski, your lawyer is a genius. Quincy, you want to see if his honor has a few minutes to help take down a white slave ring?"

Adams had to wait in the courtroom while Judge Beauchamp finished hearing the divorce case. It took some persuading, but he finally got his honor to agree to accompany Adams back to the jury room on a matter of extreme urgency related to the killing of Richard Cory. They arrived just as Camille and Cecilia were showing the federal agents that the case numbers for Cumberland County matched the dates in the same rows as the C numbers for nineteen eighteen. After hurried introductions and the display of federal agents' credentials, Adams turned the floor over to Flammonde who gave his honor a concise but compelling summary of what was afoot and why they needed his help in the form of a warrant.

Having had his own experience as a practitioner appearing before the federal judge, and having listened to innumerable war-stories from other lawyers over lunches and at bar functions and having decided that he didn't give a damn whose toes got stepped on either over at the federal courthouse or up in Augusta, Judge Beauchamp concluded "Sounds like probable cause to me.

"Miss Winters, or Miss…Durbin is it? Would one of you be good enough to type up the warrant? Mr. Flammonde, I assume you will dictate what you want? I need to excuse myself for a moment so that I can telephone Mrs. Beauchamp and tell her that I'll be late for dinner. And Mr. Adams, please make sure that what Mr. Flammonde dictates will stand up to a motion to suppress. I do not want any of these people to walk because Mr. Flammonde went too far or not far enough.

"Mrs. Dubrowski, I usually let the jury make up my mind as to whether a defendant is guilty or not guilty. In this case, as you know, I've had to make up my own mind. My conclusion, should you wish to know it, is that you had no hand in Richard Cory's death. However, although it's none of my business, someday I wish you'd tell me why in the devil you confessed to a crime you didn't commit.

"Now, Miss Winters, Miss Durbin, Mr. Adams and Mr. Flammonde, if you'll follow me back to my chambers, I'll show you where the blank warrant forms are kept so you can get started. You other gentlemen, and Mrs. Dubrowski, you're welcome to come as well, but it will be a little crowded."

"Lamar, maybe you and Maurice best get started back up to Hallowell. You'll need to get hold of Isaacson and find the two deputy marshals. Soon as we've got the warrant we'll head up there. Meet you at the foot of the hill…the one that leads up to the school."

"So we win the battle and lose the war, Emil."

"Why's that Lamar?"

"Once we execute the warrant and grab the records, what's to keep Smedley and Boyles from packin' up and high-tailin' it for parts unknown?"

"Yeah," added Maurice, "after they pick up the telephone and call the sheriff and that judge…let them know they may want to consider doin' the same thing."

"I'd be willing to bet that they're gonna put up a fuss so big that we'll have to hold them on charges of obstruction of justice for interferin' with the execution of the warrant. As for the judge and the sheriff, I don't see why we have to book Smedley and Boyles into the jail in Augusta; might as well bring 'em back down here. The warrant will be issued out of the court here, so here's where we ought to bring 'em. Time they get where they can get to a telephone we ought to have enough to get arrest warrants for the lot of them. See you at the foot of Winthrop Hill in four hours."

Chapter Thirty-Six

Esther Dubrowski was impervious to every plea that Flammonde could think of to keep her from coming along. The more dangerous he made it sound the more determined she was that she needed to be there to rescue the O'Brien girl and to do anything she could for the other inmates. Since Raymond and Morton had taken their automobile, Flammonde had no choice but to ride with Adams and the three women. After thanking Judge Beauchamp and promising to report the results of the search as soon as possible they started north on the post road.

It was after ten o'clock by the time they arrived at Winthrop Hill. Flammonde was relieved to see that Lamar and Maurice had managed to round up Deputy Isaacson. The three men were sitting in the automobile at the corner of the post road and Winthrop Avenue. "Got the warrant?" Lamar asked.

"Yes, and I see you've got the man to serve it. Where are the marshals?"

"Bit of difficulty there, Emil."

"What'd they do, Maurice? Get arrested for loitering?"

"Boyles and Smedley have decamped. Took off about two hours ago, headin' south. Same as before, she was drivin' and he was ridin' shotgun. Marshals took out after 'em but they couldn't keep up with that big Packard. Ollie...he's the one does the talkin' other one does the drivin'...says the Packard had a big wicker hamper loaded on the luggage rack. Packard had to be doing ninety, Ollie says, by the time they got to the south side of Hallowell.

"By the time Ollie and J.T.... that's what the other one goes by, just initials...got to Tilbury Town, the Packard was out of sight. They went down as far as Oakdale Hall, but didn't catch sight of the vehicle. They couldn't go in without a warrant, so they went back into Tilbury Town and cruised around for a bit just to see if maybe they're holed up in town somewhere. Didn't see anything, so they came back up here. Figured they'd take a break...you know what stake-outs are like...and then wait for someone to come along and give 'em new instructions. Well, we showed up about an hour ago and sent the two of them back down to watch Oakdale Hall. If Boyles and Smedley are there and try to leave, I told J.T. to run into the Packard hard enough that it won't be drivable."

"That's got to be where they are. We would have seen that

Packard coming south as we were going north. There are some other roads, but they aren't well-paved and you need to know them really well to make any time."

"I expect Quincy's right. They're at Oakdale Hall, and that wicker hamper's got me worried."

"How do you want to play it, Emil?"

"Maurice, you and Lamar get on down to Oakdale Hall. Isaacson will serve the warrant and I'll help him with the search. Walter, do you know whether they have matrons or whatever they call them up there?"

"I think there are half a dozen; at least that's how many are on the day shift. I'm not sure at night."

"Quincy, maybe you ought to come with Walter and me. Can't let you help with the search, but you can throw some legal-sounding stuff at the staff, keep them in line and doin' their jobs while we do ours. Ladies, I wish I could find something for you…yeah, I can. Would you mind just sort of checkin' on whatever girls they got up there; just to make sure they're okay and don't need any urgent medical attention. Anyone asks; just tell 'em you're from Portland and that you're acting under instructions. They ask whose instructions, you say it's none of their business.

"Everyone ready?"

"No! I not go up to school. If Smedley and Boyles gone, the girls there at the school are in no danger. I must go to Oakdale Hall; help sisters."

"The O'Brien sisters are at Oakdale Hall? How do you know, Mrs. Dubrowski?"

"I will tell you, Mr. Flammonde, but you must first promise that I may go with Lamar and Maurice."

"But Mother…"

"Cecilia, *zug gornischt*!"

"Please, Mrs. Dubrowski, it could be very dangerous. These are desperate people and they may be armed. It had to be one or both of them that murdered Cory."

"Mr. Flammonde, what is in basket on back of automobile? You say this worries you. You know what…who…is in basket just as I do."

"I'm only guessing, Mrs. Dubrowski. You seem certain. Why?"

"Then I can go with Lamar and Maurice?"

"You are a very stubborn woman, Mrs. Dubrowski."

"Good; then is settled. I will go with Lamar and Maurice. Now I will…"

"Where my mother goes…"

"No, Cecilia. You and Miss Winters will go with Mr. Flammonde. Mr. Adams will come to look after me. The two of you can make talk like lawyer; not good as Mr. Adams, but good enough."

"Don't worry, Cecilia, Quincy will look after her. Quincy, take this." Camille fished around in her handbag for a moment and brought out the derringer which she handed to Adams. "Emil said this would protect me; now it will protect you and Mrs. Dubrowski."

"Mr. Adams, give gun to me; I know how to use. Remember?" Before Adams could protest or put the weapon in his pocket Esther snatched it out of his open hand and held it behind her back. "I will tell you now what I know."

"Please begin, Mrs. Dubrowski. We don't have a lot of time."

"Very well, Mr. Flammonde…Emil…this is what I know: The O'Brien girls were arrested; this was on Saturday the week before Cory was shot. Sheriff take them to the jail. The judge comes also to jail; signs paper to turn girls over to Smedley and Boyles. Bridget tells me horrible things are done to them at school."

"How do you know it was Bridget?"

"Because, Mr. Adams, she tells me her name."

"But I thought she didn't…"

"In the jail cell she would speak to me. I would hold her in my arms. At first she says nothing, only cries. But next day I hold her again and she starts to whisper in my ear so the matron would not hear. She would sit on one side and Colleen on the other. I put my arms around them both. Bridget tells me of these things they do to her and sister. You know, like you see in those pictures. First night they are there, sheriff comes and rapes her.

"This goes on night after night; the sheriff, the judge, they do to both girls."

"Did Richard take part?" Cecilia asks between sobs.

"No, Cecilia, they do not say that Cory was there. Not until Thursday before he is killed. I think this is true because he told me he was going to Boston for a few days. He left on that Monday.

"On Thursday the girls escape. They tell me there is a room in basement; that is where they are taken to be raped. There is in basement a camera which they use to make those pictures. They also have whips and chains and wooden…I'm sorry…I do not know the word for this thing. It is like a man's…you know what I mean. When they are done with the girls on Wednesday night they leave them in this room. The girls tell me they cry themselves to sleep then when sun is coming up they make plan to escape.

"There is small window high up on wall; it is same place as ground outside. Window is painted over so no one can see in but still some sunlight comes in. Because paint is so thick, window cannot open. They are afraid to break glass because someone may hear. Colleen finds table knife; she stands on chair but cannot reach top of window. So Bridget sits on Colleen's shoulders and Colleen stands on chair. This way they cut away enough paint for the window to open. Bridget crawls out and then pulls Colleen up.

"They run into woods to hide during day on Thursday. That night go into town; take vegetables from garden to eat. While they are looking for food they are caught again Friday night by sheriff. He brings them back to school. They are afraid going to be beaten or raped again, but this does not happen. The next day…Saturday… they are made to bathe and fix each other's hair so looks nice. They are given clean clothes…not *shmattes* like inmates wear…kind of clothes Camille or Cecilia would wear to fancy party. This is Saturday night.

"Colleen tells me that a man…she does not know name…comes this night to dinner. It is Cory. He is dressed in dinner suit...with tails and white tie. So is Smedley. Colleen does not say what Boyles is wearing. They make Colleen and Bridget sit at table and eat. Before dinner Boyles say if they do not behave and be polite to gentleman coming to dinner they will be taken again to basement. They are given glasses of wine and told they must drink. Colleen says they do not know how to drink; have never had wine before. Boyles gives them look, so they drink. Colleen drinks some of the wine and so does Bridget.

"After this she remembers very little, and Bridget remembers nothing. She thinks she fell asleep from the wine."

"It was probably laced with chloral hydrate." Seeing the bewildered looks from Adams and the women, Maurice explained. "…a Mickey Finn…knock-out drops. A few drops can put a full-grown man down."

"You mean they were drugged?" Cecilia put a cigarette to her lips and Lamar lighted it for her.

"Yes, it's a common trick of the trade so to speak." Flammonde got out a cheroot and took a light off Lamar's match. "But go on, Mrs. Dubrowski. You said Colleen remembered very little. What does she remember?"

"She is wrapped in a cloak and put in Cory's automobile. As

they drive off he puts hand down front of her dress. He almost loses control of automobile; runs into fence around new building. Then she falls asleep; dreams someone is rubbing her leg…" Mrs. Dubrowski places her hand on her upper thigh to illustrate…"possibly he touches her…her…you know what I mean.

"She is sleeping when they arrive at Oakdale Hall. She does not remember going inside; she thinks possibly Cory carried her up the front steps and into music room. Now this part, I am making guess because Colleen does not remember. Cory must have left her sleeping on the sofa in the music room. He then went upstairs and changed from his tails to smoking jacket. He then goes back downstairs. I hear him come up stairs, but not when he goes back down. He pours some brandy into small glass which he holds under Colleen's nose so that fumes wake her up. She tells me she remembers a strong smell and then becoming awake. But she is dizzy and has no strength in her arms or legs. He pinches her nose so she must open mouth to breathe. Then he pours brandy down her mouth. This makes her choke and almost be sick.

"Colleen tells me that Cory makes her get on her knees in front of him. He is sitting in chair where I find him next morning. Colleen is now awake and frightened, but still has no strength to resist. Cory, she says, then unbuttons his trousers and takes out his…please…I do not know proper English word for…"

"Yes, Mrs. Dubrowski; I think everyone knows to what you refer."

"Thank you, Mr. Flammonde. Although I was in prison for ten years, I still think I am respectable person. To talk of these things is very hard for me."

"Please go on, Mrs. Dubrowski."

"He tells her what she must do to him. Shows to her the *tchotchke*…excuse me…brooch; says she may have fine jewelry like this and fine clothes to go with jewelry if she will do what he wants. He is squeezing her tightly between his knees; her arms are between his knees and all she can do is shake her head from side to side. She begins to cry and says she does not want jewelry or fine clothes; just wants for them to leave her and her sister alone. Cory takes her by her hair and forces her face down to his…and then she hears loud noise. Cory lets go of her hair and falls back from her. His…his…goes limp.

"She does not know that noise is gunshot; that someone has shot Cory."

"Was the shooter there in the room? Based on Dr. Goodson's

testimony he must have been standing right next to Cory. How could she not have seen him?"

"She tells me that she is crying, covering face with her hands because she is so ashamed. Man helps her to her feet; takes her in his arms and holds her to his chest until she catches breath. So she sees only his chest and not his face. He walks behind her to get her cloak. While he is doing this, she is staring at Cory. Man wraps cloak around her shoulders and tells her she must go; run away as fast and as far as she can go. He takes twenty dollars out of his pocket and gives it to her. So she runs out front door and never looks back."

"Sounds to me like she was tellin' you the truth, Esther...Ma'am. She wouldn't have known where the gun was, and we've got the pictures that prove she's tellin' the truth about what went on in that basement."

"Yes, Lamar, I believe she is telling truth when she told me. This is why I tell to Quincy...Mr. Adams...he must also be lawyer for girls."

"Did they tell you how she was captured the third time?" Flammonde flicked the stub of his cheroot into the darkness.

"Colleen will not leave behind Bridget. She hides in woods along river. Goes into Tilbury Town and takes vegetables from gardens to eat. Lives like this until Tuesday night. She keeps money man give to her so she can buy train tickets for herself and Bridget once she gets Bridget out from school.

"This is Tuesday after Cory is shot. Late that night she goes back to school to get Bridget. She goes in through window in basement which has not been sealed up since last time. It is now time the sun is coming up. Goes upstairs to room where she and Bridget are kept before. Door is locked. She is whispering through key hole trying to wake Bridget up. She does not hear Boyles come up behind her. Boyles puts hands around Colleen's neck and makes tight like this." Mrs. Dubrowski holds her hands as though choking someone.

"Boyles forces Colleen to floor and Boyles...how you say... straddles...Colleen. Boyles is too heavy; Colleen cannot breathe. She thinks she is going to die so she closes eyes; does not want the last thing she sees to be Boyles. She tells me she sees her mother holding out her hand making motion that Colleen should come with mother. Then she remembers no more. She wake up in basement; she and Bridget are in chains, legs and arms. Then sheriff comes and takes to jail. They are put in cell with me."

"Did you know they were going to try to escape when you were in court?" Flammonde looked at his watch.

"Must I answer this, Mr. Adams?"

"I'd rather she didn't, Emil. Is it important?"

"I don't know, Quincy. I'm just wondering how they knew to go to Oakdale Hall when they escaped from the courthouse."

"I will tell you this, Mr. Flammonde. I tell them if they are released on bail, they should go there and tell Mr. Silas that I said they could stay and take care of the house until I returned."

In the dim light Adams thought he saw his client wink at him. "Then Mr. Silas didn't know they were fugitives."

"No, I tell girls not to tell Mr. Silas where they meet me."

"Emil, we need to get a move on. Don't need to worry about Boyles and Smedley stayin' out of jail if and when we get our hands on 'em. What the girls told Esther will be enough to charge both Smedley and Boyles with rape."

"Not to mention the High Sheriff and that judge. But Lamar's right, Emil. We'd best get on down there. Sure as anything they're gonna murder those two girls. They know that the girls can put the pair of them in prison for life on the rape charges."

"But they've only got one of them and we're not even sure of that. How do you figure they've got both, Maurice?"

"I'm thinking they have a pretty good idea that Colleen's still hidin' out somewhere on the property. Maybe they tortured Bridget into tellin' them. They'll use Bridget like a tethered goat; threaten to kill her unless Colleen gives herself up. Then if she does give herself up they'll murder the both of them."

"Emil, this is your show. But I think we need all the man-power we can get down there at Oakdale Hall. We may have to search the grounds. Also we don't know if the sheriff and judge are with them."

"You'll have Ollie and…what's-his-name…J.T."

"That's my point, Emil. It'll be just Lamar and me. Not that we can't handle it. But what if we can't? Bullets start flyin' and maybe one accidentally hits me or Lamar. You willing to count on those two clowns…Ollie and J.T.? We haven't done any reconnaissance; we don't know the grounds; we don't know for sure how many guns they have or whether they know how to use them."

"You're saying abandon the search of the school?"

"Damn right, Emil. More likely than not whatever we'd be lookin' for at the school is already stuffed in a suitcase in the back of that Packard automobile. And if it's not, it'll still be at the school tomorrow."

"But Judge Beauchamp's warrant is only for the school premises."

"I don't think we need a warrant for Oakdale Hall, Walter. We've got probable cause to believe that the lives of those two girls are in imminent danger; we wait for a warrant, it'll be too late. It's called 'exigent circumstances.' It may be a bit of a stretch, but it's one I think the judge'll give us.

"Mrs. Dubrowski, do you know where the quarry is on the property?"

"No, I…"

"I do, Emil. I've been there. I think I remember where it is."

"Okay; then I guess we'll have to take you with us to show us the way. So Camille, you and Quincy might as well come along too. But if there's gun-play, I want all four of you civilians to get out of there the second it starts. Will you promise me that you'll do that?"

Quincy, Camille and Cecilia all nodded their heads and said they would. "Mrs. Dubrowski, Esther?"

"I'm sorry, Emil. I will not make to you promise that I have no intention of keeping. If I can do anything to help those girls, it is my duty and I will take my chances just as you are doing. I will not go in harm's way, but I will not get out of its way either.

"Now no more talk; we must go."

Chapter Thirty-Seven

With headlamps off they coasted to a stop at the end of the drive leading from the highway to Oakdale Hall. Ollie reported that no one had come in or out since they'd been there. Esther persuaded Flammonde to allow her to lead them to the house and in through the back door. She had kept a spare key hidden in a flower pot on the back porch and she knew which boards squeaked when stepped on so that if they followed her closely they could enter without being heard. Ollie and J.T. were given the task of checking the barn and adjacent garage to see if the Packard was there. Adams was given the job ramming the marshals' automobile into the Packard should things go wrong at the house and Smedley and Boyles make it to the road. Cecilia and Camille reluctantly accepted the assignment to go back to Tilbury Town in Quincy's automobile and bring Dr. Goodson back with them in case emergency medical attention was needed.

They returned with a haphazardly-dressed but alert doctor just as the two search parties arrived back at the foot of the driveway. "Nothing in the house," Flammonde reported. "Doesn't look like they even went in."

"Same thing with the barn." Ollie panted. The vigorous activity seeming to have taken its toll. "No sign of the automobile. One of the riding horses is gone too. Wagon's there, and so are the draft horses."

"Did you look in the tack room?" Cecilia asked.

"I took a quick look, Miss." J.T. spoke for the first time. "Might have been one bridle set missing; there was one empty peg on the wall there in the tack room. Could be a saddle's gone also. The others were kept on saw-horses and there was room for one more."

"Cecilia, do you think you can find the quarry in the dark?"

"I...I...think so, Emil. "There's a field road that starts at a gate in the fence that runs around the house and barn and the garden. I'd estimate the gate's about fifty yards beyond the far side of the barn."

"You reckon that we ought to try and get up to the quarry at night, Emil? Even if Cecilia's got the right field road, there'll be you, me, Maurice, Deputy Isaacson, Ollie and J.T. That's six people; seven if we take Cecilia along to show us the way. We're all going to have to walk up that road single-file. Hasn't been any rain for a good while; somebody steps on a branch, trips over a root, it's gonna make noise. Shootin' happens to start, we ain't gonna be able to spread out much."

"Lamar's right, Emil. And if my guess is right, they're waitin' 'till daylight, at least until dawn, figuring that Colleen won't come for Bridget 'fore then."

"Ollie, J.T., did you happen to notice whether the gate was open or closed?"

"I didn't, Emil. J.T.?"

"Nope; Emil, you said check the barn. That's what we did. You want us to go back up and look?"

"Maurice, you and Lamar go take a look. Ollie, you and J.T. stay here just in case. You see that Packard come barrelin' down the drive you ram it just like Lamar told you. Don't use your weapons unless they start shootin' at you. And even then, be damn sure you aim at who's doin' the shootin' and that you hit only what you're aimin' at. I don't want you to accidentally hit one of those girls. That clear? Rest of us will go up to the house. Lamar, you and Maurice come back to the house when you've had your look."

"Emil, you want me to go get my dad and my brothers? They can take over down here for the marshals. That'll give you two more guns up at the quarry."

"Mrs. Dubrowski, do you know whether there are any other ways in and out of the place by automobile?"

"No; I'm sorry. I know only this way."

"Camille, come up to the house. Does either your father or one of your brothers have a telephone? Call them up. Ask whether they know of any other ways that a wheeled vehicle—an automobile or a wagon—can get in or out. If there is, we can ask them go there and do what Ollie and J.T. are doing here. I'm sure they know Cory's Packard."

Camille managed to reach her father and brothers all of whom had home telephones. She reported that her father had held a timber lease on the estate before Cory's tenure. He knew of a corduroy road that ran north from the property to the sawmill in Tilbury Town. He figured that the road was probably unused since Cory had not renewed the timber lease, but that it might still be passable if someone needed to use it badly enough. She handed the 'phone to Flammonde who gave Harley Winters a truncated version of what was happening and what he wanted them to do. After a couple of "I'll be darns" Winters agreed that he and his sons would take up a position at the north end of the log road and stop the Packard from leaving should it come that way.

They passed the few remaining hours of darkness in the music room. They closed the heavy drapes so that they could smoke, but

Flammonde vetoed turning on any lights. After Flammonde made sure that no light from the stove could be seen from the outside, Mrs. Dubrowski managed to make coffee without turning on the lights. She found some fruit and vegetable preserves in the pantry along with some crackers so that those who were of a mind to could have something to eat.

Just before dawn they moved to the barn and then to the gate in the fence. At first light they started in with Cecilia leading and Flammonde at her side. After a few minutes Lamar, who was walking just a couple of steps behind Cecilia, put his hand on her shoulder to get her to stop. "Look," he whispered, "automobile tire tracks. Wide tires and see how far apart they are. The have to have been made by a large vehicle."

"Like a Packard," Emil added needlessly. "Cecilia, how far to the quarry from here?"

"Emil, I don't know. I was only here once and I was more interested in not falling off the horse than I was in measuring distances. But the quarry was the first place we went and my recollection is that it didn't take a very long time to get there once we were inside the gate. With the horses walking slowly on my account, I'd guess that it was about twenty minutes, maybe a bit more, from the time we went through the gate until we got to the quarry. Just before you get there, the trees are cut down so there's a clearing before you get to the shed and the quarry itself. As best I remember the distance from the edge of the trees to the shed is about ten or fifteen feet."

"Did Cory say what was in the shed?"

"He said tools and a windlass on a dolly that rolls on the rails. That's what they used to lower tools and…oh my God! He also said that's where they kept the dynamite…"

"Did he say there was any still stored there?"

"I think there is because he said he didn't like to go in the shed since when dynamite gets old it becomes unstable and extremely risky to handle. I thought he was only trying to impress me, so I said something about how dangerous quarrying must be.

"He said no one will likely ever know how many bodies lie at the bottom of that pit. Then he sort of smiled and asked if I was ready to move on."

"He was probably telling you at least part of the truth, Cecilia; at least the part about there being bodies down there. But I doubt they are the bodies of dead stone cutters. I think he was telling you what happened to those cases in the ledger with no initials, just a dash mark. Easy enough to figure how he got that separated shoulder."

As Cecilia and Emil were having their whispered conversation Lamar had gone on a few steps ahead. He knelt down on one knee next to the dirt track. "Emil, look here. Someone's been through here on horseback since the Packard went by." Lamar pointed to a set of hoof-prints in the dirt overlaying the automobile tire tread pattern. "From the spacing between the prints and the way there's no dirt disturbed around them, it looks like whoever was ridin' just let the reins go slack and let the horse sort of just mosey along at its own pace."

"How can you tell just from some hoof-prints?" Cecilia looked dubious.

"I learned a little about tracking from an old Comanche, an ex-army scout. Army retired him so he joined up with the Texas Rangers. I rode with him for a while back when we were still chasing after the Comanche. Seems he had a pretty intense dislike for Quanah Parker the Comanche chief. Something to do with a rivalry over a woman. Parker took a fancy to the scout's woman. She seemed okay with the switch, but it didn't set too well with Trebblehorn…that was the scout's name…but there wasn't much he could do about it except try to get even."

"Let's move on," Maurice urged. "It's already full daylight. If someone else is there, we'll know right soon anyway."

As Cecilia was now sure that this was the way to the quarry, Emil, Lamar, Walter and Maurice went on several yards ahead with the civilians hanging back just enough to be out of the line of fire. After a few more minutes of careful walking they could just see the clearing and a corner of the shack ahead. Emil stopped and turned around. He put one finger to his lips and with his other hand made a patting motion indicating that they should get down and stay where they were. Lamar and Maurice stepped off the road on opposite sides and went forward through the trees.

While Lamar and Maurice were on their reconnoitering mission the civilians moved up to where Flammonde and Isaacson were waiting. In a few minutes Lamar made his way back. "They're there alright. At least Boyles is. There was lantern light coming from the shack doorway which is partly open. But neither of us could get a good enough angle to see if anyone's inside. Packard's parked by the door of the shack."

"Where is Boyles?" Flammonde asked.

"That's the bad part. They've got Bridget wrapped up in a thick chain and she's dangling from the windlass cable that runs up through a gin pole and out over the edge of the quarry. Boyles is standin' next to the windlass brake smoking a cigar and looking around. She releases the brake and Bridget goes straight down. I can't tell how deep it is…"

"Richard mentioned to me that it was over sixty feet."

"Lamar do you think you can get close enough to get a shot at Boyles?"

"Yeah, I can Emil. But when I drop her, what if she pulls the brake? There goes Bridget."

"May I make a suggestion?"

"Okay, Quincy. What would you do?"

"Why not just confront her? I mean four of you with weapons drawn. What will she do? Commit murder right in front of you?"

"So we'd have a Mexican stand-off?"

"If that's the same as a stale-mate, I guess so Lamar. You can offer to let them go if they just leave the girl. You've got the two marshals blocking the drive-way. If Boyles even knows about the corduroy road you've got the Winters men blocking that way out."

"Quincy's right, Emil."

"Only one problem, Maurice." Emil frowned. "I think Camille's father and brothers can handle 'em if they go that way, but I'm not so sure about Ollie and J.T. Don't look like either one of them has seen any action in a while. Also, we don't know who's in the shack or what they're armed with. They have even one rifle and it could be another O.K. Corral with us the ones ending up on Boot Hill."

"Emil, there's another problem."

"What's that Quincy?"

"While we've been huddled here it looks like Mrs. Dubrowski's taken matters into her own hands. Cecilia and Camille have gone either with her or after her."

"Damn it!" Emil kicked the ground in anger. "That woman's gonna get herself and maybe two, three others killed. What does she think she's gonna do?"

"Probably go after Boyles with that derringer."

As the four lawmen and Adams moved closer to the clearing the three women had evidently gone into the woods that bordered the road and could not be seen. Just before the men reached the clearing they heard Boyles calling, "Colleen O'Brien, I know you're out there. I can hear you in the brush. You show yourself right this minute. If you come out and behave yourself, no harm will come to you or to your sister. We only want to talk with you."

For a minute or longer there was nothing but silence. Then Boyles started up again. "Can you see your sister, Colleen? All I have to do is to pull this lever and you'll never see her again. I know your poor ma on her death bed made you promise you'd take care of your sister. Is this how you keep your promise to your ma?"

There was still no response from Colleen if she was in fact in sight and hearing range. "Child, I've asked you nicely for the last time." Boyles released the brake lever and Bridget dropped about a foot so that only her head and shoulders were visible above the edge of the quarry. The fall brought a scream of pain from Bridget as the chain jerked tightly around her body.

"I won't ask you again. If you're not out here right in front of me by the time I count to ten, I'll release this lever and this time I won't stop it; that will be the last you see of your precious sister. You get down here right now, you ungrateful little bitch. We tried and tried to make ladies out of the pair of you; give you a chance at the good life and you pay us back by murdering our friend Mr. Cory."

Colleen stepped out into the clearing from behind a pile of broken semi-cut blocks of stone. As she passed the Packard she called out, "Bridget, Bridget. Are you okay?"

"Go back, Colleen. She means to kill us both. Go find Esther; she'll help you. You can't help me."

"Why you sorry lying little bitch. I thought you couldn't talk. I'll fix you." Boyles started to release the brake.

"Get away from her you evil woman! Colleen, get back!" Esther came running out of the woods with the derringer in her outstretched hand. She was about ten feet from where Boyles was standing. She fired and the bullet evidently caught Boyles in her thigh causing her to momentarily lose her balance and release the brake lever. As she did Esther closed the last few feet and grabbed the brake lever grinding the windlass to a stop. When Esther grabbed the brake lever Colleen took out a hunting knife that she'd concealed in the sleeve of her dress and charged at Boyles. Boyles regained her balance and picked up a large monkey wrench from the windlass platform.

This all happened in the space of a few seconds. As it was unfolding the lawmen ran into the clearing yelling "Federal agents! Federal agents! Put up your hands! Flammonde motioned to Maurice, "Maurice, take the shack. Walter, you back-up Maurice. Quincy, get Cecilia and Camille before they…"

Flammonde's order to Adams came too late. Cecilia and Camille came out of the woods just as Esther fired. They started toward Boyles intending to go around the other side of the windlass and crank Bridget back up to the surface. But Boyles swung the monkey wrench in a wide arc causing the women to stop short. The wrench struck Colleen's knife hand sending the knife flying into the wall of the shack. Boyles grabbed Colleen and held her in a choke hold. With her free hand she reached down and picked up a bundle of dynamite off the windlass dolly, at least six sticks bound with cord and with the fuses twisted together. Her cigar was clamped into one side of her mouth. She took a long pull and knocked off the ash so that the glowing tip was visible. "Get back, all of you. Do you hear me? You don't get back, I'll set this dynamite off and see all of you in hell before breakfast.

"Dowdy, you and Chivas get out of there and get the automobile started."

Cautiously the door of the shack opened and the sheriff stepped out leveling a shotgun at Maurice and Deputy Isaacson. Smedley stepped out carrying a suitcase taking care to stay behind the sheriff. Dowdy got in the driver's door and started the engine. Smedley opened the rear passenger-side door and started to put the suitcase in the backseat. Boyles, still holding Colleen and the dynamite started edging away from the windlass toward the corner of the shack. She had almost reached the shack when a rifle shot coming from behind her struck her in the back of the head. The exiting bullet barely missed Colleen, passed between Camille and Cecilia and buried itself in the thin soil. Camille and Cecilia were both splattered with blood and bits of skull and brain matter. As Boyles fell forward she landed on top of Colleen pinning the girl beneath her. The dynamite dropped from her hand and the cigar fell from her mouth landing on the dynamite fuse.

For an instant everyone stopped and stared. Camille was the first to react followed in a moment by the sheriff and Cecilia. Camille scooped up the dynamite and dashed to the edge of the quarry. Cecilia began turning the windlass crank in order to raise Bridget above ground level. The sheriff fired one round from his shotgun through the front passenger window of the automobile striking his deputy in the arm and side. He then put the vehicle in gear and started around the opposite corner of the shack in the direction of the timber road. Maurice lunged at the front passenger-side door but was knocked aside by the open rear door as the auto swung sharply to the left.

Camille reached the edge of the quarry and heaved the dynamite down and out as far as she could. Cecilia had managed to get Bridget up to ground level. Cecilia moved between Bridget and the quarry edge so that she absorbed the blast wave when the dynamite exploded. The blast wave stunned her causing her to lose her footing and she began sliding into the quarry. At the last instant she grabbed the chain wrapped around Bridget causing the girl to scream in pain.

Smedley had not been able to make it into the back seat of the automobile before the sheriff drove off. He started crawling on hands and knees toward his mother. Esther had just rolled Boyles's body over to get it off of Colleen. When Smedley saw what was left of his mother's face, he began to cry "mommy, mommy" and continued crawling toward her until Maurice put a boot on his back and pushed him to the ground.

As soon as she saw Cecilia hanging by one hand over the quarry Camille lay down at the edge and grabbed Cecilia's free hand. Flammonde reached over and took Cecilia's other arm and between he and Camille they managed to pull her back up.

Lamar ran around the shack in the direction from which the rifle shot had come. While Maurice was handcuffing Smedley and everyone else was working to release Bridget, Lamar managed to get off a couple of rounds aimed at the rear tires of the Packard as it disappeared into the woods. A minute later Lamar came back from the edge of the woods holding a rifle in one hand and leading a horse. Ellsworth Silas was astride the horse his arms in the air. He looked down at Lamar. "Mr. Lawman, you mind if I put this here blanket around me? Seems I got a bit of a chill." Silas turned his head and nodded toward a blanket that was draped across the horse's back behind the saddle.

"I reckon it's okay, old-timer. Why don't you dismount; then you can wrap up if you like."

As Silas dismounted he broke into a fit of coughing. He wiped his perspiring forehead with his sleeve and wrapped himself in the blanket. "Much obliged, Mr…." The rest of his words dissolved into another spell of coughing.

"Lamar, maybe you'd best take that horse back down to the house and fetch Dr. Goodson. Looks like Walter caught a pretty good bunch of pellets. Hope it was birdshot and not buckshot. Whichever, he's bleedin' pretty bad. Also, looks like Bridget's got a broken arm. Must have happened when Boyles dropped her down over the edge. Otherwise, I think everybody's gonna be alright. Everyone except Boyles, that is.

"Mr. Silas, can you understand me? I know you're hard of

hearing."

"Pretty well, Mister. Long as you stand facing me I can make out most of what you're saying."

"I don't know whether to thank you or arrest you." Flammonde took the rifle from Lamar as Lamar mounted the horse and dug his heels into the animal's flanks.

"No need to thank me. If you're going to arrest me for killin' that…that…" he looked over at Boyles's body and spat on it. This brought on more coughing and when it stopped he continued. "If you're gonna arrest me, can I ask one favor?"

"What's that, Mr. Silas?"

"You mind if I kill that one too?" He pointed toward Smedley who was still lying on the ground simpering."

"Wish I could, Mr. Silas, but I reckon you've bagged your limit for the season with that one." Flammonde nodded toward Boyles's corpse.

"Well now that's mighty disappointing." Silas beckoned to Adams. "Say! You that lawyer fella' sent me that subpoena?"

"Yes, Sir. I'm Quincy Adams, Mrs. Dubrowski's lawyer."

"Seems this here lawman's fixin' to arrest me for shootin' that sorry pile of cow manure." Silas prodded the corpse with the toe of his gum boot. "I expect I'm gonna need me a lawyer too."

"I don't know, Mr. Silas. I'd rather be a material witness and testify for you. But the law won't let me do both."

"Say what, Mr. Lawyer?"

"I said…"

"Hold on. Maurice, I hear a motor vehicle coming this way from the log road. Quincy, you take Mr. Silas and get over next to the shed. Camille, Cecilia, you get Deputy Isaacson over there too. See what you can do to stop the bleedin'. Esther, you and Colleen get Bridget over next to the shed also. Maurice, you get over behind those rocks Colleen was hidin' behind. I'll take Mr. Silas's Winchester and hunker down behind the windlass dolly. Mr. Silas, your rifle still loaded, or was that your only round?"

"What? I can't…"

"Never mind. Quincy, get him over there. I'll find out whether it's loaded if I need to use it."

Just as Flammonde got hunkered down in position the Winters' truck cleared the trees and rolled to a stop. Harley Winters got out of the cab and trotted anxiously toward the shack. "Thought we heard some shooting; then there was a sound like an explosion." When he saw Boyles's body, the head lying in a pool of blood, he stopped. "Where's Camille? She okay?"

"I'm alright, Daddy." Camille came around the corner of the shack almost tripping over the corpse. "Daddy, it was awful. Esther...Mrs. Dubrowski...shot Boyles in the leg. Boyles was going to...and then Mr. Silas shot Boyles in the head. He had to; she was going to blow us all up..."

"...and your daughter saved us all, Mr. Winters." Flammonde set down the rifle and pumped Winters's hand. But what are you doing here? Did you see the Packard?"

"Yup, we saw it alright. But I'm right glad to say there weren't no need to stop it. I wasn't too keen on bangin' up my new truck. Anyway, the Packard come out of the timber rear wheels runnin' on their rims. Both the back tires gone. Packard got stuck in the bar ditch where the corduroy road meets the gravel road leadin' to the saw mill. Sheriff got out asked if we had a chain and could we pull him out. I said maybe he ought to come back here with us. We thought we heard shootin' and figured that he ought to see if someone needed help.

"Well then he reaches back into the Packard and pulls out a shotgun. Fred 'n' Billy...they were in the back of the truck...pulled out their rifles and I said to the sheriff that he ought to think about puttin' his shotgun back there in the Packard. He thought about it for a second or two and decided that might be a good idea, all things considered. He asked if we know who he is and I said yup, we do. Said he needed to get to a 'phone; call his dispatcher to send some more men out here.

"I said no need for that, Sheriff Dowdy. Me and Fred and Billy, we'll give you all the help you need. Then he says we're obstructing him in the performance of his official duties and there'd be grave consequences. I said well, Sir, we'll just take our chances on that. So he says he ain't goin' back down here without more men and he'd just walk into town and get to a 'phone that way.

"He starts to walk off and Fred and Billy jump down off the flatbed and block his way. He started to reach for his side arm, but Fred grabs 'hold of his wrist and twisted it behind his back. Billy gets his other arm and twists it 'round his back. I get his side-arm and his handcuffs and handcuff him just as he was: Hands behind his back. Truth be told, I always wanted to do that. Had it done to me once or twice way back when. Fred and Billy, they manhandle him onto the flatbed and get up there with him just to make sure he doesn't roll off.

That corduroy road can be pretty bumpy. Once we got him loaded onto the flatbed we come straight here fast as we could.

He's on the back of the truck if you want to talk things over with him. Also, you might want to take a look in that suitcase that's back there with him. Found it on the backseat of the Packard. Billy brought it along just to be sure nobody happened by and took off with it while we were gone. I'm kind of embarrassed to admit it, but Billy's curiosity got the best of him and he took a look inside."

"What's in it?" Flammonde took out his cigar case and offered it around before lighting one for himself.

"Full of cash. Twenties, fifties and there's even a bundle or two of hundreds. There's some papers too that I expect you'll be wantin'."

"Mr. Winters, this is Maurice Morton; he's also a federal agent. My other colleague, Lamar Raymond ought to be back any minute with Dr. Goodson to attend to our casualties. Camille, how is Deputy Isaacson?"

"I think the bleeding's stopping. So if he doesn't get an infection, he'll be okay. Bridget's in a lot of pain. Her arm's certainly broken; you can tell just by looking. It's just a good thing they didn't have that chain around her neck or inside her arms." Camille looked down at Boyles's body and nudged the head next to the entry wound with her toe. "It's a shame she had to die that way, Emil; I mean quick, without knowing what hit her. I can think of so many other ways that would have been more just."

"Camille Winters, where'd you learn that kind of thinkin'? I didn't raise you that way…"

"No, Daddy you didn't." Camille stepped toward her father and fell into his arms crying and gasping for breath. After a minute she regained her composure. "I'm sorry. I just never knew that there could be such evil in the world. I guess being exposed to what I've just seen and been through has made me forget for a minute how lucky I've been to have you and Fred and Billy and Paul and Jesse taking care of me my whole life.

"I think I'll go speak with Fred and Billy for a minute."

"Go ahead, Camille. Sounds like Lamar's comin' back with the doc." Flammonde turned to Harley Winters. "She'll get over those thoughts, Mr. Winters. I've been working these Mann Act cases full-time now for four years. I can understand how Camille could have such ideas; I still have them myself. I've just learned I have to keep 'em to myself or just vent them with Lamar and Maurice over a bottle of sour mash.

In case you haven't figured out what happened up here, Boyles was fixin' to blow us all up with a handful of dynamite when Mr. Silas put a .44-caliber round through the back of her head. Even though Boyles was dead before she hit the ground she somehow lit the fuse. Your daughter grabbed up the dynamite and heaved it into the quarry. That's the explosion you heard. Just as we heard you comin' up the road, Mr. Silas asked if I'd mind if he killed Smedley also. I had to tell him yes, I'd mind, but my gut sure was tellin' me to say no; have at him."

As Flammonde was attempting to explain Camille's feelings to her father they began walking toward the truck. Camille was sitting in the cab on the passenger side smoking a cigarette she'd gotten from Fred. If her father noticed, he said nothing. The sheriff was laying face-down in the bed of the truck. "Fred, Billy, you mind rollin' him over and sitting him up for a minute. I'd like to have a word with him, if it's okay with you."

After Dowdy was turned over and propped against the back of the cab Flammonde hopped up on the truck bed and stood over the sullen sheriff. "Sheriff Dowdy, I'm Emil Flammonde, Special Agent, U.S. Department of Justice. I'm placing you under arrest for violation of the United States Code, title 18, section 2421."

"You're a federal officer?"

"That's what I said."

"Well thank goodness. I been after this gang for over a year now. Been workin' undercover. Finally managed to infiltrate the gang; got them to take me into their confidence. I was just about to…"

"Raping children; was that a part of your undercover operation? I need to warn you that you're in custody and anything you say will be taken down and used against you in criminal proceedings against you in the U.S. court."

"Raping children? What children? I never raped…"

"Mr. Dowdy, I'm about ten seconds away from showing Mr. Winters and his sons those photographs you removed from Cory's house and then takin' a walk in the woods for a bit; maybe enjoy a cigar while you explain to these gentlemen that you were only doing your duty while you were on their payroll as the sheriff of Kennebec County. They told me how rough the ride is on that log road. I can see how easy it'd be for a fellow in handcuffs might get himself bruised up a good bit."

"You have those photographs? You have no right to have them. They were in my custody as evidence."

"Evidence of what, Mr. Dowdy? That you're as venal and

depraved as Boyles, Smedley and the late Mr. Cory? You're as disgusting as they are; no, you're even more disgusting. You are worse because you did what you did from behind a lawman's badge. But I'm glad you told me the pictures were being held as evidence; I was a mite worried that they were your personal property. That might have raised some warrantless-search issues.

"You think Smedley's going to back up your story? Gonna take the fall all by himself? And Judge Gribble? He's not going to throw anything on you that he can?"

"The hell he will. You ask him who took most of those pictures. Ask him what's in that iron safe he keeps in his chambers. And you tell mama's boy if I'm going down, he's going with me. What about Boyles? You not charging her because she's a woman?"

"We're not charging her, but only because she's no longer in our jurisdiction. She's maybe answerin' to a much different court about now. You'll get a chance to talk to her on your way back to town. She probably won't answer back, but feel free to talk to her all you want."

Chapter Thirty-Eight

As Flammonde was persuading Harley Winters of the need to transport Boyles's corpse and Doc Goodson was attending to the wounded, Adams secured Flammonde's permission to begin walking back to the house with Ellsworth Silas. After they'd gone a ways back down the road, Silas stopped and took a worn leather bill-fold out of his overalls. He opened it and extracted a creased sepia-tone photograph of a girl and handed it to Adams. It was a formal portrait of a girl Adams estimated must have been about fourteen when the picture was taken. On the back was a date, June, nineteen sixteen and written in childish script, "To Grandpa, Love Emma." The portrait was a good one. The girl was in three-quarter view of the camera lens smiling slightly, a girl-like yet grown-up smile. Her long hair was parted in the middle with curls cascading over the shoulders of her white, lace-trimmed blouse. She sat with her hands folded in her lap and her legs crossed at the ankles and tucked slightly under the bench on which she was seated.

Adams handed the photograph back to Silas and turned to face him. Adams spoke in a normal conversational tone, "Can you understand me alright if I don't talk any louder than this?"

"Okay, I reckon. Long as you're facin' me. But I expect it's me gonna be doin' most of the talkin' anyway."

"Good. Mr. Silas, I'd be honored to be your lawyer. Anything you say to me will be held in absolute confidence." Adams held out his hand which Silas took and then they continued back toward the house.

"The photograph pretty much tells the story, Mr. Silas. I assume that somehow your granddaughter fell into the hands of these people..."

"Yup. She and her ma had a spat. Girls that age and their mothers do that a lot so I'm told. She, Emma, decided she'd run away from home, just for a day or two; teach her ma a lesson. That was the last time we seen her.

"When she disappeared I quit my work and started looking for her full time. Put advertisements in all the newspapers; started going around from town to town showing this photograph to anybody who'd look. Nobody could say for sure that they'd seen her, so I kept on looking. I started checking courthouse records, and finally about a year after she'd gone missing, I found her name in the court records in Penobscot County, you know over in Bangor. I asked the clerk-lady what happened to her. Asked could I see the case file? She said no; juvenile case files are sealed. Can't let you see 'em unless you get a court order. So I asked her, 'How do I do that?' She says I need to get a lawyer; she can't give legal advice.

"So I walk around looking for a lawyer. Lots of lawyers' offices there near the courthouse. I hunt for one that looks like I can afford him. I find one that looks like he might need the business, so I go in and tell him what I want. He says he'll charge me fifty bucks. So I give him the fifty bucks…it just about taps me out…and he says come back tomorrow and he'll have an answer for me. I said thank you, and I'll see you tomorrow. I'm thinking to myself that's darn quick. I expected that he'd have to file some paper with the judge; maybe I'd have to go to court or something.

"I go back the next day. I walk into the office, there's a woman sitting at the lawyer's desk and she asks what do I want? Says the lawyer got called out of town on urgent business. I tell her why I'm there and she sort of laughs. Made me feel right uncomfortable. I ask her if the lawyer has filed the paper to let me see my granddaughter's file. She says, 'No need to be filin' any papers; your relative, if she was a juvenile, got sent to the Industrial School for Wayward Girls over at Hallowell.' I ask her how does she know, and she says she used to work in the clerk's office and that's where they send every female juvenile delinquent.

"Then I say, 'Don't seem right; the lawyer keepin' my fifty dollars seein's how he didn't have to work none for it.' She says, 'You got the answer you was lookin' for' and she don't see no reason to give back any of the money. Well, I figure there ain't no point arguing with her so I leave and just kind of hang out where I can keep an eye on the door. Sure enough, half an hour later here comes Mr. Lawyer. I follow him for a couple of blocks until we get to a quiet place where there aren't many folks around. I come up behind him; tap him on the shoulder. He turns around; sees who it is tappin' him on the shoulder. He starts tellin' me same thing the woman said. I tell him never mind that. We trade a few words back and forth. He finally sees the fairness in my position and gives me back thirty dollars."

"Did you…"

"Naw, I mean he might have seen my old army Colt revolver tucked in my belt. But I never did take it out. Heck, it wasn't even loaded. I sure didn't want any trouble; I just wanted to get on down to Hallowell quick as I could and figured I'd need some money in order to keep goin' and see this thing through."

"How did you come to Oakdale Hall?"

"I come over to Hallowell next day; went straight to the school. I asked there at the front desk is my granddaughter Emma Silas here?" Girl tells me she can't say; same excuse the clerk in Bangor gives me: Juvenile records are sealed. I'm getting right angry at this point; maybe raising my voice some. That brings Boyles out of her office. She tells me the same thing: Juvenile records are sealed; I have to get a court order and Judge Gribble ain't gonna give me one. She says I'm not off the property in one minute, she'll call the sheriff, have me arrested for trespassin'. She pulls out this pocket watch and starts calling off the seconds. I figure I'm not likely to find my granddaughter while I'm sitting in a jail cell, so I get on out of there.

"I go into town find a rooming house and start asking around about the school and all. Who runs it? Is it really a school? What happens to a girl when she's released? Those kinds of questions. Nobody seems to want to talk about the school. Some, I think they were trying to warn me—not threatening me—said for my own good I'd best quit asking so many questions about something weren't my business and just move on. Lady owns the boarding house said I'd have to move out. My rent's paid for a week, so I tell her I'll be leavin' then.

"Next day, Cory shows up. Introduces himself and says that he knows the folks run the school real well; they're friends of his. Good people, he says. Take real good care of the girls get sent there. I tell him I just want to find out about my granddaughter; what happened to her. He tells me the same thing about the records; he says that after a year, if the girl doesn't get in any more trouble, the records are destroyed so she doesn't have that hanging over her the rest of her life."

"Cory was lying to you, Mr. Silas, same as the rest of them. There's no way those records are destroyed; sealed, maybe; but not destroyed."

"Well I sure didn't know no better, so I took him at his word. Then he asks me what I do for a living. I tell him I've done just about everything a man can do with a strong back and not much education. He asks me do I have experience with horses. I say yup, going back as far as my soldiering days. So he asks me: Do I want a job? He says he needs a stable hand; tells me what the work would be, the wages and that I'd get room and board."

"So he found you?"

"Yup. I reckon he had suspicions that I was a detective or some kind of government investigator working under cover. He and the others probably wanted me where they could keep an eye on me 'till they figured out whether I was who I said I was: Just a harmless deaf old fool lookin' for his granddaughter.

"They must have checked and found out that I wasn't some government investigator or private detective, but since I gave a day's work for a day's pay, Cory just kept me on. I was willing to stay on hoping that maybe I'd finally get someone to tell me the truth about what was going on up there at the school."

"You must have finally found something out."

"It was those picnics, 'hayrides' he called 'em. One time Mrs. Browsky, she ask me about what they did on those hayrides. I didn't know and I told her so. But her askin' got me to thinking. I couldn't figure out what was in that hamper they'd bring with them. One time I asked the sheriff could I help carry it, load it on the wagon? He said no, it weren't all that heavy. He and Mr. Cory could handle it. Told me I best just see to the horses and leave it at that. I could see that he was lying about it not being heavy. When they loaded it onto the wagon they were heavin' and groanin' a whole lot more than if it was just a picnic basket.

"Finally, back in May, I made up my mind to find out what they were really doin' up there at the quarry. So I waited about half an hour after they left and went up the road after them. I got there just in time to see that they had a body...a young girl...wrapped up in a chain like they had the one just now. They'd hooked her up just like you saw and dropped her over the side. I heard the splash when she hit the water. The chain around the body was hooked to the windlass cable with a spring-loaded clamp that's attached to a wire that runs along with the cable. So when the body hits the water and sinks to the bottom all they have to do is pull on the wire and the clamp comes loose. Then they haul the cable and the wire back up and roll the dolly back into the shack. After that they broke out a bottle of whiskey; passed it around until it was empty. Weren't no way I could get close enough to hear what they was talkin' about, so I come back down.

"Do you know whether the victim was alive when they dropped her over?"

"No, I couldn't tell for sure. I know she wasn't moving, you know, like struggling."

"Was it you that sent the letter to Washington?"

"Yup, that was me. I'd seen about enough, more than any man would ever want to see. I figured with the sheriff and the judge in on it, weren't no use going to the local law people. They'd just say I'm crazy and lock me up somewhere, or I'd end up in the bottom of that quarry."

"And when nothing happened in response to your letter…"

"Yup. I got tired of waiting for anybody to come and for anything to get done. Figured with the war on, maybe the government was too busy to worry about something going on in a small town in Maine."

"So you decided to take matters into your own hands?"

"I didn't know what I was going to do, except have it out with Cory. I got his revolver out of the chest. I didn't have any ammunition for mine; it's too expensive and hard to find. I waited up until I saw the headlamps of the automobile. He parked it in front and got that girl out from the front seat. I went up on the porch and waited until he was inside. I saw him carry the girl into the parlor and lay her down on the sofa. I was just about to go in and confront him when he comes out of the parlor and goes upstairs. While he's upstairs I slip into the parlor and hide myself behind the window drape.

"In a few minutes Cory comes back down and starts tryin' to wake the girl up. He sticks a glass of whisky under her nose and she starts to come around. Then he pinches her nose and pours some whisky down her throat. She's pretty awake by then. She starts in crying and beggin' him to let her go.

"First off, he shows her this little box, has some kind of diamond thing inside. That don't do anything to calm her down. Then he pulls her down where he's sittin' in his chair and she's on her knees in front of him. Then he unbuttons his trousers, takes out his…you know…and tries to force her to take it in her mouth. Well, that did it for me. I slipped out from behind the curtain stepped up next to him and put one round into his brain."

Adams hearing the vehicles coming toward them pulled Silas to the side of the road so that they could pass. Silas tugged the blanket around his shoulders and broke into another fit of coughing. Lamar was driving Adams's automobile with Esther Dubrowski in the front passenger seat with Colleen O'Brien sitting in her lap. Doc Goodson, along with his patients Deputy Isaacson and Bridget O'Brien, were squeezed into the back. The cab of the truck held Harley Winters at the wheel with Cecilia and Camille sitting beside him. Flammonde, Morton and the Winters brothers were standing in the back against the sideboards. The sheriff was still seated with his back to the cab. Smedley had been trussed up and placed next to the sheriff. Boyles's body had been wrapped in a piece of rotting canvas and hoisted onto the bed of the truck where it was positioned length-wise in the center. Each time the truck pitched to one side or the other the body would start to roll in that direction until someone put out a booted toe to stop it. As Silas still had much to tell, Adams motioned that the vehicles should continue on and that he and Silas would continue walking and talking.

By the time the vehicles had passed so had Silas's coughing fit. "Mr. Silas, I hope you haven't come down with the influenza."

"I got me a touch of something there in the jailhouse in Portland. I expect it is the influenza." Silas coughed a few more times and then opened the blanket and carried it over his arm. He'd broken out in perspiration on his forehead and neck and his shirt was beginning to stain from the wetness. "The police caught a couple of army deserters from that Camp Devens down in Massachusetts; locked 'em up in the county jail along with the other prisoners 'till the army could claim 'em. They were just a couple of kids trying to escape coming down with the influenza; didn't mean to desert the army. But the army didn't see it that way. Anyhow, instead of escaping the disease they brought it with them. They got real sick and then in the next day or two some of the regular prisoners started having symptoms too. Those who had symptoms got moved to the hospital.

"I figured I'd had about enough of Cumberland County's hospitality so I decided maybe I'd get me some symptoms too. It was easy enough; I just took my blanket off the bed wrapped it around me and started running in place until I broke out in a real good sweat. Then I started coughing and calling for the turn-key. Well he come and it didn't take him a minute to figure out that somehow I'd come down with the sickness even though most of the time I'd been in a cell by myself. So I got transferred to the hospital along with the next batch of prisoners. That's probably when I picked up the real thing.

"Nobody was much interested in guarding a bunch of sick prisoners. So that night, I just kind of slipped out. Since I didn't have any money on me I just hitched a ride on the north-bound freight train and come back here."

"Colleen told us how you comforted her and helped her get away. But Mrs. Dubrowski says she heard an automobile drive off. Who was in the automobile?"

"That was just me. After the girl got away, I drove it into the garage where it's kept. Would have looked kinda funny: Cory comes home; leaves his automobile sitting in front of the house; goes in and puts on his smoking jacket; then come back down to his parlor and shoots himself in the head."

"So you wanted to make it look like Cory took his own life?"

"Like I say, I didn't plan on shooting him in the first place. But after I done it, why not make it look like he done it himself?"

"But then you let Esther Dubrowski almost take the blame for it."

"Whoa now, Mr. Lawyer. Until I got your subpoena I had no idea they was tryin' to put it on her. I guess you know they told us at the inquest not to discuss the case with anybody, and that was just fine with me. I'd already made up my mind that I'd tell the truth if Pompus had asked me whether it was me shot Cory. I figured 'what the hell' I'm an old man and if anyone needed killing, it was Richard Cory. Maybe if I told the whole story in court somebody who wasn't in it with him and the others would take an interest and start a real investigation.

"But that damn fool Pompus never asked me, so I just went on about my business. I don't read newspapers, so I had no idea Mrs. Browsky was in jail charged with shooting Cory. If I'd known, I'd have come forward in a minute. Even when those girls come to stay at Oakdale Hall, they didn't tell me where they'd got to know Mrs. Browsky.

"You know that when that under-sheriff came to serve me with the subpoena, he barely got to put it in my hand; then he was off chasing after those girls. Well somehow he managed to catch one and said I was under arrest for abetting a fugitive. I didn't want to put up a fuss about it just then, so I went back to Augusta with him. They locked me up it the jail. I damn sure didn't want to talk to anyone there—the sheriff being part of the gang and all—so I kept my mouth shut until they brought me down to Portland. One of the under-sheriffs there, his daddy and uncle served with me during the war. So as a favor to me on their account he was supposed to have told you I needed to see you real bad."

"He did tell me that, Mr. Silas. It's my fault I didn't come to see you. I was so wound up with the trial, I just plain forgot."

"Well, now that you know the truth, what are you going to do about it?"

"Nothing. I'm your lawyer; unless you tell me I can, I won't tell anybody. I doubt that you'll be charged with killing Boyles. You saved ten lives—not counting Smedley and the sheriff—and that's as good as self-defense in Maine. Even if I don't get to testify, there are nine others that will. You need to get Doc Goodson to take a look at you. Maybe he's got something that'll fight the influenza, assuming that's what you have."

"Tell you what, Mr. Lawyer: I'll do what you ask. If I die, then you can tell Mrs. Browsky and them other lawmen come up with you. But I want to hire you to do one other thing for me."

"Sure, Mr. Silas. What's that?"

"See if you can find out what happened to Emma. If she's down in that quarry, get her out and give her a Christian burial. And if somehow she's alive, get her to come home. I'll write down her folks' address. Whatever she's been through, they'll want her back."

They'd reached the barn by this time and shook hands on their bargain. Silas went to his quarters. Adams turned away, brushed back a couple of tears and went to find Doc Goodson.

Epilogue

Quincy Adams survived the influenza; Ellsworth Silas did not. He did, however, live long enough to learn that Emma had been found working as a waitress in a diner in Houston. Adams had given Emma's photograph to Flammonde who had gone through the batch that he, Lamar and Maurice had brought with them. Although the innocent look was gone in their photograph, the resemblance was sufficient for them to contact the Harris County sheriff who'd managed to track her down. Another couple of telegrams to Washington and she was on the train north as an urgently-needed material witness in the case against the Boyles-Cory gang.

Men, boats and equipment were brought in and the quarry dredged. It yielded enough skeletal remains so that pathologists were able to determine there were at least a dozen corpses—all of them pubescent females. None could be positively identified.

Judge Cranston Gribble was arrested at the border trying to enter Canada. The cash and documents found in his luggage were more than enough to tie him to the Boyles-Cory gang. The overwhelming evidence against him persuaded him to plead guilty in state court in exchange for a twenty-year sentence. Predictably, he only served a few months before dying as a result of being shanked while standing in line for the evening meal. All of the inmates who had previously appeared in his court were questioned repeatedly, but none would admit to any knowledge regarding the occurrence. Indeed, none would even admit to recognizing Judge Gribble from his pre-incarceration life.

At Sheriff Dowdy's trial, his lawyer tried his best to sell the jury on the notion than his client was working undercover to bring down the Boyles-Cory gang. He even produced a photography expert to claim that the photographs had been doctored. The jury refused to buy the story, in large part because of the testimony of the O'Brien twins and Emma Silas. The time George Dowdy actually served on his life sentence stands even today as the shortest on record in the State of Maine. Despite his tearful plea, he was placed in with the general prison population. In less than a week his emasculated corpse was discovered in his cell beneath a blood-soaked blanket. A perfunctory inquiry led to an official ruling of suicide and the case was closed.

Chivas Smedley got to stand trial in federal court, charged with multiple Mann Act violations for which he received maximum sentences which were "stacked," that is, each sentence commenced upon completion of the previous one. It did not take long—indeed less than twenty-four hours—for Smedley to learn what it was like to be on the receiving end of a sodomy encounter. In time he learned to tolerate—some would say enjoy—these daily interactions with his fellow inmates. It kept him from the drudgery of hard labor and earned him frequent extra rations and cigarettes. Inevitably, one of these interactions resulted in Smedley contracting a venereal disease which led to madness and then a slow, agonizing death.

Stripped of his law license, Bascom Pommus III was no longer qualified to serve as district attorney. Unwilling to relinquish his office it took a *quo warranto* proceeding in which the State was represented by Horatio Christmas to finally have him removed. The governor, based on the strong recommendation of Reverend Christmas appointed Enoch Matthews as Pommus's successor. Matthews won election in his own right in 1920 and went on to serve several more terms with distinction.

The vacancy in the Kennebec County sheriff's office was filled by Walter Isaacson who also served with integrity for several terms.

Bringing down the Boyles-Cory gang was Lamar Raymond's last Mann Act assignment. He took his accumulated leave and when he returned he joined up with J. Edgar Hoover's anti-subversive unit. As Flammonde predicted, the relationship was not a happy one. So when the Volstead Act went into effect, Raymond was among the first to transfer to Treasury where he was placed in charge of a squad chasing smugglers running rum from Cuba and Jamaica to Florida. Although he found the Florida climate to his liking, after a while the conflict between his personal feelings toward alcoholic beverages and his duties as an enforcer of the prohibition laws became more than he could comfortably bear. Unable to reconcile the conflict, he put in his papers and moved to Hollywood where he became a technical adviser to producers of motion pictures set in the make-believe American West.

It took a while longer for Maurice Morton to burn out on Mann Act cases. Because of his background and lack of a college degree, not to mention a law degree, he recognized that his future in the modern Federal Bureau of Investigation under Mr. Hoover was not destined to be either lengthy or happy. He too put in his papers and took a position in which he could put his carny skills to good use—a Wall Street investment bank—where he made a great deal of money for himself, his employers and even a few clients. Early in 1929, in a flash of clairvoyance, he resigned his position and liquidated his portfolio.

Restless in retirement, in 1932 he bought a bankrupt forty-miler. With the eager help of as many of his former carny colleagues as he could find, including a certain magician's assistant, he turned it into one of the largest and even occasionally profitable shows on the circuit.

With his law degree and refined sartorial sense, Emil Flammonde managed to blend in—if not quite fit in—the modern Bureau. He even managed to get along tolerably well with the Chief and Mr. Tolson. Indeed, when he was in Washington and not in the field, they often invited him to dine so that he could enthrall them with tales of his Mann Act cases, the more titillating the better. When the Office of Strategic Services was formed in1942, Colonel Donovan, at the insistence of Harry Hopkins, persuaded Mr. Hoover to "loan" Flammonde to the O.S.S. for the duration.

In his retirement years after the war, Flammonde headed The Esther Dubrowski Memorial Foundation, a foundation whose charter stipulated that its purpose was to feed, clothe and provide medical care to orphaned children in impoverished post-war Europe. While the foundation did much good in its ostensible mission, its actual, covert mission—in which it also enjoyed considerable success—was the disruption, often by use of violent means, of international trafficking in pubescent children. From time to time there were rumors that the financial backing came from one of the major Hollywood motion picture studios. The Foundation's long-time legal counsel, Quincy Adams, like the Foundation's CEO, rarely gave interviews, and never discussed the Foundation's funding sources. Thus its principal benefactor has never been disclosed.

As soon as Esther Dubrowski received her $1000 bequest from the Richard Cory estate she and Cecilia decided to make a fresh start in California. They moved to Los Angeles thinking that with their respective job skills they would easily find work. Cecilia did find work at one of the motion picture studios, initially as a secretary. As happened with some frequency in those days, she was "discovered" as a potential screen star. She adopted a stage name and thereafter starred in a number of motion pictures. At the height of her fame, however, she abandoned her acting career to marry the nephew of the head of one of the great studios. In a short while she bore four children: Adam, Camille, Bridget and Colleen all of whom were relentlessly spoiled by their Grandma Esther.

Quincy and Camille declined Harrell Berman's offer to join his firm. After they married—Quincy having sensibly decided to take

Flammonde advice—they moved to Boston where Adams reestablished his law practice. When his practice was able to provide a decent living, Camille matriculated at Radcliffe where she eventually earned a doctorate in English literature. Camille went on to a successful career as a professor in her field at Wellesley. Along the way they produced two children: Emily Cecilia and Lamar Raymond.

At the end of World War II, Adams served as a judge presiding over one of the lesser war crimes trials after which he retired except for serving as legal counsel to the Esther Dubrowski Memorial Foundation.

Acknowledgments

Gardiner, Maine—Robinson's "Tilbury Town"—is today pretty much a suburb of Augusta as is Hallowell. Many turn-of-the-century buildings still grace its streets and my "Oakdale Hall" still stands south of town. If you go to Gardiner you won't find the "Red Rooster" but you will find a delightful "modern" (50's style) diner as well as some very nice folks at the Edwin Arlington Robinson Historical Center and at the public library both located in Water Street. The Industrial School still exists in Hallowell at the crest of Winthrop Hill where it serves as a pre-release center for the Maine Department of Corrections. The courthouses in Portland and Augusta are in use today just as they were in 1918.

I allowed myself to vent a little at court personnel, from judges to clerks to bailiffs. After nearly 50 years of dealing with them, perhaps I've earned the right. What's more, they're free to write their own books and vent about lawyers and this one in particular, should they choose to do so. However my venting has no application whatever to the folks staffing either the Kennebec County or Cumberland County courthouses. They could not have been more professional, and yet cordial, in assisting me in my research.

Many thanks to Susan Lawrence at the Maine Historical Society in Portland for her assistance in researching matters relating to Portland, especially the history and description of the Sharrey Tphiloh Synagogue. Thanks are also due to Charles Fischman who first introduced me to the beauty and character of Maine.

My profound thanks go to my friends and work colleagues Cherie Zalstein and Grace Stewart. Their knowledge of and proficiency in operating modern word-processing equipment has enabled you to read this work in print rather than long-hand.

Penultimately, I thank my editor (and spouse) Marsha Fischman—hater of hyphens and lover of short sentence—for her sharp and critical eye. Her efforts have made this work far better than it otherwise would have been.

Lastly, my thanks to Edwin Arlington Robinson whose sixteen short lines said so much, and in such an elegant way, about this complex fellow Richard Cory yet left room for one to imagine as I have.

www.ingramcontent.com/pod-product-compliance
Lightning Source LLC
Chambersburg PA
CBHW030012180626
46810CB00001B/5